I0556235

# Swelter

By Christine James

Copyright © 2017 BGP Publishing

All rights reserved

No part of this book may be reproduced in any form
or by any electronic or mechanical means, including
information storage and retrieval systems, without
permission in writing from the publisher, except by a
reviewer who may quote brief passages in a review.

The characters and events portrayed in this book are
fictitious. Any similarity to real persons, living or dead
is coincidental and not intended by the author.

Cover by Kristy Charbonneau
Photo Credits:
Rhonda Johnson
Angel Bara
Rennaulka/Dreamstime.com
Angelblue/Dreamstime.com

"I'm the one that's got to die

when it's time for me to die,

so let me live my life the way I want to."

— *Jimi Hendrix*

# Dedication

This book is dedicated to my Aunt Fee. An amazing, strong woman that I will forever miss and always remember. Some of my fondest memories were spent in Louisiana.

I also want to dedicate it to law enforcement. Thank you for your bravery and dedication. Thank you for putting your lives on the line every day to keep us safe!

# Acknowledgements

This list might get a little long, so hang in there.

I thank the Lord above for giving me the ability to write and the creative mind to do so. He's the reason I have this ability!

Special thanks to the real Lynn Robichaud and Levi Moss who helped me with procedures and steps that go into an investigation. While your names have been changed for this book, you know who you are.

I also want to say a special thanks to the real doctor Ross that helped me with the medical terms and fielding my wacky, off the wall questions. My childhood friend that I had the pleasure of reconnecting with. You are an inspiration, and I am so proud of the man you've become, the smiles you've helped bring to the world and the amazing things you're going to do in the future. More than anything I am glad to be able to call you a friend.

My amazing husband for putting up with my craziness during this—sometimes painful—process and cheering me on when I felt like quitting.

My parents for their unyielding support, love and babysitting skills!

My amazing in-laws for welcoming me into their family, despite my craziness and loving me regardless.

To Jen, for helping me overcome my gross sickness in order to write, as well as help me with a few other medical terms.

Rhonda for keeping my kiddos and providing me with a stunning picture to use. You're a true blessing to me and my family with everything you do. I'd be lost without you!

My editor Kat, for giving me another set of eyes and helping me untangle the mess that was this book before it was finished. I couldn't have done it without you.

My best friend and sounding board. Without your encouragement and pushing, I don't think this thing could have ever gotten finished. I love you.

Uncle Everett for encouraging me to write another mystery thriller. Last and most certainly not least, my readers, friends, and fans. If it weren't for you reading my crazy ideas, I couldn't have come this far. Thank you from the very bottom of my heart.

# Prologue

The bluish fog hovered over the water like a thick, heavy blanket as the cool surface mingled with the oppressive Louisiana heat. The shallow, flat bottom boat silently glided through the eerie stillness, leaving swirling tails of fog in its quiet wake. Gentle waves in the water drifted away from the boat, causing the full moon's reflection to shimmer and disperse. Tension rippled through the air as frogs croaked and cicadas trilled. The air was sticky, heavily saturated with humidity and clinging to his exposed skin like a layer of the blood he'd just spilled. The tiny hairs on his arms beaded with moisture as he plunged the push pole beneath the water and into the muddy bottom of the bayou. Pearls of sweat rolled down his face. His tongue darted out, tasting the saltiness on his lips.

Somewhere, deep in the darkest bowels of the swamp, an owl screeched an eerie warning. He scanned the dark shadows surrounding the swamp. Tonight he was a predator, claiming victory over his prey. He could feel the eyes of other predators watching him, gauging his movements, waiting for him to make a mistake and fall overboard. Still, he pushed on. He had a mission, and he would not fail. Cautiously, he guided the boat through the grove of cypress trees. Satisfied that he'd found the perfect place, he pulled the push pole back inside the boat and gently placed it to the side. The boat rocked precariously beneath his feet, water lapping high on the edge. It would be all too easy for the boat to tip. Halting his motions, he allowed the water to calm before taking a seat on the narrow aluminum bench.

Beneath the seat, he'd tucked a small cooler. He pulled it from its resting place and balanced it on his leg as he flipped open the lid. Immediately, the smell of rancid meat assaulted his senses. He took a deep breath and smiled. It was a smell that reminded him of home.

Carefully, he retrieved a pair of latex gloves and snapped them into place over his hands. He reached into the cooler and withdrew several rotten chunks of beef melt and chicken innards. "Ah, just right," he murmured, allowing the stuff to squish between his fingers.

The meat had been left in the scorching sun for a week straight in preparation for this night. It had to be just right, or it wouldn't work. With a gentle flick of his wrist, he dropped the chunks over the edge and into the placid surface. He repeated the process until there was nothing left but rancid juices swirling around the bottom of the maggot infested cooler.

After a few moments, he plunged his hand beneath the surface and began to splash. The sound carried loudly in the otherwise eerie silence. He didn't have to wait long before the commotion was answered by low growls from the shadows. He pulled his hand back into the safety of the boat just as several heavy splashes sounded from the bank. The boat bobbed softly in the water as he waited.

*Bump. Thump. Bump.* The aluminum echoed as it was nudged from both sides. "Hello, boys." A loud hiss and churning water was the only response.

He clapped his hands together once and rubbed them eagerly. "Excellent. It's time."

Reaching into his pocket, he withdrew a small syringe. For a moment he just stared at the man sitting across from him, hands zip-tied behind his back and shaking with fear. It was a rush and one he had to have. His pants grew uncomfortably tight as he grew hard. It wasn't his victim that aroused him, but the kill. Yes, he would have to find a whore tonight. Blood sang through his veins as his heart picked up speed. He nearly trembled with excitement.

With his free hand, he leaned across and pulled the mask from his victim's face. In the bright light of the moon, he could see the harrowing expression in the other man's bulging eyes. Immediately the man began to struggle against his bonds, but it was a futile attempt. There was no escape.

A wicked sneer pulled his mouth up as he watched him struggle. "Shh," he whispered, placing his finger against his lips. "You'll disturb their dinner."

He pointed to the water beside him. As if to illustrate his point, a massive gator lashed out at a smaller one with his dangerous tail, sending droplets of water splashing over them.

The victim's eyes shifted to the churning water all around them. Fervently he shook his head, the gag muffling his pleas. He laughed at the man's tears, but the distinct scent of urine and defecation permeating the air caused the smile to drop from his face.

"Now you've gone and pissed and shit in my boat," he snapped. He roughly slammed his fist into the side of the man's face. The bones crunched on impact. Rage tore through him, but he remained in control.

Swiftly, he grabbed the cooler and dumped the maggoty meat juice over the man's head. "I was going to make this quick, but you've gone and pissed me off." Retching sounds were muffled by the gag between his lips.

"I guess I will season their dinner tonight," he chuckled.

Leaning forward, he then jabbed the needle roughly into the man's thigh and depressed the plunger. Once empty, he withdrew it and held it up to inspect it.

"It's amazing how something so small, can do so much damage," he said thoughtfully.

The man whimpered and began to sag.

"Well, that was quick."

Withdrawing his knife, he cut the man's bindings and removed the gag. He moved to stand over his motionless victim. Frantic eyes shifted back and forth.

"I would say don't worry, you won't feel a thing, but that's a lie. You're going to feel every single tooth that tears into your skin."

He removed a pair of pruning shears and held it just below the knuckle of the man's left index finger. With a quick snip, the task was done. He dropped the finger and the sheers into the empty cooler and continued with his task.

Hefting the man onto his side, he leaned down close to his face and pried open his mouth. He roughly forced the syringe down his throat. Blood trickled from the corner of his mouth as gurgling sounds gathered in the back of his throat and rose out his mouth.

"Dinner . . . is . . . served," he grunted as he placed a boot roughly in the man's side. With a forceful shove, he sent him over the edge. The boat rocked dangerously at the sudden shift of weight.

The inky black water around him erupted into chaos as the behemoth reptiles fought over the fresh meal. He glanced over the side and saw the man's face disappear beneath the surface as he was pulled downward by two gators. Victory!

With a satisfied smile, he picked up his pole and carefully navigated the boat away from the feeding frenzy. Once again he was swallowed by the shadows of the swamp. As his boat drifted away, he glared up at the moon.

"Soon." His whispered, leaving his threat clinging heavily to the humid July night.

After loading the boat onto the trailer, he lifted the window of the camper and peered into the darkness. He heard the muffled whimpers.

"Don't worry. Your time will come soon."

Feeling pleased that his plan was finally set in motion, he closed the glass and slid behind the wheel. Everything was perfect.

# 1

With a sad wave and a strong, albeit fake smile, Cheri watched her kids disappear as she drove down the pot-hole filled street in her rusted Toyota Corolla. Once they were out of sight, she let the tears flood down her cheeks as she silently cursed her ex-husband for being such a rat bastard. Shared custody was awful, but at least she got to keep them with her, most of the time. Thankfully, her son was seventeen, eighteen before next summer. He wouldn't have to spend any more *required* time with his father. Unfortunately, her daughter was only thirteen. She had a few more years to go.

Turning, she made her way over the neglected yard. The brittle brown grass crunched beneath her feet. Carefully she climbed the rickety steps of the little two-bedroom shack. She had no doubt that once-upon-a-time the house was charming, but the peeling dinghy-white paint combined with the saggy roof and its missing shingles spoke otherwise. The front windows were open wide with an old box fan wheezing and stirring the hot air inside. A couple of the panes were held together with good ole duct tape, and one was completely missing, pitifully covered with a scrap of cardboard box.

As she stood on the porch, she cursed Alexander Bouvier vehemently. He'd gotten everything in the divorce; their beautiful house in Alexandria, the cars, even their beautiful, award-winning German Shepard. He'd told the court that she could have the kids, so long as he could have them a couple weeks out of the summer and every other major holiday. According to him, his career took up too much time, and he couldn't adequately be the parent they needed.

Translation: he was too busy bending every skirt within spitting distance over his desk. Thankfully, he carried medical insurance on both the kids, but foolishly enough, they'd agreed, outside of court, that he would

5

make monthly payments to care for their needs. Those were laughable at best, considering they were lucky to get two hundred dollars. More times than not, it was less. Sure, she could press the issue if she wanted to and knew she could take him for quite a bit. However, the last time she'd threatened to do just that, he'd retaliated by saying he'd take her back to court and demand another custody hearing. He'd be able to prove her living arrangements were unsuitable for children. It was a low move because he knew the attorney fees alone would eat her alive. So, scared of losing her kids, she'd sucked it up and left well enough alone. Talk about screwed without a kiss.

With a growl of frustration, she reached up to the ledge and pulled down a hidden and very crumpled pack of Pall Mall Lights. Sweat dotted her brow and ran in a trail between her breasts. Pressing the front of her shirt against her skin, she blotted away the sweat and then plopped her butt into the worn green chair. The metal was hot against the back of her bare legs.

"Too early to be so damn hot," she grumbled. The sun was barely in the sky, and the humidity was enough to soak her completely. She looked up and stared out over the deserted street, her eyes landed on the city dump, directly across from her house.

"Home sweet home," she sighed.

She shook a smoke out of the pack and pushed the filtered end between her lips. Jeremy would freak if he knew she was smoking again. It wasn't a habit she indulged in often, usually only when she was stressed. And, with the way she was feeling, she was pretty sure she'd be able to burn through an entire pack. She struck her thumb against the flint of the lighter and held the flame to the tip. After taking a deep drag, she exhaled the smoke through her nose. She pulled her foot up onto the chair and rested her arm on top of her knee. Taking another long pull, she fought back the urge to cough. Slowly, she exhaled and like the smoke drifting out into the stifling morning heat, she allowed her mind to wander.

Her life had been nothing but pain, disappointment, and suffering. Being a ward of the state wasn't something she'd wish on anyone. It could quite possibly explain why she had settled for the first man to bat his lashes and show her interest. The insatiable need to be loved and wanted by someone was smothering. At sixteen any young woman would fall for a tall, handsome, suave and rich twenty-two-year-old. With sweet whispered words and doting affection, she'd fallen hard and fast for such a man. Unfortunately, that man had been Alexander Bouvier.

In the end, after two years with Alexander, she hadn't gotten her fairytale. She was eighteen, a high school dropout and pregnant. Before long, she found herself in a loveless marriage. He was not the man she'd thought him to be, but it had been too late to turn back. She was stuck. The only thing that helped her make it through the screaming matches and the affairs had been her two children. They'd been her salvation and the only bright spot in the otherwise fifteen years of misery.

Cheri took a long pull on her cigarette and exhaled it through her nose. A thin sheen of sweat covered her bare arms and legs. A mosquito whined irritatingly beside her ear. She swatted at it absently as she took one last drag before snuffing it out on the arm of her chair. The chiming from the wall clock in the living room told her it was a quarter past eight. With a groan, she hauled herself out of the chair and walked from the muggy outside, into her even muggier house. She had to be at work at nine and realized it was a bit sad that the only reason she looked forward to going in was because the grocery store was air conditioned.

The divorce had been final for three years, and she'd found herself, against her better judgment, back in the town she was born in. She'd taken a job at the local grocery store to make ends meet between shrimp and gator seasons. When she came back, she'd prayed that everyone had forgotten about her. Thankfully, no one seemed to remember Cherilynn Deveau and the scandal that surrounded her. That didn't mean she could be careless, though. She couldn't take any risks.

Before moving back, she'd died her long blond hair back to her natural deep brown and added a few layers. When Jeremy had questioned her about it, she'd just shrugged it off. "New town, new look," she'd said lightly.

Dead Water, Louisiana was about fifty-five miles southwest of New Orleans and another twenty miles in the middle of nowhere. Dead Water boasted a population of twelve hundred and three people, with two gas stations, one grocery store, a liquor store, three small restaurants and one particularly rough bar at the end of town. It had earned its namesake a hundred and fifty or so years ago because of a mysterious epidemic of dead fish floating in the lakes, swamps, and bayous. It was a dying town, and she had no clue why she had bothered coming back. The town now knew her as Cheri Bouvier, ex-wife to some businessman who'd settled down in Alexandria. With any luck, twenty years would be enough time for people to forget the poor swamp wraith that had been thrust into foster care. More than anything she hoped that the rumors had been long since buried. The past needed to stay where it was. Dead.

# 2

The meat cleaver came down with a heavy *thunk*, severing ligaments, and tendons as if they were made from butter. Drying blood, splattered from his previous kill, still stained the walls as the metallic smell permeated the air. He repeated the motion, swinging swiftly in a downward motion, slicing through the skin and thick muscle. The blade spliced through nerves, causing the body to twitch. As he pulled the blade free, the flesh made a wet sucking noise. Lifting the cleaver high, once more, he brought it down with as much force as he could muster. A smile of satisfaction tugged against his mouth as the cartilage and bones finally gave, leaving the blade lodged firmly into the thick wooden block.

"Please tell me dat ain't what I tink it is," said a rough, gravelly voice from behind him.

"Dunno. Depends on what ya think it is," he responded lightly as he continued to quarter the chunks of meat.

The man climbed the remainder of the steps and walked through the door of the screened in back porch. The hinges snapped back, causing it to slam loudly back into place. The older man hobbled his way to the small ice chest resting on the porch swing. He wore a pair of well worn, faded denim overalls with an equally faded sleeveless shirt beneath. His arms were tanned dark brown and leathery with age. He pulled out a glass bottle of coke and popped the top off using one of the brass buttons holding up his overalls. He settled his five-foot-four-inch frame onto the swing, the boards creaking just as much as the old timer's joints.

His feet pushed back and forth, gently swaying the swing. After taking a long swig from his bottle he looked at the younger man. He wiped his mouth with the back of his hand and frowned. "Jax, ya know better din ta go out and hunt dem gators dis early. If ya git cawt they'll shut

9

ya down. And we both know ya don't need no more trouble with da law. Especially wit dat otha business you be runnin out da back of dis bar," Marvin said as he twisted his white handlebar mustache as he watched his nephew.

Jax flashed his uncle a wide grin, wiping the sweat from his brow with his forearm.

"Uncle Marvin, you know damn good and well no one cares if a few gators get poached. They're a menace and everyone knows it. As for the other business, no one needs to know 'bout that."

His uncle harrumphed and pulled at his mustache. "No matter if dose beast are a menace, da law don't care none for dat, and you know if you get cawt. . . ." He let the sentence fall between them as he arched a white bushy eyebrow at his nephew. "What'choo want wit dat gator no how?"

Jax shrugged, thankful for the change of subject. "Jimmy called and said something was gettin his cows and pull'n'em down into the channel. Figured we'd serve'im up as a special this weekend."

Uncle Marvin just shrugged his beefy shoulders. "Ya just be careful and keep yer head down, ya hear me?"

"Yes sir," Jax said dutifully.

"What's with all da blood on da wall? Looks like ya done killed someone," Marvin said as he pulled out a silver pouch of tobacco from the pocket on the front of his overalls. He unwrapped it and bit off a plug.

"I snared a wild boar while I was out after dis big boy," Jax said slapping what was left of the gator's back.

Marvin whistled low. "Wooo·wee, he surely did make a mess."

"Yeah, but he'll be good eat'n. He wasn't too old." Jax brought the cleaver down again. "Why don't you help me cut this beast up?"

"I don't tink so. Dat dere is yer doin's. You caught'em, you clean'em."

"Not even for Cookie's sauce picon?" Jax bribed with a sly smile.

The old man pursed his lips to the side as he contemplated the deal. He finished his coke and threw it into the trash barrel before hauling himself to his feet.

"Fine, I'll help ya, but I don't want nothing ta do with ya if ya git cawt." Marvin picked up a filet knife and set to work removing the gator meat from the bone. His old hands moved with ease and experience that could have only been brought on by years of living in the bayous.

The early morning air was heavy with humidity as the mosquitos hummed loudly around the back porch. There was, however, an occasional breeze that moved the stifling heat around. Even though it was a hot breeze, it was better than nothing. Sweat soaked Jax's brow—rolling down the sides of his face—as he worked diligently beside his uncle. The pair chatted casually about things of little consequence. Marvin had always been his favorite uncle. He was a good man with a heart of gold, always willing to help a friend, neighbor or stranger in need. He was old school, and Jax had learned a lot of life lessons from him. After throwing the meat into a metal basin of ice, Jax hefted the container and walked to the door leading into the back of his bar.

"Ya gonna come down tonight?" he asked his uncle as they stepped into the small kitchen. The smell of grease mingled with the sweet scent of homemade beignets. The heat from the grills and ovens was already smothering. The small wheezing and choking air conditioner in the window did little to ward off the heat.

"I don' know. Yer aunt has a list of tings for me ta do dat is at least a mile long," Marvin grumbled as he closed the door behind him. He ambled over to the sink and washed the blood and guts from his hands, quickly drying them again on the bibs of his overalls.

"So I'll see ya then?"

"Yep," Marvin said, smiling wide and nodding his partially bald head.

Jax set the gator on the counter in front of his cook. "Got something fresh for you t'night, Cookie."

"Go to bed," Cookie exclaimed as he picked up a piece of meat and turned it over in his hands before giving out a low whistle. "*Mon Dieu*, Jax. Dat dere is some good look'n gata," he said as he flashed a wide grin full of missing teeth. His deep brown eyes lit up against his coal black skin and black and white hair.

"It sure is. I figured we'd add some fried gator and Jambalaya to the menu t'night."

Cookie licked his lips. "I might even make up a batch of m'gator etouffee."

Jax shrugged. "Do with it what you want, man. Make them skillets sing. We're gonna be busy. I've got Rip Johnson coming in t'night for a live gig."

"Rip Johnson? How did'ja swing dat, m'boy?" Marvin asked as he poached a sugar covered beignet from a serving platter. Cookie glared a warning in his direction but Marvin just grinned, powdered sugar clinging to his lips and mustache. He licked his fingers loudly as Cookie returned to stirring whatever he had cooking in the giant pot on the stove, all the while watching Marvin from the corner of his eyes.

"He's in town visit'n family and he said he'd stop by," Jax said, as Marvin reached for another sugary treat. This time Cookie was ready, and with reflexes startlingly quick for a seventy-nine-year-old, he smacked the back of Marvin's hand with a wooden spoon.

"Keep dem grubby hands ta yerself, ya ornery ole ass," Cookie scolded shaking the spoon at Marvin.

"Ornery? I ain't da one beat'n people wit wooden spoons. Ya mean ole cuss," Marvin said with a frown as he rubbed the back of his aching hand.

Jax threw his head back and laughed at the two old men.

"Shoot. Rip's one of da best blues players in dese parts," Marvin said.

He moved his head in agreement as he made his way to the sink and poured a generous amount of dish liquid onto his hands. He scrubbed his hands and forearms until they were white with soap. After rinsing, he grabbed the towel and turned to Cookie, who was still arguing with Marvin.

"Jax, we gonna need more meal. I used da last of it yesterday," Cookie said as he put the metal bowl of fresh meat in the big stainless steel refrigerator.

"I'll make a run and get some. Do we need anything else?"

Cookie shrugged and stuck his spoon back into the giant pot, slowly stirring in circular motions. Cookie shook his head. "Damn it, Marvin, I done tole'ja, keep dem hands away from my food. Next time imma gonna cut dem finga's off!" Cookie was still stirring and though his back was turned to Marvin he never missed a beat. Marvin's hand stopped over the plate of food as he contemplated Cookie's words. He must have decided it wasn't worth the risk. With a grunt and a frown, he shuffled back.

Jax rolled his eyes and made his way through the doors that led out to the main portion of the bar. In the background, he could still hear the two men arguing, rapidly followed by the loud clanging of a pot crashing to the floor.

"Jax, you've gotta hire someone else."

Jax stopped short when he nearly plowed over the tiny blond standing in his way.

She propped her hands on her hips and glared up at him. Her blond eyebrows tugged together in a severe frown. Trixie was five foot five inches of dynamite. Her hair was cropped short, spiked on top and dyed platinum blond. Her eyes were the color of sapphires, with tiny crow's feet gathering in the corners. She was forty-eight but could easily pass for thirty-eight. Her breasts stood high and proud, revealing enough cleavage to leave a man wanting little more than a peek—also leaving Jax wondering if they were real. She had a narrow waist with flared ample hips.

"I'll set up interviews for next week," he grumbled as he moved around her and began to restock the beer cooler.

"Damn it, Jax, I can't run the bar and be on the floor at the same time."

Jax growled, annoyance clawing its way to the surface. "Fine, I'll put out some calls t'day and try to interview a few people once we are closed after lunch. Will that get you off my ass?"

"For now," she said without missing a beat. She grabbed the stack of papers he'd missed sitting on the bar.

"What are those?"

"Help wanted flyers. I'll just run out and hang these up right quick," she said simply.

"Where the hell did you get those?"

"I made'm last night," she said with a shrug.

"Trixie, I'm your boss. Not the other way around."

She huffed out a sigh. "I'm sorry, I'm just exhausted. It's Friday night and I know we're gonna be busy. I just dread it, that s'all."

"Don't worry, I'll be here and I'll work the bar and help out on the floor if ya need me."

"Okay. Hey, I heard Cookie say he needed some meal from the store. Ya want me to go and get it?"

"That would actually work out great. I got shit around here that needs to be fixed before tonight and some other stuff to take care of while we are closed." The beer bottles clinked together as he sat another case on the floor and began to fill the cooler beneath the bar.

She arched a golden brow at him. "What other stuff?"

He stared at her evenly.

She nodded and held up her hands. "All right. I get it. None of my business. Anyhow, I got some stuff I need to get from the store anyhow."

"Okay," he said absently as he went back to stocking beer.

"How's the jaw?" She indicated to the fading purple bruise spreading across the lower left half of his jaw bone.

He shrugged and ran his hand over his stubbly jawline. "Still hurts like hell."

"Serves ya right for bangin' around on another man's wife like she was some cheap ole piano," she grunted.

"How in the hell was I s'posed to know she was married?"

"Oh I dunno, ask?" she said with an annoyed shrug.

He snorted. "That was the last thing going through my mind at that particular moment."

"Well, ya got yer ass beat good this time. I knew one day you wouldn't win."

"Who says I didn't win. He didn't just walk away."

"That's not the point. I keep tell'n ya, you can't take home the trash that comes in here. One way or another you're bound ta catch some creepy crawlies, s'mthin antibiotics won't cure. You may very well be on the end of a shotgun next time."

"You've been here three months and you're already act'n like a damned mother hen." Jax frowned down at her. "I'm not paying ya to lecture me, so if you're done, go to the store and get the meal for Cookie," Jax said, his ire rising further. There was just something about the woman that sometimes pissed him off, even though she was his best employee.

Trixie just shrugged, "You've been in at least half a dozen fights since I started workin' here."

"Trixie, my business is none of yours. You'll do well to remember that in the future." There was no mistaking the warning in his voice as he removed cash from the register and handed it to her.

She didn't flinch, instead, she just shrugged and took the money. Slinging the strap of her purse over her shoulder she gave him a cool look. "If ya need anything else just call."

She gathered the flyers and sauntered toward the door, giving him a nice view of her backside as her hips twitched from left to right. She was pretty, for an older woman. The fall of her cowboy boots against the old timber floors echoed through the empty room as she walked away. The backless shirt she wore exposed tanned and flawless skin, with a tattoo in the small of her back. Trixie was cute as hell but not even close to being his type. He liked his women with more meat on their bones. Though he was fairly certain he could bounce a quarter off her ass from ten yards away, she was to slight, not weighing more than one-twenty-five soaking wet. Besides, he didn't like dipping the pen in company ink, so to speak.

Shrugging it off, he stocked the rest of the beer before looking at the list of repairs he'd made the night before.

There were several small items scribbled in his near-illegible handwriting, but there were a few that he knew would take a little bit of time. The top priority on the list would be the rewiring of the aging sound system in order to be prepared for Rip's show.

Jaxon Lawrence Marceaux III was a hot-headed Cajun and had been for as long as anyone could remember. Everyone in their tiny little Hamlet knew both he and his temper were nothing to be trifled with. His rap sheet was full of small infractions and one big one. Thankfully, he'd been released after serving only six years.

Reaching beneath the bar, he removed his toolbox. On his way to the stage, he stopped to land a well-placed thump to the old jukebox. The ancient machine whirred to life with clinking and metallic noises. Jax smiled as the soulful sounds and heavy guitar riffs from King of Blues and his guitar Lucy swirled around him like a heady fog. For a brief moment, he mourned the recent death of the King. No matter where he'd been in life, blues music had been constant. People were a letdown. Music wasn't.

He'd purchased his bar, *Voodoo Queen*, six years ago. For nearly thirty years prior, it had been known around town as *Momma LaRoux's*, the pride of Dead Water Louisiana. He'd spent every last dime of his life savings restoring the rundown, weather-beaten bar at the end of the docks. Even then it hadn't been quite enough to cover costs. The other business ventures he'd picked up along the way helped immensely. He just prayed he could stay under the radar.

Though it was infinitely better than before, the bar still needed some major repairs. The siding, weather-worn timber graying with age, had seen better days and was in desperate need of replacing. His first restoration had come when he repaired the ten fourteen-foot-tall stilts that the bar rested on. From there on out he made repairs as he needed them. It still had a long way to go before it would be exactly what he wanted, however, he had a good start.

Since he lived a good distance away, he'd added a small apartment to the back, just off the kitchen. It made it easier for early deliveries or nights when he'd had just a touch too much to drink.

The small town had been ecstatic when *Voodoo Queen* re-opened its doors. It gave the blue collar types a place to kick back after work for a few beers and some good food. Unfortunately, it also had a reputation for being a 'rough place'. Through the week it was fairly calm and quiet, with regulars coming in for lunch and dinner. But, when Friday and Saturday nights rolled around it was a different story. People came from neighboring towns to hear the live blues bands. Blues and Jazz were the only types of music allowed in his bar. Though, with the influx of people on the weekends, came the bar fights. Jax learned quickly, that on those nights, extra security was a must.

Hefting his toolbox onto the small ten by seven stage, he set to work, tearing out wires, splicing new ones, and adding more. Before long, he became lost in the music and allowed his mind to wander as his hands seemed to know what to do on their own.

Even though he'd been paroled and on his best behavior, it hadn't been enough to stop some of the citizens from looking at him as if he were the devil about to eat their puppies. Mothers would tuck their kids close to their sides when they passed him on the sidewalks. It held little effect that his parents were upstanding citizens of the community and had been for several decades. Jax was a stain on the town—a pariah.

He tried to be a good citizen. He paid his taxes, paid his fines, went to church with his momma as often as possible. Once upon a time, he'd gone out of his way to help people out. It was how he'd been raised. His parents had force-fed kindness down his throat. It was just the way of things. You see someone that needs help, you help them and you do it without expecting anything in return.

The fights that happened at the bar stayed at the bar and never drew the attention of the law. Jax and his crew made sure of that. He was a pretty good size man, so he often handled most of the major confrontations by himself. There were usually a few punches thrown and after he'd made his point—sometimes by his own punch—the offenders backed off. However, there was, on occasion, that *one* person that had to test their strength and take him on. It never really ended well for the other guy. Sometimes, though, that wasn't always the case. There were those rare occasions that Jax had narrowly escaped a fight without a major injury. Thankfully, his security team had stepped in.

There was a sizzle of electricity as he accidentally touched two wires together. "Shit. Dammit," he cursed as he burned his fingers and jarred himself rudely from his wandering thoughts. He'd thought he got the breaker turned off—apparently not.

Frowning and trying to focus on what he was doing, Jax spliced the wire. As he did, he absently flexed his jaw, flinching at the pain. It was still tender, and he wasn't all too unsure the dumb moose that had sucker punched hadn't knocked a jaw tooth loose.

"Dumb redneck," he muttered as he wrapped the wire with black electrical tape. It seemed like Donovan "Big Bubba" LeRoche didn't take too kindly to finding his wife bent over their living room couch by another man.

He tried to remember the woman's name but couldn't, and didn't feel in the least bit sorry about it. She'd neglected to mention that she was married to a river barge so she didn't really deserve to have her name remembered. In fact, she was one on a list of many that he'd forgotten their names in the last couple of weeks. He just couldn't seem to care anymore. As long as they understood it was a one-time—maybe two-time—deal he was good with the arrangement. Anything more than that wasn't going to happen. He refused to put himself through that kind of heartache again.

He worked through the morning without incident, only taking a break to grab a cold beer from the cooler. Between songs on the old juke, he could hear Marvin and Cookie still arguing in the kitchen. A few times he'd heard the loud clamoring followed by another long string of creole curses. The only thing Jax could do was laugh.

Uncle Marvin was one of his favorite people in the world. Always with a witty remark, he liked to agitate people, and it appeared that Cookie was today's victim. Jax wasn't worried, because whatever Marvin dished out, Cookie gave it right back, and sometimes moreover.

He looked down at his watch and groaned. Ten thirty. They opened for lunch in less than an hour. With no other choice, he safely tucked the wires he'd been working on back under the stage and secured the panel. He would have to finish the wiring before they opened for dinner. There were other things that needed his attention.

After stuffing his tools back into his faded toolbox, he put it back behind the bar and set off to work on more of his list.

Cheri guided the groceries from the conveyer belt over the scanner, each beep grinding against her nerves. She'd been five minutes late and her boss had been waiting, ready to pounce, not giving a damn that she had to walk to work. It took every ounce of energy she could muster not to punch him and walk out of the grocery store. But, if she did that, she would be without a job and would have no way to provide for the kids. Damn her life.

As she pulled the last of twenty bags of cornmeal across, she plastered a fake sugary sweet smile across her face. Sparkling blue eyes glittered back at her warmly.

Cheri was about to recite to total, but boisterous voice from the end of the isle halted her words.

"What the hell is taking so long?" the man complained loudly.

"I'm sorry sir, I'm almost finished," she said kindly as she bit down painfully on the inside of her cheek.

She returned her gaze to the little woman with a blond pixie haircut. "One sixteen thirty-six."

The blond smiled and handed her a two one hundred dollar bills. Cheri frowned knowing she didn't have enough change in her register to break both hundreds. "Gimme a second. I'll have to get some change," Cheri said apologetically.

"S'ok, I ain't goin nowhere," the woman said with a shrug as she looked down at her phone. Her fingers began to glide rapidly over the screen.

Cheri picked up the phone attached to the divider above her register. "Jerry, I need change on three please." After replacing the phone back on its cradle, she finished bagging the woman's groceries. The man at the end of the aisle spoke up again.

"C'mon. Are you too stupid to count money?"

Cheri's temper snapped and all the built-up stress finally came erupting forward. She was helpless to stop it. She spun around and pinned the short balding man with a frigid glare. "Listen, you greasy fat weasel. If you think you can do the job any better, then put your cookies on the belt and get up here and do it yourself."

The man sputtered.

"What? Nothing to say? Good, keep it that way." Cheri was fuming.

The man's ruddy cheeks flushed angry crimson as he stuttered angrily. His jowls quickly working back and forth as he tried to think of a clever retort. The only thing he could do was look at the other woman.

"Don't look at me for help. You're the one that thought you were tough shit," the blond said as she held up her hands in surrender. "Personally, I think she took it easy on you by calling you a greasy fat weasel. She didn't even mention your hog jowls." There was no hint of laughter or joking in the woman's voice as she glared at the man.

Cheri snickered but it was short lived when she heard the clearing of a throat behind her. When she turned she was met by her boss's disapproving glare. From behind his wide plastic-rimmed, eighties replica glasses, his beady eyes narrowed. His thin lips twitched angrily under his blond porn star mustache. His face, scarred with acne and freckles, became red and splotchy with anger. Boy, he sure was an ugly piece of the male species.

Jerry cleared his throat again. "I think you should leave and pick up your last check next week."

"But she didn't do anything," the blond protested before Cheri got a chance to reply.

"Ma'am," he started, the nasally tone in his voice grating against Cheri's last nerve, "I don't really care whose fault it is, but we don't allow our employees to disrespect customers like that."

"So you let loud, rude ass customers treat your employees like shit?"

"The customer is always right," he intoned, and he repeated the age-old customer service mantra.

"Customers are always right? Well, guess I'm right when I say that you're a sad little man that probably never had a date in high school."

Jerry's fake smile faltered and his brow furrowed. He cleared his throat and tried to continue. "We treat our customers with—"

The woman held up her hand, promptly cutting Jerry off. "I don't particularly care how you treat your customers," she snapped. Cheri watched as the woman's eyes snapped blue fire at her soon to be former boss.

"What matters is the way you treat your employees. If they are. . . . Oh, you know what? You're not worth wasting my breath. Give me my damn change" she snapped back.

Cheri was already untying her apron and pushing past him. For a brief moment, she thought about the satisfaction she would gain from wrapping the green polyester blend apron around Jerry's scrawny neck and choking the life out of him.

Stiffening her spine, she walked out the doors—not bothering to clock out. Cheri walked out the electronic doors and She was instantly blasted with a flash of hot air. She walked over to the bench resting between two soda machines and sat down heavily. Leaning forward she cradled her face in her hands. Once again her temper had gotten the better of her—only this time it had cost her a source of income.

Lost in her thoughts and misery, she didn't hear the sliding of the doors or the approach of footsteps.

When a soft hand rested on her shoulder, she started and looked up. It was the blond.

"Hey, you need a lift somewhere?"

Cheri dashed away the few tears. "No, thanks but I live just a few miles down the road here."

"Honey, it's gotta be a hundred degrees out here already. Lemme give ya a ride."

The woman's thick accent brought her a sense of comfort. "You don't have too," Cheri protested but climbed to her feet regardless.

"I insist. It's kinda my fault ya just got fired."

"Not really. I've just had a bad day."

"Bad day? It's not even ten."

Cheri nodded and gave her a sad smile. "I know."

She smiled and nodded her understanding. She shifted her grocery bags and offered her hand. "I'm Trixie."

Cheri took Trixie's offered hand and squeezed. "Cheri," she replied.

"Pleased ta meet'cha Cheri. Now, come on and lemme give ya a lift." Trixie didn't wait for a response as she marched across the hot asphalt.

Cheri shrugged and followed. The sun beat down on her head as her sneakers seemed to stick to the newly paved parking lot. The strong smell of asphalt and chemicals made her nose curl and her stomach churn. As she reached for the door handle on Trixie's SUV, an uneasy feeling crept over her.

Slowly turning around, she surveyed the parking lot and the grocery store. Nothing seemed out of place but the uneasy feeling grew more intense and the hair on her arms twitched. Then she saw it, something moved at the corner of the building. No, not something but some*one.* She squinted, lifting her hand to her brow to shield her eyes from the glaring sun. There was definitely someone standing there, hidden in the shadows. She could feel eyes boring into her, even over the distance that separated them. A shiver of apprehension speared through her.

"Hey Cheri, ya comin?" Trixie called from her open door, violently startling her.

Cheri turned and offered her an apologetic smile as she climbed into the vehicle. Her eyes moved back to where the shadow has been standing, but there was no one there.

Trixie turned the engine over and shoved it into gear. As they sped from the parking lot, Cheri didn't see anything or anyone unusual. As they disappeared down the road, however, it felt like a strange pair of eyes were following her.

He watched as her ass swayed back and forth when she walked. The way her long neck was revealed when her hair was pulled on top of her head made his hands twitch.

He groaned, envisioning his hands around her neck as he drove himself into her. His jeans became uncomfortably tight. A slow smile tilted his lips when she stopped and looked at his direction. Her plump lips were pressed lightly together as she shielded her eyes.

The two women climbed into the car as he stepped back further into the shadows. With a low growl of frustration, he slammed his fist against the rough brick at the side of the building. He felt the skin of his knuckles split but he didn't feel the pain.

"Patience," he whispered as he tried to calm down. But the thought of her beneath him would not leave his mind.

Slowly, he moved his hand away from the wall, blood oozed across the backs of his fingers. Pulling his fist up to his lips he ran his tongue across broken skin, never taking his eyes from the explorer. The metallic taste of blood on his tongue was heavy. Once the vehicle pulled out of the lot, he looked down at his hand.

A slow smile curled across his bloody lips. Soon, it would be her blood on his hands and oh how he would enjoy the feeling of it was he squeezed every last drop from her body.

# 3

Cheri and Trixie carried on light conversation as Cheri directed her toward her house. Trixie was an easy person to like. While her personality was light, there was a warning, just below the surface of her sapphire colored eyes that said she could be a force to be reckoned with if crossed. When Trixie pulled the Explorer into the shell covered drive, Cheri tried not to cringe at the pathetic shape her house was in. Squaring her shoulders and lifting her chin proudly, she prepared to defend her home from insult, but none came. The older woman simply offered a lopsided smile but said nothing.

"Well, I appreciate the lift," she said after a slightly awkward moment of silence. Reaching into the front of her jeans. She made a show of fishing around in her pocket for some money, hoping and praying Trixie would stop her. When the other woman didn't say anything Cheri's heart fell. She'd have to make an excuse. Mentally, she cursed Alex, like she did every time something went wrong in her life. She hated being a charity case.

"What are ya doing?" Trixie finally asked, arching an immaculately sculpted eyebrow.

"Gas money. It's quite a ways from the grocery," she said as if she had all the money in the world.

"Yeah, more than a couple of miles," she winked.

Cheri flushed, caught in her lie. "I must've left my cash in the house. Hang on and I'll go get ya some money."

"Eh, don't worry about it," she snorted as she batted Cheri's hand away.

Cheri released a small sigh of release. "Are you sure?" She wanted to pay the woman something. If she needed too, she could dip into the meager college fund she'd set up for her kids. Though it was something she

25

tried desperately not to do. It wouldn't be the first time it had happened.

Trixie patted her knee in a motherly fashion. "Listen, it's not that big of a deal, really."

Cheri knotted her hands in her lap. "Well, thanks! I really appreciate it." With her hand on the door handle, she began to get out but a surprisingly firm grip on her arm stopped her.

"Hey."

"Yeah?" she asked, looking over her shoulder.

Trixie pursed her lips to the side and chewed on her cheek. Absently she drummed her red polished fingers against the steering wheel, studying Cheri closely. A minute passed, and she still hadn't said anything, just sat there staring. Finally, a slow smile crossed her full lips. "Do ya have another job?"

Cheri frowned and shook her head. "Shrimp season is over and gator season doesn't start for another couple months." The fact that she'd just lost her only source of income until then only added to her stress.

"Have ya ever tended bar or been a waitress?"

"It's been a while, but yeah to both."

Reaching up to her visor, she pulled down a piece of paper and handed it to Cheri. "Come in this afternoon, round three and talk ta my boss."

"You're offering me a job?"

"I can't hire ya, my ass would be in the sling for good, but I'll put in a good word for ya," she said with a conspiratorial wink.

"Ummm, okay. But why me?"

Trixie shrugged. "Ya look like the type of gal that can take care of'er self. My boss'll appreciate that." She pulled the gear shift down into reverse and turned around in her seat, preparing to back out. "And trust me, you'll need that if he hires ya. There can be some real jackasses out there."

"Okay, sure. I'll come down," Cheri said without even bothering to look at the flyer.

"Be sure you do,"

Cheri closed the door and watched as Trixie backed out of the drive. She sped away slinging gravel and dirt up behind her. She marveled at the roller coaster ride her luck had already been on, and it wasn't even noon. She started toward her house, scanning the piece of paper in her hand. There was nothing remarkable about it; no fancy fonts or clip art designs. HELP WANTED was printed in big bold letters. Her eyes traveled down the list of requirements, all of which she'd done before. Before she reached the porch she stopped abruptly, eyes scanning the address.

"Oh hell no," she said wadding up the piece of paper.

The *Voodoo Queen* was infamous for its amazing live bands, unfortunately, that's not all it was famous for. Bar fights and deviant activities went hand in hand as far as the *Voodoo Queen* was concerned. Living in a small town, everyone and everything was subject to being the topic of the rumor mill at some point. That particular bar seemed to take its turn in the mill more times than not. The most recent she'd heard, from a friend of a friend that is a dispatcher at the local police department, was that last weekend someone had been beaten to death by a beer bottle. Another popular one was that the owner was a philanderer, not caring if a woman was married or not before taking her to his bed. Those paled in comparison to the stories she'd heard about his prison stay. She'd never met the man, nor did she really have the want or desire too. She tried to stay in her little hovel as much as she could. She didn't really like being around many people.

"That's the last thing I need," she grunted as she climbed the steps. Alex would love nothing more than to attack her for working at a bar. She started to reach up for her hidden cigarettes but remembered she'd smoked the last one just after her kids had left.

"Fantastic."

She fished her phone out of her back pocket and flipped open the top. It was a cheap penny phone she'd gotten when she signed the meager cell phone contract. The screen read two new text messages. She looked at the time the message was sent. Ten forty-six.

*Baby Boy:* just north of New Orleans. Maddy being a bitch. Can I leave her on the side of the road?

Cheri smiled. Jeremy seemed to always make her laugh. Quickly, she tapped her response.

*Me:* think ur father might object to that and watch ur mouth. It's not nice to call your sister a bitch.

A few minutes later her phone vibrated in her hand.

*Baby Boy:* hell, I'll leave her with him. Sorry.
*Me:* don't u dare. Stop texting and driving.
*Baby Boy:* u texted first.
*Me:* touché
*Baby Boy:* y aren't u @ work

Cheri chewed on her bottom lip, thankful that her son wasn't asking that question in person. Taking a deep breath, she tapped her response.

*Me:* was feeling sick. Went home early. Text me ur next stop.

A few seconds later.

*Baby Boy:* k

Cheri tucked the phone into her back pocket and walked into the house, slamming the door behind her.

The heat inside the house was nearly as bad as it was outside. Making her way into the kitchen, she opened the refrigerator but frowned when the light didn't come on.

"Seriously?" She opened the freezer and groaned. Not only was it warmer than it should be, but what little food she'd had in there was already thawed out and spoiled. It had been working perfectly at six a.m. when she'd made the kids breakfast. She looked up at the clock. It was nearly noon. Walking over to the sink she ran the tap, filling a glass from the drain stand with cold water. After draining the glass and filling it again, she reached for the fan that was perched in the window. When it didn't come on after she flipped the switch, a sinking feeling slammed into her gut.

She reached for the switch that worked the light over the sink. When nothing happened she let out a frustrated cry.

Retrieving her phone from her back pocket, she scrolled through her phone book until she found the number for city hall.

It rang three times before an overly chipper Marjorie answered the phone.

"Um, yes, I seem to be experiencing a power outage," Cheri said.

"Well, let's see where you at, honey. What's your address?"

"2736 Lumber Way."

"Ok, lemme see what I can find out for ya."

Cheri listened as the keys of a keyboard clicked on the other end of the line. Finally, she heard a soft sigh and knew what the woman's response was before she even said it.

"I'm sorry, but your bill is overdue."

"I know. Is there any way I can get a little more time?"

"I can't do that ma'am."

"Please. I've had a horrible day. I'm trying to raise my kids on my own and they just took off to their father's for the rest of the summer. I can have you the money by Monday," she said.

There was a long pause before the woman finally answered. "I'm sorry, there's just nothing I can do," she said.

"Please, Marjorie. Just a little help?" Cheri asked, her throat clogging with tears. She hated the fact that she'd been reduced to begging. She'd hit an all-new low.

Marjorie huffed out a sigh and lowered her voice. "Okay, I can get it turned back on for ya, but ya have ta have that money by Monday. If it gets turned off again, I can't help ya."

Cheri closed her eyes and smiled. Finally, something was going her way.

"How much do I owe?" she waited for the total.

"It looks like four hundred sixty-eight dollars and eighteen cents."

"Wow, that's a lot."

"I know it is, but you didn't pay last month's either. Combine it with this month's bill along with late fees and penalties, it adds up."

"Well, I'll have the money to ya on Monday for sure."

"Ya better. For both our sakes," she said firmly.

"Secret's safe with me," Cheri promised.

"Ok. Hang tight and I'll get that back on for ya in an hour or so."

"You're an angel."

"Hey, us single mothers have ta stick t'gether."

"Thank you," Cheri said again before closing her phone.

She filled her glass with water again and retrieved the newspaper from the table. Tucking it beneath her arm, she walked back out onto the porch. For once it was cooler outside than it was inside. Thumbing through the help wanted section, she began to look for a job. The longer she looked the more discouraged she became. There were only five ads seeking help. Three were searching for computer programmers in the neighboring town and the other two were for mechanics at a local gas station. Briefly, she thought about applying for the mechanic job but knew she would be fired as soon as she opened the hood of a car. Though she knew how to check the oil and the other fluids but actually working on a car wasn't on her list of special skills. The computer programmers were not an option either.

Out of frustration, she threw the paper to the ground. It landed beside the wadded up help wanted flier Trixie had given her. Reaching down she retrieved the ball and straightened it against her leg.

"The Voodoo Queen, eh?" She decided she didn't have much room to be choosy. With no other option, she went back in the house and began to get dressed. It would take at least an hour to walk to the bar. If she left at one she would be there in plenty of time to chicken out. Desperate times called for desperate measures. She just wasn't sure how desperate she really was.

"You did what?" Jax growled.

"Don't get all bent out of shape. I have a good feeling about her."

"Dammit Trixie, I can't go hiring people base on your *'good feelings'.* I have a business to run and I damn well can't do that if you go off doing your own thing." Jax's temper began to elevate. The lunch rush had been busy, so they were behind on clean-up, which meant he would be behind on the rest of the repairs he needed to make on the sound system for the show.

"Damn it, Jax. She got fired. Right there in front of me. I felt bad for her." Trixie continued to plead her case.

Jax whirled on her and pinned her with a dark brown gaze. "I'm not running a charity for every person who loses their job."

Trixie threw plates, bottles, and glasses into the bus tub and hitched it on her hip. She leveled a blue glare at him. The humor was gone from her eyes and they'd grown cold. "Well, considering the last three waitresses you hired didn't know beer bottles from their butts I figured *I'd* give it a shot."

Scrubbing his whiskered face with his hand he flinched. Damn, he needed to shave. Looking at the clock above the bar it already said half-past two. He didn't have a choice, he knew it and so did she.

"You're walking a fine line here, Trixie." He frowned at her but she was not phased. She just narrowed her eyes and lifted her chin, daring him to tell her no.

Finally, not wanting to waste any more time he relented. "She's your responsibility. If *you* want her in here, then *you* train her. I don't want to have anything to do with it. I've got enough shit on my plate without having to train another girl."

"Boss, someone be out back a wait'n fo you," Cookie said sticking his head over the swinging doors for the kitchen.

"I'll be right there," he said as he jerked his baseball cap from the counter and jammed it down on his head. "Damn females," he muttered as he made his way through the kitchen and out onto the back loading area.

Cheri stood at the end of the pier, staring at the building sitting above the murky water on lengthy stilts. The Voodoo Queen. Her stomach muscles clenched as she twisted and untwisted the crumpled flyer in her hands again. The woman had told her to come by, surely she would get the job if she was told personally to come by. Right?

She took a step forward and the weather-worn boards creaked beneath her feet. Sweat beaded and ran down her spine, causing her tank top to stick uncomfortably to her.

"You can do this. It's just another job. It's for the kids. Suck it up," she told herself. The closer she drew to the building the more anxious she become.

She'd just made it to the foot of the stairs leading up to the front entrance when she heard heated voices from around back. Unable to quell her curiosity, she walked over to where the ramp lead up to a back entrance.

"You're outside your fool mind if you think I'm paying for this shit."

"C'mon, Jax. It's my best stuff. I ain't gonna do you no wrong, boy."

There was a long pause followed by some muttered words that she couldn't make out. When she peeked around the corner, she saw a man wearing a baseball cap handing a wad of money to another man—who quickly stuffed the money inside his pocket. The baseball hat man was sexy but there was something wildly dangerous about him, but there was just something about him that piqued her interest.

*He's dangerous*, her mind screamed. She didn't need her mind to tell her that because she knew from just looking at him that he was the wrong kind of man to mess with.

"I'll let it slide this time, but if you bring me this shit next time. . . . Your body will never be found. Are we clear?"

"Yes, sir," the other man stammered already backing away and through the doors. The dangerous one disappeared as the scared one took off out the door and down the ramp like the hounds of hell are gnawing at his heels.

Cheri barely had enough time to move from her hiding spot and to the entrance steps before he appeared and all but sprinted back down the dock.

As if her nerves were already in bad enough shape, seeing some kind of shady deal going down out back did absolutely nothing to quiet her nerves. If anything, it only made things worse.

What in the hell was she getting herself into? Cheri was just reaching for the front door when it abruptly swung open. Taking a startled step back, she missed the step behind her and felt herself begin to fall. A strong hand shot out and steadied her before she could tumble into the reddish-brown water below them.

Once she was steady, she jerked out of his grasp. "Watch out asshole," she snapped trying to hide her humiliation. When she looked up, her eyes met his deep brown ones. Her throat went unexpectedly dry.

"Asshole? I just kept you from falling into the water and you're calling *me* an asshole?"

Annoyed that she'd been caught off guard, she narrowed her eyes. "If you would've been watching where you were going in the first place, then I wouldn't have tripped."

"Next time, I'll let you fall, let you risk your pretty little neck with the gators," he grunted as he jammed his hands in his tight-fitting jeans and removed a set of keys.

Cheri opened her mouth to reply but snapped it shut when he shoved passed her, the conversation clearly over.

She watched his retreating back as he marched down the dock. His long strides stretching his jeans tight across his backside. His boots thumped heavily, echoing against the water beneath him. It was him, the man from the back, and good lord he was sexy as hell. She'd seen it from a distance but up close was something completely different. She'd been right with her first guess; he was most definitely dangerous but more than anything she hoped he didn't work there.

Shifting her focus to the task at hand, she took a few deep breaths and tried to calm her nerves. She stood outside the unremarkable building and heaved a defeated sigh. "Don't have much of a choice, do I?"

With that, she pulled on the handle and stepped inside. It took a few minutes for her eyes to adjust to the dimly lit interior. Once they did, she was astonished that the inside looked far better than she expected. The smell of fryer grease mingled with a hint of cigarette smoke. In fact, it felt comforting, for some reason. It wasn't a high-class joint by any means, but it looked decent. To her right was a long L-shaped bar, maybe fifteen feet in length. Behind the bar, on the wall, hung a large mirror surrounded by neon lights advertising one brand of beer or another. Liquor bottles of all kinds were presented on shelves. At the far end were a set of swinging doors that disappeared into what sounded, judging from the banging pots and pans, to be the kitchen. It was pretty standard and almost cliché.

In front of her were six, small round tables, each with three chairs around them. In the center of the tables were ashtrays and laminated menus. Just beyond those tables were two pool tables, complete with the hanging stained glass lights over them. To her left, against the walls, rested three high-back sets of booths, with tables also sporting the menus and ashtrays.

The very front of the room boasted of a decent size stage, complete with drums, monitors and in the corner a soundboard. The dance floor in front and to the side wasn't large but looked like it would serve its purpose well. The room was far larger than she'd expected, based on appearances from the outside.

She saw Trixie come partially through the swinging doors, stopping with her back to the bar. "Marvin I swear if ya do that one more time, I'll let Cookie throw yer ass it the fryer."

A round of male laughter sounded from the kitchen as Trixie stepped fully through the swinging doors and picked a rag up from the bar. She was muttering violently to herself, something about ornery old Cajuns.

"Um, hello?" Cheri said.

Trixie's head snapped up. The harsh expression on her face softened and turned inviting. "Oh hey, girl. Ya scared me." She looked down at her watch and nodded. "Early. Good, I like that."

"It's a long walk."

"You walked from your house?"

"It's ok," Cheri said with a small shrug. "So where's the boss?"

Trixie slapped the bar towel over her shoulder and put her hands on her narrow waist. "He's not here right now."

Cheri's face fell. As she had walked here, she'd psyched herself up for the job. She'd thrown out every reason there was for not taking it and focused only on the positive ones. That list had been significantly shorter.

"But, he told me to do whatever I wanted," Trixie reassured her.

"Oh, okay?"

"He was pissed when I told him about you coming by."

"Oh," and like that she deflated. Coming here had most definitely been a bad decision. So, squaring her shoulders and lifting her chin she refused to be beat down. "Well, can I grab a beer before I head back? It's a long walk and I'm thirsty.

Trixie just watched her for a few moments before finally speaking. "It's my decision," she said as she walked around the bar and came to a stop in front of her. She was about three inches shorter than Cheri, but her stature made her seem like she was six foot. It was kind of intimidating. "And I'm in a tight spot right now. We're short-handed, ya said you had experience waiting tables and tending bar. Ya don't look like you'll put up with no crap and right now, I don't have any other choices. I don't have the time or the patience to train another one of Jax's bimbo waitresses. If you want the job, you start right now.

We have a long and hard night ahead of us. In three hours this place will be full. Can you handle yourself?"

"I believe so."

"Good. Grab a cloth from the tub over there and finish wiping down those tables. Run a broom over the floor and when you're finished, go clean the bathrooms, you'll find the supplies under the sinks. Come find me when you're finished, and I'll show ya how to run the register."

"Ummm, how much is the pay?" Cheri asked.

"Oh, right. It's minimum wage. You keep the tips from your tables and if you have any joint tables with another girl, you'll split."

"Wow, that's generous." She'd waitressed before and it was very rare that waitress got paid regular wages. Maybe the job wouldn't be so bad.

"The minute I see ya slacking or doing anything but working your ass off, I'll kick your butt out da door. We clear?" Trixie said firmly.

Cheri nodded and Trixie breezed away, stopping to place a thump on top of the jukebox. It whirred to life and soon smooth blues blasted out. "A little music for ya," she said as disappeared back into the kitchen.

Cheri threw her purse on the bar and grabbed the towel. Quickly but thoroughly, she cleaned the tables and swept the floors. The music allowing her to focus on her work and nothing else. Feeling a little lighter, she sang softly to the music she knew all too well.

After an hour, all her tasks were done. She'd removed her outer shirt so it wouldn't get too dirty. Now she was wearing a simple black tank and was thankful because it was a little warm inside the bar. She was tying the top of the trash bag together and walking out of the men's restroom when the sudden sound of a deep voice caused her to stop dead in her tracks.

"What the hell are you doing in there?" he said tightly.

It was *him*.

"I'm cleaning. Is that okay with you?" she challenged, arching a dark brow in his direction.

"I gathered you were cleaning them, but *why* are you cleaning them?"

Cheri leveled an annoyed glare at him. "Because they're disgusting."

"That's our new girl," Trixie said appearing from what appeared to be nowhere and interrupting the conversation.

"Her?" The man gave her the once over, slowly dragging his eyes over her body.

Suddenly, Cheri felt like her white shorts were too short and her black tank-top too revealing. She crossed her arms under her breasts. His eyes boldly flickered to her chest, and she could feel the heat rising to her cheeks. Had he just checked her out?

She cleared her throat, pulling his gaze back up to hers. "You have a problem with that?" she challenged.

"And if I do?" he challenged, widening his stance and crossing his arms over his chest, mirroring her.

"I'd say that's just too damn bad," she said with a simple shrug. She moved around him and walked behind the bar to where she dropped the dirty towels into the hamper.

He was quiet for a long moment as he watched her move around. Then suddenly he threw back his head and laughed. "Oh I like her," he said to Trixie.

Cheri spun around and glared at him. "Congratulations. Now, tell me why in the hell I should care if you like me or not?"

"Because, honey, *this* is Jax," Trixie said with a chuckle. "He's owns this place."

Cheri stopped and gaped up at him. Heat climbed up her neck and settled into her cheeks. She wondered if she left now if the line at the unemployment office would be very long.

# 4

Trixie hadn't been kidding when she'd said they were going to have a packed house. People from all walks of life began to filter in for an early dinner around six o'clock. Some were dirty and dusty just looking for a cold drink and hot meal, while others were dressed a night out on the town—a thought that struck her funny considering the current size of their town. There were women in simple attire such as jeans and t-shirts while the younger women chose to dress in more revealing clothing. By the time eight rolled around there was barely any room to walk. She was amazed that they were all gathered in one place, getting along as the guitar riffs of Rip seemed to lull them into some trance.

Once Cheri got used to the menu and the register, everything fell into place. Even Jax seemed to be more tolerable as the people kept coming in. Around eleven the crowd began to grow rowdy. After a few stern warnings from Jax and his Louisville Slugger, the point was made and there weren't any further incidents. Trixie and Jax had both warned her that some of the men could get a little handsy and suggestive with each drink. Thankfully, she hadn't had to deal with much more than a few slurred come-ons.

As the evening wore on, she finally felt herself begin to relax. However, she couldn't shake the feeling that she was being watched. The feeling had followed her all day after leaving the grocery store—after seeing figure lurking in the shadows. Several times, while she was behind the bar, she found herself scanning the room for the source of her unease, but nothing stood out so she tried to shrug it off as first night jitters.

Rip packed up his gear and left the stage just shortly after one, and as he left, most of the patrons trickled out. There were still a few men and women enjoying the blues blaring from the jukebox. Some of them danced so suggestively Cheri felt like she was encroaching on a personal moment.

She made her way to a booth in the corner to check on a scruffy looking gentleman missing several teeth. He couldn't really have been much older than forty-five, but the Louisiana sun and heat hadn't been kind to him.

"What else can I get ya?" she asked as she cleared his empty bottles from his table, placing them on her tray.

He looked up at her through drunken and bleary eyes. She suppressed the urge to gag as a sleazy grin climbed across his face.

"I tell ya what ya can git fo me sweetheart," he said as he suggestively grabbed at the front of his jeans.

Cheri stared coolly down at him, refusing to let him ruffle her feathers, even though she could feel her anger starting to bubble to life. She glanced over her shoulder and found not only Trixie but Jax watching her. *Fantastic.*

She turned and pasted on the fake smile she'd been using all evening. "Sorry love, I'm taken, but I can get ya once last drink if you'd like. It's last call," she said with false sweetness.

Leaning forward, she reached across his table to retrieve the last empty bottle. Instantly she realized her mistake when a rough hand slap across her backside and squeeze painfully.

Jax watched from across the room as the events between Cheri and the old man unfolded. Anger flared through him as he stepped around the bar to intervene.

"Hang on," Trixie said with an arm in front of his chest. "Let's see what she's got."

Jax didn't want to but he knew she was right. If Cheri was going to be working in his bar she needed to be able to take care of herself. He'd been watching her all night, or when time could allow it and had been impressed by the way she'd handled the intensity of the crowd. The minute her green eyes flashed fire at him, he knew she would work out just fine. He watched, there was just something about her that intrigued the hell out of him.

"Get your hands off me," Cheri said through gritted teeth, though she was still trying to keep her smile firmly in place.

"Ooo we dat ass is nice'n'tight." With his free hand, he rubbed the slight bulge in the front of his dirty jeans as he continued to grope her.

She set her tray on the table with a loud thump. The beer bottles that had been safely resting on the tray scattered across the table and bounced to the floor noisily.

"I said. Don't. Touch. Me," she snarled.

*Keep calm. You're going to lose your job on your first day.* Her inner voice chided.

When he didn't head her warning, her resolved snapped and so did her temper. When his hand began to run down the back of her bare thighs and then tried to make its way back up and under the hem of her shorts, she'd had enough. Blind with rage, she reached for the man's hand and with a quick jerk of her wrist, wrenched his fingers back savagely.

He howled in pain and tried to swing at her with his other hand. Whether she was too quick or he was just too drunk, it didn't matter because she easily dodged his drunken punch. The fact that he was willing to punch a woman only added fuel to her already growing fury. While still holding the man's fingers and wrist awkwardly bent back, she roughly grabbed him by the back of the neck and slammed his face down onto the table. There was a sickening crunch as his nose met the hard surface.

She held him there and bent close to his face. The ripe odor coming off of him nearly made her wretch. "When a woman tells you to get your hands off of her, ya better listen. Do you hear me?"

When he didn't answer she lifted his head and slammed it down again. He howled in pain.

"Do you hear me?" she said applying more pressure to his neck, smashing his bloody face harder into the table.

"Yes," he gurgled through the blood.

She released him and took a quick step back, making sure she was out of reach in case he came up swinging.

When he lifted his head, blood was oozing from his nose and mouth. He gingerly touched his face.

"Ya broke my nose ya crazy bitch." He stood drunkenly to his feet and took a step closer.

Cheri balled her fist at her sides, ready to defend herself further. She could have walked away, but she'd learned early on in life to never turn her back on a mean drunk. It never ended well. She braced her feet and prepared as the man got closer. Her heart sped through her chest.

"Everything okay here?" Jax appeared at her side, putting himself partially between them. He towered over the other man by a good eight inches. He had the ball bat casually slung over one of his shoulders.

"Dat crazy bitch done gone an broke m'nose," he said as he spit a stream of blood close to Cheri's feet. She wanted to recoil but held her ground.

"I didn't see a thing," Jax said lightly, "Trixie, did you see anything?" he called over his shoulder without taking his eyes off the other man.

"Nope. Sure didn't."

He took a step closer to Jax, puffing out his chest. Apparently, the alcohol had made him invincible.

"I should kick yer ass boy," he seethed.

Jax, unphased by the threat, smiled down at him. The smile was slow and lazy, but Cheri saw the darkness lying just beneath the surface. This man, her new boss, was dangerous. "You can try, but I promise, a broken nose will be the least of your problems." His voice was low and tight, and his gaze was steady.

That seemed to have gotten the man's attention because he backed down. He started to walk around them heading toward the exit, but Jax big hand landed heavily on his shoulder.

"Pay your tab at the bar."

The man glared at Cheri through swelling eyes. "You'll pay fa dis," he grunted as he made his way to the bar. Jax watched as the man left, followed by the remaining patrons.

When he turned his attention back to her, their eyes locked and held for a few moments. Deep brown eyes searched hers. She tried not to falter under the gaze. His strong jaw was covered with a couple days' worth of stubble. His hair was deep black, cropped short in the back and a little longer on top. There was a small cut above his left eye, just below his eyebrow, that seemed to still be healing. He was probably the sexiest man she'd seen in a very long time. With his hands on hips, legs braced apart, she didn't miss the tan expanse of chest that showed through the v of his t-shirt, or the definition of his legs beneath his worn jeans.

"What in the hell were you planning on doing?" he demanded.

"Excuse me?" she asked, a little confused.

"You looked like you were about ready to take him on."

"So?" she said as she stooped to pick up the scattered beer bottles.

"So?! Woman, are you out of your damn mind? He would have killed you. A woman has no place fighting a man."

Cheri frowned at the sexist remark. Slowly, she climbed to her feet, trying to choose her words carefully. It was hard considering adrenaline was still pumping through her veins. Couple that with the fury still raging through her and it made for an explosive combination. "Is there a rule somewhere say'n that a woman can't fight a man?"

He snorted. "There should be."

Her scowl deepened as she watched a smug smile spread on his beautiful lips. "Yeah well, it wouldn't be the first time I've had to fight a man. Sure as hell won't be the last."

The look on his face softened a margin and he licked his lips as he blew out a low sigh.

"Women can't fight men. It's stupid."

*Bet those lips taste good.* Inwardly she scolded the hormonal teenage girl that was more focused on her sexy boss than focused on his incredibly sexist remark.

"Do you have a tail to go with that snout?" she snapped as she quickly wiped her towel across the table. The white rag turned pink as she mopped the man's blood up, careful not to get it on her.

"Did you just call me a pig?" he scoffed.

"If the shit fits!" she slung back at him.

He glared at her for several long moments before finally throwing his head back letting out a large bark of laughter. When his eyes landed back on hers they were twinkling. The deep rumbling sound made her stomach flutter nervously and that pissed her off further.

"Do you get off laughing at me?"

"Got a bit of a temper on ya, eh?" He propped the ball bat against the table and stooped to pick up a stray beer bottle that had rolled beneath the table.

"I've dealt with men like you my entire life."

He arched a brow. "Men like me? Do tell, because I am curious to hear this." He pushed himself back up to his full height and placed the bottle on her tray.

She frowned at him. "I'd like to keep my job, so no, I won't be telling you," she said as she grabbed the tray and pushed around him, his heavy footfalls right behind her.

"You've not held your tongue so far. C'mon Mrs. Bouvier, don't hold back."

She slammed her tray on the bar and the bottles went plinking in different directions, *again*. She really needed to stop slamming stuff down when she got pissed. She whirled around on him.

Try as she might she couldn't hold back. "I've dealt with pigs my entire life. They see women as nothing but play things they can use until they're bored. Then, they move on to the next pretty toy. Men treat women as if they belong in the kitchen or laying on their back while they grunt and rut on top of them. I've enough in my life to deal with. The last thing I need right now is to have to constantly worry about satisfying or stroking your delicate male ego." By the time she finished she was breathing heavier and her hands trembled with rage.

"Woman, there isn't a single thing delicate about me." His voice was low and even.

She snorted, unsure if she should be amused or turned on.

"You've got a big ole brass pair on you," he scoffed.

She lifted her shoulder in a shrug as she tossed the bottles in the trash. "If ya don't want to know the truth then don't ask." She blew out an exaggerated huff and swatted at the strands of hair that had come out of the sloppy bun on top of her head. "Listen, if I'm fired then fine. I'm not here to make friends. If I didn't need this job, I wouldn't have come all the way down here. I'll smile and play nice, but I'll be damned if I let men paw at me, or talk down to me, and *that* includes you."

Casually he leaned on the end of the bar, resting his elbow on the surface while lacing his fingers together in front of him. He watched her with a smug smile. Obviously, he'd misjudged her from the very beginning. "Fighter are ya?"

"Yeah, well, when you've lived like I have, you don't have a choice." She moved around him and walked behind the bar. Trixie smiled evenly at her but didn't say anything.

Jax was quiet for a while before chuckling. He admired her spirit but knew her razor-sharp tongue would eventually begin to rub him the wrong way. "Just don't make a habit out of beating the hell outta my customers," he said as he moved away and began to upturn chairs and place them on the table.

"Then you need to tell them ta keep their hands to themselves," she shot back.

Jax frowned his good humor quickly beginning to fade. Perhaps the woman had just a little too much brass. "I can't always come to your aid when ya get into a situation like that."

Cheri scoffed. "You're awfully presumptuous, thinking I need your help. I didn't ask for your help."

"No, but you sure as hell needed it."

Cheri's hands balled into fists again as she clenched her teeth together. She itched to claw the smug look from his face. She'd managed to get away with breaking a customer's nose, somehow, she didn't think doing the same to her boss would end with the same result.

"How about a shot to welcome the new waitress," Trixie said, breaking up the tension between the pair. She poured three shots of liquor and nudged one to Jax and then one to Cheri.

Cheri and Jax glared at each other for a few minutes longer, neither one willing to back down. It wasn't until Trixie cleared her throat that the pair looked away.

"So, I get to get to keep my job?" she asked as she picked up the shot glass.

"You wouldn't I had anything to say 'bout it," Jax muttered.

Trixie shot him a warning glare but turned to Cheri. "No, honey, you're not fired and despite his rudeness, he's impressed with how ya handled yourself. He would'a done just the same. Truth of the matter is, we need someone too badly and he knows it." Trixie spoke to her like Jax wasn't standing three feet away.

Cheri smiled smugly up at Jax before tossing back the shot. It burned like wildfire as it burned a trail down her throat, but she somehow managed to keep her face blank.

Not wanting to be outdone by a woman, Jax tossed back the shot and slammed the glass down on the bar. "Get back to work. I'll be in my office if you need me," he said pointedly to Trixie and ignoring Cheri.

By the time 3:00 am rolled around, her feet were screaming and her body felt as if it had been steamrolled. She massaged her lower back as Trixie walked over to her and handed her a bundle of bills. "Not bad for your first night," she said.

"Thanks," Cheri said as she stuffed the bills in her back pocket without looking.

"Hey, I've got to take off," Trixie said, slinging her purse over her shoulder. "Do you mind telling Jax I bolted early?"

"I don't guess. Do I need to stay?"

"Normally someone stays so he can take a deposit to the bank, but he doesn't always go home. A lot of times he just sleeps here."

"Here? As in, the bar?"

Trixie nodded and walked around the bar. "Yeah, he has a little apartment in back. You did good. See you tomorrow at four?"

"Guess so," she said.

"Good."

Trixie walked across the room and through the front door. Wearily, she collapsed into a chair. Her entire body ached. She'd forgotten just how truly exhausting waitressing could really be. She removed the wad of money she'd stuffed into her back pocket and began to count. "Wow," she muttered, stunned that her tips totaled one hundred and fifteen dollars.

Taking out her phone, she dialed her son, knowing that with his sleeping issues he was likely still up.

She was right.

"Hey, baby. How are ya?" she asked.

*"Good. Why are you still up?"*

"I'm just getting off work."

*"Work? Why work? The grocery store closed hours ago."* She could hear the skepticism in his voice.

"I got fired today, but a lady offered me another job."

*"Where at?"* She heard the sound of rapid key punches from his end and knew he must have been writing or playing a game.

"Are you writing?" She was trying to redirect the conversation. It didn't work.

*"Yes, and ya didn't answer my question."*

She took a deep breath. "The Voodoo Queen."

*"Mon Dieu, mom,"* he said angrily. *"What the hell do ya think you're doing working at that place? Do you have any idea what kind of sick bastards lurk there? I mean—"*

"Hey!" she snapped, abruptly cutting him off. "First of all, *young man*, you'd do well to remember I'm still your mother. I don't let grown men talk to me the way you just did and I'll be damned if I let my own son talk to me that way. Am. I. Clear?"

*"Yes ma'am,"* he grumbled into the phone.

"Secondly, I needed a job. There was no way around it," she said sadly.

*"Mom? What's wrong?"*

"Nothing you need to worry about. I'll have it all taken care of by Monday."

*"I'm coming home tomorrow!"*

"No. You need to spend time with your father."

*"And you need me at home. You're more important than he is anyhow.*

"Don't be like that." She couldn't deny the fact that the petty part of her mind was screaming with joy at the thought of her son liking her more than his father.

*"Mom?"*

"I promise, Jeremy, I've got everything under control."

*"Are you okay? Do you have food?"*

"Yes, baby, I have food. Now stop worrying." He started to interrupt but she cut him off. "Kiss your sister for me and get some rest."

*"But . . . I can come—"*

"No. Now goodnight," she said firmly.

*"Love ya,"* he muttered.

"Love ya too."

She snapped her phone closed and sagged back into her chair. Reaching up, she unwound her hair and let it fall down her back, immediately easing the headache she'd developed. Closing her eyes, she rolled her neck from side to side. If she had another good night tomorrow night, she may be able to come up with enough money to pay at least half the electric bill.

She pinched the bridge of her nose. Taking a deep breath, she tried to calm herself. Slowly she exhaled. Leaning forward—resting her elbows on the table—she cradled her face in her palms. Her eyes kept drifting closed. She wished Jax would hurry the hell up.

Jax stood at the door to his office, catching the last part of her phone conversation. She had kids. Were they home alone while she worked? There wasn't a ring on her finger. Was there a man in the picture? He watched as she let down her hair and nearly groaned when the dark waves fell past her shoulders. He'd always been a sucker for brunettes.

As he watched her roll her neck and shoulders he found himself wondering things about her he shouldn't even been considering. She'd proven her temper was just as salty as his own. The two of them would be a bad combination. Still, the very male part of him wondered what it would be like.

Shaking the dangerous thoughts from his head, he made his presence known by clearing his throat.

Cheri jumped and turned.

"Where's Trixie?"

"She left. Said I needed to stay and wait for you."

"Well you can go now," he said dismissively.

"Do I need to report my tips to you?"

"Nah, what ya do with it is your own business, I don't really care. I pay regular minimum wage, so ya don't have to."

"Okay, well, thanks."

Slipping her phone in her back pocket and her keys into her front pocket, she walked toward the door. "See ya tomorrow," he called.

"Yeah," she said waving over her shoulder. She was nearly out the door when she stopped and turned.

"Thanks," she said awkwardly. "Ya know, for the job."

He nodded once. "You're welcome."

With a smile, she stepped out into the night. The air was heavy with moisture and the dense humidity saturated her skin immediately. With each breath, she felt as if she were swallowing buckets of rancid swamp water. Quickly, she coiled her hair back on top of her head. She'd taken five steps and her clothes were already sticking to her uncomfortably. In the distance, she saw a flash of lightning. As she walked down the dock, she prayed the rain would hold off until she got home, but then again maybe the rain would provide some relief. Stuffing her hands in her pockets and around her keys, she set off toward home. Each step she took, her aching feet made protest. As soon as she got her electric back on and things caught up, she was going to have to retire her three-year-old Goodwill Nikes.

Thunder rumbled behind her and despite her pain, she picked up her pace.

Night vision binoculars zeroed in on his prey. He watched from his boat as she left the bar and began to walk home. It would be so easy to take her, to just grab her and do all the things his body was screaming for, but that would be entirely *too* easy. It was about the game and his impatience would just ruin it. The hunt was always more fun than the kill. Well, in most cases.

Blood begin began to sing through his veins in excitement. His placid member began to jerk to life. The image of her on her knees, hands bound behind her as she begged for mercy only excited him further. Oh, he was going to enjoy every second he had her.

Perhaps he *should* just take her now. A dark scowl crossed his face. If that happened, he knew he would be less than satisfied. Maybe, just maybe, he could take her and keep her for a while, using her until there was nothing left. This made the thought of taking her sooner than planned a little more appealing. Sure, he was still going to carve every inch of flesh from her body while she was still alive, but he might as well have a little fun beforehand.

He watched the sway of her shapely ass with each step, and then finally, the darkness swallowed her. Deciding to stick with the original plan, he took up his oars and slowly rowed from his hiding spot. It wouldn't be long before the bar owner came out. He'd taken a risk actually going inside tonight. Thankfully he'd been able to slip in and out without being noticed. For an hour straight he'd watched her move around the room, flirting and earning money. Whore. She was nothing but a filthy whore.

Rage burned through him all over again, burning away the lust that had been in his veins. His hands tightened around the oars as he silently emerged from beneath the bar. Thunder rumbled closer, the charge in the air becoming more tangible thanks to the incoming storm. No, he would not take her tonight. It just wasn't time. There were still things that needed to be done. Things had already been set into motion. The games had only just begun.

# 5

Her sodden shoes squished against the pavement as she stomped through the puddles. She'd barely made it half a mile before the summer storm unleashed its torrent. With each step, she violently cursed her life and everything about it. She cursed Alex for leaving her in ruins. She cursed her former boss at the grocery store for being a pitiful excuse of a man, and then she cursed both men at the same time. After a good rant about them, she moved on to curse her new boss.

Angrily she pushed the soaked stands of hair out of her face, but they stubbornly fell right back in place. She seriously contemplated even showing back up to the bar. Was it actually worth being subjected to the lewd comments and the groping, not to mention the obnoxiously handsome yet infuriating owner?

She let out a frustrated sigh, beads of water flew off her nose and disappeared into the downpour. Of course, it wasn't worth it, but what choice did she have? If she didn't work at the bar, where would she go? She hardly had any food in the house, the power was barely on.

Lost in her thoughts, she didn't hear the blaring of a horn until it was right behind her. "What the hell," she screeched before flipping the truck the bird as it passed, splashing warm and muddy water all over her.

She screamed at the tail lights but her curses were drowned out by the rolling clap of thunder that made her jump. Another vehicle rolled passed her, but this one slowed to a stop. She stopped and stared at the bright red lights of an older model truck. There weren't many people out and about at four in the morning, except for lunatics and even then that's pushing it. They had to sleep too, right?

The reverse lights switched on and slowly the truck backed toward her. Cheri's hand tightened around her keys as it came to a stop beside her. The door flew open

51

with loud popping hinges screaming of their need of WD-40.

"Why are you walking?" Jax's baritone timbre sounded from the inside of the darkened cab. She could barely hear his voice over the downpour. His features glowed eerily in the green lights of the dash.

"Felt like the thing to do." Despite the heat, the rain was making her cold.

"It's raining."

"No shit?! Is that what that is?" She rolled her eyes.

"You know, you're a real smart ass!"

"Better than being a dumb ass," she shot back.

"Oh, that's clever. Did you come up with that one on your own?"

"What do you want, Jax?"

"Well, I thought I was being nice and offering you a ride."

"You didn't offer me anything but a stupid question and a very stupid observation."

"You don't want a ride? Fine by me."

Without bothering to close the door, Jax pressed the gas and sped off, the door slapping shut on the way.

Cheri just stood watching his tail lights disappear around the corner, dumbfounded that he'd actually left her. He hadn't even really offered her a ride as much as just open the door.

"I freaking hate men," she muttered, forcing her aching and stiff legs to get moving again. As she rounded the corner, on the side of the road sat Jax's truck.

Biting down on her pride and pushing it aside, she opened the passenger side door and slid in.

"What took you so long?" he asked as he took a long drag off his cigarette. The cherry glowed to life. Leaning over in the seat she plucked it from between his lips and put it between hers. After taking a deep drag she slowly blew out the bluish smoke into the truck.

"Would you like one?" he asked, shaking one from his pack and offering it to her.

After taking another drag from his, she handed it back to him and took the offered one. He flicked the lighter in front of her and she flinched at the sudden light. Cupping his hands with hers to hold the flame still she inhaled and lit the cigarette.

She moved away and exhaled, already feeling a bit calmer. "Thanks," she said as she blew a stream of smoke through her nose.

"I just didn't want to give you mine. Where too?" he asked as he pushed the gearshift on the floor into first.

Cheri told him her address and he just looked at her through the darkness.

"What?" she asked, squirming under his gaze.

"You were going to walk all that way tonight?" he asked incredulously.

"Didn't feel like flying," she muttered.

"Why? Is your broom broke?"

Cheri frowned. "Do you make a habit out of being a dick, or is this a special occasion?"

He chose to ignore her and focus on something else. "All ya had to do is ask for a lift. I would'a given ya one."

"Yeah, that would'a been an awesome first impression."

"Your first impression wasn't that great, nor was your second or third."

"Are you nearing a point here soon or do we need to stop for supplies?"

Jax sucked on the filter one last time before cracking the window and flicking it out.

"Are you always such a bitch to people who are trying to help you out?"

"I don't need help from anyone. I can do just fine on my own," she said stubbornly.

"Listen, I was just being nice. It's not safe for a beautiful woman to be out walking this time a night. Not in this area and definitely not in a storm."

Had she just heard him right? Did he really just call her beautiful?

"Pfft, no one is going to mess with me. I look like a drowned rat!"

Jax opened his mouth to reply but it snapped closed again. There was no use. The woman was infuriating. She had a comment or remark about everything. He was afraid if she kept talking he would throw her ass back out on the side of the road and be done with her. Instead, he shook another cigarette from the pack and stuck it between his lips. The lighter flared to life and he rolled the window down.

They rode in silence before he pulled under the lit awning of the only twenty-four-hour gas station in town. As he fueled up the truck Cheri went inside and bought herself a pack of cigarettes. She knew she shouldn't, but until things started to calm down, it was her only outlet.

The storm raged on around them, the protective awning doing little to protect them from the downpour. Sliding back into the truck she lit another smoke and stared out her window. Water drops gathered and then slid down the glass, leaving silvery trails behind.

The driver side door popped open, causing Cheri to flinch. She looked at Jax but he was looking at the gauges on the dash. He turned the key in the ignition and the old beast rumbled to life.

"How old is this thing?" Cheri asked, tired of the silence between them.

"I've had her for a few years," he said, patting the steering wheel affectionately.

She chuckled. "What is it with men and their trucks?"

"There are very few things in life that a woman can't take from a man."

"Really now?" she said with a slight smile.

"Yep."

"Are you going to share this little bit of wisdom?"

"Nah, not t'night," he said with a grin as he pulled back into the storm.

Finally, they pulled into her driveway. He shifted into park and killed the engine, leaving the lights on. Cheri looked at her house and shivered. It looked like an evil beast in the shadows of the storm.

"Thanks for the ride," she said as she tried to open the door. She jiggled the handle, but nothing happened.

"Hang on." He jumped out his door and walked around the front of the truck. With a firm tug, he pulled the door open.

"It sticks sometimes," he said by way of explanation.

"Worked fine earlier," she muttered as she slid out.

She stumbled into him when he didn't move out of the way. His hand landed on her hip as he steadied her.

"You have a thing with gett'n in people's personal spaces don't ya?" Cheri said, trying to ignore the lingering smell of his cologne.

"Hey, you're the one that can't stand up. C'mon, I'm tired of getting wet," he said allowing his hand to linger a moment longer than necessary. He dropped his hand and moved to her side.

She took a step toward her house and he followed. Stopping, she turned and looked at him. "I'm perfectly capable of walking into my own house on my own."

"My momma taught me better than that," he argued.

"I don't see your momma here, so run along," she said dismissively already making her way to the house.

She could hear his heavy footfalls behind her. When she reached the safety of the porch, she spun around and pinned him with a look.

"Well, thanks for the ride and the chivalry. G'night," she said brusquely.

"I'll wait until you're inside," he said stubbornly.

She groaned, knowing that there was no way that he would be deterred until he walked her *into* the house. She just prayed that her power had been turned back on. If push came to shove she could blame an outage on the storm.

Tugging open the torn screen door, she turned the knob and kicked the bottom of the old storm door. Before entering fully, she reached in with her hand and brushed it against the switch. She said a silent prayer of thanks when the room was suddenly bathed with harsh yellow lighting. She flinched. It looked better in the dark. The couch was strewn with blankets and pillows. On the coffee table was a coffee cup with old coffee in it as well as a few empty Red Bull cans.

"Sorry about the mess. The maid's out," she snorted as she gathered the cans and disappeared through the door that lead to the kitchen.

"You a bit of a caffeine junkie?" he called after her.

"Something like that," she said tiredly as she tossed the cans and walked back into the room. She leaned against the door frame, crossing her arms.

"That stuff'll kill ya," he said.

"Thanks for your concern," she said dryly.

"You good here?"

"Of course I am. Why wouldn't I be?"

He lifted a shoulder. "I'll come get ya tomorrow for work, or I'll send Trixie," he said as he walked to the door.

"What makes you think I'll need a ride?"

"Because you needed one tonight and I don't see a vehicle in the drive. 'Sides, this storm is s'pposed to last til Tuesday."

She frowned. "You're kind of a pain in the ass."

"And you're stubborn."

He turned to walk out and she let out a long sigh. "Thanks," she said softly.

Jax stopped and turned, giving her a stunned look. This caused her to chuckle. "I know I come off as a bit of a bitch. I'm just. . . . Thanks," she said again before she could ramble any further.

A genuine smile curved on his face. He tilted his head in her direction. "You're welcome." That was all he said as he walked through the front door, down the steps, and into the pelting rain. The horn blasted once and then he was gone, tail lights disappearing behind a curtain of rain.

There wasn't much she liked about her house. However, the one thing she did love was the claw foot tub in the tiny bathroom. The elegant tub looked sorely out of place against the chipped wall tiles and peeling linoleum on the drastically uneven floor. However, she enjoyed a good long soak.

It was nearly six in the morning before she slipped beneath the bubbles. Her body ached. She was physically and mentally exhausted. Steam rose and curled around her as the storm beat its fury against the window. The sky was trying to lighten to day but the heavy saturation of black clouds prevented the progress. Three candles rested on the closed toilet lid. Their flames sent dancing shadows skittering across the wall and up the ceiling. Her eyes grew heavy and soon she began to drift.

Black water swirled around her, filling her nose and mouth with putrid, rotting swamp sludge. She tried to scream, but it oozed down her throat and choked her. Reaching out through the darkness she tried to grasp for something to pull her to safety, but the only thing she grabbed was darkness.

She struggled to kick her legs, trying to propel herself to the surface but nothing happened. Something was tightly wrapped around her ankles, pulling her deeper into the abyss. Her lungs burned for air, begging for relief. None came.

Her movements became sluggish and she began to grow lightheaded. With one last desperate attempt, she reached through the inky blackness for something to cling to. This time her hand brushed against something. She tangled her hands in what felt like fabric and tugged with all her might. The darkness around her began to lighten to a pale shade of gray. As her vision began to clear, she slowly turned her head and looked in front of her.

Her mouth opened in a scream as a bloated face appeared in front of hers. Its flesh was split and rotting, eyes missing from their sockets. She struggled to release the body but its engorged fingers moved and wrapped tightly around her wrist. Slowly, its mouth inched open in a silent scream. She watched in horror as a snake slithered through black and broken teeth, circling the corpse's throat before making its way into the empty eye cavities. Water filled her lungs as she kicked and screamed. There was no sound—only terror. It was him. He was coming to get her and this time, she wouldn't survive.

Cheri bolted upright, choking and violently spiting up streams of water. Water sloshed over the edge of the tub and onto the floor. Feeling momentarily disoriented, she looked around, trying to get a grip on her surroundings. Her heart sprinted so hard through her chest that she was certain there would be bruises. The room was dark, the candles on the toilet having gone out. She frowned because they weren't melted down. Smoke still curled up from their extinguished wicks.

Her breathing had yet to return to normal as she once again looked around the room.

Careful not to slip, she gripped the edge of the tub with trembling hands and stepped from the still warm water. She reached for her the towel she'd left on the towel rack, but there was nothing there. Cheri's stomach turned and her throat grew dry as a feeling of unease settled over her. Reaching for the light switch she flicked it but nothing happened.

"Seriously?"

A loud clap of thunder reminded her that the storm was still raging as her house gave a little shutter. She grabbed a t-shirt from the back of the door and tugged it over her trembling body. Making her way down the dark hall, the unmistakable sound of creaking floorboards caused her to stop. It wasn't until her lungs began to burn that she realized she'd been holding her breath. Slowly, she let it out.

*Creeeeeak.*

The short hall felt like it was twenty miles long. Her blood pulsed in her ears and goosebumps puckered her skin. She flattened herself against the wall and slowly inched her head around the corner. It was exactly at this point when she watched movies, she would be screaming at the woman on the television about her stupidity. *Don't look around the corner.* It was too late to go back.

*Wham. Wham. Wham. Crack.*

The sudden loud noise made her scream. The front door was standing wide open as the screen door was being slammed into the wall by the howling wind.

Why was the door open? She could have sworn she'd closed and locked it before taking a bath.

Her entire body trembled as she crossed the living room on shaking legs to pull the screen door closed. As she was about to turn away a flash of lightning splintered the sky. A dark figure stood at the end of her driveway. Her eyes grew wide and terror slashed through her as the lightning faded. Had he been in her house? Maybe she'd been imagining things. Another jagged streak of lightning lit the sky, causing her squeeze her eyes closed. However, when she opened them again, the figure was gone.

Taking a shaky breath, she jerked the heavy door closed and twisted the rickety deadbolt, knowing it wouldn't be much in the way of protection, but at least it gave her a small measure of security. Her hands shook violently as she tried to calm her nerves.

The power flickered back on and she breathed a small sigh of relief. However, her relief was short lived when something on the carpet caught her attention. Kneeling down she examined the old, yellowing carpet. Footprints—muddy footprints, making a trail through the living room and disappearing into the hall. Cautiously she followed them, switching on more lights as she went. Electricity bill be damned. The prints went straight to the bathroom and stopped in front of the toilet, right beside the tub where her head had rested on the back. How had she missed them earlier?

Cheri's entire body was overcome with violent tremors, and bile began to rise to the back of her throat. Someone had been in her house, watching her sleep, naked. Tears welled in her eyes. This just wasn't happening. She looked at the mirror, still slightly fogged from the fading steam of her bath. Dripping letters made her take a quick step back. Her feet became tangled in the floor mat, and she fell, ripping the towel rack from the wall as she collided with the wooden storage cabinet.

She couldn't focus on the pain shooting through her side or the bruise she was sure to have on her shoulder. The only thing she saw was the fading words.

"I know."

# 6

Jax hadn't wanted to play taxi to the new waitresses, but the fact of the matter was, he couldn't bear to let her walk to work. Trixie and Kimmy were swamped with the cleanup following the lunch rush. They would be spending the rest of the afternoon preparing for the evening rush. He'd been the only other option.

He pulled into her drive at half past three and switched off the ignition. The roof of the house was missing shingles and one portion was covered by a large blue tarp, partially blown aside. He frowned. Life definitely was not being kind to Cheri.

He climbed from the truck and made his way up the front porch. The storm had taken a break, leaving behind thick and sticky air. The heavy black clouds in the distance reminded him that the storm was far from over. By the time he reached the front door, his shirt was sticking to him. Lifting his hand, he tapped his knuckles against the glass. The single pane rattled loudly and he was worried that the thing would shatter. The curtain moved aside and Cheri's pale face appeared on the other side. He stepped back at the sound of the deadbolt turning.

"Hey," Cheri said, as she got the door open after a few solid jerks. She slipped through the crack, preventing him from seeing further into her house. Her skin was slightly pale and her green eyes were red-rimmed. Dark circles had formed under her eyes as she stared wearily at him.

"Are you okay?" he asked.

A frown pinched her face. "Yes. Why wouldn't I be?" she asked said in a clipped tone.

"You just look . . . tired," he said.

She rolled her eyes as she pulled the door closed behind her, locking it. She turned and looked up at him.

"You know that's just a polite way of sayin I look like shit, right?"

Jax's mouth fell open and then snapped shut. "No, I was saying you look tired," he said with a frown.

She shrugged. "Outta coffee," she said as if it explained it all.

"Noted. Well, your taxi service is here," he said sarcastically.

"I wasn't . . . I mean I thought it would be Trixie," she muttered.

"We had a busy lunch," he said by way of answer.

"Oh." She moved passed him and walked down the steps.

"You know, with a door like that, anyone can just walk right in."

She spun around. Her abruptness brought him up short. A strange look crossed over her face, but then it was gone. It happened so quickly he thought he'd imagined it. Fear?

She slid her sunglasses down over her eyes. He could see his reflection in the lenses. A deep frown pulled her full lips downward. "Did ya come to criticize my house or give me a ride to work? Because I only need one of those. I'll let ya guess which one."

Jax bit down on the inside of his cheek. "I only meant—"

"Well save it. I'm not interested."

That was the end of the conversation as she marched around the mud puddles and to the side of the truck. Her denim shorts hugged her round backside nicely. Her short legs were tanned and well defined. There didn't appear to be anything other than muscle on them. Today she'd chosen to wear a dark pink halter-top. A giant feather tattoo was in the middle of her back, the top of it tearing away and turning into birds. He hadn't really noticed the tattoo before, but something about it was appealing. However, the tattoo wasn't the only thing on her back that he noticed. A dark purple bruised marred her shoulder.

"What happen to your shoulder," he asked as he followed her to the truck.

She stopped and turned. "Nothing. I don't remember."

It was a lie. He knew it and she knew he knew it.

He watched as she struggled with the passenger door before finally getting it open. Climbing in she slammed the door closed and angrily crossed her arms over her chest.

"Damn women," he muttered as he walked around the truck.

Over the next several days, Cheri fell into a comfortable routine at the bar. Once she was familiar with everything, she discovered that she actually liked it. She and Trixie had become friends and even Jax had been somewhat tolerable. By tolerable, it meant she rarely saw him. He was usually holed up in his office or out running errands. The only time she saw him for an extended period of time was when he took her home after work, which was usually about three in the morning.

On some days she walked to the bar, her pride never allowing her to call for a ride. Sometimes, however, Jax's uncle Marvin had taken to picking her up in his rusty old yellow Chevy. She'd instantly taken a liking to the old Cajun, finding his playful banter and kind demeanor oddly comforting. If she'd had a grandfather, Marvin was what she imagined him to be like. He always had a way of making her laugh and found that while Jax was as tough as nails and as mean as a gator, he had a soft spot for his uncle.

Thankfully, nothing else happened at home, and after three days with very little sleep, she figured it was just someone playing a sick joke on her. She'd called Roux Sunday morning and told him about what had happened. After an hour of talking, he'd managed to convince her that she was just under a lot of stressed and that the footprints she'd seen were her own. Though she'd spent the next day scrubbing up the prints, she'd somehow managed to convince herself that she'd imagined the whole thing.

Roux always had a way of calming her down and finding logic with everything. This time had been no different. He was still looking out for her, even though they'd been out of the system for years.

While she'd pushed the events that happened in her house out of her mind, she still couldn't shake the feeling that she was being watched.

Her finances weren't in much better shape, but she'd managed to pay part of her electric bill with the tips she'd made the first weekend working at the bar. After some more begging, she'd even convince the sweet clerk to allow her to pay the rest of the balance on Friday.

It was Saturday—a week after starting work at the bar—and she begrudgingly made her way into city hall—a day late—with what was left of her tips after buying limited groceries. It wasn't enough and she knew it. She still owed well over two hundred dollars, but she was hoping to get one more extension. She could have waited until Monday but she'd decided that it was better to show up as a good faith gesture. It was a good thing they were open half a day.

Cheri waited patiently in line behind an older woman. Finally, it was her time to face the music. She stepped up to the long wooden desk.

"Please tell me you got the rest of yer money, *cher*," the older heavyset black woman said in a hushed whisper. Her thick accent was indicative of being raised deep in Louisiana. Her hair was pulled into a frizzy bun on top of her head, harsh silver strands poking out in all directions. She looked over her black framed glasses at Cheri.

"I've only got a hundred," Cheri said softly.

The woman frowned. "Honey, I cain't give ya no mo time."

"Even with this? I'm working all weekend and I can have the rest by Monday mornin." The front door opened bringing in the hot air from outside. Cheri was too focused on trying to keep her power on to pay attention to anything else.

"Dats what ya said Monday, that you would have it on Friday. It's Saturday. Honey, I've helped ya all I can, but I've got my own family I gots ta think about."

"Please, Marj. Just a day and a half. Ya'll aren't even open tomorrow." Cheri hated begging, but it was all she could do. If Marj couldn't keep her power on then, Cheri would do without until she could get it turned back on, even if that meant paying the extra fees.

"I'm sorry, *cher*. I jus cain't."

"Well, how much is left?"

Marj clicked away on an old keyboard. "After ya pay t'day, you'll still owe a hunnerd and eighty-three dollas."

Cheri slid the stack of ones and fives across the counter with a heavy sigh. "Thanks for doin what ya could."

Marj took the money and gave her a sad smile. "Thin's'll start look'n up for ya honey. Don't ya give up."

Cheri laughed sadly. "They really can't get much worse." Hitching her purse over her shoulder she turned. She jolted to a stop and her stomach landed with a splat at her ankles. She was wrong, things just got much worse.

"What are you doing here?" she said as she found Jax staring down at her. Her face flamed with embarrassment. It was obvious he'd heard everything that had just happened.

"Just pay'n bills. Hey Marj," he said taking Cheri's spot at the desk.

"Hey, Jax honey. What can I do fer ya?"

"Just need to pay the bar's utilities."

"Sure thing."

While Marj clicked away on her computer he turned to Cheri, who was still standing awkwardly behind him. "Ya work today?"

"You made the schedule, shouldn't ya know the answer to that?" she snapped hatefully.

He frowned.

She sighed. "Sorry. I just had some stuff I had to take care of here, and yes I work today."

"Hang on and I'll give you a ride." He turned around and talked to Marj but she couldn't understand what he was saying. She wasn't about to turn down a ride. It was over a hundred degrees and she'd just about smothered walking to city hall.

She watched as Jax reached into the back pocket of his faded jeans and removed his wallet. He took out some cash and then stuffed the faded leather back into its place. A few minutes later she heard Marj giggle like a school girl and Jax's deep laughter. He turned to his side and leaned an elbow onto the desk.

"When ya gonna run away with me, Marj?" he flirted.

"Jax honey, what choo gonna do wit a woman as big as me, eh?"

"What can I say, I like a woman with curves." For a brief moment, his dark gaze lingered on Cheri. She frowned and looked away, feeling blush burn her cheeks.

Marj batted at his hand. "Get on outta here wit dat mess, you. Keep outta trouble."

"Now ya know that ain't gonna happen'n. You've known me for too long," he said with a wink.

"Dat is true. How's yer momma?"

"Ornery."

"Boy, she 'as ta be wit a son like you." Marj giggled again and Cheri wondered if it were possible for the woman's accent to get thicker.

"Now, don't get ugly," he teased.

"Ya tell'er I said hi, will ya?"

"Yes'm," he said politely.

"Now git outta'ere b'fore I take ya up on yer offer," she said swatting at him with her hand.

"Offer still stands." He pushed away from the counter. "We gotta get ta work," he said pointedly to Cheri. He walked passed her and made his way to the door, but a loud *pssst* stopped her before she could leave.

"I tol'ja things would get better," she said with a nod in Jax's direction.

Cheri frowned at the woman's meaning and left the blessed air conditioning to step into the oppressive heat. The harsh sun beat down on her scalp, making it tingle uncomfortably. It wasn't until she was in the truck, the old leather bench seat hot beneath her legs, that she realized what had just happened.

She turned to Jax and frowned at him.

"Did you just do what I think you just did?"

He snickered. "Boy that's a mouth full, and what is it that you think I just did?" he asked as he cranked the engine. He flipped the switch and warm air blasted through the vents, but soon it turned cool. He shifted into reverse.

"You know damn well what I'm talk'n about."

"I'm fairly certain I don't." He pulled to the four-way stop and then turned right, heading toward the bar.

"You paid my electric bill didn't you?"

He was quiet for a long time. "Damnit Jax, answer me!" she demanded.

"So what if I did? It looked like you were having a hard time."

"It's none of your business."

"*Têtue*," he muttered.

Cheri whipped her head around. "Stubborn woman? Really?"

He eyed her a smidge of surprised in his eyes.

She nodded. "Yeah, that's right. I understand perfectly what you said. And you know what? *Embrasse mon tcheue,* I didn't ask for your help," she snapped.

Cheri had no idea what she was expecting but his laughter was not one. "I'll be damned. Kiss your ass? Kiss. Your. Ass?"

Once he got his laughter under control she looked at him. "Are you quite finished?"

"You're a real piece of work, you know that?"

Her frowned deepened. "I don't like owing people. Especially, strangers I barely know," she grumbled.

"We're hardly strangers."

She turned in her seat and looked at him, squaring her shoulders proudly. "Jax, I work for you. We're not friends, we barely know each other, and hell, we can barely be in the same room without fighting."

"Because you're a stubborn female," he muttered, this time in English, as he pulled the truck to stop at the end of the pier.

"That's like the pot calling the kettle black."

Jax turned and stared at her. His arm stretched out on the back of the seat. "Listen, we may not know each other well, but ya proved yourself at my bar. We don't get along because we both have apparent attitude problems. But, I take care of my own. You work for me, therefore you've become part of that. If ya don't like it, well, that's just too damn bad."

"I'm going to pay you back."

"Fine. If that's what ya feel like you need to do, then ya can start tonight." He arched a brow and a lazy smile tipped his mouth up.

"W-what?" she squeaked.

Jax looked at her smugly. Her eyes grew wide as she studied him. Good Lord, she hoped he wasn't suggesting *that*.

*Would it be a bad thing?* She shook the thought from her head, even though it had her shifting uncomfortably in her seat. Heat flamed through her extremities. Okay, so perhaps the thought wasn't altogether unappealing.

He laughed, the sound low and rich. "You need to relax. I've got a catering job t'night. I need a hand. You interested?"

"You cater?"

"Not normally, but this is a special circumstance." When he saw her hesitate he then added. "I'll pay you extra."

Cheri thought about it for a little longer, he added. "The money would be good."

She lifted a shoulder. "Sure, but who's going to watch the bar while you're gone?"

"Trixie can cover it and I've got a couple of the other girls coming in to cover."

"Okay."

"Great. Cookie should be finishing up now. We'll get the kegs and coolers loaded, then the food and we'll be on our way."

"Kegs?"

"Yeah, this is a private gathering."

"Oh," was all she could say before two guys appeared on the ramp from the back of the bar. One was wheeling down a keg while the other was carrying two cases of beer.

"C'mon," Jax said climbing from the truck. "We need to help Cookie get the food down, and knowing him, there's gonna be a ton."

Jax hadn't been joking. When they got to the kitchen Cookie was covering the last pot of gumbo. There were at least two dozen containers covered with foil.

"Good lord, Cookie, ya cooking for an army?" she asked as she walked in and plucked a freshly boiled shrimp from the pile before he could get it covered. She peeled away the shell and popped it into her mouth. Flavor immediately exploded on her tongue as the butter and spices blended together.

"Eh, ya know us Cajuns like ta eat, we do."

"Mmm, dat dere is some good stuff," she said, imitating a thick Cajun accent.

"Dats fo'sho babuh girl. Don' ya go forget'n it. Ole Cookie be da best cook in dese parts," he said flashing her a wide gaped tooth grin.

She just chuckled as she began hefting container after container to the truck. Finally, when the last had been loaded and a new tarp secured over the bed, she and Jax climbed into the truck.

"So where exactly we headin?"

"Out to Bayou Jons."

"Bayou Jons? That is in the middle of nowhere!"

"Yeah, this family likes their privacy."

Cheri frowned. "Are they criminals?"

Jax laughed. "No. The furthest from it. The woman used to actually work for the government. They just like their solitude."

Cheri tensed. She was going to be around someone that had worked for the government. She tried not to panic, for all she knew the woman could have worked for the post office. At any rate, she grew more nervous.

The drive to Bayou Jons was a solid thirty-minute drive. Jax had told her they could have went by boat and it would have been much closer, but carrying that much food would not have been a good idea. He turned onto a dirt path barely wide enough for a vehicle to fit down. It was barely discernible from the road. On both sides of the drive, nailed to two massive pine trees were bright yellow "no trespassing" signs. Both signs were riddled with holes from buckshot.

The truck bumped and bounced over the washouts from the previous storm for over a mile before they finally pulled into a circular driveway. There was at least a dozen or more vehicles parked haphazardly everywhere. Mostly large trucks covered in mud and sporting giant wheels. A single story, blue sided house was the center point. It was an old dwelling that had mismatched wooden shingles on the roof, some old and some very recently added. A tin covered porch jutted out from the front. Bright, paper lanterns were strewn between the railings. Twinkling white lights were draped between poles.

The house sat about three hundred yards from a small dock. Kids were running and screaming as they plummeted themselves off the end, into the reddish-brown water. Swimming in the bayou could be very dangerous. Cheri knew this first hand, which is why she never swam anywhere she couldn't see what was around or under her.

As soon as she slipped from the truck, she was struck by sounds of zydeco music, loud laughter, and singing. Kid's laughter filled the air as she saw more children darting between vehicles while playing a game of what appeared to be hide and seek. The humidity in the swamps and bayous were more oppressive due to the extreme moisture. With the humidity and moisture came mosquitoes the size of Volkswagens. The strong scent of citronella drifted from the dozens upon dozens of tiki touches scattered about. Some were scattered among the pine trees while others lined the water's edge.

"Wow," she said as she moved to the back of the truck and began to remove the tarp.

Jax just laughed and placed two fingers between his lips and whistled obnoxiously loud.

"Damn, warn someone next time," Cheri said, flinching away from the shrill whistle.

"Oh, hey I'm going to whistle," he said smartly.

Before she could retort, three men and two women appeared.

"*Mon Dieu*, Jaxon, do ya think ya brought e'nough food?" said one of the men. He looked to be in his mid-twenties with copper orange hair and freckles covering his face.

"Ya wanna eat, no?" Jax said, handing the boy a foil covered tray.

The women took some and after a few more trips they finally had all the food unloaded.

"What do you want me to do?" Cheri asked.

"Just set up the tables and start uncovering the food. I'll be there in a second to help ya."

Cheri went to the large line of tables and began to uncover the food while placing serving spoons in each one.

"Oo-we dat Cookie done gone and outdone 'imself dis time."

When she looked up she found Uncle Marvin hovering over the sugar covered beignets. His hands stuffed in the pockets of his worn overalls. She smiled. "Uncle Marvin, I didn't expect to see you," she said, glad to see a friendly face that she knew.

"*Cher*, look at'choo. You is purtier dan a lily on de swamp," he said, releasing a low whistle.

"Are you flirting again?" she teased with a wink.

"Mehbe. Is it work'n?" his blue eyes twinkled mischievously.

"Keep it up and it just might," she said with a wink. He laughed heartily and ambled off.

As she continued to uncover and prepare dishes. She heard strong creole accent. When she turned she found an old man staring expectantly at a much younger one. His eyes were gray-blue and slightly clouded from what she guessed were cataracts. However, there was still a sharpness of knowledge and wisdom that lingered in their depths. The old timer's face was leathery and creased with age, creating extra folds of skin along the sides of his face and down his neck. An old, trucker-style cap, was perched on top of his head. He sat in an old metal chair with his hands neatly folded on top of a twisted cypress cane, staring expectantly at the other gentleman.

The younger man looked miserable and sorely out of place. He was wearing a long sleeve dress shirt with the sleeves pushed up past his elbows. His black slacks were already covered with mud and sweat was pouring from his face. It was a handsome face but in a clean-cut, country club sense.

It was obvious that the old timer was speaking to him, but he looked helpless as he struggled to understand what was being said.

"*To pale kreyol?*" the old man repeated in a rough, gravelly voice.

The young man just looked at him confused. Many of the older generation only spoke creole, making it difficult for outsiders to understand.

"He's asking if you speak Creole," Cheri said as she continued to work. He perked up when she spoke to him.

"N-no, I don't."

"Then say, *non, mo pale pa kreyo*," she instructed.

He repeated the phrase, after stammering through it.

The old man nodded knowingly and smiled. He didn't have a single tooth.

"*Ki non ou?*"

The younger man looked to her. "He's asking your name."

"Oh, J-Jerry."

She told the old man but he said nothing else as he studied the people around him.

"So, Jerry, you're not from around here are ya?" It was more of a joke than a statement because it was painfully obvious that he wasn't from anywhere nearby.

"No. I'm from Chicago. I moved down here a few months ago."

"Ah, I see. That would explain why you're ... overdressed."

"Yeah," wiping the sweat from his brow. A few minutes later a petite blond wearing a bright yellow sundress came bouncing over. She looked to be close to Cheri's age.

"Hey baby," she said sitting on his lap and pressing her mouth to his.

Cheri went back to her business, ignoring the couple and focusing on her job. The blond came up for air and turned a bright smile toward Cheri and slipped off Jerry's lap.

"You must be the new waitress. I'm Desire, Jax's sister, and this is my boyfriend Jerry." She thrust her hand out and Cheri winced. After wiping the sauce that was on her hands on the seat of her shorts she took the girl's hand.

*Jax's sister?*

"It's nice to meet you, Desire."

"Jax has talked about you."

Cheri started a little. "Well, don't believe everything he says," she said. She had no idea how to respond to that. The fact that Jax talked about her at all was a surprise.

Desire chuckled. "Yeah. Says you're a right pain in the ass with a stubborn streak a mile long."

Cheri chuckled, not at all offended. "Yeah, well your brother isn't all rainbows and unicorns either."

She laughed and nodded. "Which is exactly why I like you already. He says you argue with him at every turn."

Cheri nodded. "I do."

"I think we're going to get along just fine, Cheri. Not many people stand up to him."

"Well, I'm not particularly scared of him."

Desire smiled sadly. "That's good. There's not a lot of people around here that can say that ya know?"

Cheri nodded. "I've heard the rumors, but nothing substantial and nothing I really care about." She lifted a shoulder casually. "I don't judge people on rumors. I try not to judge them at all. Jax has been nothing but good to me, and believe me, that's not easy at all."

"So you don't know what these rumors are?" There was something of a hint of panic in her voice, but she hid it well and passed it off as curiosity. Cheri hadn't missed it there was something else there.

"I've heard everything from embezzler to kingpin in some drug cartel. I don't know and not to sound harsh, but I really don't care. He's given me a job and aside from being a pain in my ass, he's done right by me. I'm not scared of him."

Desire's bright blue eyes glittered with unshed tears. There was just something in there that made Cheri wondering what Jax's story really was. Before she could think any more about it, Desire spoke again. "It's nice to hear that for a change." She pulled Cheri into a sudden hug. Cheri's body tensed as she awkwardly patted Desire on the back.

Desire pulled away and sniffed, blushing slightly. "I'm sorry. I'm a bit of a hugger."

"No problems there."

She laughed again and Cheri realized that Desire and Jax were polar opposite. Desire was sunny and bubbly while Jax was dark and broody. No matter their differences, though, she could see the love Desire had for her brother.

"Well, I need to introduce Jerry around. This is his first time meeting everyone," she said taking her boyfriend by the hand and tugging him behind her.

"That explains why he looks so terrified."

"He'll make it just fine," she said sliding up to his side.

The couple walked off hand and hand. Cheri almost felt bad for the poor guy. Jax was intimidating to most normal people. She could hardly imagine what it was like to be his baby sister's new boyfriend.

Her dour mood beginning to lift, she got back to work. Once the food was set up, she searched for Jax but had no luck. She made her way up to the porch, heading for the front door.

"Cherilynn Deveau? Lawdy, child is that really you."

Cheri froze and her heart began to race through her chest. No one was supposed to know her by that name. It was a name that was supposed to have died. She squeezed her eyes closed and took a deep breath. Slowly, turning around, she saw a face from her past. The porch tilted dangerously beneath her feet as her hands began to shake.

"It *is* you," the older woman said with a gasp, her hand resting on her large ample chest and her eyes filling with tears.

# 7

"I'm sorry, but I think you've got the wrong person," Cheri said evenly as she tried to move around the older woman. Though her emotions were stampeding all over the place, she kept her cool.

"Cherilynn, don't gimme that line of bull, young lady, ya know damn good and well who I am," the older woman scolded moving to block her path.

Cheri really saw no way out of it. She released a heavy sigh. "Hello, Mrs. Marceaux. It's been a long time."

"It has, honey, gimme a hug." She said as she closed the gap between them and folded Cheri into a big embrace. The years had been kind to the woman, who had to be nearing her mid-fifties when Cheri had known her all those years ago. Her brown hair was now streaked with traces of silver, and small wrinkles gathered at the corners of her eyes. She'd lost quite a bit of weight, but she was still a good, sturdy woman reaching nearly five foot ten. The woman was old school. She believed in spankings with belts but knew where the line of abuse had been drawn. Her accent was true Cajun, despite her college degree.

Cheri had to admit, the hug felt nice, familiar and comforting. The older woman had always seemed like the only adult in her life that had actually cared for her, but seeing her only brought a wealth of memories to the surface, making her more than a little bit nervous. Lizabeth Marceaux was from her past and that was not something she was in a hurry to visit. In fact, Lizabeth was one of the few people that knew the real story about Cheri, and despite the risks to her job, she'd gone out of her way to help bury everything. Lizabeth had been Cheri's caseworker. Regrettably, Cheri hadn't kept in contact, but it had been for the best. She'd been fairly successful. Until now.

Lizabeth stood back, holding Cheri out at arm's length. "Look at'cha. Ya sure did fill out and become a look'er. Why, Cherilynn, you're downright beautiful."

"Thanks, but can you please call me Cheri. No one knows me by Cherilynn Deveau and I'd really like to keep it that way."

"Of course honey. What on earth are ya doing out here? Not that I mind you be'n here. I love ya like my own."

"I'm working. My boss needed my help catering."

"Ahhh, so you're da new waitress work'in for Jaxon?"

Before Cheri say anything Jax appeared at their side.

"I see you've met our hostess," Jax said, wrapping his arm around Lizabeth's shoulders fondly.

"Jaxon, ya didn't tell me that Cheri worked for you."

Jax looked down at her, a little confused. "You know Cheri?"

"We met at the grocery store a few times," she spoke up, not giving Lizabeth a chance to respond. The older woman's warm eyes met and held hers as Cheri silently pleaded with her.

"That's right. I loved going through dis girl's line. Always s'friendly."

"You were always my favorite," Cheri assured her. It had been the truth.

"So this is your party," Cheri said, trying to steer the conversation away from herself.

"It's our family reunion," she said squeezing Jax's into her side.

"Our?"

"Yep. You're workin for muh *bébé*," she said proudly as she reached up and gave his chin a gentle squeeze. Jax flinched and move slightly out of her reach.

Cheri felt herself grow pale and she clutched the porch rail. This was the last thing she needed. The less Jax knew about her the better. The air around her grew warmer as she struggled to maintain her composure. Panic seized her. Jax was Lizabeth's son. Why hadn't she put two and two together? The same last names should have been a giveaway.

"Cheri, we need to get the coolers set up before everyone starts to eat," Jax said over his mom's head.

"S-sure," she said, trying to clear her throat.

Jax walked down the stairs but as she tried to follow, Lizabeth's hand shot out and gently grabbed her by the arm.

"Honey, your past is your past. Ain't no one gonna hold it against ya. 'Sides, I would've done it too."

Cheri just looked at her with pleading eyes. "But if you're worry'n bout me sayin somethin, then don't. Cause I couldn't if I wanted. This damn thing with the cases being sealed or something like dat," she said with a smile and a wink.

She pushed out a sigh of relief. "Thank you," she whispered.

"I can only imagine how you've had ta work so hard ta get your life back ta normal. I'll not mess it up, but honey, stop hidin from it. Alway's look'n over yer shoulder ain't a way ta live."

"Yes'm," Cheri said, unable to really think of anything else to say.

Cheri walked down the steps and to the tables where Jax was talking to Uncle Marvin.

"Shoo-we, honey if I was a few years younger," Uncle Marvin said as he nudged her gently in the ribs.

Jax snorted and laughed. "You wouldn't know what to do with someone like her, old man," he teased.

"You be surprised at what dis ole horse can still do."

Cheri frowned, unsure if Jax's statement was a compliment or an insult. She didn't have a chance to question it further before a loud whistle summoned everyone around the food.

"So, what do you want me to do?" she asked.

He lifted a shoulder. "I'm sure you can figure it out," he said before striding off.

"What the hell is that supposed to mean?'" she grumbled as she watched him disappear into a crowd of cajuns.

"Don't mind him none, *cher.* Ole Jax, he comes off as rough as sandpaper, him, but he got a heart a gold. Don't

matter none what dem town folks say. He done paid 'is
time and moved on he did. Mmhmm, you make a friend in
him, you got a friend fo life. Dats fo sho."

"I'm too old to make new friends," she grumbled as
she picked up a beer can someone had tossed to the
ground.

"Never can have too many friends, *cher*. Never."

The old man ambled off in search of who knows what,
leaving Cheri alone with her thoughts. Thankfully, as the
party made its way into full swing, it didn't take long for
her to forget about her former social worker. She thrust
herself into work, cleaning up after people and chatting
casually to most of Jax's family.

Some of them were young enough that their Cajun
was muddied by modern times. However, there were the
old-timers, like the man from before, that spoke in Creole
or with such a heavy accent, that it would be hard for
anyone else to understand. Thankfully, she understood
both very well.


Night time had finally cast its touch amongst a party that
showed no signs of losing steam. The torches glowed
brightly as the colorful paper lanterns swayed in the hot
summer breeze. She had to admit, even though she'd been
on her feet all evening, the light and playful mood of Jax's
family was contagious. Jax even seemed to loosen up as
the evening progressed. Everyone was having a good time.
Even the out of town guy seemed to be enjoying himself as
he spun her around to the beat of the light and playful
zydeco music. The serving tables had been pushed aside
to make room for a makeshift dance floor. People laughed
and twirled about. From just beyond the reach of the tiki
torches, peals of laughter could be heard ringing out
through the darkness. Children darted in and out of the
shadows as they play hide and go seek.

"Ya'll gonna done fool round and get on'a gator,"
Lizabeth called to them. But when no one answered she
just laughed and walked over to Cheri.

"Ya have'n a good time, honey?"

Cheri nodded. "I really am."

"E'ven though ya have ta work?"

"It's okay. It keeps me busy and reminds me that there are still good people."

"Honey, they always was good people. You just happen onto da bad ones."

"Or the bad ones found me."

"Either way. You happy now?"

"Most of the time," she said and then her face brightened. "I have two kids. A boy and a girl."

"They from that one man?"

"My ex-husband, yeah."

"I never did like him none. I was always so scared for you when you was run'in a'round with'im. He was bad news, no?"

"Not really. For a while, things were good. We moved up to Alexandria and had a good life, but after a while, things began to. . . ."

"Turn ta hell, eh?"

"Something like that."

Lizabeth grabbed Cheri's hand and gave it a squeeze. "Honey, you got two bebes outta dat man. I've no doubt they be as pretty as their momma. Dats all you need to worry about. Ya doin' okay, though? Otherwise?"

"Mostly. I'm just wait'n till gator season gets here."

"I'm not surprised you gator hunt," she said with a knowing chuckle. Cheri laughed with her and continued to talk as the festivities carried on around them.

A while later she looked for Jax, needing to ask him a question about the leftovers when she saw him walk around the side of the house. Quickly, she followed and once more she found herself in a situation much like the one she'd been in the first day at the bar.

Jax was talking to someone in the shadows but she couldn't hear what was being said. However, the one thing she did see was money exchanging hands. The guy handed Jax a roll of cash and Jax passed something to the man. Her heart drummed in her chest. Who in the hell was she working for? Quickly, she made her way back to the party, pretending that she didn't see whatever it was she just saw.

Deep in the woods ey` ched as she moved around the party. She laughed and acted as if she was on top of the world. Fists clenched and unclenched, wanting desperately to wrap around the woman's neck. Fifteen feet in front the hiding spot, a child scrambled to find a hiding place. So easy. It would be so easy.

Piercing eyes moved from the youngster and watched as Cheri moved to the side of the house. She was keeping to the shadows, just like a predator, watching as Jax did his shady business. The bastard was no better than Cheri. Maybe, just maybe, Jax would be another victim. How sweet would that be?

A slow smile tilted angry lips as the shadow once more slithered back to the darkness.

# 8

Jax sat on the front steps, beer dangling between his fingers. He watched as his momma and Cheri laughed and chatted. There was something off there. They looked like they'd known each other for a long time. The more time he spent around Cheri, the more he found her to be an enigma. She was maddening as hell but there was something else about the way she kept her guard securely in place. She seemed to be hiding something, but so was he. There was just something about her that kept pulling at his mind. Like there was something he should know, but just couldn't put a finger on it.

He watched as his mother wandered off to talk to his aunt, leaving Cheri alone. She went back to work picking up the bottles, cans, and cups that his family had tossed askew. She stopped for a moment to pull the tie from her hair. Long dark hair spilled down her back as she leaned her head back to gather the heavy mass once more. With expert hands, she quickly wound it into a sloppy bun high on her head.

She must have sensed him staring at her because she turned. Even from the distance, he could see the brilliance of her green eyes studying him. There was no smile, just an even gaze. He tilted his bottle to her as a salute and took a long pull. That earned him a severe eye roll. She turned away and with bag in hand, began once more picking up trash.

"Boy, give dat girl da rest of da night off. You's workin her ta death," Uncle Marvin said as he lowered himself beside Jax. He grunted and groaned until he got his bulky frame situated.

"She's here to work," he said pointedly.

"I know dat and she has been, but she's not taken a break to eat or s'much as drink a thing e'ither."

Jax turned. "What?"

Uncle Marvin just shook his head. "I off'ad her a plate and she refused. Said she was work'n."

"*Mon Dieu*, that woman is stubborn as hell," Jax grumbled.

His uncle exploded in laughter, slapping him roughly on the back. "Boy, you done call'n da kettle black on dat one."

Cheri had said the same thing to him earlier. "Shut up, ya old goat," he scoffed playfully as he pushed himself from the step and walked into the house. A few minutes later, he returned outside carrying a plate piled high with food in one hand and two long neck bottles in the other. He crossed through the crowd to where Cheri was tying closed the black bag. She was bent over and Jax stopped abruptly. It was only up close that he noticed exactly how nice her backside truly was. He groaned. This woman was nothing but trouble.

When she straightened and turned abruptly, he took a startled step back.

"Ya scared the hell outta me. What are you doing sneaking up on people?" She asked irritably.

He tried not to focus on the thin sheen of sweat covering the skin that was exposed above her tank top. His efforts were futile as a bead of sweat started from her shoulder and rolled down into the valley between her breasts.

"Hey," Cheri snapped her fingers in front of his face. "I asked you a question."

"I brought you some food. Take a break," he said gruffly.

"I don't want a break—wait. Were you just staring at my chest?"

Busted. "Kind of hard not to." There was no use in lying.

"What is that supposed to mean?"

"Means they *are* just . . . there." There was a slight teasing edge to his voice.

"Don't beat around the bush do ya?"

"What's the point of saying something if you're not going to say what you want to say? No use in sugar coat'n shit."

She shook her head. "If you're finished being a smart ass and staring at my chest, I've got work to get back too."

Jax shook his head.

"What?"

"Time for you to have fun."

"I didn't come here to have fun. I came to work. If you're done with me, you can take me home."

"Sorry, no can do. I can't leave, so you either have to find your own way or wait until I say we go. In the meantime, I brought you something to eat. Sit down and relax, have a few beers. Looks like you need to have a good time."

"I don't need to have a good time," she said stubbornly as she took the plate and sat it on the table. He watched her and sensing that he wouldn't give up, she plucked a piece of fried shrimp from the pile and popped it into her mouth. Her stomach rumbled loudly in thanks. She took a few more bites.

"There, are you happy now?"

"Getting there. Now for the good time part."

"I told you, not here to have a good time," she said as she grabbed the trash bag and began to walk away. His hand closed around her upper arm. She stopped and looked at him.

"Have you forgotten how to have fun?" He offered her the bottle.

She held his gaze for a while but then relented. "You're such an ass."

She jerked the bottle from him, popped off the top and tipped it up. Jax watched in wide-eyed wonder as she drank without coming up from air. A few of his cousins turned and saw her slamming back the beer. They cheered loudly.

After the bottle was emptied, she suffocated a belch and smiled up at him. "Oh, I know how to have fun. I just can't ever find people that can keep up," she said saucily, in a silent challenge as she took the other bottle from him and slammed it like the first one.

"Is that a challenge?"

She finished the second one and threw it to the can and then shrugged. "Take it how you want it."

He smirked, his eyes raking shamelessly over her. "I usually do," he said.

A cold chill settled at the base of her spine at his words. There was no hiding the implications, nor did he even try as he grabbed a bottle from the cooler and removed the top. He emptied it far quicker than Cheri had hers. Then they just stood staring a silent challenge at one another. It was going to be an interesting night.

As time wore on, Cheri's inhibitions slowly began to slip away. She and Jax continued to drink and it wasn't long before she found herself actually having a great time.

By the time midnight rolled around, she was feeling pretty good—having lost count of how much she'd drank. It had been long time since she'd drank more than a couple drinks.

"Dance with me," Jax said suddenly standing. He grabbed her by the arm and pulled her from her perch on top of the picnic table. Even though it was late, the band was still going strong. People were still dancing and laughing cheerfully.

"What? Why?"

"Because you need to have fun."

"Why do you keep saying that? I *have* been having fun, and why are you so hell-bent on me having a good time?"

"Why are you so hell bent on arguing with me at every turn?

She shrugged as a response because she really didn't have an answer. Jax laughed, his brown eyes lighting up and a genuine smile spreading across his handsome face. At the bar he was always tense but surrounded by his family, he was at ease. Since knowing him, she couldn't recall seeing him laugh or smile as much as he had over the past couple of hours.

He tugged on her arm, breaking her out of her thoughts.

"Oh fine," she said with an exaggerated sigh.

He tugged her onto the dance floor, never letting go of her hand. Not giving her a chance to adjust, he gave her a quick little spin and then pulled her hard against his chest. The move was awkward and clumsy, but she couldn't help the bubble of laughter that slipped through her lips.

The band had taken a break, and someone had plugged in blues from a pa-system. Together they dance to the sultry beats of a saxophone and electric guitar. Jax's right hand rested just below the small of her back, dangerously close to her backside. He held her tightly as, and they moved to the music.

She draped her arms over his shoulders and clasped her hands together behind his neck. He smelled like cologne and all male causing her heart to flutter in her chest. The music was slow, making it easy for their bodies to move in time. "So, tell me. What does your girlfriend think about you dancing with the hired help?"

He looked down at her, smoky brown eyes pulling her into them. The corners crinkled in amusement. "If you wanted to know if I have a girlfriend, all you had to do is ask."

"Fine. Do you have a girlfriend?" she said with a cheeky smile.

There was no smile. In fact, it almost appeared as if he were sad. Finally, he shook his head. "No. There is no girlfriend. There was one, but . . . things ended a while ago."

"Oh." That was all she could say. What was the proper response when someone tells you their relationship had ended? Still, a small part of her felt a little giddy at the fact that he was single. Maybe it was the alcohol talking.

He lifted a shoulder. "It was a rocky relationship anyway."

Even though he said it, she could tell that the relationship might have been more than a little thing to him.

"You're thinking?" he said, his voice breaking through her thoughts. He pressed his thumb lightly between her eyes. "You get a wrinkle right here when you are lost in thought."

She rolled her eyes and batted his hand away, partially because there was something intimate in the gentle way he touched her face. Her heart fluttered. "I'm thinking that I need another beer."

Cheri pulled away as if she were going to get another drink, but he grabbed her hand, gave her a dramatic spin, and then pulled her to him. Her back landed against his solid chest, and her breath hitched in her throat. The song changed, and the rhythm became low and sultry. He moved against her back, keeping time with the music with his body. Cheri could feel heat rising in her cheeks. Her mouth went dry, and her eyes drifted closed as the tips of his fingers skimmed the bare skin of her arms. She could feel his mouth near her ear and his warm breath on her neck. His left hand snaked around and rested on her stomach, something she normally would not have allowed. Holding her tightly to him his right hand continued to move down her arm and resting on her hip. She gasped, feeling the evidence of his arousal press against her backside.

Feeling bold, she lifted her arm and snaked it behind his head, threading her fingers through his silky hair. Her body was reacting to his, and she was too drunk to really care. In the back of her mind, she knew that she was playing a deadly game. This was her boss, and she needed this job. Somehow that just wasn't connecting for her. Perhaps it was the alcohol. Perhaps it was the fact that he was a strong veral man and it had been a long time since she'd been with a man. At any rate, common sense wasn't really rating too high up on her moral compass. Slowly, she rolled her hips and backside against him. A small smile drifted across her lips when she heard him growl. It was a low, rumbling sound that made the butterflies in the pit of her stomach stir and the muscles between her thighs twitch.

Closing her eyes, she tilted her head to the right, exposing her neck fully to him. He didn't disappoint as he blew gently on the sweat-dampened skin, creating a cooling sensation. Her body reacted instantly, muscles tensing as goosebumps dotted her arms.

His lips teased the side of her neck. She gasped and pulled her bottom lip between her teeth as tiny jolts of electricity zipped through her. There was no denying the fact that this man, this infuriating man was nothing but pure, raw sexual energy. Her eyes fluttered closed as his mouth fastened fully on her neck, sucking it gently and teasing lightly with his tongue as he went. She really needed to get her head on straight before she did something she would regret.

She spun in his arms and through fuzzy eyes she looked up at him. "Why are you such a pain in the ass?"

"That makes the second time you've mentioned my ass tonight," he murmured against her ear. "It would make a man wonder if ya had a fascination with it."

"Oink, oink, oink," she said playfully.

"Are you calling me pig, again?"

"Maybe."

He skimmed her hips and beneath the hem of her shirt. His large, calloused hands resting on her ribs. His mouth pressed against her ear. "I may be a pig, but you're the one who will be squealing."

He gave her another spin and brought her crashing against his chest. A tremor of desire washed through her, causing her inner muscles to tighten. Her tongue darted out and moistened her lips.

Feeling bold she smiled up at him. "Your ass is actually the last thing, I'm thinking about right now," she whispered.

"What exactly are you thinkin?" he asked, arching a dark brow. His dark eyes shone with raw, hungry desire.

"I'm thinkin that you're a painfully obnoxious and arrogant man that thinks he can have anything he wants."

"Not, *anything*."

"I find that hard to believe," she said as she traced her index finger over his nipple through the fabric of his t-shirt. She pressed her hips more fully against him.

*You're playing a dangerous game.* Her mind screamed loudly at her.

He sucked in a sharp breath and lowered his face closer to hers. His warm breath teased her lips. "You're right. I typically do get what I want and right now I can think-,"

"Jax, baby, I think it's time you take Cheri home."

Cheri jumped away from Jax—staggering and clutching to his arm for support. She was startled by Lizabeth's sudden voice. Embarrassment colored her cheeks as she looked at the older woman. Why did it feel like she was a teenager just caught making out with a boy?

He shot his mother an annoyed look but didn't argue. "Let me get my keys," he said as he walked passed his mom and into the house.

"I-I'm sorry," Cheri stammered after he was gone. "I didn't mean to be inappropriate."

Lizabeth tsked. "Honey, it's not him I was worried a'bout. I love my *bébé*, but he's kind of a hound when it comes to women."

"He's a player?"

"You can say dat. Don't like being tied down. He's smooth, but sometimes I wonder what dat boy would do if he stopped running from his demons long enough ta look at da world around 'im."

"Demons?"

"My *bébé* is a complicated boy, he is. People talk. I love dat boy, but honey, I love you too. As much as it'd make this ole heart happy to see ya'll t'gether, I just don't wanna see ya hurt. Ya done both come too far and had ta live through too much hell. I'd be worried that this path for ya'll wouldn't end well." The old woman shook her head. "Those demons'll eat ya 'live, *bébé*."

In that moment, she saw the depth of the woman's love for her son, but at the same time, she could see the sadness in her brown eyes.

Before she had a chance to ask any questions Jax's voice reached them. "Ya ready head out?"

"Are you really okay to drive?"

"I quit drinking quite a while ago."

Cheri looked at Lizabeth and got a look that vaguely resembled an 'I told you so.' She frowned up at Jax. Red tinted Cheri's vision as she glared up at him. He just smiled lazily down at her.

She pushed passed him and wrapped her arms around his mother. "Thank you for all you've ever done for me," she whispered.

"Take care, *bébé*," she whispered.

Cheri moved away and pushed passed Jax. Angrily she marched over to his truck. Her pride was stinging as well as her ego. He'd just been toying with her the whole time. Damn it. She was sick and tired of being toyed with.

As they rode in silence back to Cheri's house, it dawned on her exactly how much alcohol she'd actually had to drink. Her eyes began to grow heavy and while she didn't exactly have the urge to vomit, her stomach still did somersaults. She rested her head against the window, allowing the glass to cool her. Before long, her eyes slid closed and everything vanished.

"Slut!"

The word hissed angrily into the night as the taillights disappeared around the corner.

# 9

The lantern light bounced off the old stone walls as he walked down the hall. Rats skittered around the floor at his feet. Water slid over the stone in slimy rivers. It was all so beautifully cliché with the musty smell, the odd shadows, everything right down to his echoing footfalls. The wheels on the gurney squeaked loudly as he pushed it down the long hall.

Finally, he reached the large metal door. After hanging the lantern on the hook, he turned the knob and pushed the door with his foot. The hinges echoed eerily as he stepped over the threshold into a warmly lit room. There were no windows, so he could use as much light as he wanted without being detected.

He wheeled the gurney inside and closed the door behind him.

"It's finally your turn," he said with a sneer as he looked down at the terrified body secured to the gurney.

"W-what do you want?" the guy's voice trembled with fear.

He didn't answer as he tightened the straps holding the guy's hands and legs securely in place.

"We have a friend in common," he said, being sure to keep his voice low.

"W-who is our mutual friend?" When he received no answer, he sucked in a deep breath and yelled as loudly as possible. "Help. Someone help me."

"You can yell all you want. Go ahead if it makes you feel better. No one knows about this place."

Moving carefully, he removed an alcohol pad from the foil packet and cleansed the bend of the man's arm. Choosing a blade from the surgical table beside him, he held it up, inspecting it. Perfect. He replaced it and began removing the man's shirt. Picking up a syringe, he pressed the plunger and watched as the cloudy liquid bubbled and rolled over the tip of the needle.

"I would say this isn't going to hurt, but then again that'd be a lie. I would also say that I'm sorry but . . . I'm not." He chuckled but then it died on his lips. Anger began to surge through him. However, he remained in control as he administered the medicine. Rage filled him. They were all oblivious to the danger lurking at their backdoors. He could have easily reached out and taken *her*, but it hadn't been time. More than anything he'd wanted to feel his blade slice into Jax, stabbing his heart.

"She thinks she has the right to be happy, after everything she did? That bitch doesn't deserve happy," he growled. His hands began to shake with blind rage. The guy on the table whimpered as his movements began to slow and the medicine spread through his veins. Tears rolled from the corners of his eyes. He couldn't move. The only thing that he was able to move was his eyes.

"In about five seconds you will be completely unable to move," he explained. He reached over and turned a knob on the tank beside the bed. A *whooshing* filled the room.

Making a show of snapping on his rubber gloves he smiled. "Time for work, but first, let's remove these." Slowly and ever so gently, he removed the gold, wire-rimmed glasses from the man's face.

"Now, where was I? Oh yes, that's right."

He picked up the instrument and held it over the man's eye. "She'll see what she's done, and if not, giving her extra insight might just help her see a little more clearly."

He worked quickly, sliding it behind the eye tearing the muscles and tissues away. The man's good eye rolled back in his head, presumably due to pain and shock. A wet sucking sound filled the room as he removed the eye from its socket and gently placed it on the gauze, next to the glasses.

"Now that the hard work is done, let's have a little fun, shall we?"

He removed a scalpel from the table and drew it over the man's chest. Low, barely audible whimpers slipped through partially parted lips. Blood seeped down pale skin and dripped off the table. The *splat, splat, splat* of blood dripping to the floor mingled with the steady *beep, beep, beep* of the machinery.

"No, this will never do," he said pursing his lips. Moving away from his table, he pushed play on the portable stereo and soon the dulcet tones of Moonlight Sonata drifted around them.

"Ah, yes, much better. *Now* I can get to work."

And work he did, slicing away layers of skin from random parts of the body. He took care, never to puncture too deep. He couldn't risk nicking an artery or vein that would cause the man to bleed out before his task was through. Finally, when he was finished, he tugged off his gloves and threw them into the trash. The coppery scent of blood mingled with the musty smell of the room. It was a familiar smell and one that brought him comfort and arousal. His erection strained behind his zipper. Maybe he would ease the pressure while buried inside a whore. He would even picture *her*. He throbbed again and he groaned.

"Time to go for a ride," he said. He needed to get out and take care of things, but first things first. Blood oozed from the empty socket of the man and pooled beneath his head. He removed another syringe and filled it with a sedative. He couldn't afford for anyone to hear or see him transporting the . . . patient. The clock on the wall told him he was running out of time.

Moving quickly, he filled another syringe with the cloudy liquid and put a cap on it.

"Time for dinner." He was on a mission, but he had one stop to make first and if he was going to make it on time, he had to hurry. He pushed the gurney back down the hall and within moments, he as back out in the world, leaving his playroom behind for the moment.

The gravel crunched softly under his feet as he slowly walked up the drive. So *he* was here. No doubt the bar owner was inside buried between her thighs. He could picture her stretched out beneath him, moaning like a whore and begging for him to give it to her harder. His jeans grew uncomfortable as he pictured himself in the place of the bar owner. He would not be slow or easy with her and then, he would slit her throat. The thought of seeing her life's blood ooze from her neck made him hard all over again.

Anger poured through his veins like acid, creeping into the back of his throat. He clamped down on the end of his tongue until the metallic taste of his own blood filled his mouth. Slowly, he approached the house and made his way up the stairs. He knew exactly where to step to keep them from squeaking.

He peered in through the screen door. *He* was asleep on the couch, arm thrown over his forehead.

With ease he slipped into the house, laughing to himself at how stupid they were. Quietly, he slunk across the living room, the old threadbare carpet muffling his footsteps. He stood at the end of the couch for a moment, contemplating what he was going to do. The bar owner stirred slightly. It would be so easy to slide the knife between his ribs, extinguishing his life before anyone knew what was happening. The prospect of feeling his blade slice through flesh and bone excited him. He imagined the blood covering his hand and dripping onto the carpet. Jax would struggle, but it would be in vain. It would be too late.

His hand flexed at his side as he slowly reached for his knife. So easy.

"That's not part of the plan," the voice inside his mind chastised. With a frown, he begrudgingly backed away and slipped into the hallway, making his way to her bedroom. He knew where each and every squeaky floorboard was. He'd been in the house numerous times while she slept. She made it all too easy for him.

He slipped through the open bedroom door. Cheri was curled into a ball on her side, cheeks pillowed on the backs of her hands. He stood at the foot of her bed, watching as she slept. A slow smile slipped across his face as he silently moved to stand beside the bed. He knelt down, her face inches from his. Her plump lips were parted slightly as she snored softly. Reaching over, he barely brushed his knuckles against her cheek. It would be so easy to extinguish her light. All it would take would be a quick flick of his wrist and her neck would snap like dry twigs.

That couldn't happen, though. The game had already been put into motion. The stage had been set and soon, she would be the star. Very soon he would know what her life felt like as it slipped through his fingers.

Excitement bounded through him as he slowly climbed to his feet and slipped back into the shadows.

Jax's eyes snapped open, unsure of what had woken him. His heart beat like a jackhammer through his chest. The entire room was cast in complete darkness, the only light coming in was from the half-moon. His skin prickled as a heavy feeling of dread settled over him. Something felt off.

He swung his legs over the edge of the couch and pushed himself upright. A clammy sweat broke out over his body. Something was wrong.

What had woken him?

Quietly, he eased through the house and made his way down the hall to Cheri's room. The blueish light from the floodlight shone on her face. The tightness in his chest eased up when he saw her resting peacefully, and yet something was still bothering him. She was beautiful and for a moment, he just watched her sleep. It was the only time that he recalled seeing her relaxed. The tension in her face was gone. Dark lashes fell across beautiful cheeks.

Reaching to the foot of the bed, he gently pulled a light blanket over her. It was warm in the room but for some reason, there was a damp chill lingering about. He then walked over to the window and scanned the yard beyond the house. There was nothing out of the ordinary. So why did he feel like someone was watching him?

Jax cast one last glance over his shoulder as he left Cheri's room. Content that she was okay, he made his way back out to the living room. He reached for the light switch but his hand stopped before turning it on. Why was he turning the lights on? Was he suddenly scared of the dark?

Deciding that his uneasy feelings were figments of his imagination, he lowered himself back down onto the ungodly uncomfortable couch. It didn't take long for sleep to tug him under once more.

From the shadows of her closet, he watched as Jax stared at Cheri. He'd known something was wrong. Yes, Jax might prove to be a bit more of a challenge than he originally imagined, but he knew one sure way of getting the convict's attention. It wouldn't take long and it would be most effective.

For a few more moments he watched as they slept, dreaming about the day when he would finally feel her heart in the palm of his hand. He would relish that day. He counted the seconds, minutes and hours until he could take her for his and then extinguish her light. That's what murderers deserved!

# 10

The persistent pounding in Cheri's head sent pinpricks of light flashing beneath her lids. Groaning, she shifted uncomfortably, momentarily confused as to where she was. The clock on the wall chimed nine-thirty and she realized she was in her room. She searched through her cloudy mind, trying to remember how she'd gotten to her bed. She frowned and rolled over. On the nightstand beside the small bed sat a glass of water and a bottle of aspirin.

Another round of banging went on and this time she realized it wasn't going on in her head, well at least not all of it. "What the hell?" She grumbled. Her eyes were gritty with sleep and her tongue was glued to the roof of her mouth.

She, very sluggishly, moved to a sitting position and squeezed her eyes closed. The hangover reared its ugly head. How much had she actually drank? "Ugh," she grunted as she cradled her head. Snatching the bottle off the table, she shook four white pills into her hand. After popping them into her mouth she drained the entire contents of the glass. The water effectively washed away the sludgy feeling in her mouth.

*Bam, bam, bam.*

Slowly she stood, the floor only tilted slightly, or maybe it hadn't. Considering the state that the floor was in, it wouldn't have been that farfetched. She listened for the beating again and this time she realized it was hammering and the racket was coming from outside.

After adjusting her clothing, she walked down the hall, across the living room and out onto the front porch. A blue tarp, her blue tarp, was laying on the ground in a forgotten heap. She turned around and looked up to her roof. Even though the sky was gray and overcast, the light still stabbed through her retinas like red hot needles.

"It is nine in the morning, why in the freaking hell are you on my roof like a giant woodpecker?"

"Good morning to you too, sunshine," Jax called down to her with a wide smile.

"What are you doing?" she asked, ignoring his cheery mood and shielding her eyes.

"I'm getting a tan, what in the hell does it look like I am doing." She briefly noticed that he was shirtless and their little dancing interlude played back through her mind. That wasn't the only thing. The warning from his mother did as well.

"I know *what* you are doing, I just don't know *why* you're doing it."

"It needed to be done," he said simply as if it were the most logical thing to have a near stranger standing on her roof.

"You mean you dropped me off last night and came back to fix my roof, on a Sunday?"

"No," he said as he knelt down to position another shingle in place. His Levi's clung to his hips and thighs as he worked. Her mouth went dry all over again.

"What do you mean, no?"

He stood and looked down at her. Even though the distance between them, she could still feel the intensity of his. "I mean that no, I didn't drop you off, leave and come back. By the way, that couch of yours is kind of a nightmare to sleep on."

"You . . . you slept in my house?" she sputtered.

"I did. You snore," he said lightly as he began hammering shingles onto the roof once more.

"I do not, and get off my roof. I didn't ask you to fix it."

"And your door."

"What?" she turned and looked at the front porch and noticed her front door wasn't the only thing he'd fixed. Her frown deepened. How had she not noticed that he'd fixed all those things, and how in the hell had she not heard him cutting, sawing and hammering? It was hard for her to accept any kind of help because that kind of help always had strings attached. Nothing in her life had ever been that easy. He *had* to want something. She just couldn't figure out what it was.

"I fixed your door, the porch railing, and those steps. This place should be condemned," he said.

*Ouch.* The dig at her house stung. She knew it wasn't a mansion, but it was the only thing she could afford.

"Get off my roof, Jax and get the hell out of here."

Turning, she angrily marched up the new stairs and through the new door, slamming it loudly behind her. She tried to ignore the stab of pain she felt inside her head at the loud noise. Damn hangover.

Jax stared at her. Despite the heat, her dark hair fell past her shoulders in a wavy disarray. He sat back on his haunches and watched her march angrily back into the house. He was dumbfounded and his irritation prickled. Thinking he would help her out on a few things, considering the fact it was obvious that she didn't have anyone else to help her, had apparently been a mistake.

He wiped the sweat from his brow with his t-shirt and climbed down from the roof. He walked up the steps, his boots falling heavily on the new boards. With a frown, he pushed through the front door, but she wasn't in the living room or the kitchen. He walked into the hall and stopped at the first bedroom. He stopped in his tracks. She stood in the room with her back to the door. Jax's irritation vanished and it felt as if all the air had been sucked from his chest.

Cheri was shirtless, only wearing a bra and in the process of pulling on a pair of old cut off denim shorts. As she tugged them on she shimmied her hips to the left and right and he nearly groaned. Just before she got them pulled up completely he saw a thin scrap of lace disappear beneath the shorts.

She was stunning with curves in all the perfect places. The small of her back swayed gently allowing for a nice flare into her beautifully rounded backside. A backside he remembered all too well from the night before, as they had danced. His eyes traveled up, studying the black tattoo that twisted and turned along her ribcage. Thorny vines with black roses were depicted as they pierced into her skin. It looked remarkably realistic. However, his eyes stopped when he saw crisscrossing scars marring her lower back. Some were faint, having faded with time, but the others had healed poorly, leaving behind angry purple slashes.

A blinding and an inexplicable rage burned through his veins. Someone had beat her and done so very badly.

He must have made a sound because she whirled around. Some of the welts and scars carried over to her sides and stomach. Cheri clutched her shirt to her heaving chest. The image of her white lace bra and dusky tipped nipples forever burned into his brain.

"What in the hell do you think you are doing?" she sputtered. Deep crimson creeping into her cheeks.

"I—uh . ." he stuttered. It wasn't often that he found himself speechless, but now was one of those instances.

She frowned at his dumb response. "Are you kidding me right now? You sleep in my house, without permission. You assume I need help. You insult my home and NOW you're standing in the door of my bedroom, watching me change. Did I miss anything else? Are you also skulking outside my house at night?" Fury tinted her voice, but it didn't match the humility and shame she was feeling. She'd been completely exposed.

"Who did that to you?" he asked as he stepped into the room, heedless of her rant.

She immediately backed away, feeling like frightened rabbit cornered by a predator. Her heart began to thunder in her chest as he got closer. "N-no one. Get out," she said, pointing her finger at him. Her hands trembled, but he could see that she was trying to hide it.

Jax watched with confusion as the anger in her face melted and was replaced with sheer terror. He stopped and then backed away, holding up his hands.

"Whoa, sorry."

"Get out," she hissed clearing her throat and hardening her voice.

He only nodded once as he backed completely out of the room and pulled the door closed behind him.

A few minutes later she came down the hall, wearing a purple and pink tank-top. Her hair was pulled into a ponytail.

"Why are you still here?" she glared at him, crossing her arms over her chest.

She didn't have on a stitch of makeup, having washed the remaining off from the night before. She was more beautiful without it. Deciding it would be in the best interest of everyone if he just let everything go— pertaining to her scars—he frowned at her. Maybe being annoyed with her would take his mind away from the dangerous path it was wandering down.

"You know, you're seriously ungrateful."

Cheri's scowl deepened as she met his hard look with a cool one of her own. He wanted to pick a fight with her. The so be it. "And you have a lot of nerve."

"*I* have a lot of nerve?" he scoffed.

"I didn't ask you to sleep on my couch, but you did, and bitched about it. I didn't ask you to fix my door, but you did. You bitched about that the other day. Then you fixed my steps and my roof. Don't get me wrong, I appreciate you helping, but what I don't appreciate is the fact that you are disrespecting my home." Her voice was rising along with her temper.

He opened his mouth to respond but she cut him off. "And that's not even including the fact that ya just barge in here whenever ya damn well please and lurk in the doorways watching me get dressed like some sick perv."

"Your door was open."

"So ya just came right on in," she said sweeping her arm open.

"I was just tryin to be nice. Had I known you'd be so ungrateful, I wouldn't have bothered. I'm surprised I didn't break my damn neck on that piece of shit ladder out there. Do you have any idea how old that thing is?"

"It came with the house and I've survived on my own for years. I don't need a man in my life. I've made it on my own for years, even when I was married. I know how to fix a roof, door, and anything else that breaks."

He crossed his arms over his chest. "Is that so?"

"Yes, damn it, it is. You know why? Because I learned a long time ago that no one is reliable. Everyone is out to get something. So I do it on my own." Her blood was boiling with rage now and Jax's was beginning to simmer as well.

"Wow. No wonder you are single," he said incredulously.

"I'm single because I *choose* to be and because I've yet to find a man to satisfy me." She eyed him challengingly, thinking that it would deflate his ego. However, it backfired when he took a slow step closer. His brown eyes were liquid pools of lust. A shiver danced its way across her body as he stared at her like a panther stalking his prey

"That's because you've not found the right man." His voice was low and silky, making her tremble despite the heat.

"And *you're* the right man?" she asked as she cleared her throat and crossed her arms tightly over her chest. She arched a mocking brow at him.

"Haven't ever had any complaints," he said with a shrug.

She let out an annoyed growl. "You're the most arrogant, self-absorbed asshole I have ever had the displeasure of meeting."

Jax took another step closer. "Am I now?"

Her nostrils flared. "Damn right you are. You think that just because you're good looking that all the women will throw themselves at you." Cheri uncrossed her arms and jabbed a finger into his chest. "Well, I got news for you, pal. I'm not one of those girls and I sure as hell ain't easy like them."

A lazy smirk slid across his face and Cheri's heart sped up. Damn him.

"Couldn't have proved it by me last night!" he fired back. His voice turned low and sultry. "In fact, I'm pretty sure that you were more than just a little willing to be one of *those women.*"

"Pfft, you wish," she snorted, wishing she'd had a better comeback. The embarrassing fact of the matter was; he wasn't that far from the truth. Had their little encounter not been interrupted, she very well could have become just another notch in the bedpost for him. She curled her hands into tight fists, her fingers twitching with the need to claw the smug look off his face.

He smirked at her retort and she bristled. "Has anyone ever told you that you've got quite the nasty little temper?"

"A time or two," she hissed.

Their eyes remained locked together, neither one willing to back down. Then, all of a sudden, he closed the last fraction of distance between them and brought his mouth crashing down against hers. Her entire body tensed as his tongue swept passed the barrier of her soft lips and into the warm cavern of her mouth. In moments, the rigidity left her body and she swayed into him as she began to meet his kisses eagerly. Their tongues dueled as he teased her bottom lip with his teeth. He sucked on it roughly and bit down, causing a low husky moan to slip from her throat.

The pure, raw sound of it had him hardening in seconds. With a deep growl, he backed her against the wall, a picture frame clattering to the floor. Her hands plowed through the hair at the back of his head, roughly pulling him tighter against her mouth. The roughness surprised him and stirred the flames growing in the pit of his stomach. His palm rested on the swell of her hip while the other roughly gripped her backside and pulled her against his arousal.

Jax tore his mouth away from hers and kissed her jaw—making his way down the column of her neck. Using his teeth, he lightly bit down on her shoulder, causing her to arch away from the wall. A smile tilted his lips when she shivered and clung to him.

To say Cheri was shocked by Jax's abrupt kiss was an understatement. However, that wasn't what shocked her the most. No, the most startling thing was that after a few seconds into the kiss, she'd become swept away. He tasted like coffee and spearmint. She shuttered as tiny goosebumps fanned out over her arms and down her legs.

For a few moments, she became lost in his kiss, his touch and the hardness of his body as he pulled her tighter against his. There was no mistaking his arousal as it pushed eagerly against her. His lips burned trails of fire along her neck with promises of desire to come.

Her mind was beginning to grow cloudy and Jax's hands slipped beneath the hem of her shirt and touched her skin. The instant his fingers brushed against her scars, it was as if she were doused with a bucket of cold water. Reality began to sink in. This was her boss. There were lines she refused to cross and *this* . . . this was most definitely being one of them.

Cheri put her hands against his chest and shoved him with as much strength as she had. She wanted to be calm but the only thing she could feel was confusion and fury as it simmered through her. No man had ever kissed her like that and no man had *ever* made her feel like that. Conflicting emotions spun around. She chose to focus on the one she was the most familiar with. Anger.

At first, he didn't move but the second time she shoved, he took a step back.

"Get off me," she hissed.

Jax's eyes were glassy with desire and hazy with confusion.

"What the hell was that?" she snapped, wiping the back of her hand across her mouth. She had to get the taste of him off her mouth. She couldn't be reminded of what had just happened.

Jax scowled down at her. "Has it been so long since you've been kissed that you have no idea what it was?"

Her eyes narrowed into dangerous slits. "You have no right to violate me like that," she shot back angrily.

"Whoa?! Hold on a minute," he said holding up his hands. "I didn't *violate* you. Yes, I kissed you but you kissed me back, just as eagerly I might add."

"I had no choice. You can't assume every woman within a hundred feet wants to drop their panties for you. I most certainly don't," she said tersely.

A slow smirk tilted his lips as he cocked his head to the side. "Is that so? Tell that to them." He ticked his chin toward her chest. She didn't have to look down to know what he was referring too. The tips of her breasts stood painfully erect, straining through the fabric of her shirt.

Flummoxed by his boldness and more than a little pissed she landed an open-handed slap across his cheek. Her breaths were coming out in short, frustrated pants. Her nostrils flared and her palm stung.

At first, her outburst had been amusing, but now she'd crossed the line.

"Your gross intrusion into my personal life is unacceptable."

"And you're being an ungrateful bitch," he spat back vehemently.

She raised her hand to slap him again, but this time he caught her wrist in his hand, squeezing it tightly. The pain was startling, but she refused to allow him to see it.

"Don't *ever* do that again," he said quietly. There was a dark edge to his voice. It carried menace as well as a promising threat. The tone made her want to step back. She'd seen that darkness before and it hadn't ended well for her.

"What? You'll hit me?" she challenged, still unable to get control over her tongue. She lifted her chin in defiance. "Go ahead. It's nothing that I haven't had done to me before."

And then, like that, his anger was gone. Someone somewhere in her past was the cause for this. They were the reason she was as rough as sandpaper and as sharp as broken glass. It was all about defense. This was how she protected herself.

He released her hand and put a little space between them. He raked his hands through his dark hair before resting them on his hips. "Listen. I'm sorry. I shouldn't have watched you get dressed, and I most certainly shouldn't have kissed you."

Cheri blinked and looked up at him. His abrupt shift in mood confused her. "What?"

He scrubbed his whiskered face. "I shouldn't have done all of this without asking ya. I was only trying to help, and the only reason I slept on the couch was to make sure you were okay."

"To make sure I was okay? Why wouldn't I have been?"

"Yeah, ya were pretty out of it last night when we got here. I couldn't get you to wake up. So after I put you in bed, I stayed."

"Oh," was all she could say.

She felt weird, knowing that he'd cared enough about her to make sure she was okay. Maybe she'd misjudged him. Guilt over her little temper tantrum gnawed at her. "Have you had breakfast? I can make ya some pancakes or something."

"Thanks, but I ate when I went to get supplies. Listen, I can go if ya want. I just wanted to fix that spot on the roof before the storm hit tonight."

The two of them stood awkwardly staring at each other—both at a loss for words. Finally, she let out a long, pent-up sigh. "Listen, I'm sorry. I just don't take charity well," she said begrudgingly.

He scoffed. "Trust me, it's not charity. If that roof falls in on you it'll be on my hands because I didn't fix it. Then if you're hurt I'm going to have to find a replacement for you, and I sure as hell just don't have that kind'a time." He watched as she crossed her arms tightly over her chest. After seeing the scars on her body he knew now why she did it. It was a way of protecting herself. Though, he really doubted she even knew she was doing it.

"Glad to know where your concerns lay," she bristled.

"What? You think I'm worried about *you*?"

*Ouch.*

"No, you made *that* abundantly clear last night." It was his turn to flinch. Damn, he had been a complete jackass the night before.

If he let on how much last night had actually affected him, it would scare the hell out of her. No, he would play it the other way. "Did you think something was going to happen last night?"

Her eyes widened and her mouth gaped. *Yes*. "No," she snapped.

"Good, because I don't make a habit out of sleeping with my employees."

"But you go around kissing them at random?" she said through tight lips.

He just smirked and leaned in closer, his warm breath smelling like coffee. Reaching in, he placed a hand on each side of her, resting them against the chipped countertop. He caged her in with his body and her breathing changed. "Touché, but don't try to kid yourself. We both know that we'd be dynamite between the sheets, *mon cher.*"

His tongue darted out to moisten his lips and she tried her hardest not to look down but failed.

"Bastard," she hissed—though it was only half-hearted. Placing both palms on his chest she shoved him with all the force she could muster.

"I swear your arrogance knows no bounds. Does it?"

"Nope."

She groaned. "Why don't you just leave?" *Before I do something stupid.*

He shrugged and chuckled. There was some sadistic part of him that enjoyed seeing her ready to shred him alive. The main reason being because she was damn cute. "I'll leave when the roof is finished," he said stubbornly.

"That wasn't the option," she fired back.

"Yes, pretty sure it is." He was goading her, finding some sort of morbid pleasure in watching the way her cheeks pinked with her anger.

Cheri's hands twitched at her sides, itching to reach for something and launch it at him as hard and as fast as she could manage. She had to get her temper under control. So, after a staring match, she took a deep, calming breath before steadying her voice.

"I can't afford to pay you," she finally said, swallowing her pride. Maybe if she could get through to him another way. It was obvious that she wasn't going to get anywhere using the aggressive route.

All the fight left him when she saw the humiliation in her eyes. It was honest and sincere and not solely based on pride. "I'm not charging you."

"I can't let you do that."

"Woman, do ya have to always be so damn pigheaded? Is it so hard for you to accept when someone is trying to be nice?"

"But you aren't doing it to be nice," she replied hotly.

He watched as she spun around and reached into the cabinet, removing a box of *Captain Crunch*. His eyes roamed over the tantalizing amount of tanned and sculpted legs, especially as her shorts rode up a couple inches higher.

When she turned back around he quickly looked somewhere else. She hopped up on the counter, her feet dangling over the edge, kicking the cabinets below. After opening the top of the box she plunged her hand inside and pulled out a hand full. Cereal was the perfect hangover food and honestly, it was keeping her focused.

Having lost most of her energy to fight but still slightly annoyed she sighed. "Jax, I can't let ya do that. I already owe you money. I can't afford the materials it would take for you to fix everything that needs fix'n."

"Well, at least let me fix the roof. My way of sayin' thanks for the help last night!"

"I'm getting paid for working last night, remember?" She popped a handful of cereal into her mouth and chewed. The loud crunching echoed through her head like cannon fire.

"True, but ya could've said no and face it, you had fun," he said wagging his brows playfully. Cheri just stared at him suspiciously. How in the hell could he go from being infuriating to playful in a matter of seconds? Inwardly she rolled her eyes, his mood swings were going to give her whiplash.

She thought about it for a long moment before opening her mouth. "Ok, on one condition, though."

"No promises, but I'll bite."

"I'm helping."

He looked at her as if she'd lost her mind. "Do ya have any idea how to work on a roof?"

"First of all, I'll ignore that incredibly sexist remark, and secondly, you'd be surprised at how well I can use a hammer."

Jax sensed a tone of smugness in her last statement and he wondered about it, but only briefly.

"What's it going to be? The storm is supposed to move in late this afternoon."

"Fine, but I'm not responsible if ya fall off the roof."

She jumped from the counter. "And I won't be responsible if you accidentally get shoved off," she said as she walked passed him and smirked. "I'm going to change into my work clothes." She went into the hall but then stuck her head around the corner. "Stay," she said pointing to the floor, the command dangerously close to the command she'd give a dog. When he looked up at her, he realized that was exactly how she'd meant it.

"You're cute," he said dryly.

She lifted a shoulder and said a simple "I know" before disappearing down the hall.

When she reappeared a little later, he was surprised to find her wearing a pair of old, work-worn jeans that hugged her full hips and backside perfectly. Just beneath each of the back pockets were holes but someone had sewed red bandanas on the inside, keeping from exposing too much skin. She wore a red tee-shirt that was covered with white paint. The deep v of the shirt revealed her ample cleavage. Her thick brown hair was pulled through the back of an old trucker's hat. She looked like she was ready for a day of hard work, all the way down to her old boots. He had to admit, he'd never seen a woman look more stunning than she looked in that moment standing in front of him.

"Ya weren't kidding when ya said work clothes, were ya?"

She looked up at him puzzled. "Why would I kid about that?" She removed a pair of gloves from a drawer in the kitchen. Like the rest of her clothes, they appeared worn but in otherwise great shape.

"I just never pictured ya doing a lot of manual labor."

"Again with the sexist remarks. I'm no stranger to manual labor. I 'gator hunt during the season and when I can, I work on shrimp boats."

"Really?" This was news to him and honestly, he found it a little more than sexy, exactly what he *did not* need.

"I have a family to support," she said with a casual lift of her shoulder. "Now, c'mon, we have a roof to fix," she said as she walked passed him, tucking the gloves in her back pocket.

Jax just watched as she left the room, leaving him speechless to stare after her. He was finding out that Cheri was quite the quandary. She was harsh, brash and belligerent yet at the same time, he could see compassion and warmth resting just beneath the surface of her exterior. All of these things were a dangerous combination for Jax. Because, in the past, it was these kinds of women that had always lead him down some dangerous paths, but it wasn't because he didn't want to go. No, it was because he was attracted to beautiful things and if they were a little crazy and dangerous, all the better. The bad thing was, Cheri was all of them. She was wild and crazy but the one thing that struck him deep was that she was broken. He'd been told by his momma a long time ago that one day a girl was going to come around and she wasn't going to be able to be fixed. Was Cheri that girl? Was she the one that was broken beyond repair?

He shook his head as he stepped out onto the porch and into the steaming heat of the morning. It was going to be a long day.

# 11

"Are you kidding me with this mess?" Detective Lynn Robichaud said as he stared at the file his partner slapped down in front of him.

"Happy Sunday," he smirked. His partner, a behemoth of a man by the name of Levi Moss, lowered his frame into the chair.

"I should be watching football in my recliner, not here going over case files," Lynn grunted.

"You and me both, man." Levi was still young by detective standards, but he'd more than proven himself in Lynn's eyes. At first, he hadn't been thrilled about the youngster being assigned to him, but after taking a few bullets for one another, things changed. Levi was a good cop with a heart of gold. In his young life, he'd already been through a marriage and a divorce. A lot for a young man to deal with at only twenty-seven.

"This is the report from the body found yesterday morning?"

Levi nodded. "Just got it from the ME."

Absently, Lynn thumbed through the report and photos from the scene. He'd worked for the Louisiana State Highway patrol for thirty years. Just out of the academy and ready for action, he'd started as a patrolman working in different parishes all through the state. He'd met the love his life, Cindy, in New Orleans and that's where he'd settled down, working from the troop located just a town over. He looked at the picture of his family on his desk. A wife that kept him on his toes and out of trouble, a son in the military and a daughter in the academy following his footsteps, he felt truly blessed. Several years later he'd been promoted to detective and was now one of the top in the parish with the second highest solve rate in the state.

The pitiful excuse of an air conditioner wheezed behind him, pulling him out of his daze. Lynn drew his dark eyebrows into a deep scowl as he studied the case closer.

Lynn wiped his handkerchief across his sweaty forehead as he stared at the gruesome pictures. Then he turned dark eyes to his partner and grunted. "How in the name of hades can you stand that?"

Levi arched a bushy brow at him. "What?"

"Man, it looks like a damn bear crawled up onto your face and died."

Levi absently ran his hand across his bushy red beard and shrugged. "Didn't have a chance to shave it, besides, the woman I was with last night said she liked it," he said wagging his brows suggestively.

Lynn rolled his eyes. "You need to at least trim that thing. It's a fire hazard."

"Fine dad, I'll trim it later."

"Don't call me dad. I'm not that much older than you," Lynn grunted.

"*Yeah, okay!* Anyhow, that's the report."

"Let me guess, it wasn't some drunk cajun that fell over the boat and got himself ate?"

Levi shook his head. "Nope."

"Of course not," he grumbled as he began to look further at the files. He'd heard about the body being found and hoped that it was just an accident. Unfortunately, that didn't seem to be the case at all.

Levi nodded. "I know, and you're not going to like this, either. Chief said he wants this to take top priority."

Lynn's head snapped up. "What?! Why?" There were a million reasons why he could think that this particular case could wait over the ones that he was currently losing sleep over. One case involving a kidnapped little girl. Anger bubbled in his gut and he pulled open the top drawer and popped the top open on a bottle of anti-acids.

Knowing there was no use in taking his anger out on the kid, he sighed. "What do we know?"

Levi shrugged his big beefy shoulders and briefly Lynn thought that the kid would be better suited as a pro-wrestler. "Not much. It looks like there was evidence of Succinylcholine being used."

"Succinylcholine but how?"

Levi nodded. "According to the ME, it's a neuromuscular agent. It's used on patients before they go under for surgery. It's typically used for smaller surgeries. She gave me a whole list of others that are used for bigger surgeries."

Lynn shook his head. "Were any of them present?"

"No."

"Then it's irrelevant. Go on."

"When the succinylcholine is used it paralyzes the patients, keeping them perfectly still for any of the procedures. While their muscles may move on their own, this drug works to keep that from happening."

"So they found succinylcholine with the tox screens?"

"Not exactly."

Lynn's brow furrowed and his dark eyebrows drew together. "Then how in the hell do we know it was used.

"While it's not evident, traces of it are very rarely left in the system because the body immediately begins to break it down. The affects don't last long roughly between four to six minutes before the affects wear completely off."

"Okay?"

"There were signs of its broken down components. When she did the autopsy on his brain, she found succinic acid, the main broken down metabolite. The ME said she still had some other tox screens to run, though. She thought this one was weird so she did it first."

"Shit," Lynn grunted as he flipped through the papers. "Okay, so what's to say this . . . uh. . . ." he said as he flipped through the papers.

"Guy," Levi supplied.

"Right. So what's to say this guy just didn't have a surgery and the neuro junk is just from the surgery?"

"Well, that would be well and fine. Small doses could pretty much go undetected by a tox screen."

"Okay, and I am guessing the amounts found were not small."

Levi shook his head. "No. The broken down particulates were still pretty evident, even with the level of decomp. Whoever used it, used a large dose and a lot of it. The ME was not happy about this either. The level of decomp was ridiculous. She did point out the marks." Levi slid an eight by ten photo out of the sleeve and placed it on top of the pile. Then he tapped the picture.

Lynn pulled his glasses from the top of his head and held up the picture to examine. He frowned. The severed arm was pretty badly mangled and gashed open. "This is the arm pulled from the swamp? Are any of these from the killer?" he asked as he pointed to several large tears in the sickly purple and grey limb. There were large chunks of skin and muscle torn away, revealing nothing but rotting tissue. The tissue breaking down was no doubt due to the conditions of the swamp.

"No. The examiner said those are all from gators."

"Gators? As in plural?"

Levi pursed his lips and crossed his arms over his chest. "Yeah. She said there were at least four other gators that snacked on this arm before it wound up at the bottom of the swamp. We got a call a little bit ago from some swampers that found some more human remains in the belly of another gator."

"Awesome," Lynn groaned. "Okay, so it was gators that killed this guy?"

Levi ticked his head to the side and pursed his lips. "That initially killed him, yes. However, I seriously doubt he injected himself with a Succinylcholine and rolled himself into the bayou after cutting off his own finger."

Lynn's eyes looked at the fingers in the picture. They were all miraculously intact, except for the index finger. He squinted and pulled the picture closer before looking up at Levi. "It was cut off."

"Yep."

"Probably for a trophy."

"Most likely."

Lynn placed the file back in the folder and closed it. "Do we have an i.d. on the vic yet?"

Levi nodded. "They were able to lift prints from the hand they found. Travis Anderson, and he's got a list of priors a mile long."

Lynn frowned and looked through the paperwork. "Drugs, theft and oh look he's a sex offender too."

Levi snorted, "Yeah he was a real upstanding citizen. Infractions start when he was thirteen years old. Was bounced around from home to home until he was thrown in juvie when he was seventeen for the rape of a girl in one of the homes he was in. A grudge kill? Maybe he owed somebody?"

Lynn shrugged and shook his head. "It's possible—we don't want to rule anything out just yet, but one of the officers already checked in with Anderson's parole officer. He said Anderson had been on the straight and narrow for about four years. Passed every random drug test thrown his way and was even holding a steady job."

"So what the hell made him a mark?"

"Hell if I know. Wrong place, wrong time maybe?"

Lynn frowned and skimmed through the file once more. Something just didn't feel right. "Do we have time of death?"

Levi looked over his notes. "ME has it at about twenty-eight hours before discovery, give or take before the rest of the body was found. So looks like he was killed and dumped sometime late Friday night."

Lynn pushed away from his desk and stood. After grabbing his holsters from the back of his chair, he slung them over his shoulders and then grabbed the file. Lynn grunted. "Looks more like twenty-eight days," he grumbled.

"That's what I thought, but with the weird weather we've had. All the rain and the heat accelerated the process. I guess."

"Yeah. Decomp rate increases within certain weather conditions. It would stand to reason that is what happened here."

"This is going to be like finding a needle in a mountain of haystacks," Lynn grunted as he walked from his office.

"Especially since we're going into this blind and with no leads. Where do we even start?" Levi grumbled as they walked through the room filled with desks and criminals waiting to be processed.

"Start where the arm was found and then we'll go talk to the damn rednecks that are poaching gator. If they know anything they'll spit it out. Chances are, the body was dumped not too far from there. We'll get some units out there and start canvassing the area to see what we can come up with. Then I guess we go check out Anderson's apartment."

"K. I'm gonna stop by Sweeties and grab a couple doughnuts. You want any?"

Lynn frowned at him. "I hate doughnuts."

"Just cause you do, don't mean I got to," Levi chuckled as they pushed through the double glass doors and into the miserable heat of the Louisiana evening.

"And you're doing everything you can to perpetuate the cop stereotype."

They walked down the sidewalk to their dodge charger.

"Don't use big words like that," Levi chuckled, already shuffling away and into the bakery just down from the station.

Lynn rolled his eyes. "Just hurry the hell up."

He watched the black clouds on the horizon as they slowly crept closer. Their inky blackness left the air feeling heavily charged with electricity. The hot breeze blowing around did nothing to stifle the oppressive heat. If anything it only made it worse. They were fighting an uphill battle because if it rained it could easily wash away whatever evidence there was a small chance of finding. Even then their chances were close to zero of even finding anything.

As he waited for Levi he flipped through the pages again. A heavy feeling landed in his gut making him briefly wish he'd taken up a smoking habit. As he stared at the gruesome and mangled limb, something began to bother him. He had a feeling that this case was going to be one for the records.

Before he had any more time to ponder his sinking feeling, Levi appeared carrying a bag in one hand, two cups of coffee in the other and a big white powered doughnut in his mouth. Lynn took his coffee and eyed the powdery confection getting all over the kid.

"You better think again if you think you're eat'n that mess in my car."

Levi smiled. "And get Baby dirty? Perish the thought." That was all he said as he shoved the remainder of the doughnut into his mouth. His cheeks puffed out like a chipmunk he gave him a wide smile.

Lynn slipped behind the wheel and closed the door. It was going to be one hell of a day.

# 12

"What's your story?" Cheri asked as she hammered another nail into the shingle. The kiss from earlier had been somewhat forgotten. That didn't stop her from desperately wanting to ask about what she'd seen last night and the other day at the bar, but somehow she didn't think asking her boss if he was a drug dealer would go over too well. So, she kept her thoughts to herself.

"What? You mean you *don't* know who you are working for?" he said as he hammered.

"I've heard rumors."

"Then what you hear must be true. Right?" he slammed the hammer down on the head of the nail a little harder than necessary.

Cheri frowned. "I have no room to judge others. You don't want to tell me, fine. No skin off my nose. I was just trying to make conversation."

He blew out a sigh and looked up at her. "A long time ago someone hurt someone I care about." She watched the dark cloud of anger pass over his face. She knew that whatever happened in the past would likely haunt him for the rest of his life, and something about that left her feeling severely unsettled. From the serious expression he always wore, it seemed like it had been a very long time since he'd been happy.

She accepted his vague answer, sensing that he really didn't want to say more. She wouldn't push. More than anyone, she understood what it was like to keep a dark secret.

They went back to working and the sound of the hammers was oddly comforting to her. She'd lost track of time and become lost in thoughts when his words startled her.

"I went to prison when I turned twenty-two. I was in there for six years."

117

"Oh," Cheri said, wiping her forehead with the back of her gloved hand. Of all the rumors she'd heard, the prison one was constant. She'd surmised that he'd served time, but the reasoning was still unclear.

He opened his mouth to say something but snapped it shut and turned his attention back to sliding another shingle into place.

"It's okay. You don't have to tell me. Either way, I'm not afraid of you."

Jax dropped his hammer to the roof and lifted his gaze. "You should be."

"Why? Because everyone else is, or it's just what I'm supposed to do?" she scoffed.

"Both."

She snorted and looked at him. "I don't do well with people telling me what to do."

He chuckled and muttered. "Don't I know it?"

She resisted the urge to stick her tongue out at him. She continued. "Listen, I really don't give a shit what you did or didn't do. I believe you're a good person. You've been nothing but good to me so I don't rightly care. I'm not a good person. I've got things in my past that I pray never sees the light of day. I still try, though. We should never stop trying."

"I find that very hard to believe."

"What? That I have secrets?"

"No, that you're not a good person," he said as he hammered another shingle into place.

Cheri was quiet for a while, processing what he'd said. When she picked up and placed a shingle and began to nail it she finally spoke. "Things aren't always as they seem, Jax." She blew out a heavy sigh. "Listen, I'm really sorry for the way I've been acting. My past has made me this . . . cold person. I'm not proud of it and I'm not trying to justify my behavior. I've been more than a little ungrateful and for that, I'm really sorry. I'm not used to someone actually being nice to me because they want to be nice. It's typically because they always want something in return."

"Not everyone is bad, Cheri," he said thoughtfully.

A small smile drifted across her face. "I'm beginning to see this."

Another long stretch of silence passed between them as they worked. The humidity was relentless. Gnats buzzed and overhead, buzzards circled. More than likely due to the city dump being directly across the street.

When the silence had gone on for too long, Cheri finally spoke. "So how did you come to own Voodoo Queen?"

"When I was in prison I was hell-bent on making something of myself. I started taking business classes. By the time I got out, I had a business degree. I didn't have much money so I worked on the pipelines in Oklahoma until I was almost thirty. During that time, I'd managed to save up as much money possible. When I finally came home, seven years ago, I began the process of buying the Queen. It took a year but I finally got her."

Cheri watched the fondness that came over him when he talked about his bar. It made her realize how lonely she really was.

"You got what you wanted," she said.

"Wasn't easy," he said.

"Nothing ever worth anything ever is," she said matter-of-factly.

"This is true." His brown gaze met and held hers. Everything around them ceased to exist. The stifling heat grew warmer and if her cheeks weren't already pink from heat they would be from the intensity of his gaze. Her pulse quickened as he licked his lips. Beads of sweat rolled down the sides of his face and onto his bare shoulders.

"I think we need to . . . take a break. Do you want some tea?"

"That sounds like a good idea." His voice crackled a little bit as he swallowed and nodded. His Adam's apple bobbed and she knew if she didn't get off that roof that minute, she was going to do something incredibly stupid. She decided to chalk it all up to too much heat.

Jax straightened and pulled his bandana from his back pocket. After quickly swiping it over his face he smiled and nodded.

Cheri adverted her eyes, trying to look anywhere but his bare chest. He was built, there was no doubt about that. His skin was tanned dark brown from hours working in the hot sun. There were tattoos on his ribs. She tried to catch glimpses of it but she could only make out *there is a killer in us all.* There were two tattoos on his back, just by his shoulder blades. After a while, it dawned on her what they were. It was a depiction of wings that had been torn off, leaving behind broken and bleeding holes. Her heart buckled. What had really happened?

Tossing her hammer down beside a stack of shingles she climbed from her knees to her feet. She felt Jax's hand at her elbow helping her up. There was a desperate need to change the subject, move or do something because suddenly everything felt as if it were pressing down on her. She placed her hands in the small of her back and massaged away the ache of being bent over for an hour straight.

She looked at their progress and forced a smiled. They'd managed to cover and repair just about half the front side of the roof. Thankfully there hadn't been any water damage so no major repairs were needed.

"Another hour and we should be done. The back side is fine, a few shingles could probably be replaced but it ain't nothing that needs to be done t'day," he said.

"I really do appreciate it," she said rolling her neck side to side.

Jax smiled broadly revealing perfectly white—slightly crooked—teeth. He swiped at a bead of sweat that was dripping of the end of his nose. "It's hotter than the hinges of hell out here t'day," he said looking up.

"Yep and the sun hasn't even show his damn face either," she remarked indicating to the increasingly darkening sky. She began to make her way down the ladder. Once on the ground, she turned and held the old, wooden contraption steady.

It was hard not to appreciate his backside as he climbed down, however as he placed his foot on the third rung from the ground the sound of splintering wood caught her attention. Acting on instinct she reached out to try to awkwardly steady him but it was too late. He was already pitching back and she was in his way. Together they landed on the ground in a tangle of limbs and curses. Jax's elbow caught Cheri in the ribs, causing the air to leave her lungs in a whoosh.

His weight pushed the air from her lungs and she was struggling to regain it. She awkwardly pushed at him, as she fought for air. As soon as she was free from his weight she sucked in a sharp breath, feeling her lungs expand in her chest.

"Why in the hell weren't you holding the ladder?" he grumbled as he offered her his hand.

She just stared at him, astonished. "I was holding the ladder you asshole." She batted his hand away and despite her aching, protesting body, she climbed to her feet.

"Apparently not," he challenged.

"The damn rung broke," she said pointing down to the offending ladder as she bent over to assess the damage. Her shirt was plastered to her back by the thick and awful smelling mud.

She straightened and glared at him. "If I wanted ya to fall, I would've pushed ya from the roof. And I'm fine, thanks for asking," she grumbled twisting her arm to see where the radiating pain was coming from.

"Here, let me see," he said taking her arm and inspecting the sting. She tried to jerk away but he held her tight. "Let. Me. See," he said slowly.

"I'm fine," she muttered but let him look at her arm.

After pushing and poking around her arm he released her. "It's just a scrape."

"Thanks, doc," she said drily.

He ignored the jab. "What about your ribs?" His hands were on her, lifting her shirt, gently pressing and testing. She flinched at first from the pressure, but then because of his touch.

"I'm fine," she said as she abruptly pulled away from him. "Let's get something to drink," muttered as she turned and made her way up the stairs.

Jax scowled as he watched her go. Damn stubborn woman. With a sigh, he followed her into the house.

"Listen, I'm sorry," he lamented as she moved around the kitchen slamming cabinets and banging doors. Her shirt was caked with mud but she wasn't letting that bother her. He couldn't help but smile.

"Whatever," was her curt response as she continued to slam cabinets.

"That ladder is older than Methuselah. It's a wonder we didn't break our necks beforehand."

"It came with the house," she replied, still not turning around.

"Well, that would explain it."

At that, Cheri whirled around and glared at him. She had a smudge of dirt on her cheek. He wanted to reach up and wipe it way, but snapping fury in her green eyes made him rethink that.

Her nostrils flared with anger as she narrowed her eyes, her mouth opening and then snapping shut. She pressed her lips into a tight line. He watched with mild amusement as she fought with herself. He quirked his eyebrows, challenging her to unleash her temper on him.

She held his gaze for a few moments longer before whirling around to retrieve another glass from the cupboard. She'd tracked mud all through the house but she no longer cared. She was just trying to focus on anything but her increasing desire and fury for Jax. The man was absolutely the most infuriating creature on the face of the planet, and heaven help her if that same man didn't turn her on at the same time.

Jax didn't say anything as watched her move around the kitchen. Her shirt lifted, revealing dark purple scars. The muscles in his jaws flexed. Was there any wonder that she had trust issues? He couldn't blame her one bit.

As he watched her mix the tea, he remembered the conversation he'd had with his mother the night before, when she'd found him sitting on the porch watching Cheri work.

"Ya leave that girl alone, Jaxon" she'd told him.

"What do ya mean?" he asked, never taking his eyes off of Cheri. He'd gone into the house to grab a couple more beers after they'd danced for a while.

"She don't need no man in her life muckin things up."

He'd eyed his mother suspiciously. "Ya know her from somewhere other than the grocery store."

"That is none of yer concern. I know ya like yer women loose and fast, Jaxon. She's neither of dose things. She's a good girl."

True, the women he took to his bed were far from being angels, but he never expected to hear his momma call him out on it.

"I've not been with a woman in a long while momma."

"Go ta bed!" she exclaimed skeptically.

"You don't believe me?" He eyed her, somewhat shocked that his own mother thought so little of him.

She chuckled and patted his hand. "Nah, honey, I don't. Because you're too much like yer daddy was *when he was your age.*"

Jax sighed and rolled his eyes and returned his gaze back to Cheri. She was laughing and dancing with his cousin. She tucked an escaped strand of hair behind her ear as she laughed at something Jean-luc had said to her. "There's nothing there, momma," he said as he pulled from his beer. Even as he said the words, he wondered how much he actually believed them.

"Jax."

"Huh?" Jax blinked, pushing aside the conversation with his mother.

Cheri was standing with her hands on her hips, a dark brow arched at him. "Come in space cadet. I asked what ya wanted. I have water, tea, and lemonade."

"Tea's fine," he said.

She walked to the fridge and pulled open the door. Jax's attention turned to the pictures hanging on the wall.

The frames were cheap, some with chunks of wood missing and others with cracks in the glass. A couple of the frames were hand-made, seashells glued to popsicle sticks with glitter and ribbons attached. There were several photos of a boy and a girl. Some starting from when they were toddlers going up to what appeared to be recent. The boy was thin but had the same green eyes as Cheri. The girl was the spitting image of her momma and looked to be every bit the firecracker.

They were from a different time and place. The woman in the picture was younger, somewhat thinner. Her hair was a different color and styled differently but there was no doubt that it was Cheri. The haunted look he recognized was evident, even though it was years ago. In those photos, the smile never quite reached her eyes.

Then, there were the candid ones where she wasn't staring into the camera but at her children. That was when he caught a glimpse of her smile. The genuine smile. Her guards were down and he could actually see her.

"These your kids?" he asked, already knowing the answer but needing to fill the strained silence between them.

"Yep," came her short reply. She opened the freezer door and Jax resumed looking at the pictures, but the sound of shattering glass pulled his attention back to the kitchen. Seconds later came Cheri's piercing scream.

He rushed to her side. It took him a few moments for his eyes to register what exactly he was seeing. Resting on a block of ice was a severed finger, pointing at her. The inside of the freezer was coated in frozen blood.

# 13

"Why's there a bloody finger in your freezer?"

"How the hell should I know?" she sputtered, unable to take her eyes from the small horror scene. Her hands shook violently and her knees threatened to buckle. Her heart was hammering so loudly, she was certain it was going to explode from her chest at any moment.

Grabbing a paper towel, he reached in.

"Don't touch it," she said grabbing his arm.

"Well, would you like me to leave it in there?"

"Not especially."

Reaching in, he clutched it through the paper towel. Under the block of ice was a piece of folded paper. Reaching in the freezer, she removed the paper.

"You probably shouldn't touch that," Jax said.

"Why not?" she asked as she unfolded it.

*I know,* was scrawled in red. Her hands grew clammy and her mouth grew dry.

"What does that mean?" Jax asked, reading over her shoulder.

She lifted her shoulder and tossed the paper in the trash. "I-I don't know."

"Bullshit," he spat.

She frowned. "How would I know what the letter attached to the finger in my freezer means? Seriously?"

"I'm sure the cops—"

"Um, no. There aren't going to be any cops," she said pointedly.

He stared at her a brief flicker of fear flashed behind her eyes. "Why in the hell wouldn't you call the cops?"

Her shoulders stiffened and she slammed the freezer door closed. "I'm just not getting the cops involved."

He studied her for a moment, contemplating what he wanted to do. "I'm calling the cops," he said finally as he tugged his cell phone from his pocket.

"Don't," she pleaded, reaching out and grabbing his arm. The desperation in her voice caused him to pause.

He looked down at her hand, he could feel her callouses scraping against his skin. "Why don't you want the cops here, Cheri?"

"I just don't, okay!" she said hotly.

"Are you hiding something?"

His probing gaze made her shift uncomfortably. "We're all guilty of hiding something," she replied softly as she lowered her gaze. She took a deep breath and tried to steady her nerves before starting again. "Listen, I've dealt a lot with cops in my life. I'm not interested in having them root'n around my business. Just leave it alone, will ya?"

"I'm not a fan of the authorities myself, but something like this. . . . Well, it's something that they need to be takin care of. If anything to rule you out of anything. What would happen if they found the body this belonged too and somehow it was linked to you?! What if someone is framing you for murder?"

The question knocked the wind out of her like a swift blow to the gut. He was right. The room buckled and the walls warped like a funhouse mirror. The floor tilted as the anxiety attack threatened to choke her.

"Hey! Whoa there," Jax said tossing the finger to the counter quickly before reaching out to steady her. She sagged into his arms and he led her to the couch where she sat heavily. Leaning forward, she cradled her head in her hands, taking deep breaths until the room stopped spinning. Vaguely she was aware of the sound of the water being turned on and then off. It had been a long time since she'd had an attack. She concentrated on regulating her breathing. Quietly she counted, keeping her eyes tightly closed. Her stomach clenched and unclenched as bile climbed to the back of her throat.

*Breathe.*
Inhale.
*One, two, three. . . .*
Exhale.
*Four, five, six.*

"What was that all about?" he asked. A cool cloth was gently pressed to the back of her neck.

"I don't know. I probably got too hot," she lied.

"That was more than getting hot," he said pointedly. "We're calling the cops," Jax said standing.

He was dialing the number when her hand flashed out and caught his and for the second time in ten minutes, he was caught off guard by her touch. "Please," she whispered. Her soft plea twisted in his gut. As he looked at her, for the first time since meeting her, the mile high wall she had around her crumbled slightly. Her green eyes were wild with panic.

"What are you so scared of?" he asked, sitting on the coffee table in front of her. One of his knees pressed between her thighs. His closeness forced her to look at him. He held both of her hands tightly between his, caressing them slightly with his thumbs. Odd as it was, it gave her comfort, something she'd never really experienced before.

Cheri had two options. She swallowed past the lump in her throat and licked her dry lips. "He'll take my kids away from me." It wasn't *that* far from the truth.

"Who will?"

"My ex-husband. He's looking for any excuse he can to get full custody. He's already tried to use the living conditions as one."

Everything began to click into place, the reason she was so defensive about her house, the reason she was so angry all the time. There was still a burning question that bothered him.

"Is he the one that left those marks on you?"

"What?" she blinked confused as to what he was talking about. Then she remembered that he'd seen her back. He'd seen the lashes. She shook her head. "No. Alex was a lot of things, but he was never physically abusive. That was courtesy of my stepfather and a couple different fosters. Anyhow, my personal life isn't important right now. Someone left a finger in my freezer." She needed to move his attention somewhere else.

Slowly standing she made her way back into the kitchen and retrieved the finger. Careful not to touch it, she turned it this way and that, inspecting every inch of it. Where it had been cut away was bloody, with bits of flesh still clinging. She could see the bone, and it made her stomach roll. The flesh was purple and lifeless. The nails were dirty and grimy, reminding her of some of the mechanics she used to work with.

"Do you recognize it?"

She frowned up at him. "What the hell kind of question is that? Of course, I don't recognize it. It's a damn severed finger. Unless there's a head hidden in the toaster oven, it's pretty safe to assume I don't know who it belongs to."

Even as she said it, she studied the offending object. There was a small faded cross tattooed in green ink just below the fingernail. Something about the tattoo bothered her but she couldn't put a finger on it. She chuckled and soon it bubbled into out of control laughter. Her ribs ached from the fall but they ached more as she laughed like a lunatic.

Jax just stared at her as if she'd lost her mind. Perhaps she had.

He frowned. "What are you laughing about?"

After several long moments, she got her laughter under control. She swiped the tears from her eyes. "Nothing." Suddenly, the intrusion from the other night came bouncing back with the force of a tornado. Maybe she really was being watched. There was someone outside the grocery store the day she'd gotten fired. Then, that same night at the end of her driveway.

Maybe someone else knew her secret. It was this thought that sobered her, pushing away all the laughter and filling the space with stone cold panic. It skittered up her spine with icy fingers, reaching around her throat and threatening to choke her. She squeezed her eyes closed and took another series of deep breaths.

She opened her eyes, and while Jax stared at her with heavy concern, she tried to focus on details. How long had it been since she'd opened the freezer door?

Surely she'd been in the freezer in the past week. Hadn't she? She struggled to remember but was coming up blank.

Cheri pulled her hands from Jax's and slowly pushed to her feet. With determined steps.

"Where are you going?" Jax asked.

She walked over to the counter and picked the finger up, careful not to touch it outside the paper towel. She lightly squeezed it. When it squished she let out a shiver of revulsion, her stomach rolling dangerously.

"It's not frozen all the way through. I mean my freezer isn't that great and it typically takes things forever to freeze."

"You think someone could've put it in there last night?" he asked, looking at the slightly bloated, purplish digit.

She walked into the living room and tossed it onto the coffee table before sagging onto the lumpy couch. She propped her feet on the edge of the chipped table and stared at the finger. The air in the room seemed to grow thick as she tried to catch her breath. The morning heat was doing nothing to improve the situation. Couple that with the hangover that was still lingering about, it was just downright miserable.

Everything she'd worked so hard for over the past two decades was slipping away. The shadows of her past were creeping out from their hiding places. It was only a matter of time before they came screaming into the light. She'd been foolish to think she could hide for so long.

Someone was tormenting her, but who? Only two people knew what happened, Roux and Lizabeth. Roux wouldn't have told anyone, so she ruled him out immediately. However, Lizabeth, she wasn't so sure about. Could she have told her son about Cheri's past?

"Who would have done something like this?" she whispered afraid she already knew the truth.

"Is there anyone that would want to scare you?"

*Only one.* "No."

Jax shook his head.

"Things have just been so weird lately."

The hard look on his face softened a little. "Weird how?"

"Like someone is watching me."

"Someone watching you? What do you mean?"

She quickly told him about the man she thought she saw standing beside the grocery store and then paused.

"What? What is it?"

"Then that first night that I worked at the bar. I fell asleep in the tub after I got home, and something woke me. I don't know what it was. When I came out to the living room there were muddy footprints and the front door was open. I thought I saw. . . ." She paused, wondering how crazy she really sounded.

He sat on the couch beside her. "What? What did you think you saw?"

"I thought I saw someone at the end of my driveway, watching me. But it was raining and pretty dark. It could have been anything. I was tired."

"Why are you just now telling me this?" he asked tersely.

"Because I thought I was seeing things."

If she thought that the look on his face could grow any harder, she'd been wrong. The look that was there now, was bordering on murderous. "What footprints," he growled.

"The next day, there were muddy footprints on the carpet," she said pointing to where she'd scrubbed them up. "I thought that maybe I'd been the one to track them in. I didn't say anything because it was foolish," she admitted.

"You should have told me," he snapped.

Anger boiled through her, so much so that she missed the edge of concern in his voice. "First of all, it happened over a week ago and nothing has happened since. Secondly, it was after my first night of work and I didn't know you from Adam."

"Until now," he cut in.

"What?"

"Nothing has happened until now."

She ignored him and continued. "And lastly, you're not my keeper and I don't need a babysitter," she snapped back.

"Someone is obviously stalking you."

"Really?"

"You just said—"

"I know what I *just* said. I also said I was tired. I could have imagined the whole thing. I could have left those muddy footprints and the door could have blown open while I was in the tub." No matter how much she said it, she still couldn't shake the eerie feeling she had.

He frowned. "I still think we need to call the cops!"

"I said no cops," she said standing. She winced as pain shot through her side.

"You're hurt," he said.

"I'm fine," she said waving him off when he reached for her.

"Jax, I don't like cops, never have. There are things. . . . Well, just believe me when I say I don't need them in my life to further complicate things."

He stepped forward and looked down at her. She could feel the heat of his skin next to hers. The way he'd held her, danced with her the night before drifted through his mind. "What are you hiding?" His dark eyes bore into hers, leaving her feeling more than a little exposed.

She gulped. "N-nothing."

"You're afraid of something," he continued, his voice was low as he held her gaze.

She swallowed hard, the lump in her throat refusing to go away. She wanted to be angry at his intrusion, but the truth of the matter was—she was just too tired. "Nothing." It came out in a whisper and she mentally cursed herself.

He just nodded once in understanding and took a step closer. Reaching up he pushed a strand of hair away from her face, tucking it behind her ear. "If you're in some kind of trouble. Something that is preventing you from going to the cops. . . ." He let the thought die on his lips as he knuckles grazed against her cheek.

Her eyes drifted closed for a brief moment at the comfort that just the slight touch brought her. Then she remembered where she was and what was happening and moved away from his touch. Her barriers slipped firmly back it place. *Don't let anyone in and don't get hurt.* That had been her mantra for so many years, and it had to stay firmly in place.

"Listen, I'm not in any kind of trouble and I'm sure this is just a sick joke. Just leave it alone." She brushed past him and stood by the front door. She tugged it open and looked at him expectantly.

"You need to go," she tried to keep her voice firm. If she showed any signs of being scared then he would never leave, and that wouldn't work.

"And leave you here alone? Not likely."

She rolled her eyes. "Seriously? I'm pretty sure that if anything were going to happen to me it would have by now," she defended. Even though she said the words she didn't believe them.

He frowned at her, trying to read her emotions. She lifted her chin a notch, daring him to push the issue. He huffed. "You're not staying here alone."

She narrowed her eyes on him. "The hell I'm not."

"It's not safe."

"It's a prank," she said weakly. She wanted to believe it.

"Prank or not, I'm not letting you stay here tonight. So, this is what you're going to do. You're either going to stay at my place, in the apartment at the bar or I'm going to stay here with you. Those are your options."

Cheri crossed her arms defiantly over her chest, thrusting her breasts up. She didn't miss the flicker of his eyes to her chest. "You have a lot of nerve thinking you can come in here and tell me what I am or what I'm not going to do."

"It is what it is," he shrugged.

"I'm not going to stay with you," she said stubbornly.

"Then it looks like you've got a new roommate."

Cheri sputtered angrily, trying to get the words out that she so desperately wanted to call him, but nothing came out besides an angry mixture of stuttering nonsense.

"I'll be back to pick you up for work after a while. I've got some things to pick up in town." He turned and marched to the door and then stopped. He turned and faced her. "I'll put the ladder away but I'm finishing that damn roof for you tomorrow. If I'm going to have to stay here, then I'm not going to have it cave in on me while I sleep."

That was all he said as he turned and marched from the house. He stopped and turned. "Lock this door after I leave and don't open it for anyone that you don't know. Do you understand me?"

When she didn't answer he turned fully and faced her. "So help me, Cheri. I will toss your ass in my truck right now and you'll have a new shadow for the rest of your life if you don't do as I say."

Pissed at being ordered around in her own house, she marched over to the door and slammed it, causing the walls and windows to rattle. Still, he didn't move until she twisted the lock. He gave her a smug look of satisfaction before turning on his heel and marching down the steps.

Once he was out of sight, she grabbed her cell phone and a pack of cigarettes from the coffee table, careful not to touch the finger. She went into the bathroom, shutting the door firmly behind her. Sitting on the edge of the tub, she shoved open the old creaky window. For a second she thought the thing was going to fall out, she was relieved when it just protested.

With trembling hands, she shook a cigarette from the pack and jammed it between her lips. It took three tries with the lighter before the tip began to glow bright red. The smoke filled her lungs and she held it for a minute before exhaling. It did nothing to calm her.

She flipped open her phone and dialed Roux's number. After ringing three times it went to voicemail. It was Sunday morning. He was usually home reading the paper and treating himself to waffles, something he only did once a week. Roux was a creature of habit, he had a slight case of attention deficit disorder mixed with a touch of obsessive-compulsive disorder. His routines were very important to him and any deviation from them really bothered him.

She didn't leave a message but disconnected and tried again. She crossed her legs and bounced her foot anxiously as the phone on the other end rang. After flicking her ashes out, the window and took another drag. "Please pick up," she whispered. The results were the same. This time she did leave a message.

"Roux, I don't know where you are, but something is going on here. I think someone," she swallowed past the lump in her throat before finishing. "Roux, someone knows. I don't think I was imagining the other night. I think someone was really in here. I'm being watched. There's some weird shit going on." She paused, deciding not to say anything else. "Just call me. Please."

She knew she was on the edge of hysterics so she took a deep breath. Everything was spinning and if she didn't gain control soon, things would get out of hand in a hurry. She smoked the cigarette down to the filter before dropping it in the toilet and flushing.

Leaning over the sink, she splashed cold water on her clammy face. She looked at her reflection as she gripped the edge of the chipped sink. Water dripped off the end of her nose and landed soundlessly in the sink.

"You're just hung over. Get a hold of yourself." She took a deep breath through her nose and slowly blew it out through her lips. After doing this three times, she felt her nerves calm, but just a little. She loosed her grip on the sink and blood rushed back into her hands.

Maybe she would go into work early. She frowned, if she did that, she would see Jax. That was a whole new set of problems. Granted, not as important as the severed finger but still something to think about. Broken images flashed through her mind from last night. His hands gliding up and down her back. The way he held her close while they danced. The feel of his hips pressing into her backside as they danced front to back. The scent of his cologne mingling with body wash. Just thinking about him made her heart race.

"Get your shit together," she growled at her reflection.

She scrubbed her eyes with the heels of her hands and splashed on more cold water. She had more important things to worry about than some stupid rampant hormone issue.

"Screw it," she muttered. She walked from the bathroom and into her daughter's room. Her daughter had the biggest closet in the house, so naturally, it was where Cheri kept her clothes. Hurriedly she changed into a pair of black shorts. As she tugged a black tank top over her head she looked out the window at the heavy clouds steadily getting closer. If she hurried and if luck was on her side, she could make it to the bar before it started to rain. Then again luck never had been particularly kind to her.

Jax leaned the old ladder back against the house where he'd found it. As he was turning to walk back to the front, he heard a voice coming from an open window. He knew he should mind his own business, but something about the frantic tone in Cheri's voice pulled him up short.

He listened as she talked, or left a message for someone named Roux. He couldn't hear all of what she'd said, *but someone knows* and *I'm being watched*, came through loud and clear. What exactly was Cheri hiding? Whatever it was seemed to be finally getting to her. Tiny cracks in her armor were starting to show. As he walked back to his truck, he was left thinking about Cheri and the questions that he was beginning to form. Last night, he'd caught glimpses of a carefree woman and even a few times today he'd seen it, but when he got to close, she slammed the walls back up and forced him out.

The biggest question that was nagging him was: why was there a bloody finger in her freezer? He knew he should call the cops and report it, but the sheer terror in Cheri's eyes when he had mentioned it was the only thing that stopped him. If Cheri was in some kind of trouble and he called the cops, he could be the one responsible for making her life worse, and no matter how much she annoyed him, he couldn't do that to her.

He'd been on the wrong end of the law before, and if he had to be honest with himself, he still was in some areas. Sure, bootlegging wasn't a major offense, however, if he wasn't careful, he could wind himself back up in prison. The allure of the dangerous always appealed to him. *Which is why you got sent to prison in the first place.* His brain reminded him. He understood there were risks and understood all too well about not wanting to involve the cops, but this was something far different than illegal moonshine. He had a feeling that the secret Cheri was harboring was much darker and could quite possibly leave her in a world of danger.

He knew he should stay out of it, but couldn't. There was one person that he was certain to have the answers. His mother. Jax hadn't missed the awkwardness between Cheri and his mother the night before, and if he had to place money on it, he would bet his business that his mother knew more than she was letting on.

He looked at the poor house once more. The dark swells of storm clouds were beginning to boil overhead.

"Storms coming," he muttered as he put his truck into gear and pointed toward his mother's house. It was time to get some answers.

# 14

The bar was quiet, but then again it was Sunday night. Too many people spent the day in church repenting for the sins they'd committed the night before. It was a good thing business was slow because Cheri's mood was as volatile as the storm raging outside. She hadn't seen much of Jax since she'd arrived. The one time she'd seen him, he'd spent fifteen minutes yelling at her for walking by herself.

As a result, another screaming matched had occurred and was followed by the slamming of his office door. Since then, he'd come out of his office once for a beer and then disappeared behind his closed door with grunted curses and muttered annoyances.

With little else to do, she pulled her phone out of her back pocket and leaned against the bar. She pressed the speed dial, trying Roux's number again. Not only was it unlike him to deviate from his routine, but he always called her back.

She closed her phone and frowned down at it.

"What's da matter, honey, boyfriend ain't call'n ya back?" Trixie asked, coming up behind her and depositing empty beer bottles in the trash. One of the bottles didn't make it and as it landed against the rough planks of the floor, dark brown shards of glass exploded everywhere. "Shit," Trixie grunted as Cheri jumped and yelped. Her sudden movements sent the salt shaker she'd been filling as well as a flurry of salt all over the bar.

"Jeez, honey! What da hell's got ya so jumpy?" she asked as she grabbed the broom and began to rake the glass into a pile. The *plinking* of the broken pieces was like razors against Cheri's already frayed nerves.

"Nothing, just a little bit on edge." With a damp towel, Cheri raked the spilled salt into her hand and tossed it in the trash.

"Why?" Trixie's blue eyes sparkled with concern.

"My friend's not answering his phone."

"Maybe he died?" she offered.

Cheri's head whipped around. "What did you say?"

Trixie started at Cheri's sudden movements and took a step back.

"I said maybe *it* died. Ya know, the phone?"

Cheri breathed a sigh of relief. The thought of anything happening to him made her stomach twist into knots. She shook her head. "Sorry. No, Roux has o.c.d and is very particular. His phone never dies and he's never without it."

"And he's not answer'n, huh?" Trixie propped her hip against a stool.

Cheri frowned and nodded.

Trixie offered her a shrug and drew the broom across the floor. "He'll turn up. Maybe he just try'n out somethin new. Everything'll be okay. You'll see."

Cheri wished she felt the confidence that Trixie put out, but she didn't. She gave her a small smile before turning back to the task of refilling all the salt shakers.

Moving around the bar, Cheri made her way to the table that still needed to be cleared from dinner dishes. As she was wiping the table she heard a low whistle come from Trixie.

"What?"

When she turned, she found Trixie staring up at the television mounted in the corner, remote poised in hand.

"Hey, turn that up." Cheri placed the dirty dishes on the bar and watched the newscast.

There were police officers in boats with nets and push poles. "What are they doing?" Cheri asked. She didn't have a television so new she was somewhat behind on news.

"Shh," Trixie admonished, pushing the volume button up higher.

The reporter's voice continued the report. "Early Saturday morning a call came in from two fishermen out in Johnson's Bayou. Terrance Brix claimed that while reeling in his line something felt off. What the men found when they pulled their line from the water can be

described only as something straight out of a horror film."
Cheri's heart froze. Johnson's Bayou. She clutched the
edge of the bar to keep from losing her balance. She forced
herself to keep breathing.

The camera shifted to the two cajun men. Terrance
appearing to be in his mid-sixties while Eli early forties.
He spoke adamantly about what had happened, his
dialect so hard to understand, the station had to put
captions across the bottom of the screen. She tried to focus
on what they were saying, but blood thundered in Cheri's
ears.

The camera cut back to the reporter and she
continued. "It is believed that this could be part of an
investigation involving body parts found in a gator, not
five miles from here. Here is Detective Lynn Robichaud
from the Louisiana State Highway Patrol." The woman
chased after a man with dark hair and silver around the
temples.

"Detective, can you tell me if you have any leads as to
who would be responsible for such a grisly crime?"

He cleared his throat and made his voice firm. "As of
right now we are not ruling this out as an accident. It's
very easy for fishermen to get turned around in the
swamp, especially at night. This is why we highly
recommend people follow the game and wildlife
regulations about hunting after dark. Now, if you'll excuse
me." For a moment his eyes locked with the camera and
Cheri felt as if he were staring right at her. Her heartbeat
quickened. She could feel his deep brown eyes on her
through the television and she shuttered.

The detective didn't give the persistent reporter a
chance to respond before he spun on his heels and crossed
under the yellow crime scene tape, bear of a man close on
his heels.

Johnson's Bayou was a place filled with nightmares
and things unspeakable. That particular stretch of swamp
was known to house some of the biggest gators in the
parish. Along with deadly snakes, it was a place that
people with common sense left alone. It was theorized
that God had created that portion of swamp to dump the

animals that were too mean to be out in the world. The dense vegetation provided shelter and perfect hiding spots.

Because of its location, few people ventured back there. The animals weren't the only threats. There were snarls of roots, cypress knees and underwater stumps that would tear the entire bottom out of a boat. It was a dangerous labyrinth and unfortunately one she knew all too well. Was this a message for her?

Her hands trembled as she clutched the plates. She tried to drag air into her lungs but it just wouldn't happen. Tears burned the backs of her eyes as the floor seemed to shift. She could feel the attack coming on and she was helpless to stop it. She swayed heavily.

"When was this news report?" she asked with a shaky voice.

"I think it was from earlier today. I caught a clip earlier saying that the police are out dragging the swamp for more body parts." Trixie shrugged and disappeared into the kitchen.

Cheri tried to swallow but her mouth felt pasty. Her tongue stuck to the roof of her mouth and her stomach twisted.

A heavy hand landed on her shoulder, causing her to cry out and drop the stack of dishes. Bits of food, broken glass and cutlery bounced over the freshly swept floor. When she whirled around, she found Jax behind her. His expression was dark and his eyes cloudy.

"I—I'm sorry. I didn't mean to. . . ." She didn't finish her sentence as she knelt and began to hastily scoop the broken dishes into a pile with her hand.

"Easy there," Jax said as he knelt down and helped her.

"I didn't hear you," she sputtered.

"Clearly. You looked like you just seen a ghost. What the hell is going on?"

"Nothing," she said as she stood and dumped the broken glass into the trash can.

Jax grabbed her by the arm and all but dragged her back to his office. Once inside he kicked the door closed and spun on her.

"Damn it, Cheri. What the hell is going on? I feel like I've been jerked into the middle of a movie and have no clue what's going on because I missed the beginning. So you'd best be spilling whatever it is up in the pretty little head of yours."

She squared her shoulders and lifted her chin. "Nothing, Jax. Please just leave it alone," she bit out. She tried to hide her fear but her trembling hands betrayed her.

"Not going to happen. I heard you this morning. You were on the phone."

She stared at him with wide eyes. "You were spying on me?"

"No. I was putting the ladder back behind the house. You were in the bathroom and I heard you talking to someone. I heard what you said." He took a step closer, his frame towering over her.

"I don't know what you're talking about." *Keep calm. He doesn't know anything.*

She tried to push past him but he stopped her by grabbing her shoulders holding her at arm's length, pinning her arms to her sides.

"Damn it let me go," she hissed as she struggled.

"Not a chance in hell. Not until you tell me what is going on."

"I told you this morning I don't know anything," she struggled against his hold on her, but his grip was too firm.

"Bullshit! Try again," he growled.

"Jax, I swear if you don't let me go I'll detach your balls and throw them in Cookie's fryer." She struggled again, kicking out her foot—aiming for his shin. When easily stepped out of the way, a frustrated cry worked its way from her mouth.

He ignored her threats and lowered his face closer to hers. She gulped. He was so close that she could see the flecks of gold in his brown eyes. "What are you hiding Cheri? What did you do? What are you running from?"

All the fight left her, leaving her feeling deflated. "I can't," she whispered. She wanted to stay angry with him for intruding but she couldn't. Everything was coming apart at the seams and she couldn't figure out why. She'd been so careful over the years. She didn't have the energy to stay mad. When she looked up, she felt herself getting pulled into his deep brown eyes. He was just trying to help. What would it hurt to let him?

He just stared at her, his gaze holding on to hers. Slowly he loosened his grip. It was obvious that forcing her to talk wasn't the way he needed to go about getting the answers. With a reluctant sigh, he released her arms and backed away. He plowed his hands through his hair and then allowed his hands to rest on his hips.

"Listen, I'm sorry, okay? I was only trying to offer a hand."

She fidgeted with a piece of skin on the edge of her thumbnail before bringing it to her lips. Her legs bounced anxiously up and down.

"I'm sorry," she muttered. "I've been on my own for so long. Even when I was married, I was alone. I just don't know how to handle it."

Jax moved to stand in front of her, perching his backside against the edge of the desk. He crossed his feet at the ankles and then his arms over his chest. Cheri tried not to stare at the bulging muscles in his arms or the way his black t-shirt was pulled tightly over his shoulders. Feeling uncomfortable she pulled her legs beneath her in the chair.

"If I felt that me helping you out was the only thing bothering you, I would leave it alone, but Cheri, we both know you're hiding something. Are you in some kind of trouble?"

She squirmed slightly under his gaze. Could she trust him with her secret? Part of her wanted to say yes, but the side of her that needed to protect her family more than anything was screaming at her to keep her mouth shut. She didn't know what to do. She wanted to trust

Jax, but she trusted no one. His mother used to work for the state. If he chose to go to the cops with her information everything she'd worked to accomplish over the years would vanish. She would lose her kids and there was the very real possibility of going to jail.

Feeling conflicted, she leaned forward and covered her face with her hands, slowly shaking her head. Tears were burning the backs of her eyes again, but the last thing she wanted to do in front of him was cry.

Jax watched as another small crack formed in Cheri's armor. Whatever struggle she was wrestling with internally was major. She was so close to just letting go. Just a little push. That's all she needed.

"Hey," he said softly as he lowered himself in front of her. His large hands resting on her folded knees. When she didn't look up at him, he gently grasped her by the wrists and pulled her hands away from her face. When her gaze met his again her eyes were watery.

"You can trust me," he said, gently holding onto her hands.

"I don't know you," she whispered, her eyes falling to their hands.

Something inside his chest tightened, and he knew without a doubt—in that second—that he would not let anything happen to her. Whatever it was she was hiding or running from, he would help her with it.

"Look at me," he commanded softly.

She sniffed and shook her head slowly. Tendrils of hair slipped from her ponytail and fell around her face. Without thinking he reached out and brushed them back, tucking them behind her ear. Then he gently gripped her chin with his thumb and index finger, lifting her face.

"Whatever we discuss within these walls will stay here. I promise you're safe. I won't go to the cops. No matter how bad it is."

Cheri looked at him and knew he meant it, but he couldn't always keep her safe. Sooner or later things were going to catch up with her, and in light of recent events, it was looking like that might happen sooner rather than later.

She took a deep breath. "What do you want to know?"

Relief washed over him because for a minute he thought she was going to close those walls back up. Now, she was allowing him in.

"I wanna know how you know my mother."

Jax stood and backed away, in large part because being so close to her was doing things to him that it shouldn't be. The smell of her perfume was pulling him in. Her beautiful heart-shaped mouth with plump and perfect lips were begging to be kissed. "I told you how I met your mom." He'd hoped to get the answers this afternoon when he went to his mom's house, but she wasn't home.

His face hardened. "Cut the bullshit, Cheri. I've been around enough people to know when they're lying and both of you were doing just that."

"I've known your mother since I was barely a teenager," she finally said. It all came out in a rush. "Your mother was my case worker. She placed me into the system."

Cheri watched his face, gauging his reaction as she began her story. "I was placed with my first foster family when I was thirteen. They were okay, for the most part, until the dad got drunk. Then things changed. He was mean to the other boys in the house. He would beat them and threaten his own kids. I only lasted there for a couple of months before your mom found out what was going on. As soon as she did she pulled me before anything could happen.

"I don't really remember *all* of the houses I was in. I got older I started acting out. I got made fun of a lot because my clothes weren't the right ones, I didn't have a mother or father, ya know standard bullying bullshit. I started to defend myself with aggression. That lead to me getting suspended a lot. When that happened, I went home and packed my bags because I could expect your mother to show up the next day. I was always right."

She drew in a ragged breath, looking to see if Jax was still listening. She was afraid to see into his eyes. For some reason, she didn't want him to think less of her, but when her gaze did venture to his, the only thing she saw was compassion. There was also a tinge of anger there, but he didn't say anything. He just nodded for her to continue.

"It was in one of the last homes that I met Roux."

"The guy I heard you talking to?"

She nodded and chewed on the side of her thumb, tearing the skin back until it bled. Jax handed her a tissue from his desk and she continued. "The guy who I've been calling all damn day long. Anyway, he's a couple years older than me. It was always the same thing at the new homes, especially if there were several other kids. The older ones would pick on the younger ones and torment them mercilessly. Well, this house was worse than all the others, because it was primarily made up of boys ranging from fifteen to seventeen. At this time, I was fifteen. I mostly kept to myself because boys and men made me uncomfortable." She clamped her lips together realizing what she'd just said. She hoped that he hadn't picked up on it and asked why. When he didn't say anything, she continued. "I tried to keep my head down and keep to myself. It wasn't not wanting to be noticed so much as it was self-preservation. If I became invisible, then no one would bother me. At least, that's what I thought."

Cheri took a deep ragged breath as the memories chipped away at her brain, opening up old wounds that—after almost twenty-three years—had yet to heal. She rolled her neck from left to right, trying to ease some of the tension. "Apparently, I wasn't as invisible as I had thought. One night, after I'd just gotten into my bed I heard my bedroom door open. I shared the room with another girl, but she always snuck out. I pretty much always had it to myself.

"It was a small, stuffy room in the attic. It wasn't much but at least we got our privacy. Well, most of the time.

"Anyhow, he walked through my bedroom door. I didn't have to see his face to know who it was. I'd felt his eyes on me, watching every move I made. I'd been hoping that he would ignore me, like everyone else. Turns out, hoping did me no good."

Jax felt bile rise to the back of his throat and adrenaline began to push through his veins. He knew what was coming and as much as he wanted to stop her, he couldn't. This had been like a cancer she'd been carrying around for so long. It had slowly eaten away at her. If listening was the best way to help her, then that's exactly what he would do.

She took a deep, shaky breath and he watched as the memories pulled her under.

"I don't really remember much. I remember him holding me down the first time and when I tried to fight and scream he punched me. He must have knocked me out because when I came to he was pulling his clothes back on."

Tears rolled down her cheeks but she didn't stop them. Her chest constricted painfully as she relived the memory. A memory she relived every single night. A memory that she was reliving for the first time in decades for someone else.

Jax knelt back down in front of her, taking both of her hands into his. He squeezed them and brought them up to his lips and gently kissed her knuckles. He had no idea what to do. All he knew was that he wanted to give her comfort and this was the only way he knew how.

Cheri wanted to pull her hands away. She didn't want him to see her like this because, after so many years, she still felt dirty and tainted. She'd been damaged before, but after that night, she'd been broken.

"Didn't anyone do anything?"

She sniffled and shook her head. "He threatened me. It's cliché, really, but at that age, you're terrified and have no one to talk to. You want to live, so you do what you can to survive. In my case, surviving meant keeping my mouth closed. All these adults always say "you can trust me" or "you can talk to me". It was all bullshit. It was because of adults that I was in the situation in the first place. When your life is threatened like that—at that age—you believe it. There is no such thing as trusting an adult. There was no word for the terror I felt.

"He had cupped his hand over my face and nose, cutting off my air supply and just before I would black out, he released me. Told me to keep my mouth shut or the next time he came to me would be much worse."

"The next time?"

"Yes," she said softly. "He'd decided that the boys in the house weren't doing it for him anymore. I was his new plaything."

Rage so powerful it nearly took his breath away zipped through him. Very slowly he climbed to his feet, feeling a familiar darkness deep inside his being creeping forward. It was a darkness that he'd buried in the very deepest part of his mind. It was that same darkness that had landed him in jail over a decade ago. He could feel it clawing its way to the surface. He clamped his jaw together tightly, breathing deeply through his nose.

Cheri continued, seemingly lost in her story. Her eyes were glazed as she stared at a spot on the wall across the room from them. "I don't really remember how long it went on for, I guess I lost track of time. He would come into my room just about every night. On the nights he didn't show up, I lay awaked all night, scared to hear that door. On the nights he *did* show up, I learned to just lay there and take it. I was scared for my life, but one night, Roux happened to walk in. We'd been spending a lot of time together. He was about as close to normal as any of the kids were, and he didn't even have to talk. I just liked sitting with him. There were days that he'd just show up to my room and we'd sit for hours. Sometimes we talked, other times we just sat there. He was my safe place.

"That night he was coming to my room to tell me how his date had gone. When he came through the door, he found me face down in the mattress. I don't really remember what happened. All I know was the guy was thrown off of me and I could breathe again. Everything happened so fast that it was just this big jumbled mess.

"The guy was taken to jail, and they'd threatened to take Roux, but decided against it. That night, your mom came for not only me but Roux as well. She's the one that kept me us together. If it weren't for them I have no idea what would have happened to me."

"What happened?"

She lifted a shoulder. "Nothing much really. I had to testify against him. He was old enough to be tried as an adult. He got put away for a while."

"Did he get out?"

Cheri lifted his shoulder. "I think so but I'm not sure when."

The overwhelming urge to hunt down the sick bastard burned his throat like battery acid. Higher and higher the darkness crept. He took a deep breath, forcing his anger back down.

Cheri continued. "Pretty soon after the trial, your mom moved Roux and I to a different place. This one was good enough but the mother was a little heavy handed with the punishment. Other than that, it was probably the best out of all of them. Roux aged out a year after we were placed and I was left alone. He tried to keep tabs on me but the fosters thought it was weird and made it so I couldn't see him. He moved to N'Orleans shortly after that."

Cheri let out a ragged breath but oddly enough felt relieved. Roux and Lizabeth were the only ones that ever knew what had happened—and the court. She brushed away the tears that had slipped from her cheeks. She continued and told him the story of Alexander.

When she was finished he was just staring at her, his face a dark mask hiding his emotions. She tugged nervously on her bottom lip with her teeth and began to fidget. Without asking she grabbed his cigarettes from the desk and shook one out of the pack. Jax took the pack from her and shook out his own before offering her the lighter. After she took a deep drag and exhaled, she looked up at him through the curling smoke.

"I've never told anybody any of that," she finally said. "Your mother risked everything to help me. After I aged out, I did some research and found out that had someone discovered what she did for me . . . she could have gone to jail. She risked so much. So I left and didn't look back. I figured if I left her alone then no one would find out what she did."

"She was just doing her job. She was good about that."

Cheri shook her head. "It was so much more than that." Realizing what she'd said and that she'd almost said too much, she clamped her lips together.

Jax gave a small chuckle and nodded. If he'd noticed her slip, he didn't say anything. "That's my mother. She's got a stubborn streak a mile wide. Not really one people wanna cross."

"You don't seem surprised."

"Because I'm not, not really. I mean, I know my mother has bent the rules before. Honestly, when my momma sets her mind on something, there ain't no changing it."

"Gee and here I wondered where you got it from," she teased softly. For a brief moment the mood was lightened, but all too soon the heaviness returned—erasing the smile from her lips.

"It's a good thing you finally told someone. But I do have another question."

Cheri swallowed but nodded. Jax had proved himself to her by sticking around and allowing her to talk. That alone was more than anyone—other than Roux—had ever offered.

"Okay?"

He took another drag and flicked his ashes into the ashtray on his desk. He exhaled twin streams of smoke from his nose and clenched his jaw before finally asking.

"How in the hell did you end up in foster care in the first place?"

There it was. *The* question. The one *only* she and his mother knew the answer too. The question that had the darkest possible answer.

"Believe me when I tell you that no one can hold onto a secret better than I can."

She stared at him, searching the deep pools of his eyes and realized that she wasn't the only one hiding secrets. Jax had one too, possibly more. Cheri's heart began to race. She wiped her clammy palms against the hem of her shorts. She squeezed her eyes closed and when she opened them she took one last drag before crushing the half-smoked cigarette in the tray. Slowly, she exhaled, blowing smoke from her lips.

Her eyes slid up and met his. "When I said there was stuff your mother could have gone to jail for, I wasn't referring to the rules she bent with my foster placement."

"Okay?" Jax's scowl deepened and his mouth turned down into a frown. She hesitated. "Jax, I killed my step-father. Your mother helped me by covering it up."

# 15

Lynn sat at his desk shuffling through the case files. The soft sound of footsteps came up behind him. The scent of jasmine reached him before she did. Arms reached around his shoulders as she wrapped him in a warm hug.

"Another bad one?" his wife asked as she pressed a soft kiss to his whiskered face, reminding him that if he didn't shave soon he'd look like Levi.

He closed the file and removed his glasses before leaning back into her arms. It was the only place he truly found solace. With a heavy sigh, he scrubbed his dry and burning eyes. "Yeah. It looks like it's going to be."

"Why don't you step away for a while? Come to bed, get a little bit of rest and then look at it again."

The idea of climbing into his bed and succumbing to sleep was all too tempting. "I'll be up in just a little while," he finally said.

She hugged him tight and he patted her folded hands before giving them a slight squeeze.

He watched as she disappeared up the stairs, her satin pajama bottoms catching the slight glow from the desk lamp before she disappeared. He had no idea how the woman had put up with him for so many years because heaven knows it hadn't been easy on her. The long sleepless nights alone. The interrupted birthday parties. The broken dates. Yet, through it all, she'd remained at his side. Sure, they'd had problems just like any other married couple, but they'd gotten through it. He couldn't picture his life without her, nor did he want too.

He looked at the case spread out in front of him and looked at his notes. He and Levi had searched Anderson's apartment. The place was littered with empty soda bottles and boxes of moldy pizza. Anderson's work schedule had been posted on his refrigerator along with the times and days he was supposed to meet with his parole officer. There was nothing that indicated that Anderson was into anything nefarious. It had been a complete bust and waste of time, so they'd gone to talk to the parole officer again. The man was consistent in stating that Anderson never showed for their last meeting, something he assured him was completely out of character.

Their next stop had been at the twenty-four-hour meat packing plant where Anderson worked. Apparently, Anderson was the model employee and was up for promotion until he suddenly didn't show up for work on Friday morning. Lynn couldn't help but feel as if they were chasing their tails, and what pissed him off further was the fact that there was possibly a killer out there somewhere, watching and knowing they were chasing their asses.

"Shit," he muttered as he pinched the bridge of his nose and squeezed his eyes closed, deciding that getting a few hours of sleep would be a fantastic idea. As he was putting the files in his desk, his cell phone began vibrating. Levi's face popped on the screen. Lynn looked at the time. *1:56 am.* He groaned as he picked up his phone. Nothing good ever came from a call from his partner at that hour.

"Yeah," he said gruffly.

"We have another one." Levi's voice was tight.

Lynn muttered under his breath and looked at the clock on his desk. They'd found a body on Saturday morning, and another one showing up *this* soon did not bode well. Not at all.

"Well, that was quick—less than three days between kills if he killed Anderson on Friday."

"This one is missing an eye."

Lynn muttered a curse. "So we have the full body then. I'll swing by your place in ten," Lynn said.

"Don't worry about it. I'm pulling into the drive now."

"Okay." That was all Lynn said as he disconnected the call. Through the living room windows, he could see the glow of Levi's headlights. With a groan and protesting joints, he hauled himself from his chair and strapped on his guns. He cast a glance up the stairs as he made his way to the door. Cindy was standing on the landing.

Slowly, she walked down and stood on the steps in front of him.

Leaning forward she kissed him softly. "Always come home," she whispered. It was something she'd whispered to him every day since they'd been married.

"Always back to you," was his automatic response.

After another quick kiss, he left the house, making sure it was locked soundly behind him. The air was heavy and even though it was two in the morning, it was hot. He could see Levi behind the wheel of the Dodge Charger as he walked down the sidewalk. He tugged open the door and slid into the seat.

Levi handed him a covered coffee and Lynn stared down at it. "You had time for coffee?"

Levi chuckled. "I was already out when I got the call. Thought I would grab you one too."

Shaking his head, Lynn took a slow sip. The strong chicory sent jolts of energy through his system, shocking him awake. Levi backed out of the drive with alarming speed and flipped on the red and blue lights.

"So where are we heading?"

"Bloody Point," he said dryly.

Lynn muttered. Unlike Johnson's Bayou, Bloody Point wasn't as obscure. Sure it was a labyrinth of cypress knees and stumps; it was easily accessible by someone that knew what they were doing. It also had a junction to where it ran into Johnson's. Bloody Point had earned its name eons ago due to the red tint in the water. It was another peril making that particular stretch of swamp deadly. The murky depths held many secrets and dangers.

"So what's the story?"

Levi turned his car onto the highway that would carry them the forty-five-minute ride south. The highway was surrounded on both sides by dense trees and he knew just beyond those trees were miles and miles of swamps.

"It appears that the body was found by a couple out checking their crawfish traps. They spotted the body half in and out of the water. It appears that it had been drug by gators and then left."

"Makes sense. Gators don't typically eat people," Lynn said absently.

"True, but they have been known to. Look at what happened in Johnson's."

"Yeah. There are some big ole gators back there. Do we know anything else?"

Levi shook his head. "Only that the body is mostly intact and the call came in about an hour ago. It's south of where the other body was found."

"South, hmm. Well, it's likely we disturbed his dumping ground so he moved. And what do you mean by 'mostly intact'?

"It was mangled by the gators pretty badly, but from what the on-scene told me, the guy's eye was missing."

"Great."

"It's too soon to know for sure if this has anything to do with the other one we found."

Lynn knew that but the lead ball rolling around in his gut told him differently. He had a feeling that they were looking at a serial killer, but typically a serial case was three bodies or more. Was there another one out there?

The pair rode in silence until they got to the scene. The drive into the bayou had been blocked by barricades and after they flashed their badges they were moved, allowing them to proceed further in. They pulled to a stop beside several other police cruisers. Red and blue lights fractured the night. Harshly lighting up the dense foliage briefly with their flashes.

They climbed from the car and made their way to the scene where couple were leaning against a Ranger's truck.

"I'm Detective Robichaud and this is Detective Moss. Would you care to go over what happened for us?"

The man nodded while holding onto his wife's hand. "We was just out checking our traps. We heard some big noise on da bank over dere and when I put the light on da bank we saw sometin half in da wata. Dere was a gator but he run off when we got closer."

"Why did you set traps here? Isn't it kind of murky for them?" Levi asked as he jotted down notes.

The man nodded. "Typically yes. But we put our traps where da wata is movi'n. Over where it is clear before heading out to da otha swamps."

Levi nodded and scribbled down more notes.

"Did you see anything or anyone?" Lynn asked.

The man shook his head. "No suh. Dey ain't no way to drive ova dere. Can only get ta it by a boat."

Satisfied with their answer, Lynn fished a card from his pocket. "If you think of anything else, please give us a call."

The couple nodded and made their way back to their vehicle. "Do you think they saw anything?" Levi asked as they walked over to where the body was on a stretcher.

"Nah, I think they were just at the wrong place wrong time."

Reaching down, Lynn unzipped the body bag and the image he saw would forever be burned into his brain. A pale body lay in front of him, naked from the waist up. His left arm had been mangled by the gators and was barely hanging on by the ligaments.

"Why do you think the gator's didn't eat him like the other?"

"Maybe the couple interrupted their dinner?"

Lynn frowned. "Look at his chest." He pointed with his pen at several of the gashes. Some were long while others were short and precise. However, that wasn't what caught his attention the most.

*I know*, was carved deeply into his chest.

"I know? What the hell is that supposed to mean?"

Lynn frowned. "It's a message."

"I get that, but to who? Us?"

"I have no idea, but we need to start looking at connections." Lynn turned to one of the uniformed officers. "Have we got an ID yet?"

"Not yet sir, but we're are working on it."

Lynn nodded and turned back to the body. "Look," he said pointing with his pen to the area around the nose and mouth.

"Are those burns?" Levi asked with a frown.

"Yeah. Those are the kinds of burns chloroform leaves behind."

"Chloroform? Who the hell still uses chloroform? Isn't that a bit old school?"

"Yes, but still no less effective."

"Where are boats usually put in?" Levi asked as one of the patrol officers walked by.

"Up there about fifty yards," the cop said.

"Thanks, we're done here," Lynn said zipping the bag and thanking the corner. He and retrieved a flashlight from the trunk of a squad car. Carefully, they walked up the path. It was a long shot but maybe they would find something.

The white-blue light shone on leaves and mud. The smell of rotting vegetation permeated the air. With it also mingled the scent of rotting meat and death. When they reached the edge, they swept the beams of their lights out over the water and then back again. Somewhere in the darkness, the heavy sound of a gator splashing into the water splintered the night.

"There are footprints here," Levi said as he squatted close to the water's edge.

"That could be from our couple."

Levi shook his hand. "No. The man's foot wasn't more than a size ten at best. The woman's much smaller."

Lynn arched a brow. Levi shrugged.

"I figured we'd look for tracks, so I observed."

"How perceptive of you," Lynn said dryly.

"I try." Levi placed his foot next to the print. "I would say it's at least a size thirteen."

"That's a bigfoot."

"I wear a fourteen, so it's not that big. It also looks to be recent."

"And you know this how?"

"Because I grew up hunting and tracking. The print is still wet."

Lynn stood and turned back to where one of the officers were walking toward them. "I need to get a cast made of this print."

"Yes, sir."

As Lynn was turning around, something on the ground caught his attention. He removed his gloves and picked it up.

"What is it?"

Lynn held it in front of the light. "It looks like the lid off a syringe."

Levi groaned. "So it looks like this is a serial?"

"Not yet, but I'd be willing to bet if a tox screen is ran on our boy back there, we'd find Succinylcholine particulates in his system."

Levi held open an evidence bag. "We'll send it to the lab."

They searched around for a while longer but found nothing else. After signing the documents and leaving their cards, they climbed back into Levi's car.

Lynn watched their surroundings. Several years had gone by since he'd worked a serial case. It had been one for the record books, and one that still haunted his dreams to this very day. People just kept getting sicker and more deranged. What was wrong with the world?

# 16

Jax didn't know how to respond. He didn't know how to react. The only thing he could do was to crunch his cigarette out in the ashtray and light another. What had he stepped in the middle of? Why was his mother involved in a murder? He watched Cheri as she stared at the cigarette between her fingers, seemingly hypnotized by the curling smoke.

"What kind of a murder?"

She lifted her gaze to him, confusion a mask on her beautiful face. "What kind of murder? I didn't know there were different kinds. You kill someone, it's murder plain and simple."

He snorted. "I'm aware of that. Listen, maybe you should start from the beginning."

"I'm putting a lot of faith in you," she said softly, looking at the ash dangling at the end of her cigarette.

His face darkened a bit. "You don't have a choice. It involves my family; therefore, it has become my concern. If you don't tell me, then I will find someone who will."

Seeing the determined look on Jax's face spoke volumes. There was no way to avoid it. She took a final drag on her cigarette and extinguished it. Jeremy was going to kill her when he got back. *If you're not dead already,* she thought glumly.

She reached for the bottle of beer resting beside Jax's hip. She didn't bother asking and he didn't bother questioning. As soon as the warm liquid filled her mouth, she winced. Nothing worse than hot beer. Nevertheless, it seemed to wash the grit in her mouth away, allowing her to start her story.

"My mother was a real piece of work. When I was ten she worked as a waitress over at that truck stop that closed down a couple years back."

"Dolly's? Wait, you mean you've lived here before?"

"Well, I lived outside town a little ways, but this is where my life all started." The tone in her voice was bitter.

"And you came back? Why?"

She lifted a shoulder and snorted. "I don't have a clue. Just felt like this was where I was supposed to be."

He nodded. "Go on."

"Well, she met this trucker and fell in love instantly. She had a habit of doing that, ya know? They eloped and got married a week after meeting. Anyway, this man was a sick bastard. I could always feel his eyes on me. One time I woke up and he was sitting in my bedroom, in the dark watching me. He was. . . ." She cleared her throat. "It was his *grunting* that woke me up." She shivered in repulsion. "At that point, he'd never touched me.

"Anyway, my mom worked overnights, so I was used to staying at home alone. Well, I didn't have to be alone anymore because there was Carl. After he and my mom got married, he'd stopped working. Wanted to be a *family man*," she said using air quotes.

Jax swallowed, his Adam's apple bobbing and the muscles in his jaw clenching tightly. The back of his throat burned with stomach acid. As badly as he wanted to look away, he couldn't. The strong and determined woman he was so used to now sat in front of him, reliving a part of her past that he was certain she'd rather not talk about at all. She'd already peeled one layer of her life away from him to see. Now, she was doing it again.

"More times than not he would pass out drunk in front of the television. On occasion it would be his snorting or shooting up that would sometimes knock him out. I loved it when that happened. It was really the only way I felt safe.

"Sometimes he would fly into a rage at the littlest thing. One time I sneezed and for no other reason than that, he decided I should be punished."

"And your mother didn't do or say anything to stop him?" Jax couldn't fathom a mother being so oblivious to her child or putting her in harm's way. Then again, he'd been raised by a mother that—while sometimes ruling with a strong hand or belt—loved her kids. It wasn't only her children she loved but all children. That's why she was so good at her job. His eyes drifted back to Cheri, watching and waiting as she gathered her thoughts. She looked like a lost child, and in a way, he supposed she was.

Hating the helplessness, she was feeling, Cheri climbed to her feet and began to pace the room. She tucked her hands in her back pockets only to pull them out again and fidget. Jax just watched, patiently waiting for her to continue. Finally, she found herself back in the chair with her legs pulled up to her chest.

"He always made sure to hit me in places that wouldn't show. His favorite, though, was a piece of cane to my back. That's where most of those scars came from. I tried to tell my mom once, but I'd been beaten by her for lying. 'Carl would never do something like that,' she'd said. I'm not altogether sure how much my mother stayed in reality. She liked her pills." She let out a ragged breath and continued.

"One time he pinched me for dropping a glass. I'd never seen a bruise turn that shade of purple before. How he 'disciplined' me really depended on his mood. Sometimes he wouldn't hit me at all. Those time were the ones I'd come to dread the most. It was those times I truly caught a glimpse of the monster he was."

"What happened with those times?"

Cheri hugged her legs tighter to her chest. "He would take me out into the woods, in the swamp and just leave me."

"Shit!" Jax growled. He rubbed his face with his hands and then crossed his arms over his chest.

"You know what I got on for my eleventh birthday?" she asked bitterly. "Not a damn thing. He took me out to the woods and left me. Said since I was older I should know how to survive. I was out there for three days before he came back to get me. I was dirty and covered with mosquito bites. He told my mom that I went out to explore and got lost. I spent days in the hospital. When it was time for me to go home, I cried.

"I was thirteen when he tried touching me for the first time. It wasn't like the boy from the foster home, though. These were subtle pats on the ass or he'd stand too close behind me when I was doing something pressing himself into me. Little things like that. On the plus side, the beatings had stopped." She gave a brittle laugh. In her ears, it sounded a bit maniacal. She gulped in a deep breath. Her heart was racing and her stomach was rolling. She prayed that she wouldn't lose what was left of her dinner. Her hands were clammy and she felt chilled, despite the oppressive heat that lingered in the room.

She slipped from her chair and wiped her sweaty palm against her shorts before tucking them into her back pockets. Once more she began to pace the small room, feeling like a caged animal. The walls felt like they were closing in on her, but as long as she kept moving, they stopped.

Her eyes slid toward Jax. His face was carefully blank, but she could see in his eyes that his mind was rolling a mile a minute. The muscle in his jaw ticked as he tightly clenched his teeth together. His mouth was set into a thin line and his arms were crossed tightly over his chest. Before she lost her nerve she continued.

"Anyway, one night he made me go out to the swamp to check his crawfish traps. He was especially wasted that night. I knew that if I got in that boat with him, I more than likely wasn't going to come home. Not this time. There was just this sick feeling in my gut, ya know.

"When he wasn't looking I put one of the kitchen knives in my boots. It wasn't big, but I'd learned how to defend myself pretty well. I told him I wasn't going to go and he flew into a blind rage. He grabbed me by my hair and dragged me through the house."

Cheri grimaced. She could still feel the pain in her scalp. Absently she ran her hand over the spot that her hair had been ripped violently from her head. She could still feel it, the slight bald spot as her fingertips grazed against it. The words seemed to get stuck in her throat as she stared at a blank spot on the wall. The memory began to swallow her and she stood locked in fear.

Jax watched as Cheri zoned out. She stared at the wall blankly, tears rolling down her cheeks from her glazed eyes. Not knowing what else to do, he slowly moved from the desk. He didn't want to startle or frighten her. Carefully, he moved behind her and placed gentle hands on her shoulders, pulling her back into the solid wall of his chest. The smell of honey and jasmine clung to her skin and hair. He took a deep breath and gently rubbed her bare arms. He could feel the rough goose bumps beneath his hands and she trembled once more before leaning back.

"I've got you," he whispered against her ear.

Cheri trembled, the feeling of his body pressed tightly against hers should have excited her, but right now, she was too far gone in the memory to feel anything but fear. She did feel his support radiating from him in waves.

Taking a deep breath, she continued.

"He pulled me by my hair to the boat. He tried to throw me in but my footing slipped and I landed against the side. I felt my ribs break but no matter how much I cried out or screamed it didn't help. This was the first time he ever struck me in the face. I had never felt anything like it before in my life. I thought he'd killed me, and I don't know, perhaps a part of me wished he had. 'Get in the boat or I'll put you in there myself,' he'd said. I don't know how I managed it, but I did."

She took a deep breath realizing that she'd been talking faster and faster. The story was pouring out of her like a dam bursting. There was no going back and there would be no stopping it. "As soon as he started the motor, I knew where he was taking me, and I knew for certain I would not be coming back, not this time. He was taking me to Johnson's Bayou, up the river aways from his tiny hovel that we all lived in. For a long time, he was quiet, but I could feel his eyes watching me. When he spoke I finally knew what he had in mind. He kept saying that it was time to perform my womanly duties."

Here it was. This was the part that was important and very likely would change Jax's opinion of her. Despite how good his body felt against hers she turned and lifted her eyes to his. His face was cloudy. She continued.

"I was sitting on the bench of the boat when he began to unfasten his belt. I waited. I waited until his pants were down around his ankles. Then when he came at me I plunged the knife as deeply into his gut as I possibly could. He fell back and I don't know what came over me. I stabbed him over and over again. I don't know how many times I did. He wasn't dead when I finished. The knife was small so I knew it wouldn't reach any of his vital organs. I just kept stabbing. There was so much blood that my hand slipped down over the blade. That's how I got this."

She held up her hand, revealing the long scar that started just beneath her index finger and ran across her palm.

"He was so shocked—or maybe he was too drunk— that he didn't fight back. I didn't know what else to do. I knew I was going to go to jail if I got caught. I panicked and somehow managed to roll him into the water. I don't know how long I sat there, but when I saw the sun coming up, I managed to make it home.

"When I got home I just sat on the kitchen floor. I lost track of time. My mother still hadn't come home. I couldn't eat. I couldn't move. That evening your mom found me."

Jax stiffened. "My mother?"

Cheri nodded. "Yeah."

"But how did she know where you were?"

"The school counselor had called her. Apparently, they'd been watching me and when I didn't show up for school, they sent someone out there."

"But how did she help you cover this up. It's state law that cops accompany social workers."

She lifted her shoulder slightly. "I don't know. Your mother was a no-nonsense type woman. I don't know why or how, but there weren't cops with her that day."

"Cause she probably told them to take a hike. She hated it when they tagged along. Said it always made the kids nervous, especially the local yokels back then."

"She found me on the floor of the kitchen, covered in dirt and blood. I told her what had happened. I was so scared she would give me to the police. After all, she was evil and was coming to take me to a place that would do nasty things to me. At least that's what I'd always been told. She surprised me, though. She helped me clean up. She cleaned all the blood from the house with peroxide and burned my clothes. I was confused. I was in a daze. Everything seemed so surreal, ya know. To this day I have no idea why she didn't involve the police. I later figured out I could have claimed self-defense. It didn't make sense."

Jax nodded knowingly. "Peroxide breaks down blood and eliminates all evidence. It's less harsh than bleach so there is no chemical smell."

Cheri nodded. "She did the same to the boat and we buried it in the woods under a lot of leaves and bushes. She promised me that things would be better and that everything that happened would be our little secret. Your family gathering was the first time I've seen your mother in eighteen years."

"So that is why you looked like you saw a ghost when you saw her."

"Because it was like seeing a ghost. Jax, I've tried so long to forget about everything that happened to me. I had no clue that your mother actually lived here, and when I found out she was your mother. . . ." She let the words die on her lips.

He tilted her chin up with his finger forcing her eyes to lock with his. "Listen, you don't have anything to worry about."

"What if it's him?" she asked softly.

"You mean Carl?"

"What if he didn't die that night? What if he's found me and he wants his revenge?"

"I doubt very seriously that is the case. From what you told me he couldn't have survived all those wounds, and even if he had, the gators probably finished him off."

"So who is doing this?"

Jax pulled her into his arms and hugged her. "I have no idea, but we'll get to the bottom of it."

For a moment she just allowed herself to be held. Her cheek was pressed against his broad chest. The fading traces of fabric softener mingled with cologne and the light scent of smoke. She could feel each breath he took in and released as his heart thundered against her cheek. One hand lightly cradled the back of her head, pressing her tighter against him while the other moved in comforting circles against her back.

Her arms wrapped around him and she could feel the taut muscles rippling beneath her palms. His chin was just above her head, and with each breath he took, her hair stirred. The noises in the room seemed to quiet; the low roar of the air conditioner; the ceiling fan as it spun and one of the pull chains clacked against the light globe. There was a sense of comfort she felt and for the first time in a very long time, she allowed herself to feel it. She allowed him to give her the comfort.

She pulled away slightly and met his gaze. Her breath hitched in her throat as his face hovered just inches above hers. She pressed the tip of her tongue along her dry lips. His eyes flicked down to her mouth and she felt the air around them snap with electricity.

Slowly, his mouth slanted over hers. The tension left her body as she leaned into his chest and his hands tightened on her waist. Her eyes drifted closed as she allowed herself to be swept away by his firm yet soft lips. The stubble on his chin raked against her face but she didn't notice. She opened her mouth wider for him, his tongue sweeping against the inside of her mouth. This kiss was much different than the one they'd shared earlier. It was full of promise and trust. It was the comfort that she'd been needing but couldn't find.

Her arms lifted and went around his neck, her fingers teasing the silky hair at his nape. Jax deepened the kiss, causing her heart rate to rise and liquid fire to spread through her veins. She heard a soft whimpering sound as he pulled her closer, flattening her body against his. The whimpering, she realized had come from her. He tasted like sweet scotch. Not even a hint that he'd been smoking.

His hands skimmed beneath her shirt and rested on her bare skin as his lips slid from her mouth to kiss the line of her jaw. Firm pressure was pressed against the jumping pulse in her neck as he teased the tender spot with the tip of his tongue. She could feel the evidence of his arousal pressing against her and she groaned throatily. Things were about to get entirely out of hand. Again!!!

More, her body screamed, but slowly she backed away. Jax stared down at her, eyes wide and dilated with desire. She could feel that her lips were slightly swollen and more than anything she wanted to see where this was going to lead, but she couldn't.

She took a deep shaky breath and stepped further away from him. This wasn't right. She was vulnerable and he was available. There was nothing about this scenario that would end well. Putting a little distance between them seemed to be a good idea because if she didn't, there was nothing stopping her from finishing what they'd started. She pushed her hands back through her hair and took another ragged breath.

"We can't," she said softly.

He nodded once and leaned back on his desk, taking a deep swig of his beer and shaking another cigarette from the pack.

"We can't call the cops," she said quietly, trying to completely avoid everything that had just happened. She needed to focus on the task at hand. If she let her heart get in the way of her head, there would be nothing but trouble.

Finally, after several long moments, he commented. "I think you're right, besides I can't have them digging into my past no more than you can."

Cheri couldn't help the sigh of relief that slipped through her lips. Thoughtfully he watched her for several long moments, his dark eyes searching for something. His gaze made her stomach flutter anxiously.

"Will you please stay with me?" She opened her mouth to protest but he moved in front of her so quickly she took a startled step back, bumping into a chair. He pressed his finger to her mouth. "Damn it, woman, for once don't argue and just listen." The tone in his voice wasn't unkind. If anything, it was almost playful.

She arched a brow at him and resisted the overwhelming urge to bite him, but she ignored it and just nodded.

"Stay with me. Just for a few days until we can figure out what's going on. I've got a buddy we can talk to. He can tell us everything there is to know about the finger."

"Buddy?" A slight wrinkle formed between her eyes when she frowned.

Lightly he pressed his thumb against the wrinkle and rubbed it softly. "You're much too young and pretty to have wrinkles," he said softly.

Her heart fluttered like a school girl with a crush. "Please? It will give me some peace of mind until we get things figured out."

She weighed her options. As much as Jax intruded on her privacy and annoyed the hell out of her, she had to admit she trusted him.

The thought of staying with him was both dangerous and appealing. Maybe she could get some sleep for a change and the nightmares would stop. On the other hand, after what just happened, she wasn't sure she was safe with him at all. However, those reasons were completely different than the others.

There was a look in his eyes, a dark cloud following him around that he just couldn't shake. There was a lot about Jaxon Marceaux she still didn't know. She found herself wondering what exactly it was that *he* was hiding. She recognized a dark secret when she saw one. Jax was holding onto something dark. She just hoped she hadn't been wrong in trusting him.

# 17

"Tiny cuts. Tiny cuts. That's all it takes to see the red," he sang as his hand slowly drew the blade of the scalpel across the creamy white flesh.

Wide eyes filled with tears and pain stared—unmoving—up at him from his table. "You've got exquisite breasts. I can see why he liked you. Too bad you're such a slut," he growled as he reached down and palmed the globe roughly. Dipping his finger in the bright red blood that ran in tiny rivers down her sides, he created a masterpiece.

The girl whimpered softly but still stayed immobile. A sudden and blinding rage burned through him as he imagined her on his table. Those eyes staring up at him defiantly.

He landed a backhand roughly against her cheek. The woman's head snapped to the side and he repositioned it to where he could see the terror in her face. This was going to be the one. It was so close he could taste his desire. Soon, the one that he truly wanted on his table would be there.

"Now, time for some more fun. The other two were for her, but you . . . you're especially for him," he said as he clapped his hands together.

Reaching over he turned the woman over, exposing her smooth back. Carefully he kept the sheet pulled over her backside. He had a plan.

"Soon," he whispered as he pressed the scalpel to her back. With slow, movements, he sliced through her supple flesh. The wet slicing sound made him hard with desire. His jeans tightened as he drew line after line. Blood beaded up and rolled down her sides. *Splat. Splat. Splat.* The drops landed on the stone floor. "Very, very soon."

Jax leaned against the door facing, watching as Cheri slept in the middle of his bed. Through the windows, the sun was beginning to show its face. What was it about her that made him want to throw away everything he'd worked so hard to get?

He sipped his coffee and tried to will away the darkness that was scratching at his brain. It was so close now. Last night, while listening to everything Cheri had been through, his demons had broken free. Now, they swirled around in his head, whispering dark things to him.

*You're two of a kind*, it whispered. *You're both killers. Admit it, you loved what you did. You loved the powerful feeling.* He squeezed his eyes closed and took three deep breaths, pushing the darkness away.

When he opened his eyes again, they were on Cheri. She was wearing one of his t-shirts. He remembered all too clearly the effect of seeing her standing in front of him, hair tumbling around her shoulders in soft waves, face scrubbed clean of makeup had on him. It wasn't something he was likely to forget.

The soft cotton shirt was too big for her, but he could still see the outline of her curves beneath it. The tantalizing shape of her breasts as they'd strained against the front, the swell and curve of her hips. She was beautiful and what bothered him the most was she didn't even know it.

Now, he watched as she slept, one shapely leg uncovered and revealing a scrap of black lace panties. It had taken a bit more arguing, but he'd finally managed to talk her into staying at his place for a few days.

He frowned as something nagged at him. If his mother was involved with all of this and she was the only one that had known what Cheri had done to her stepfather, was that going to make his mother a target?

The thought of his mother in harm's way did not sit well with him at all. In fact, nothing about this was setting well with him. He was going to help her, but if someone went digging too deeply into his past, his own dark secrets would come to light—dark secrets that would have him hauled away for good.

He took a swig from his tepid coffee and moved from the room, closing the door behind him. If he was going to keep her safe, then he needed to get ahead of the cops. It was only a matter of time before they found a connection, and he had a feeling that part of that connection was the finger that had been left for her. There was no doubt it was a warning, but what was it meaning?

Taking his phone from his pocket he stepped out onto the screened in front porch. The humidity was already climbing as the sun scrambled higher. It was Monday morning and already he felt as if he'd been put through the ringer.

He dialed a number he knew by heart but before he could hit send, a picture of his sister's smiling face popped onto the screen. A soft smile touched his face and his heart softened.

"What in the hell are you doing up so early? Isn't it against your religion or something to be up before noon?" he teased.

"And isn't against your religion to be. . . ." she paused causing him to chuckle.

"Ya got nothing," he taunted.

She huffed playfully into the phone. "I'll think of something. Listen, I was wondering if you'd like to go to lunch with Jerry and me? He really wants to get to know you."

Jax scanned his brain and then remembered that Jerry was Desire's new flavor of the month—city boy with a side of Yankee. He rolled his eyes.

"Now's not really a good time, D," he said, casting a look over his shoulder.

"Why? It's not like you have a social life," she said playfully.

"Ouch," he laughed.

"See, told'ja I would come up with something."

"Took ya long enough."

They both chuckled but then she grew serious. "I really like him, Jax. It's been a long time since I've been with someone. I mean ever since. . . ." She let the sentence die. Jax knew exactly what she was referring to and it made his gut sour. His joking mood was gone.

"Listen," she continued. "We've never really talked about what happened."

"Because there's nothing to talk about," he said shortly. "We don't talk about this, Desire. Ever. That was what we agreed too, remember. It's been a long time. Better to just let sleep'n dogs lay."

She sighed and he could see her twirling her hair, a habit she had when she was annoyed or upset. "I know, Jax. I just worry about you. You lost so much of your life because—"

"Stop!" he barked into the phone. He flinched, hoping he hadn't awakened Cheri. He lowered his voice. "Seriously, D. Just drop it. What's done is done, nothing is going to change."

She was silent for a long time before finally relenting. "You always carry so much and I just worry that while you are busy looking out for everyone else, no one is looking out for you. Don't you get lonely?"

Jax glanced into his house. After holding Cheri in his arms last night in his office, he realized how alone he really was. Taking care of people was something he'd always been taught to do. Perhaps that's why from the minute he saw her, he felt so drawn.

"I'm fine," he said when he realized the silence had lapsed a little longer than he'd intended.

"What about that girl you brought out to mom's Saturday? She's cute and spunky."

"Who the hell says spunky?"

"Sounds like I just did. Anyhow, I saw the two of you dancin'. Ya'll looked mighty close." Her chipper voice grated against his nerves, but not nearly as badly as it did knowing that she'd been right.

"Shit, D, you're like a dog with a bone. She's my employee. There's nothing going on."

"You're a shitty liar. You can't dance with someone the way you two was dance'n and say there ain't nothing there. I mean damn, Jax, that was hot."

Jax rolled his eyes, annoyed that she had a point. "Drop it, okay?"

Staying true to her nature, Desire did nothing of the sort. "I like her," she said. In the background, he could hear her rummaging around the kitchen.

"Are you trying to cook?"

"Shut up. I picked up a few things while I was traveling, and don't change the subject. Cheri. She doesn't seem like your type."

"She's not," he relented.

"Ah ha!" Desire claimed excitedly. "I knew there was something there. You do like her! You have a crush! Do you want her to be your giiiiirlfriend?" Her giggle chimed through the phone.

"Oh for the love of Pete. Are you twelve?" he asked, smiling despite himself.

"Somebody's got a crush," she sang back to him.

Jax groaned and Desire giggled. "Seriously, though. She looks like she can hold her own against you and your moods."

"What's that supposed to mean?"

"You know damn well what it's supposed to mean. You're meaner than a gator with a toothache when the mood suits ya. No, I can see the fire in that one's eyes."

Desire had always been perceptive, except when it came to her own love life. That was a completely different story.

"She's got a lot of baggage," he said. It was a weak excuse and he knew it.

"Don't you? Don't we all? Listen, I really think Jerry could be the one and I really want you to get to know him. You're really going to like him," she said abruptly changing the subject back to the lunch date.

He groaned. He really didn't want to get to know another one of his sister's passing fancies, but when it came to Desire, he couldn't say no. After all, she was his baby sister and from the day her big blue eyes and blond hair came into his world, he'd never been able to say no to her, and she knew it.

"Fine," he finally lamented.

She squealed, forcing him to hold the ear away from his phone. "How about tonight?"

"I can't tonight. I've gotta go up to NOLA and I don't know how long I'm going to be."

"What you doing up there?" she hedged.

"I'm going to go see Michael and Quinn."

"Ooo, how is that fine doctor these days."

This made him chuckle. Of all the men that came in and out of Desire's life, Michael Ross was the one that had gotten away. Well, he was the one she'd never caught. She was his best friend's kid sister and no way in hell was Michael going to go there, and it wasn't for the lack of trying on her behalf. Desire all but slathered herself in whipped cream to get his attention, and had that been an option, she probably would have done that as well.

"He's doing good. Works at the University Medical now."

"So he finally finished his residency?"

"Yeah."

"What took him so long? Isn't he like the same age you are?"

"Yeah. He took a couple years off to travel abroad before starting school."

She made a humming sound. "And Quinn?"

"He's working for NOLA P.D."

This made her snort. "Well, that's ironic."

When they were in school, Quinn had a love for his illegal substances. It was after one close call that he'd decided to get his life on track.

"We can do lunch tomorrow if you want."

Desire paused for a minute. "I'll have to check with Jerry, but that shouldn't be a problem. He's in Baton Rouge for a few days but I think he'll be back Tuesday."

"Come by the Queen around noon and I'll have Cookie cook for us."

"That's awesome."

"Okay, I've gotta get off here. I'll see ya Tuesday."

"Don't let her go. There's just something about her. I think she'll be good for you. It's in her aura. Ya'lls match," she said abruptly.

"Goodbye, baby sister."

Jax disconnected the call. Desire was a bit of a wanderer. She'd spent several months traveling the United States before extending her travels overseas. When she came back she was a little different. She'd decided to take up studying chakras and auras while visiting some remote place in India.

Remembering what he was doing before Desire had called, he quickly dialed a number.

The line rang twice before a gruff voice answered.

"Hello?"

"Hey, it's me. I need you to look into something for me."

The warm sunlight streamed through the windows, arching across Cheri's face. With a slow smile, she stretched and turned into the warmth. It was the first time in days the sun had made an appearance and it felt amazing. The dreams hadn't come. It was the first night in a long time she'd slept without waking up in a cold sweat or on the edge of hysteria.

Slowly, she opened her eyes and realized that she wasn't in her bed. A fact that she should have guessed because her body didn't ache from the lumps in the mattress. She brought her fingers up to her lips, still imagining that she could feel Jax's mouth against hers. Despite everything that had happened, she felt as if a giant weight had been lifted from her shoulders. As if somehow confiding in Jax had been the soothing medicine her soul needed.

There were so many reasons not to get involved with Jax, and she knew it, however, she allowed herself a brief moment to simply enjoy the memory of it; the way her body had reacted to his; the way she fit against him as if they were two pieces of a puzzle that fit perfectly together.

Cheri rolled her eyes at the cliché. Jax was off limits. That's all there was too it. He was her boss, she was his employee and that was that. Sure, he helped her fix her house, let her sleep in his shirt, slept on the couch so she could sleep in his bed, and fried her brain with two scorching, toe-curling kisses—but what did all that matter.

Needing to think about something other than the way Jax's mouth had felt on hers, she lifted her arms high above her head and uncurled her legs before slipping from the bed. She'd been so exhausted after they'd left the bar that she didn't want to go home and get clothes. Jax had given her a shirt and thrown her clothes in the machine for her. She took a deep breath as the smell of fabric softener and man hugged her.

She walked across the hardwood floor and quietly pulled open the door. If Jax was asleep, she didn't want to bother him. The bedroom door opened out into an open living area. The furnishings were sparse, only containing a desk in the back corner of the room, a couch with a rumpled patchwork quilt tossed aside, massive fluffy recliner, coffee table and a giant television hanging from the wall. As far as decorations went, it was pretty plain and proved just how much time he spent at the bar. It barely looked like anyone even lived there.

The walls were made of cypress timbers, sanded and polished to a beautiful shine. There was a stuffed alligator head hanging behind the desk but that was pretty much it. A partial wall separated the living room from the kitchen. This wall was completely made up of shelves holding various items—pictures, miniature figures, a box of crystals, seashells. She moved closer to inspect the picture frames. Some were of Jax and his sister, his father, and mother and some with a few men she'd never seen before. This was his family.

There was one particular picture that caught her attention. It was one of Jax, his sister, and another woman. It looked to be a few years old. The woman looked lovingly up at Jax as he looked down at her. There was a smile on his face—one that since knowing him—she'd never seen before. He looked like a completely different man. Softer. Was this the girl he'd talked about? Something scratched at the back of her mind. She lifted the photo closer to study the girl—the smiling face, the brown hair with blond streaks. There was just something about her that seemed off—or familiar.

Pushing down the small bubble of jealousy she felt, she placed the picture back in its place and wandered into the kitchen. On the counter sat a half-full coffee pot. There was a chipped mug in the drying wrack so she grabbed it and helped herself. As she was taking a sip, she heard Jax's raised voice coming from the front porch.

*"Stop! Just drop it. What's done is done, nothing is going to change."*

Cheri moved a little closer, curiosity getting the better of her. Unfortunately, she didn't hear anything after that. What was done? Who was he talking to? Feeling guilty for listening, she moved away and walked back into the bedroom. She climbed into the window seat and looked out over the lake. The surface glittered in the sun's early morning light. A crane stood in the shallow water, its head bowed as it searched for breakfast. She watched as its head disappeared beneath the water and came up seconds later, a fish flopping in its powerful beak.

As she sat and contemplated where her life had taken her, she heard the front door open and close. Jax's footsteps were solid against the floor and seconds later he appeared in the door, startled to see her awake.

"Mornin," he said with a slow drawl.

"Hey," she said. "I hope you don't mind." She lifted her coffee mug.

He shook his head. "Not at all. How'd you sleep?"

"Surprisingly well, actually. You?"

He lifted a shoulder. "I don't sleep much," he said as he stepped further into the room.

"Why not?" she asked, genuinely concerned.

"Can't seem to shut my mind off," he said tapping the side of his head with his finger. He sat on the corner of the bed across from her. There was an awkward silence between them.

Unable to take it anymore, Cheri swung her legs around and put her feet on the floor. She flushed when Jax's eyes lingered on her bare legs. "Listen, about last night. I don't want you to . . . I didn't mean. . . ." She took a deep breath and slowly released it, trying to gather her thoughts, but he was the one that spoke.

"It was a mistake. Something that should've never happened. You're my employee and nothing more. I shouldn't have crossed that line. You were vulnerable and I took advantage."

Cheri looked at him, feeling as if he'd just punched her in the stomach. Talk about a straight shot to the feels. She studied his face for a moment, trying to see if he was lying, but there were no traces of emotion. In fact, he looked almost bored with what had happened between them. He leaned casually against the door frame, crossing his legs at the ankles and lifting his coffee cup to his mouth.

She nodded, hoping that he couldn't read her emotions. Trying to remain indifferent she lifted her shoulder in a shrug. "It was what it was. Heat of the moment kind of thing. Didn't mean anything to me." If the kiss they'd shared last night didn't mean anything to him, then there was no reason for it to mean anything to her.

He watched her for a moment, gauging her reaction and the intensity of his gaze made her squirm. Before he could say anything she continued. "I didn't tell you all of that crap so you would feel sorry for me. You have your own shit to deal with. You don't need to add my problems to them," she said coolly.

Jax watched her change right in front of his eyes. She went from warm and open to cool and closed off. What in the hell had just happened? Had he misjudged what she had been about to say? He frowned. He wasn't sure what had happened but something had changed.

"If I didn't want to know, I wouldn't have asked. We all have demons, Cheri," he said using his mother's exact words.

"And the only power those demons have is the power we give them," she responded in kind.

He snorted.

"Jax you're a good guy," she said, even though she was still smarting from his earlier comment. Because despite everything, she truly believed he was.

"I'm *not* a good guy, Cheri."

A long silence lapsed between them. "Why?" she found herself asking. She wasn't sure why she asked.

It was in that moment—as he wrestled his own personal demons—that she realized they were both truly broken. She realized this because she could see herself in him—always struggling, always fighting.

They sat in silence for a long time, staring at each other before he shifted his gaze away from hers. Jax knew if he answered her question with honesty everything would change. It meant that he finally found someone to trust. Was that a risk he was willing to take?

"What are you hiding, Jax?" she asked, breaking the silence between them.

When his eyes met hers again, he made the decision. "You're not the only person in this room with blood on their hands, Cheri. You're not the only one that has killed."

# 18

By the time Lynn and Levi made it back to the office the sun was beginning to climb into the sky. Monday morning sucked. There were mountains of reports to be made, files to go through and other open cases to examine. Lynn's eyes felt like they were coated with a layer of sand. He rubbed the heels of his palms over his eyes and blinked away the gritty feeling. Reaching into his drawer he pulled out a bottle of antacids and popped a couple into his mouth.

Idly he chewed on the chalky tablets as he shuffled papers around on his desk. He'd already checked in with the other cases he'd been working. Unfortunately, those cases had grown cold.

Now, on top of his other cases, he had to worry about the possibility of a serial killer. Levi had gone down to the lab to await results from the newest murder. Lynn gathered the files and walked over to the giant cork board. He pinned a photo of the first victim—Travis Anderson— in place. Beneath it, he placed a couple of the crime scene photos.

Next, he pinned up the most recent crime scene photos. After pinning the photos of the second victim in place he took a step back. Victim number one was missing a finger. Victim number two was missing an eye.

He scrubbed his eyes once more and let out a long, slow breath. Until he had the details of the second victim, it would be hard to compare. Lynn walked back to his desk and sat down. Behind him, the air conditioner clicked and choked. He made a mental note to call maintenance to see if they could do something about the dying piece of metal.

Levi knocked twice before entering the office. Lynn looked up expectantly. "Do we know who the second victim is yet?"

His partner shook his head and tossed the folder on the desk. Lynn snatched it up and began to read. The details making his already upset stomach churn.

"So it looks like there's succinic acid in this one's brain, just like Anderson's."

"Shit," Lynn grumbled. He'd known already that they would find the stuff in the tox screen.

"And the syringe cap?"

Levi's face grew grim and Lynn did not like the look at all. "Not sure. There wasn't anything finite on it. What little there had been, was compromised."

"Damn."

"There are millions of those syringe caps. To narrow it down would be close to impossible."

This news caught Lynn's attention. "Can't get a print off it anyway, there are ridges on the cap. Which means, that it was an accident that it was there. I find it hard to believe that the killer would have been so careless as to drop something like that," Lynn grunted as he slapped his hand down on his desk. He popped another tablet in his mouth and rubbed his temples.

"Where are we on Anderson's juvie records?" Levi asked.

"It's taking a bit of time. Records are sealed and the only way we can get them is if he was tried as an adult."

"It looks like he was tried as an adult, but he was released when he was nineteen. After that, it was a string of petty larceny, theft and a couple b and e's. The last time he got sent away was for selling and distributing narcotics."

"And there is no way what so ever to find out who his foster parents were?"

Lynn shook his head. "Nope. Those records are destroyed."

"Why are they destroyed?"

"Because a lot of the foster families don't want their identities known. Also, the circumstances with some of these kids are pretty dangerous. If that information got into the wrong hands, then the kids could be in danger."

Levi nodded. "Figured as much."

With a frown, Lynn sifted through the file and scanned the report.

"Do we know who the girl was?"

Lynn skimmed the papers. "Doesn't say, but I can probably see if I can find that case. Since there were formal charges brought against him, her name should be on file."

"Well, that's something."

Something scratched at the back of Lynn's head as he read the rest of the report. "The eye was removed just like Anderson's finger was."

"Yeah. The ME said that the eye removal was precise."

"Precise how?"

"Anderson's finger was cut neat and clean. She said it was also done perimortem."

"Meaning that if Succinylcholine was in his system, he'd be able to feel it every little thing, but unable to fight. What about the eye?"

"Same thing. There were no signs of the eye having been removed postmortem. In fact," he said taking the file and flipping through it before finding the page. He handed it back, tapping the sentence. "She said the eye was also done perimortem, but it was strange."

Lynn scanned the notes but they were hard to read. "Sum it up for me because her handwriting sucks."

Levi chuckled. "While it seems that the eye was removed while this victim was still alive, it also seems like it was done with accuracy."

His eyebrows shot up, meeting his hairline. "Accuracy?!"

"She said it looks like it was done by a skilled hand. There were no rough cuts or tearing around the tissue of the eye. In fact—and this is nasty as hell—but the nerves and everything were removed. Almost as if the person doing it had intimate knowledge of surgical procedures."

Lynn groaned. "Awesome, exactly what we need. A serial killer with surgical knowledge."

"Well, we were already aware of that to some degree thanks to that neuro-blocking bullshit. Did you find any leads on that?"

He shook his head. "There are thirty-one hospitals in the surrounding areas. All hospitals have Succinylcholine. Trying to figure out if someone was taking some to the side would be like finding a specific needle in a stack of needles, and going through the staff that has access to it would take twice as long. We don't have the time nor the manpower for that."

"The examiner also said that someone injected with Succinylcholine wouldn't be able to live but for a few minutes."

"Why?"

"Because it paralyzes everything, including the muscles and vessels in the lungs. It'd only take a victim minutes before they suffocated."

Lynn skimmed the notes. "Tissue shows elevated signs of oxygen." He looked up and his eyes met his partners. "Which means, this bastard is hooking them up to a ventilator to keep them alive."

Levi scratched at his beard—which Lynn noted was considerably shorter. "We're not dealing with a typical killer here. He's organized, and while he's taking his time with the torture, he's not spending that much time with them. Look at the cuts on each victim. There are no hesitation marks."

"Which means he's confident. He's smart because he knows we'll find all of these particulates and clues, but knows there will be no way to link him to them because they are so commonly used."

"My question is, where is the missing finger and missing eye?"

"Trophies, more than likely," Lynn grunted as he studied the pictures.

Levi grimaced. "It takes one sick sonofabitch to do that."

"Well, it wouldn't be the first time body parts were taken for trophies. You have the psychos like Bundy that would keep heads, Dahmer that kept genitals and Ed Gein that kept his victim's faces."

Levi shuddered and made a face. "Sick as that is, wouldn't it be the same thing every time?"

"Not always. It depends on what his connection with the victim was. For some reason, the trophy thing just isn't sitting well with me."

"Why's that?"

He pursed his lips and frowned. "I don't know. Just weird feeling I have."

"Is this one of your freaky gut things?" Levi teased.

"I don't know what it is, but this case is really starting to piss me off and we're only a couple days in."

"I hear ya."

"Do we know how long it's going to be before we get an ID on this latest victim?"

"She said she would move as quick as she could, but she's backed up. I caught all kinds of hell for making her rush these tests."

"Why don't you see if you can't talk to some of Anderson's co-workers again. I'll go through this list of hospitals again and see if we can't narrow it down."

Levi pushed his massive form out of the chair. "I don't like the feel of this one, Lynn. I mean the murders we have are usually pretty cut and dry. This one. . . ." he scratched his beard and frowned.

"I know what ya mean."

He watched as his partner left his office, closing the door behind him. He knew exactly how Levi was feeling. They'd worked several murder cases together. However, this would be his partner's first serial case. He could understand the frustration. He'd only worked on a couple in his lifetime.

His eyes scanned the room and landed on the board he'd started of the victims. More times than not, the killers grew overconfident. When that happened, they made mistakes. It was when those mistakes were made that all the pieces fell into place. He had a feeling it wasn't going to be that easy this time.

He was lost in thought when Levi suddenly pushed through the door. "You're not going to believe this."

"What?"

"Anderson's parole officer is in holding."

"What the hell for?"

"Because when the unis went back to talk to him, apparently they struck a nerve. Confessed to lying about Anderson passing his drug tests. He never gave the drug tests because Anderson was his supplier."

"You've got to be shitting me?!"

Levi shook his head, a wide smile breaking out on his face. "And that's not all."

Lynn didn't get a chance to question what Levi was talking about. "Apparently Anderson was taken into University Medical last week with a staph infection."

Lynn was already jumping up from his seat and slinging his holsters over his shoulders. "Then University Medical is where we start. Because if he was treated there, there is a very good chance that our killer could have seen him."

"And the needle stack gets whittled down to one," Levi said.

"We can hope," Lynn muttered as they walked out the doors. "We. Can. Hope."

# 19

Cheri sat in silence for a long time as she processed what he'd just said. Did he really just admit to killing a man? She wasn't sure why, but it struck her with the force of a wrecking ball. Of all the things she'd pictured, she hadn't pictured murder as the thing he was hiding. However, she figured one could probably say the same thing for her.

"Was it on accident?"

Jax took a deep breath and let it out through his nose, his nostrils flaring softly. He pushed his tall frame away from the door. "No."

Cheri did a double take, her eyes growing wide. When she'd killed her step-father it had been somewhat of an accident, at the very least self-defense. What Jax was saying was completely different.

"You killed a man in cold blood?"

Jax nodded, looking down at his hands. Her eyes lowered to his knuckles and then slid to his face. His eyes were somewhat vacant as he flexed his knuckles and then absently rubbed them on his jeans.

"What happened?" she asked shakily.

He looked at her and opened his mouth, but it snapped shut. His demeanor changed and the startling look he gave her was surprising.

His eyes narrowed. "What? You scared of me now? I'm not the man you confessed your deepest, darkest sins to?"

"What? No. That's not—"

"I can see the way you're judging," he snorted derisively.

Cheri frowned, confused as to why his anger was suddenly directed at her. She jumped to her feet, her own anger boiling to the surface. "Now wait just a minute. I was not judging you. You can't just dump something like that on me and expect me to be all happy-go-lucky-woolet's-spend-a-day-at-the-freaking-carnival," she said dramatically waving her hands around.

It was his turn to do a double take. It struck him once more how beautiful she was when she was angry. Her full lips were pulled into a tight frown. He tried to recall if he'd ever actually seen her with her hair down before.

"Why not?! It's what you did with me."

She closed her eyes and pressed her fingers to her temples. *Don't engage. Don't argue.* After getting herself under control, she opened her eyes once more. "Is that why you went to prison?" she asked softly.

"No." His voice was flat and void of all emotion. His clipped tone told her that he wasn't going to give her any more details.

Cheri's heart hammered in her chest as she watched emotions cover Jax's face. This was it. This was why he was so haunted. This was his secret. Well, it was one of them. She waited for him to continue. He stood stock still, staring at her and she knew he was gauging if he could trust her or not. It didn't matter that she'd laid everything out for him less than twelve hours ago. This was something different. Much, much different and yet, this was what had pulled them together. They'd been brought together because it was as if their souls had been seeking each other out.

Taking a step forward, still vaguely aware that she was only wearing lace boy shorts and a t-shirt, she stopped in front of him. They were inches apart. His eyes watched hers as she stared at him. There was mixture of emotions swimming in the warm depths of his eyes; fear, heartache, loss, and . . . something else.

Lifting her palm, she pushed it to his chest, just over his heart. She ignored the tight feeling of muscle beneath her hand and focused on the erratic beating. "You can trust me," she whispered softly.

He brought his hand up and covered hers. "You're scared of me. I can see it in your eyes." His voice choked as he spoke.

"I am," she admitted but then softly added, "but not for the reasons you think."

She watched as he wrestled with his demons. He backed away and released her hand. "I can't," he said, his voice gravelly with emotion.

Cheri nodded once, allowing her hand to fall back to her sides. Her heart fell, and even though she tried not to let it bother her, the rejection she felt stung. "I understand."

The spell around them was broken and the heaviness of disappointment was left in its wake. Jax cleared his throat. "You up for a little road trip today?"

"Where?"

"I need to go up to NOLA. I have a doctor friend that can take a look at the finger."

Reality came slamming back into her. She remembered why she was staying at Jax's house in the first place. It was almost like she'd forgotten that it wasn't some sort of sleepover. Mentally she cursed herself. This was what happened when she let someone get close. She left herself vulnerable last night when she revealed everything to Jax. In turn, she'd forgotten that she was in a very serious situation. She'd also learned that Jax didn't trust her as much as she trusted him. Her pride was wounded and her ego deflated.

"Oh, right." She lifted her shoulder. "I guess."

Jax nodded. "I'll go grab your clothes."

She watched as he disappeared from the room. Feeling like a fool, she sank onto the bed and waited. Jax returned carrying her clean clothes, neatly folded. He placed them on the bed beside her and backed away.

"Are you hungry? I can make us some breakfast before we leave."

"No. I'm good, thanks."

Jax nodded. "We will leave as soon as you're ready," he said before walking out the door. He stopped and turned. "There's an extra toothbrush in the drawer to the left of the sink," he said ticking his head toward the door that lead to the bathroom.

"Thank you. I won't be long," she said.

It was only after he pulled the door closed, that she let out a pent-up breath. The constant up and down in her life was beginning to get overwhelming as well as exhausting.

Cheri climbed to her feet and rolled her neck and shoulders, trying to ease the tension that had once again settled there. She should have known that her good night's sleep wouldn't have lasted long. After grabbing her clothes, she made her way into the bathroom. She stared at her reflection and flinched. There were dark circles under her eyes and her skin looked pale.

She turned the tap water on cold and cupped her hands. As water dripped off the end of her nose and down her chin, she couldn't help but wonder what the hell had she gotten herself into with Jax. Had she just jumped out of the frying pan and into the fire?

Jax felt like an ass as he stared at the closed bedroom door. She'd taken a huge leap of faith telling him about her past, and no matter how badly he thought he wanted too, he just couldn't bring himself to do the same. She'd wanted details and he just couldn't let them go. They were his cross to bear, and with everything she already had going on, it wasn't something he wanted to burden her with. What was truly holding him back? Was it his ego or the fact that he truly didn't know if he could trust her? If he let go and trusted her with it, that meant he was no longer in control. Was that something he was ready to let go of?

Jax paced the living room, debating if he wanted to tell her the entire story or if he should just leave well enough alone. The second option sounded much better, however, he knew that eventually, Cheri would bring it up again. When she did she would press for the answers until she got them.

"Damn women," he muttered.

A few minutes later his room door opened and Cheri stepped out. Her hair was pulled into a tight ponytail at the back of her head. Her face looked freshly scrubbed, and she had a healthy glow in her cheeks.

"All set."

"Do you want some coffee for the road?"

She shook her head. "Can't drink any more coffee on an empty stomach, and I'm not especially hungry."

"Okay then," he said as he grabbed his keys and shoved his cell phone in his shirt pocket.

As the two of them left the house, a sudden chill washed over her. She stopped at the bottom of the steps and slowly turned. Her eyes landed on the dense forest surrounding Jax's small house. The interior was dark— seemingly much darker than it should have been.

Goosebumps covered her arms and the tiny hairs on the back of her neck stood on end. Straining her eyes, she looked into the menacing shadows, trying to find the source of her unease. Sweat dotted her brow as her gaze swept by each tree, each stump, and each shadow. Something definitely felt off. She squinted her eyes and then she saw it, a shadow looming next to one of the giant cypress trees.

Cheri's eyes widened as she stood rooted in fear. Her heart raced, and her mind scrambled to make sense of what she was seeing.

"Hey?"

Jax's hand suddenly touched her shoulder, causing her to jerk around. A small surprised yelp slipped from her lips before she realized it was him. He was frowning down at her.

"What's going on?" he asked.

"I, uh. . . ." she turned and looked back over her shoulder but there was nothing there but an old tree. She frowned. She had to be imagining things because of all the stress.

"Cheri, what is it?" There was a sharp edge to his voice.

She cleared her throat and shook her head. "It was nothing. I thought I saw something."

Jax's frowned deepened. "Wait here."

He didn't give her a chance to respond as he walked to the edge of the dense vegetation and looked around. When he disappeared from her sight around the side of the house, her anxiety kicked up a notch. It was only when he was striding back to her that she was able to relax.

He shook his head. "Must have been a deer or something," he said. "There weren't any tracks aside from animal out there."

Animal or not, she wasn't able to shake the creepiness that had clung to her. She felt chilled down to the very marrow of her bones. Maybe it was because of everything that was happening that she felt someone was watching her at every turn. Without another word, she climbed into the truck buckled her seatbelt. Jax started to truck and pulled out onto the muddy one lane path that lead from his house. Time to see if they could find some answers.

# 20

They rode in silence up the two-lane highway as they made their way to New Orleans. Cheri kept her attention focused out the window. What she was looking at, she had no idea, but she hadn't uttered so much as a syllable since leaving his house. The tension between them was so thick it could be cut with a knife.

"Bootleg," he said suddenly.

Cheri jumped at the sudden sound of his voice as it intruded in on her thoughts. She turned and looked at him confused. "Excuse me?"

"Bootlegging. That's why I went to prison. That's what you're seeing, that first day at the bar and then the other night."

"You're a bootlegger?" she asked incredulously.

Jax wagged his dark brows at her and a slow smile tilted the corner of his mouth. "It's one of my many talents."

Cheri's stomach fluttered lightly. She'd gotten a glimpse of some of those talents in the single kiss they'd shared. She swallowed hard and tried to ignore her nerves. "So you went to prison for bootlegging and you're doing it again?"

He lifted his shoulder in indifference. "I guess some never learn, eh?"

"What happens if you get caught?"

He snickered. "If I get caught I'll get sent away for a long time."

She snorted. "You were gone for a several years—all because of bootlegging?" she asked, a disbelieving eyebrow at him

He shrugged. "There might have been a drunk and disorderly and resisting arrest somewhere in there. Didn't help that I had a fling with the judge's wife."

Cheri rolled her eyes. Now the prison sentence made more sense.

"The judge's wife? Really?"

He lifted a shoulder. "That was the rumor at that particular time in my life. I was sleeping with the judge's wife while deflowering his precious niece." There was a playfulness to his voice.

"So you were that kind of guy, huh. The one that didn't give a shit whose woman he was tapping as long as he got off himself?"

He looked at her and wagged his brows salaciously while placing his hand over his heart. "You wound me with your words."

Cheri found herself laughing for the first time since everything had started, and she realized it felt good.

"You need to do that more often," Jax said thoughtfully.

She looked down and stared at a freckle on her thigh before looking back up. "Maybe if we out of this alive, I will."

"I didn't sleep with those women," he said after a while. "The niece was a friend of my sisters who had a crush on me. We kissed once and it felt weird, and the judge's wife was sleeping with one of the guys that worked for me. She was seen coming out of the back of my bar one night and everyone just assumed it was me. So, I had the bootlegging to give me the danger I looked for. I know the risks if I get caught again."

"Then why do it at all?"

Jax's brows furrowed a little and she knew he was trying to find the right answer.

"I've always had a habit for doing things I'm not supposed to. I do what I want when I want, and how I want."

"Sounds kinda like a dick thing to do. Don't people get hurt?"

A dark looked passed over his face but vanished quickly. "Not unless they deserve it."

It was Cheri's turn to frown. What in the hell was that supposed to mean? He must have sensed the direction her thoughts had taken her because he continued. "I take care of the people that are close to me. I protect them."

"What do you mean by that?"

He took his eyes off the road and looked at her. "It means . . . if someone I care about is in trouble, there is absolutely nothing I wouldn't do for them. *Nothing*." His gaze returned to the road. His chiseled features tight as he stared straight ahead.

Jax may be a lot of things, but a bad guy was not one of them. Was it? The remainder of the drive was quiet. The thoughts that clamored around in her head, however, were definitely not. Each time she thought she was getting closer to understanding what made Jax tick, he said or did something that threw her entire world off balance.

An hour later, they pulled off the highway and into the heart of New Orleans, slowly creeping down the crowded streets. Even though they were only a mile from the ever famed Bourbon Street, the traffic was still heavy as tourists tried to find their way around. She found herself people watching as all walks of life milled about. It would be so easy to get lost in life and completely ignore everything around them. Even the people with cameras were escaping as they snapped photos of this building or that statue. Smiling faces laughed into the cameras as people took selfies in front of monuments.

Cheri realized she was jealous of those people—the ones she'd never met. They were here, having fun and oblivious to the fact that there was a murder on the loose as they puckered their lips and made ridiculous faces in front of the lenses. She was jealous that she'd never been able to feel so carefree—jealous of people she'd never met.

It didn't stop her from loving New Orleans, though. Despite her current mood and outlook on her life, she absolutely loved the city. It was a beautiful, brimming with culture, amazing food, and brilliant music. The locals were colorful and the most important part of what made it so eccentric. If she could afford it, she would have moved there instead of Dead Water. Maybe if she had moved somewhere else none of this would be happening.

Jax turned onto Canal Street and followed the signs to the parking garage. Finally, after they were parked, she slipped from the truck and stretched her arms high above her head before rolling her shoulders. Cautiously she looked around, surveying every tiny detail around her. There was just something immensely creepy about parking garages, or maybe she'd just watched too many movies. Nevertheless, it made her skin crawl. The air was still, reeking of exhaust fumes and the brackish smell of the Mississippi River nearby. She felt cold despite the heat and moved a little closer to Jax as they walked up two flights of stairs to the main entrance of the hospital.

By the time they made it to the sliding glass doors, sweat trickled down her back and between her breasts. She breathed a sigh of relief as the doors slid open with a silent *whoosh.* She was greeted with a blast of cold air that dried the sweat on her skin as they stepped into the bustling lobby.

She watched as Jax navigated the halls with ease. It was apparent that he knew his way around. Someone had tried their hardest to mask the strong scent of disinfectant with some sort of lemon fragrance. The smell was sweet and cloying, making her nose burn. Nurses in bright scrubs went this way and that as they tended to the sick. Pregnant women walked around with doting husbands as tried to speed up their labor. Cheri took in her surroundings and was in awe by the structure alone. It was simply beautiful.

They arrived at an elevator and Jax pushed the up arrow. They waited patiently until the doors easily slid open with a ding. They waited as doctors and nurses stepped clear before climbing onto the lift. Thankfully nobody joined them.

With the doors closed, Jax pushed the button that would take them to the eight floor. She felt the soft jolt and squeezed her eyes closed, taking deep steady breaths.

When she opened them again, Jax was looking at her with an amused look.

"Don't like elevators?"

"Nope." She decided to try to focus on something instead of her intense dislike for elevators and hospitals. "Have you been carrying that damn finger around with you this whole time?" she asked in a hushed tone.

"I wanted to ask my friend to run some tests on it."

"That's so gross."

She was about to make another comment when the elevator stopped and the doors slid open. "Here we are," Jax said, stepping out in front of her.

They set off down the hall and Cheri practically had to run to keep up with him, her much shorter legs having problems keeping up with his long strides.

After taking several turns and going down many different halls, they stopped in front of a wooden door with the words *Michael Ross* embossed. Her eyes widened. "He's a plastic surgeon?"

Jax nodded. "Yep." He rasped his knuckles against the door.

"How in the hell is a plastic surgeon going to help? I hardly think this has anything to do with tits and nose jobs," she snorted.

"Michael doesn't just deal with tits and nose jobs, as you so eloquently put it. He also does rounds in the ER on occasion and just because he's a plastic surgeon doesn't make him any less of a doctor."

Cheri held up her hands in surrender. "Damn, my bad. I was just asking."

"Michael has done a lot of good with his position, and even though he is just getting his feet under him with his practice here, he's traveled all over the world to help those less fortunate."

Before she had a chance to comment the door swung wide. They were met by an extremely handsome man— close to Jax's age—with dark hair and a warm wide smile. It was the kind of smile that was genuine and sincere. It immediately calmed her and made her feel guilty about her earlier comment.

"Jax?" he said as he extended his hand and then pulled him in for a manly hug.

"Hey, man. It's good to see ya!" Jax said returning the hug and clapping him soundly on the back.

"What do I owe this unexpected surprise? Come in. Come in." Michael said as stepped aside and allowed them to enter. They stepped into a room that smelled vaguely of citrus. Once he closed the door, Jax turned.

"This is my friend Cheri."

Michael firmly cupped her hands in his strong warm grip. "Nice to meet you."

She smiled. "Likewise."

"Please, have a seat. Can I get you something to drink?"

They both shook their heads, settling themselves into two chairs in front of Michael's desk as he took his seat.

"Did we catch you at a bad time?"

"Not at all." The smile slipped when he noted the seriousness of his friend's face. "Jax, what's going on?"

Cheri just stared at Michael for a moment. It was uncanny at how easily he read Jax.

"I need your help with something," Jax said as he reached into his shirt pocket and pulled out a paper towel and placed it on the desk.

Curious, Michael reached out and gingerly unfolded the paper. His eyes grew wide and shot up to Jax's. "What the hell?"

"Yesterday, this was left in her freezer."

"What? Why?" Michael's eyes darted back and forth between them.

Cheri felt a tremor settle through her as she shrugged. "I don't know." Okay maybe she knew, but it wasn't something she really wanted to share.

Michael frowned and opened the top drawer of his desk, producing a pair of purple gloves. After snapping them on, he lifted the finger and began to inspect it under his desk light.

"Well it was a clean cut," he said picking up a pen and pointing to where the finger had been severed. "See here—how the skin and bone are cleanly severed. It was cut between the joints and the skin is slightly folded down. Looks like it *might* have been cut with something like pruning shears." Michael turned the finger over and a frown furrowed his brow. It looked to Cheri as if he were trying to solve all the mysteries of the universe.

"What is it?"

"I'm not sure, but. . . ." He moved the desk lamp down a little closer to inspect the finger. "I can't be certain, but I think I've seen this tattoo before."

"Really?"

Michael nodded but only slightly. "It's hard to say. I see a lot of people, especially when I take a round in the ER."

Jax nodded. "Are there any tests that can be run to see about DNA or something?"

Michael studied it a little further before looking back at them. First, his eyes rested on Jax and then slowly studied her. He was assessing and trying to get a read on her. She wanted to shift under his scrutiny but decided it was probably better that she hold her ground.

Cheri met his gaze evenly, and a slow smile slipped across his face, revealing perfectly white and straight teeth. There was a subtle nod before he turned his attention back to Jax. It was almost as if he'd been testing her and she just passed. He pursed his lips.

"I've got a buddy down in the lab I might be able to call in a favor to. We can't lift prints or anything like that, but we have a few things we can do. Ya'll in town for long?"

Jax lifted his shoulder. "Depends on how long it will take for results."

Michael smiled. "Couple hours at the most. I can try to get it pushed through as soon as possible."

"Really?"

He nodded, the puzzled look still on his face. "I'm just as curious as you are about this. You got anything else to do while you're in town?"

"Thought about going to see Quinn," Jax offered.

Michael nodded. "That should give us enough time. I'll shoot you a message as soon as we get the results."

The three of them said their goodbyes and soon they were back in the elevator.

"So who is this Quinn guy?" Cheri asked as they walked back to where they'd left the truck.

"He's a cop with the NOLA police department," he said as he opened the passenger side door for her. Her chest tightened at the chivalry that seemed to be just as much a part of him as breathing was. The seat was warm against the backs of her thighs and she rolled the window down as Jax walked to the other side of the truck.

"He's a cop?"

"I know we said no cops, but believe me when I say, you don't have to worry about Quinn."

"Why are we talking to him anyway?"

"I thought I'd have him do some digging into your step father's past."

Mentally, Cheri smacked herself. With everything going on, she hadn't even considered looking into his background. In fact, until recently, she'd tried to forget all about him entirely. Apparently, someone else had something in mind.

"What do you know about him?" Jax asked as he turned the engine over and pulled away from the garage.

Cheri lifted a shoulder. "Not much really. I was too young to know about him and by the time I got older, I just couldn't think about it. The more I remembered, the worse the nightmares became. When your mom first placed me I didn't sleep more than a couple hours each night."

Jax nodded as he pulled out onto the street and into the bustling midmorning traffic. The sun beat down through the windshield and onto her bare legs.

"Hey. Would you care if we stop by Roux's place before we go see your friend?"

"Sure. Where does he live?"

"On the outer edge of the garden district."

He pulled his phone out of his pocket and dialed a number. "What was your step father's last name?"

Cheri's heart seized and her hands grew clammy. Even at the very thought of him, her insides turned cold. She took a deep steady breath. "Briggs."

"Hey you dirty animal," he said by way of greeting to someone on the other end of the line. "Yeah, I'm going to swing by in a little bit. Have another stop to make first. I got that name for ya. Ready? Carl Briggs. I'm sure he has a record. He's dead."

There was silence for a few minutes. "Yeah, I know. I'll owe you a dozen and a big favor."

There was a deep rumble of laughter and it made her heart flutter.

"Don't be a greedy prick," Jax said good-naturedly. "All right. See ya in a bit."

He disconnected the phone and tucked it back into his pocket.

"Quinn sounds like something else," she said thoughtfully.

Again he chuckled, scratching at his stubbly jaw. "You could say that."

# 21

The whole way to Roux's tiny house she tried suppress her anxiousness, however, the closer they got the more the butterflies in her stomach turned into bats. She'd been trying to call Roux every couple of hours since Sunday night. Each time she was sent to voice mail and each time she grew more worried. The final time she didn't even get his message. Instead, she got an automated voice. "The caller's mailbox is full. Please try again later." This only made things worse.

Her hands shook as she snapped her phone closed. When she looked up, they were pulling to a stop in front of Roux's tiny yellow house. The front yard was well manicured and cheerfully adorned with bright flowers. There was a small garden to the side where she and Roux had often sat in the cool evenings of fall and talked about their dreams and goals. Even though those moments spent together were fewer and fewer each year, she cherished each one. Trees hugged the old crumbling brick wall beside the house as the Spanish moss dripped from the trees, stirred slightly by warm breeze. There was a heavy feeling of foreboding in the air that she prayed was just the coming storm.

She and Jax walked through the iron gate and up the sidewalk. As they reached the front porch, she frowned. There were three newspapers rolled up and still laying where they'd been tossed. The mailbox by the front door was full of envelopes.

"He's not been home in a few days," she said as she reached under the mailbox and withdrew a magnetic hide-a-key.

"Maybe he stayed with a friend."

She pressed her lips together and shook her head as she unlocked the front door. "Roux has OCD and doesn't stray from routine. He's rarely away from home unless his job takes him there."

"Maybe he's away on business?" he offered.

She shook her head. "He could be but he wouldn't have left without telling me first."

As soon as she pushed open the door the heavy feeling returned, this time worse than before. The house was really cool but had an odd smell too it. Roux had an air conditioner, but when he left the house—in order to save on utilities costs—he often turned it off. He wouldn't have gone somewhere for days without turning the air off.

She walked further into the house and was greeted by the low and anxious meow of a cat. Bending down, she scooped the orange tabby into her arms.

"Where's daddy at, Rufus?" she cooed as she pushed her nose into the soft fur at the cat's neck. The cat mewled softly and purred with affection. Panic was beginning to claw its way out. Where was Roux? Her fears were becoming realized with each second that passed and they didn't find him.

*Please be okay! Please, please, please, be okay*, she silently pleaded.

"The cat's name is Rufus?"

Rufus turned his head sharply, as if he was just realizing there was another person in the room. His ears flattened against his head as he let out a low growl followed by a hiss.

Jax held his hands up and backed away. "Sorry, dude," he said.

"C'mon, let's get you something to eat," she said carrying him into the kitchen.

She removed the bag of cat food from beneath the counter and knelt to fill the dish, along with the water. She dusted her hands on the back of her shorts and climbed to her feet. Her hands felt clammy and she felt like she was about to be sick.

Taking a deep breath through her nose, willed herself not to panic. Maybe he was just trying to change his routine up.

"He's not been here in a while. He could have tried something new," she said doubtfully. Her eyes scanned the small room and settled on the counter. There was an empty coffee cup in the sink as well as a couple glasses and plates. One glass was half full of orange juice. The pulp floating lazily on the top as fruit flies buzzed around the top and landed inside the glass. The juice was cloudy and pale.

She turned when she heard a beeping sound. The answering machine on the small bar was blinking with new messages.

"What are you doing?" Jax asked.

"Listening to his messages."

"That's an old answering machine," Jax said absently.

She shrugged. "I know. I have no idea why he liked it so much. I've tried for years to get him to upgrade but he refused. Said he liked 'old school'."

She pressed the button and the machine buzzed and clicked, then beeped. She listened to the robotic voice as it began stating the day and time of each call.

*Wednesday, ten-fifty-eight pm.*

There was nothing but silence followed by the sound of the line being disconnected. Cheri frowned but remained silent.

The machine beeped as it clicked over to the second message.

*Wednesday ten-fifty-nine pm.*

There was nothing but a long pause followed by the click.

*Wednesday, eleven pm.*

There was another beep and the clicking of the tape. Cheri's blood began to run cold in her veins. There was no mistaking that these calls were intentional.

*Thursday three-fifty-three p.m.*—a telemarketer with a barely unintelligible accent.

*Friday, ten-fifty-eight pm.*—complete silence.

Cheri moved closer and listened. The faint hint of someone breathing in the background. Goosebumps broke out on her skin. The machine clicked and beeped again.

*Friday, ten-fifty-nine pm.*—more breathing, this time a little more pronounced then . . . *click.*

*Friday, eleven pm.*

This time there was breathing followed by what sounded like heavy footsteps on gravel.

*Saturday, ten-fifty-eight.*

She listened closely. This time it was no longer silent. There were sounds of music and laughter in the background followed by *click.*

*Saturday, ten-fifty-nine.—"Hello?"*

Cheri's heart surged through her chest when she heard Roux's voice. Tears burned her eyes as they spilled over her lashes and down her cheeks. She continued to listen.

*"Hello? Who the hell is this?"*

There was still no answer. The music and laughter in the background was only getting louder. The voices were getting more and more distinct. Her eyes widened and she looked up at Jax unable to believe what she was hearing.

*"I'm calling the cops,"* Roux threatened.

There was still no response. The line went dead. The machine clicked over to the final message.

*Saturday, eleven, pm.—"Hello!!!!!"* Roux's voice was strained and frantic.

As the message began to play, Cheri's eyes grew wide as she listened in horror.

*"You can say dat. Don't like being tied down. He's smooth, but sometimes I wonder what dat boy would do if he stopped running from his demons long enough ta look at da world around 'im."*

*"Demons?"*

*"My bébé is a complicated boy, he is. People talk. I love dat boy, but honey, I love you too and as much as it'd make this ole heart happy to see ya'll t'gether, I just don't wanna see ya hurt. Ya done both come too far and had ta live through too much hell. I'd be worried that this path for ya'll wouldn't end well. Those demons'll eat ya 'live, bébé."*

The voices faded and then there was nothing but heavy breathing and what she could have sworn was laughter.

After the machine clicked off, she looked up at Jax who was staring down at her with rage in his eyes.

"That bastard was there?! He was at my mother's house Saturday night." He jabbed his finger toward the machine. "That was you and my mother talking, no?"

Cheri's head felt light as she went through everything. She nodded. "That was us, but there was no one around. You knew everyone there, right?"

"He must have been lurking in the woods. How else could he have done this?" His gaze looked down at her accusingly.

"What the hell have you drug me into?"

Cheri took a step back, almost as if she'd been slapped. "W-what have *I* drug *you* into? *You're* the one that insisted on helping me. *You're* the one that kept pushing and wouldn't let stuff go," she said, her own anger growing. "I told you to leave me alone but you wouldn't listen."

He took a step back and drew a deep breath, raking his hands back through his hair. "I'm sorry. I just—" The sound of a creaking floorboard coming from the back of the house brought them both spinning around. They both stopped, holding their breath as they listened. *Creeeeak.* Jax moved in front of Cheri, shielding her with his body as they both stared at where the sound was coming from.

"Stay here," he hissed, pulling a knife from the butcher's block.

"Are you insane?" she squeaked in a frantic whisper. "Have you never seen a scary movie?"

"This isn't a scary movie, Cheri. Someone else is in this house. Stay. Here."

"Screw you," she snapped and moved around him. His hand flashed out and closed around her arm.

"Damn stubborn woman," he growled.

She ignored the barb as they moved through the small kitchen. Cheri's heart felt as if it were going to explode. Blood was pounding in her ears and it was like everything around them slowed down. She could hear her breaths coming out short and quick. Jax was right. They weren't alone in the house.

Just as they reached the corner, a loud crash followed by shattering glass caused Cheri to scream and latch on to Jax's arm. Behind them, Rufus growled and hissed.

Jax bolted around the corner, Cheri hot on his heels. She stopped abruptly at the back door, nearly colliding with the solid wall of his back.

"Did you see who it was?"

He shook his head. "No, but whoever was there is gone now," he said.

All around their feet, glass glittered like shattered diamonds.

"We need to get out of here," Jax said again, this time with more urgency.

Cheri didn't have to be told twice. She watched as Jax walked back into the kitchen, lifted the hem of his shirt and wiped down the answering machine.

"What are you doing?"

"If something did happen to Roux, the cops will dust for prints. We don't need anything showing that we were here."

"But we didn't do anything."

"They won't care."

"What about the messages?"

"Leave them. No one will know who they are."

Taking her by the hand he jerked a paper towel from the stand and they went out the front door. Jax wiping away any signs of them being there. She was curious as to how he knew to do what he did, but then again, he had confessed to killing someone in cold blood. That thought alone should have terrified her but it didn't.

They walked back to the truck as casually as possible. As they climbed into the truck and pulled away, Cheri turned in her seat. Her gaze was pulled to the side of the house. A large form lurked in the shadows.

"Jax, there's someone there," she said frantically.

He tapped the break and looked back at the house. "I don't see anyone."

Cheri looked to where she'd seen the figure, but it was gone. She wondered if maybe she was imagining things, again.

"He's playing with us," she said, unable to keep the shakiness from her voice.

A deep scowl crossed Jax's face. "I know."

She chewed on her bottom lip and fidgeted with the hem of her shorts.

Jax reached across the seat and took her hand. It wasn't a romantic gesture but one meant to bring comfort. "You're going to be okay. I promise."

She stared at his hand as it covered hers. Her stomach tightened. The way he said it, the conviction behind each word made her realize that he was telling the truth. She could trust him. While that did bring her some amount of comfort, she wondered if this was even out of his hands.

He watched from the side of the house as the pair pulled away in the truck. A slow smile twisted his lips. It wouldn't be long now. The end game was in sight. She would be his, and it would be happening soon. Finally, all her skeletons would come screaming from the closet and he would enjoy watching her beg for her life.

His fists tightened at his sides as bitterness filled every pore of his being. The bastard she was with was no better than she was. They would both pay for their past sins. He grew hard behind his jeans as he thought about Jax watching as the whore's lifeblood drained from her body. The things he was going to do to her in front of her lover made his mouth water.

"Soon," he growled.

Cheri and Jax walked into the police station and as soon as her feet stepped over the entrance, a wave of apprehension covered her like a heavy blanket. There were people in the waiting room, pacing anxiously as they waited. The walls were stark white and littered with propaganda about calling for help, respecting the law or something else. Cheri was thankful for law enforcement, but they made her nervous regardless. The faster they could get out of there the more at ease she would feel.

Jax stepped up to the window. "I'm here to see Officer Quinn?" For a split second, the woman looked more than a little annoyed, but the minute Jax flashed his thousand-watt smile her chilly disposition thawed.

"Name please, sugar?" her drawl thick and sweet.

"Jax. He's expecting me."

"Of course. Let me see if he's in."

"Thanks, sweetheart," he said with a wink.

Cheri smothered a chuckle when he looked back at her. "What?" he asked innocently, his eyes twinkling with mischief.

She just rolled her eyes.

"Officer Quinn is out right now, but he left something for you. If you'll have a seat, I'll go grab it."

"I appreciate it," he said, his voice dripping with sweetness.

The officer cast a quick glance at Cheri over Jax's shoulder. The look was a mixture of jealousy and contempt.

The lady moved away from the window and disappeared through a door. They didn't have time to talk before she came back carrying a manila envelope with Jax's name scrawled on the top of it.

"Thanks, Cher. Have a good day," he said tilting his head toward her.

"Same to ya," she said with a wide smile.

"I—I don't know if I can look at this," she whispered once they were outside.

"Do you want me too?" he asked as they slid into the truck.

She didn't want to feel like a coward but there was just something about seeing her stepfather's history on paper that made all the demons out of the dark. Despite actually wanting Jax to read it to her, she shook her head.

For a few moments, she stared at the envelope on her lap as if it were full of snakes.

"No. I can do it."

Fingers trembling, she unfastened the clasp and slid the stack of papers out. Her eyes grew wide.

"He was a registered sex offender. Going all the way back to the 60s." Her stomach rolled. Her mother married a sex offender and had left her own daughter alone with him.

"He was released three years before he met my mother. There are three pages of minor infractions since his release but nothing that really sticks out."

"Does it say last known address?"

Cheri scanned the contents and her mouth grew dry. "It does," she lifted her gaze. "It was the cabin we lived in."

Something else caught her eye causing her to frown.

"What is it?"

"A missing person's claim was filed about a month after I was put into foster care."

"Was it your mom?"

Her eyes scanned the pages and finally, she shook her head.

"It says here it was a Tianna Briggs."

"Briggs?"

"It says report filed by twenty-five-year-old Tianna Briggs. Briggs made report stating that Carl Briggs had not returned to his cabin nor had he been seen by anyone for an extended period of time."

"So who is this woman?"

"His daughter. Carl had a daughter." She muttered.

"I take it you didn't know?"

She just shook her head and kept reading. Each line filled her with more and more trepidation. A folded piece of paper slid from the file. She unfolded it.

"It's addressed to you," she said handing it to him as she kept studying the pages.

Jax took the note from her and opened it and read out loud.

*Jax,*

*This is all I could find on Carl Briggs. He looked to be a mean piece of work. There was a report filed about his disappearance. The report is still open. There's one other thing. I did some deeper digging. Carl Briggs doesn't have a death certificate.*

*You owe me big for this.*

*Q.*

# 22

Cheri's heart pounded ferociously.

"He's a-alive?" panic welled in her chest.

"We don't know that for sure," he said calmly as he tucked the note back into the envelope.

"It's him, Jax. It has to be. He's the one doing all of this. He's getting even with me for what I did. That's why he's doing all of this. He's playing a game." Her fears tumbled from her lips just as rapidly as the tears rolling down her cheeks. "He survived and now he's coming for me. He was in my house, he left that finger for me and now he has Roux," she said hysterically.

Jax wrapped his arms around her shoulders and pulled her into his chest. He folded her tightly in his arms as she sobbed into his shirt. He stroked the back of her head and tried to calm her. "We don't know that it's him."

"It has to be," she sobbed, though her words were muffled by his shirt front. Suddenly she sat up, terror widening her eyes.

"My kids. Jax, we have to go get my kids. They're in danger."

"I don't think that's a good idea. I think they are probably safer where they are right now until we can get this figured out. I wouldn't want to risk bringing them back and wind up putting them on his radar."

She sniffled and finally pulled away. "You're right. If they were in any danger, I would know it. We still have Roux to worry about, though."

He nodded solemnly. They both knew that the chances of finding Roux alive were slim to none, but neither wanted to say as much. Jax picked the file up from her lap and thumbed through the pages, stopping on one.

"I don't think it could be him. Look at this." He held the paper out to her, pointing at a date. "He'd at least be in his mid-seventies according to this. So taking that into

210

consideration as well as the night you stabbed him, he can't be in that great of shape. He had a daughter you didn't know about?"

"Apparently but how would she even know about any of this?" The dull ache that had started behind her eyes earlier was now a raging headache. "I don't know, Jax. I don't know what to do. Should I run?" It wouldn't be the first time she ran from her troubles, but what would happen if she did. There were too many people she'd be leaving behind. People she'd come to care for. Whoever was doing this would find a way to get her to come back. Running wasn't an option.

Jax grabbed her hand and squeezed it. The pad of his calloused thumb brushed over her knuckle. "We'll get through this, ok? You just have to trust me."

It was almost as if Jax's calmness was surging through his hand and into hers. She looked into the dark depths of his eyes and she felt herself calm. "I trust you."

A smile split his face. "Good. Now, let's head back to the hospital to see what Michael found out and then get the hell out of this place."

She buckled her seatbelt as he turned the engine of the truck over. "Works for me," she muttered as he pulled out of his parking spot and into traffic.

A few short minutes later they were pulling back into the hospital parking garage. As they walked through the hospital entrance and through the different crowds of people, she noticed that Jax never left her side. His hand rested on the small of her back—a gesture she appreciated more than anything.

As they rode the elevator up to the eight floor in silence, she stole a look at Jax from the corner of her eye. What was it about this man that made her feel safe enough to crumble in front of? The minute she'd met Jax, she'd been unable to keep her defenses up. It didn't matter how hard she tried, he'd always managed to slip through the cracks.

When the elevator dinged open they stepped out into a somewhat deserted hall. They were just making their way to Michael's office when the door was abruptly opened. Two men stepped through. One was a massive hulking giant with a neatly trimmed beard and deep hazel eyes. The other was considerably shorter, stockier with a head of thick black hair—silver peppered at the temples, a black mustache, and intense dark eyes.

Cheri's step faltered as she made eye contact with the men. It was the detective from the news—the one that was working the body dump in the swamp. Their gazes locked and she took a startled step back. "Excuse me," she said looking down at her feet and standing as close to Jax as possible. However, it was too late, she'd been seen by both men. Their eyes slid to Jax and gave him the once-over.

"No problem. You here to see Dr. Ross?" the taller one asked.

Jax beamed a bright smile at him. "Yes, sir." He then draped his arm around Cheri's shoulders and hugged her against his side. He shoved his other hand into his hip pocket. "The girlfriend wants to get implants."

Cheri was too stunned to say anything. Her cheeks flamed brightly as she averted her gaze. The older detective cleared his throat and nodded once. However, the tall one just smiled widely at her. It was a goofy and endearing grin and if the circumstances were different, she'd actually like to have a beer with the guy.

"We'll be on our way then." He turned to Dr. Ross. "You have our card."

Michael flashed them a broad and convincing smile. "Yes, sir." The short detective met her eyes for a moment, and she felt her insides wither. *Stay calm. Don't look nervous.* She flashed him what she hoped was a sincere smile. A moment passed as he studied her before a hint of a smile crossed his face.

Cheri watched as the detectives stepped onto the elevators. *He knows something. Did he know she was guilty?*

Relief washed over her as soon as the doors slid closed. When she turned to look at Michael, his smile had completely vanished and was replaced by a grim expression. "You two better get in here," he said in a hushed voice.

This couldn't be good.

Once inside the office, Michael closed and locked the door before turning to face them, "What did you say to them?"

Jax shrugged. "Just that we were here to ask you about getting Cheri a new set of tits."

Michael rolled his eyes before looking at Cheri. His eyes landed on her chest and she felt heat rising into her cheeks. His gaze wasn't violating. It looked more like a professional curiosity. It only lasted for a few seconds and when he looked back up, she could have sworn she saw his handsome face turn pink. This caused her to smile.

"She clearly doesn't need any work done," he said kindly.

She laughed. "Thanks."

He just flashed her a bright smile and turned his attention back to Jax, who was scowling at his friend.

"Clearly she doesn't," Jax said tersely. The tone of his voice caught her attention and made her snicker. Was he jealous?

"Anyway! What did they want?"

Michael leaned against the front of his desk. "I got the test results back on your finger, and that's not all. Those two detectives," he said pointing to the door, "were looking for the same thing."

Jax frowned. "The same thing? What do you mean?"

Michael swallowed and raked a hand back through his hair and then loosened his tie. His hands rested on his hips as he stared at them. They shy look from earlier was gone. "They have the body that belongs to that finger."

Cheri felt the color leak from her face and the room sway. If it weren't for Jax's hand on her back, she was fairly certain that she would have fallen over.

Michael leaned back against his desk and crossed his legs at the ankles. "They wanted to know if a man matching his description had come in for treatment while I was working in the ER."

"How did you know who he was? Are you certain that the man they showed you is the same man missing the finger?"

"They had a picture of the guy. I recognized him all right, once they told me the name I was able to find his file. When I did, I looked for any noted indicating markers. The man that came into the hospital and the one in the picture are the same one. He had a tattoo on his right finger, a cross, just below the fingernail. He was treated for a staph infection and released. They didn't do a tox screen on him in the ER, but I did see what the ME's report said. The tox screens on him were through the roof. There were opiates as well as amphetamines in his system when he died, and judging from the levels that were in there, I don't see how the guy was able to walk upright. Also," Michael paused and looked back and forth between them. His brow was furrowed with worry.

"What?" Jax asked.

He let out a long breath. "There were also minute traces of neuron-blockers. Well, not so much the blockers themselves as the metabolites left behind from the broken down version of the drug."

"Okay, forgive me if I'm not following ya here, doc," Cheri said.

"What it all boils down to, that if this guy had this stuff in his system his body would have been paralyzed but he'd still be very much aware of what was going on around him. Not only that, but he would be able to feel everything that was being done to him."

Cheri's eyes widened. "That's awful."

Michael's eyes were sad. "It really is. I wish there was more I can do."

Jax shook his head. "You've done more than enough, Michael," he said clapping his buddy on the back.

"You don't need to be involved any more than you already are. You've stuck your neck out enough for us already," Cheri said, her voice firm. She'd be damned if she jeopardized someone else.

"Well, if you change your mind and need more help, you know where I'm at."

Jax nodded once and held Michael's gaze for a moment. Cheri didn't miss the look and wondered what was about.

"Okay, man, we're going to make tracks south."

Michael nodded and moved away from his desk, clapping Jax on the shoulder. "I don't know what's going on, but be careful. Whoever took out this Anderson guy is bad news."

Cheri's head snapped up. Her eyes widened. "What did you say?"

Michael looked puzzled for a moment.

"What name did you say?"

Michael turned around and picked up a piece of paper on his desk and read over it again, just to make sure he'd gotten the name correct. "Yeah, the victim's name was Travis Anderson."

Cheri blanched, and her stomach rolled. The walls seemed to warp around her as the blood pounded furiously through her ears. Her entire body shook. "I need to go. We need to get out of here right now," she said frantically. She was gasping for air. It felt as if someone had their hand around her neck and was squeezing. She didn't wait for either man as she raced to the door. It took her a few tries, but she finally managed to get the door unlocked. She all but tripped into the hall, startling an older woman wearing lime green scrubs.

"Honey, are you okay?" The nurse's words roared in her ears.

Cheri managed to nod but she couldn't speak. Her tongue was heavy and coated with a paste. Her throat was dry and she felt as if it were closing up.

Jax turned and quickly took Michael's hand. "Thanks so much for your help man. I really appreciate it."

Jax turned and began to walk away when Michael's grip on his arm stopped him. "Jax, be careful. I have a feeling you're about to get in the middle of something that won't end well for you. Is she worth it?"

Jax met Michael's steady gaze. It wasn't unkind, it was just one full of concern for his friend. Both of their gazes shifted down the hall to where Cheri was walking quickly toward the elevator—hand braced on the wall. Jax couldn't answer, even though he knew what the answer already was. He knew he was getting in the middle of something again, and this time, he had a feeling the stakes were much higher.

"Thanks, man," was all Jax could say. Michael gave him a knowing nod before releasing his grasp.

Jax hurried down the hall to where Cheri was standing in front of the elevator, his boots squeaking against the tiled floor. Gently, he grabbed her by the arm startling a yelp out of her. Her face had grown dangerously pale, and he realized that for the first time, Cheri was legitimately scared. Before she'd been worried and anxious, now he was only seeing pure, unadulterated terror. She no longer looked like the headstrong pain in the ass he'd come to know.

"Hey. What was that all about?" he asked.

She didn't answer.

"Who is Travis Anderson?"

Stubbornly, she shook her head and stiffened her spine. "Not here." She looked around the hall, causing Jax to follow her anxious glances. The elevator slid open and thankfully it was empty.

They quickly made their way through the hospital and back to the truck. It was only after they were in the safe confines of the sweltering cab of his truck that Cheri turned in her seat and looked at him with haunted eyes. "Travis Anderson is—was—the boy that raped me. He's the one I sent to jail when he was a teenager."

Jax's face grew dark. Well, someone had saved him a job because he was going to hunt Anderson down himself. "Okay."

"What does it mean? The boy who raped me was brutally murdered and his finger just showed up in my freezer. Why?"

"Someone giving you peace?"

Cheri snorted. "Not likely. I just. . . . None of this is making sense. If it was Carl, then how could he have possibly known about Travis?"

"The media?"

Cheri shook her head. "I was a minor in the system. That kind of information is not released."

"Could someone have leaked it?"

Again she shook her head. "No. There were only a few people even allowed in the courtroom. There were armed guards outside the courtroom doors. In fact, I wasn't even allowed in the same room as he was."

"Was my mother there?"

Cheri nodded. "Yeah. She was my case worker at the time. She had to be."

"Did she know Travis?"

"I don't know."

Jax frowned. "None of this is making sense. Travis Anderson, someone from your past that tormented you, is dead. Did you have any friends in common?"

Cheri tried to rack her brain. "I can't remember. That house was made up of mostly boys. There was one more girl there."

"Were you close with her?"

"We weren't *best* friends or anything but we hung out sometimes. She was a couple years older than me. I haven't seen her since your mother removed me."

"And Roux was there, right—at the house?"

Her heart pinched when she suddenly remembered that Roux was still missing. "Yeah," she said feeling the tears burning the back of her eyes.

"Maybe my mom will have the answers. Someone knows something. Someone is filling Carl in on the people in your life."

"But who. All juvenile cases are sealed. Not even the cops can get into them, and Roux is the only other person in my life."

"I don't know, but there's a hole in this bucket because it's not holding water. Things just aren't fitting right."

"I know," she said, wearily rubbing her eyes.

"Well, let's grab something to eat and then we'll head to my mother's house. See if she can shed some light on this giant shit pile."

They pulled away from the garage and as they passed people on the streets it felt as if all eyes were on her. Was he out there, right that second, watching her? The thought turned her blood to ice.

Cheri stared out the window as they put New Orleans behind them. The scenery whizzed by them in a blur. She was to lost in her thoughts to really process anything on the other side of the glass. The sun was beginning to slip down into the sky. She hadn't even realized what time it was. They'd spent the entire day in New Orleans.

She was beginning to doze when she felt Jax's hand on her arm. "You can lean over here if it would make you more comfortable."

She was too tired to protest as she scooted across the bench and lay on her side. Her head rested on a rock hard thigh. It was the safest place she could be. In a slow comforting motion, Jax stroked her hair and soon her eyes began to grow heavy. With a yawn, she let sleep claim her, and with it came the worry, dread, and fear that something far worse was coming.

Lynn stared at all the papers. They'd been through the records of all the hospital personnel at least a dozen times and not one employee on the list threw up a red flag.

"Maybe they won't have a record," Levi said as he walked in and handed Lynn a fresh cup of coffee.

"You can bet they won't. The hospital has strict policies. They won't hire a surgeon if they have any kind of criminal history."

Levi sat at the table and began to shuffle some papers around. "Okay, so what if we're not looking for a surgeon?"

"Well, we've already ruled out custodians, orderlies and anyone that wouldn't have access that kind of stuff," Lynn said.

"Right, but what I'm saying is surgeons don't typically administer the drugs for surgery prep."

"So an anesthesiologist."

Levi nodded. "It's likely."

"That's a possibility. We've narrowed the list down to the people that have access to that kind of drug. It's smaller but there is still a hell of a lot of people on it."

"And we're certain that the General is the one we want to go with?" Levi asked.

Lynn nodded. "To me, it would make the most sense. Anderson could have been picked out as a target there."

"Yes, but *what* made him the target?"

Frustrated, Lynn let out a growl and popped a chalky anti-acid between his lips. "That, my friend, is the million-dollar question. Have we got an ID on the last victim?"

"No," Levi grunted as he thumbed through the files.

"Why the hell not?"

"Apparently there was another set of bodies found over in Shreveport and their lab is under construction. They ordered it done immediately."

Lynn slammed his fist down on the table and shot to his feet. "Damn it, my case takes priority. I need an I.D. on the victim now. Without it, we're dead in the water."

"I'll go see if I can hurry the process along."

Levi moved from the meeting room they'd been using, and Lynn sat down and crossed his arms tightly over his chest. His mind wandered back to the conversation with the doc—which hadn't really told them much more than they had already known. He'd placed Anderson in the Emergency room two nights before his body was found, which meant they could have been the last ones to see him alive.

Then he thought about the man and woman they'd run into as they were leaving the doctor's office. There was just something about them that bothered him. The story the man had fed them about his girlfriend getting implants wasn't sitting well with him at all.

He was mulling it over when Levi stepped back in the room. Lynn looked at the clock and back at his partner. Only ten minutes had passed.

"That was quick."

Levi beamed. "I used my charms."

Lynn rolled his eyes and took the folder from Levi, but before opening it he looked at his partner. "Hey. Did you get a look at that girl that was at the hospital today?"

Levy arched a bushy eyebrow. "There were several women at the hospital today. Care to be more specific?" he asked as he leaned a hip against the table and flipped through the pages.

"The girl and guy we met as we were leaving that plastic surgeon's office."

"Ahh, *that* girl. Yeah, I got a good look at'er. She was kinda hot. Why?"

"Did she look like she needed implants to you?"

Levi chuckled. "If that woman is getting implants her boyfriend is one lucky sonofabitch. She was pretty stacked already."

Lynn nodded and tugged at his mustache. "That's what I thought."

"Why?"

"I don't know. Something just felt off about them."

"Maybe they were just visiting the good doctor?" Levi offered.

"True, but why lie about getting work done?"

Levi shrugged. "I don't know, man, but you're grasping at straws now. What are the chances that completely random strangers at the same doc's office would have anything to do with this case?"

Lynn pushed it to the back of his mind for later as he turned his attention to the file he held in his hands. He knew Levi was right, but there was something about the couple that just felt off.

"Roux Devin LaTour. Lives at 3344 Crescent Drive," he read out loud.

"Looks like we're going to Crescent Drive, huh?"

"Looks like."

Lynn shouldered his side arms and shoved a roll of antacids in his pocket. He had a feeling it was going to be a long night. Again.

# 23

"Shit," Levi cursed as Lynn pulled his car behind the police cruiser parked at the curb. Red and blue lights lit up the area, pulling neighbors and passersby from their homes and onto the sidewalks.

"This doesn't look good," Levi said as he shoved the car into park and cut the engine.

His partner shook his head. "No, it really doesn't."

The two men climbed from the car and stepped around the caution tape.

"Detectives," one of the uniformed officers greeted with a nod.

"What we got?" Lynn asked.

The young officer looked down at his notes. "A neighbor called in and reported hearing glass being broken next door. Said she saw someone leaving through the back door. Then she said a little bit later, a man and woman left through the front."

"Did she see anything else?" Lynn asked as he jotted down the notes.

"Said the pair got into a late model Ford pickup— dark in color, possibly blue or black. She said they left in quite the hurry."

"When did she make the call?"

"Uh, looks like the call came in a little after five."

Lynn frowned and looked at his watch. "It's half past six. What took so long to get out here?"

"Had a robbery had to deal with, sir," the young officer stammered.

"Did you find anything else?" Levi asked as Lynn stepped around him and surveyed the yard. Groups of people were gathering in small clusters and media vans had already began to descend on the scene. In minutes the place would turn into a media circus.

The guy shook his head. "Just the broken glass in the back door. Aside from that, there doesn't seem to be have been anyone home for a couple of days."

"We need to get CSU out here and do a sweep," Lynn said as he walked over to his car and popped open the trunk. He removed a pair of booties to cover his shoes as well as a pair for Levi and a pair of gloves for each.

"CSU, sir?"

Lynn nodded. "This is the residence of one of the bodies found out at the bayou last night."

The uniform nodded once and spoke into his shoulder mic. Lynn handed the booties and gloves to Levi.

"Come on. We're going in." He stopped and looked at the crowd. The tiny hairs on the backs of his neck stood on end. Slowly he surveyed all the faces, but none were more incredible than the other.

"Sir?" The officer asked.

"Get someone to take photos of the people in the crowd."

The officer bobbed his head and hurried away.

At the front step, they covered their shoes and donned their gloves. Carefully they walked into the house. It was clean, obsessively so. They inched their way through the living room and hall, Lynn's keen eye looking for any signs of something being out of place. As they were walking by the kitchen, the sight of a full cat food bowl caught his attention.

"Someone's been here," he said, ticking his head toward the half eaten bowl of food.

"Okay but who?"

Feeling frustrated Lynn continued to sweep through the kitchen, picking up stacks of bills and unopened envelopes. As he did this, Levi went to inspect the rest of the house. While he was gone, a picture beside the phone caught his attention. He picked up the frame and studied the photo. In it, their victim smiled brightly back at the camera, his arm slung around a pretty young woman. Lynn frowned and lifted the picture for closer inspection.

"I'll be damned," he muttered.

Levi rounded the corner carrying a framed photo. He held it up, showing Lynn as Lynn was holding up the picture he'd found.

"You've got to be kidding me," Levi grunted as he took the picture and inspected it. "Are you sure this is her? I mean it looks similar to her, but. . . ."

"It's her, alright. People can change their hair color and style, but they can't change a look in their eyes."

"What are you talking about?"

Lynn pointed to the photos. "Look at her eyes. She's smiling and looks like she's carefree, but there's an emptiness there, like a shadow that is haunting her. The smile doesn't quite reach her eyes."

Levi arched a bushy brow at him. "You got all that from one picture, eh?"

He shook his head. "No. I saw it today too. People get nervous around cops, it's natural, but there was something about her that seemed . . . off."

Lynn turned his attention back to the woman in the photographs, holding them side by side. One was from several years ago. She was younger, blonde, smiling widely and without a care in the world—so it seemed. In the second picture, the woman was still smiling but the haunted look was more noticeable. She'd aged more, tiny wrinkles lined her face and her hair was dark brown. There was a sadness around her and a tiredness in her eyes, but it was the same woman from the hospital. He would stake his career on it.

"I would say this is hardly a coincidence."

Lynn shook his head. "In our line of work, there are no such things as coincidences."

"Do you think they were lovers?"

"Hard to tell from the pictures, but we need to find out who she is. I'd be willing to bet she knows more than she's letting on."

Levi walked over to the answering machine. "Hey, there are messages on here, but the numbers not blinking."

Using the end of his pen, Lynn pressed the play button. They listened as all the messages clicked through.

After they cycled through, Levi looked up, his skin pale. "What the hell did we just listen too?"

"He was being taunted."

"But whoever called sounded like they were at a party, and who was the two women talking?"

Lynn just shook his head. "The call came through on Saturday night. According to the M.E, he hadn't been dead for more than twelve hours."

"He's moving quicker."

"If he snatched LaTour by midnight, sliced him up and then dumped him, we're looking at him only keeping this one for a couple of hours. He kept Anderson for much longer than that."

Levi moved to the back of the house, Lynn following him. "So, he taunts LaTour for days. Then Saturday he calls with a final taunt. Before he knows what's happening, our guy breaks in and blitz attacks him. LaTour weighed maybe a buck fifty. It wouldn't be too hard to overpower him."

"There's no signs of struggle though, and the broken glass just happened today according to the call that came in."

"Maybe he snuck in the house?"

Lynn turned. "Have there been any other calls coming in from this house?" he asked one of the passing officers. He shook his head but another one came forward.

"I came by here Saturday night, responding to a call about phone calls."

"And did you find anything?"

"No. I did a sweep of the property but nothing seemed out of place."

Lynn frowned. "You were here, meaning that you were likely the last one to see him alive and you're just now telling us this?"

The cop scowled at him. "Listen, do you have any idea how many calls we get on a daily basis. I did a sweep and there was no signs of threats. I then patrolled by here for the rest of the evening and nothing looked out of place. I don't appreciate that you are insinuating that I didn't do my job, *detective*."

Without giving Lynn a chance to respond, the man turned and stomped from the room.

The officer was right. Lynn didn't have a right to say anything, but it still got beneath his skin knowing that the criminal was able to get in and out without being detected.

"So, he got in and out without anyone knowing or seeing anything. This bastard is smarter than what we gave him credit for."

"And he's leaving us with more damn questions than he is answers," Lynn grunted.

Lynn was about to make a comment when his phone buzzed in his pocket.

"Robichaud," he said gruffly. He listened as his partner continued to walk around the room. "What the hell does that have to do with us? You're shitting me. Way down there? Fine. We're on our way." He disconnected the call.

"What was that all about?"

"We've got another body," he said grimly.

"Please tell me that you're joking."

"I wish I were, kid."

They were just walking out the door when the crime scene unit arrived. "You're not going to find anything, but I want every inch of this house dusted for prints. Cabinet doors, banisters, hell find the cat and the dust him. I want every set of prints you can find."

"Yes, sir," the uniformed officer said before hurrying off.

Levi and Lynn climbed into the car. "Where are we headed?" Levi asked as they sped out of town.

"Dead Water," he said stiffly.

"Dead Water?! Why in the hell are we going down there?"

"That's where the body is."

"You sure it's one of ours?"

Lynn frowned. "Local brass seemed to think so. I don't really know at this point, but there is one thing I *do* know."

"What's that?"

"I'm sure as hell 'bout to get pissed the hell off."

Lynn's knuckles tightened on the steering wheel as they sped away from the city, making their way about as far south as they could before meeting the gulf. The only lead they had was the mysterious woman and man that was with her. Was it a lover's quarrel? Was it a case of jealousy? Was that why the woman looked so scared? Something wasn't adding it up and come hell or high water he was going to figure out what that missing piece was. There was no way this case was going to fall through his fingers.

"Cheri! Cheri! Wake up."

She could feel Jax's hand on her shoulder gently shaking her awake. It wasn't the movement that woke her, but the urgency in his voice. With a fuzzy head, Cheri pushed herself into a seated position. It was completely dark and it took her a few moments to realize that they were creeping down the road that lead to his mother's house. However, there was something up ahead that caused her to frown. Through the thick copse of trees police lights danced ominously.

She rubbed the heels of her hands over her eyes. The truck inched forward until he finally pulled to a stop beside one of the cruisers.

"What's going on?" she whispered.

The muscle in Jax's jaw twitched as he shook his head. He cut the engine and through the windshield, he could see several officers already making their way to where he was parked. "Stay here," he said tightly.

"Uh, how about no?!" she said defiantly.

His focus was too intent on the officers to argue as he pushed open the door and held it open for her to slide out beside him.

"Sir, this is a crime scene. We're going to have to ask you to leave," one of the younger officers said in an authoritative voice. The man couldn't have been more than twenty. He squared his shoulders and tried to look intimidating to Jax, who was a good head taller than he was.

"This is my parent's house. I'm not going anywhere," Jax said firmly as his gaze shifted to the second officer. "What is going on?"

"I'm sorry sir, but you cannot be here," the second officer insisted.

"Let them through," said gruff voice from behind the two men. The two officers gave Jax the once over and then parted as another officer stepped forward.

Jax gave the man a curt nod. "What the hell is going on, Howard? Where are my parents?" Jax's voice was beginning to raise as worry began to seep from him.

"Calm down, Jax. Your mom and dad are just fine. There's been a bit of an . . . incident."

Jax's eyes narrowed. "What kind of *incident?*"

"Jax? Honey?"

Lizabeth came rushing up from behind Howard. She elbowed past him to get to her son. When she did, she threw her arms around him, hugging him tightly. Jax folded his mother into a comforting embrace and when she stepped back, the woman's cheeks were wet with tears. It shook Cheri to the core to see the strong woman look so terrified. Because if Lizabeth Marceaux was scared, something was truly the matter.

"*Mère*, what is going on?" he asked, holding his mother out at arm's length.

"It was awful. We came home and someone sitt'n on da porch. When we got out and went up dere. . . ." Lizabeth's skin paled further, given her a waxen, ashy look. Her already thick accent became thicker.

"What happened?" Jax urged.

"Dat girl. Dat girl, she's dead. An lawd have mercy, she's all cut up and nekkid as da day she was born." Lizabeth's accent grew thicker the more stress she was under. It was something that Cheri had noted from a young age.

Jax nodded once. "Stay here with Cheri while I figure out what's going on."

Lizabeth nodded and Jax stalked away from them. Lizabeth turned and met Cheri's gaze head-on. "Baby, have you told Jax anythin'?"

"He' knows everything."

"I thought so. Listen, dere was somethin else with da body."

Cheri's brows drew into a frown. "Something else? Lizabeth, what are you talking about."

The older woman cast a careful glance over her shoulder to make sure they were alone. She reached into her pocket and removed a slip of paper, folded twice over. With shaking hands, she handed it over to Cheri.

For a long moment, Cheri just looked at the piece of paper as if it were going to bite her. Then slowly she reached out and took it. With unsteady fingers, she opened it. The edges were smeared in blood and the writing was dark brown and smeared. Cheri realized in horror that the writing was in blood. She swallowed past the lump in her throat and read.

*Guilty. You both are. Their blood will be on your hands. Their blood will cover you all.*

# 24

Cheri felt the color drain from her face as she looked up at Lizabeth. "What does this mean? Why in the hell did you take it off the body? You know what will happen if someone finds out that you did that," she hissed in a harsh whisper. Her eyes darted around to make sure no one was listening.

Lizabeth waved a dismissing hand. "I'm not worried bout that none. I'm more worried bout dis. Ya know what dis means, *bebe*," Lizabeth said quietly.

Cheri's stomach did a backflip and her lungs constricted. She shook her head slowly. "But h-he's dead. I saw him go overboard," Cheri stammered, lowering her voice.

"Yeah, but are ya sure ya saw him get taken by da gators?" Lizabeth asked, arching her dark eyebrows.

Cheri wracked her brain, trying to remember that night close to twenty-five years ago. She did see the gators pull him under. Didn't she? With horror, she realized that she never did see the gators take him down. It had been too dark. He could have very easily swum to shore. Could he have survived? Maybe she didn't hurt him as badly as she thought. What if he'd been plotting his revenge all these years? Carl had been a big man; it would be simple for him to overpower all these victims. It was him. It simply had to be. There were no other options. Her stomach lurched. Clapping her hand over her mouth, she ran around to the side of Jax's truck—still concealed by the shadows—and lost the contents of her stomach. She felt a strong hand on her back.

"It's okay, *bebe*. We gonna figure dis out," Lizabeth said with more conviction than Cheri felt.

Wiping her mouth with the back of her hand, Cheri shook her head. "You can't—I can't get you involved anymore. Jax is already in it enough. If something— No."

Lizabeth frowned and propped her hands on her ample hips, her features pulling down into a severe frown. "*Tuat t'en grosse bueche*," she barked.

Cheri blinked several times startled by the woman's harsh tone. "Did you just tell me to shut my mouth?"

The old woman nodded once. "I did! Now, ya listen ta me. We gonna figure this out. We just have ta be careful for a while." She nodded with finality, then as if nothing was happening behind her she eyed Cheri suspiciously. "What you two been doin t'day?"

"We went up to New Orleans."

She arched a graying eyebrow. "What you go to Nawlins fo'?"

Cheri wondered how much she needed to say. She swallowed. "There's been other . . . things happening."

"What. Things?" she asked slowly.

Cheri quickly explained everything.

Lizabeth pressed her hand to her ample bosom her brusque demeanor vanished. "Oh lawd, not Roux." There was a glimmer of tears in her eyes.

Cheri felt her heart break even more. Roux was gone. She didn't have proof but the deep feeling of dread in her gut told her that she would never see her beloved friend again.

Lizabeth folded her into her embrace as Cheri wanted to cry, but she didn't have the energy. Instead, she just took solace in the arms of the only woman in her life that had actually given a damn about her. After a few long moments, she pulled away. Lizabeth reached up and cupped her face.

"I'm so proud of you, *bebe*," she said.

"Why? I'm nothing special."

"Shut up, you. Outta all my kids, you the one that has had the most success. A lot of them poor souls just disappear or get thrown in jail, but you," she pointed a finger at Cheri's chest, "been bust'n your ass."

This time tears misted Cheri's eyes. Someone was actually proud of her. It was the first time she'd ever heard it. Cheri opened her mouth to say something but a new set of headlights coming down the drive caused her to stop

Lizabeth frowned. "Lawd, they gone tear up my yard. Honey, stay here. I need ya ta stay outta sight till we git dis mess figured out. Can ya do dat?"

Cheri nodded and Lizabeth turned and stalked away.

Cheri was still on the passenger side—hidden in the shadows. She pressed herself deeper into the darkness as an unmarked police car rolled by Jax's truck. She watched as Jax walked between two of the police cars and made his way back to where she stood, gently resting his hand in the middle of her back.

"Are you okay?" he asked quietly. Bits and pieces of her hair had fallen from the elastic holding in place. Reaching up he pushed it away from her face and tucked it behind her ear as he gently cupped her cheek.

"Not really," she croaked. Her throat was raw from heaving, and she was fairly certain her breath smelled like stomach acid and the onion rings she'd had earlier. If she'd been of sound mind, she might have winced at the thought of Jax standing so close. However, having Jax close was exactly what she needed.

His face was grim and Cheri's stomach fell to her feet. The expression on his face was a fluctuating mixture of relief, anger, sorrow and possibly regret. He stopped just in front of her.

"What's going on?" she asked quietly. "Does it have anything to do with . . . me?"

He shook his head. "I don't think so. This. . . ." He swallowed hard and he realized that he was having a hard time answering her because of his emotions.

Concerned she looked up at him. "Jax? What is it?"

He swallowed again. "This one wasn't about you. It was about me *or* my mom," he said hoarsely.

"What do you mean you or your mom?"

"It's the girl I ended things with a few months ago." Sadness was etched into the already tired features of his face.

"The woman in the pictures at your house?" she asked.

He nodded once.

"What happened?"

He just shook his head. "It's bad. Whoever did it left a messaged carved on her."

Cheri's eyes widened. "Carved?"

He didn't answer, but he didn't have to. They both knew she'd heard him correctly.

"W-what did it say?" she ventured, wondering if she really wanted to know the answer to that. As soon as he opened his mouth, she already regretted asking him, but it was too late to stop him.

*"All things point to you. Eye for an eye. Three down. Two. Too. Go."*

"What the hell does that mean?"

Jax lifted his big shoulder. "I don't know, but. . . ." His words drifted off as he looked down at her hand.

"What's that?" he asked.

She looked down at the piece of paper she still held clutched in her palm.

"Oh, uh, your mom."

Her gaze darted over to the car that was idling beside the police cruisers. It was obvious there were two people in there, but they weren't getting out. It made her more than a little nervous. She was about to comment when both front doors swung open. Cheri's stomach heaved once again, and her chest felt as if someone were sitting on it. Grabbing Jax's hand she pulled him deeper into the shadows beside the truck, the blood written note forgotten.

When he began to question her, she pressed a finger to her lips and pointed over his shoulder. He followed where she was pointing and let loose a low curse. The two new men on the scene were the same two men that they'd run into at the hospital. Detectives.

Things just got a whole lot more complicated.

# 25

"Thanks, Sam," Levi said as he disconnected the phone. They'd just pulled up to the new crime scene when Levi had gotten a call.

"Damn, this place is already a circle jerk. Think these backwater rent-a-cops know what the hell a murder even is?" Levi scratched at his beard.

"Don't like small town cops?"

He shrugged his shoulders. "Not that, just— Hell, never mind. Anyhow. That was Sam. He got LaTour's information. It turns out that his only emergency contact is one Cherilynn Bouvier."

"Okay. What do we know about her?"

"You're going to love this. It seems that Ms. Bouvier is a resident of Dead Water."

Lynn frowned, not liking where this was going at all. "Okay, so Ms. Bouvier was close with LaTour. Have we gotten anything back from LaTour's cell phone records?"

"Should have the records and his phone unlocked any time now. They found his cell under his bed. It was password protected, but they were able to crack it easily enough. They are just waiting to get everything from the company."

Lynn grunted. Things just kept getting complicated. Every time they thought they were getting somewhere, there was another screw thrown into the mix. It was getting tiresome and they'd only been working the case less than seventy-two hours. Bodies were piling up and there were no answers in sight.

"Well, let's see if the local department are standing around with their dicks in their hands, shall we?" Levi said.

Lynn chuckled at his partner's crudeness. They got out of the car and walked through the throng of officers— each attempting to investigate.

"Please stand back," Lynn barked as he made his way up the walk. The body was lying face down on a bench, her lifeless and purple face resting on the backs of her folded hands as if she were just taking a short nap. Blond hair was matted with blood and sticking to her face. The carving on her back caused him to stop in his tracks.

"*All things point to you. Eye for an eye. Three down. Two. Too. Go,*" he read out loud. The words started at her shoulders and had been carved with a precise and steady hand. The covered her back and ended on her bottom.

"Is she missing anything?"

"E-excuse me, sir?" a young officer looking more than a little green questioned. "Missing something?"

Lynn nodded impatiently as he squatted down to get a closer look. Using his pen, he lifted one of the girls neatly manicured fingers and frowned before looking back up at the officer. "Yes, you know a body part. Eye, ear, finger whatever."

The man shook his head. "Not that I've seen."

"Do we have a time of death?"

The young officer gulped. "The ME said best he can tell was around 10pm to 1am this morning."

Lynn nodded and jotted down some notes. "He dumped one and went directly to work on another. He has no cooling off period. This wasn't done here. The killer posed the body. See," he said pointing to the worn boards of the porch. "There's very little blood."

"So the killer is killing them somewhere else and then dumping," Levi said thoughtfully.

"It appears that way."

"But are we sure the same guy did this? It's nothing like the others. Maybe he's changing up his patterns to throw us off. Forensic countermeasure?"

Lynn looked doubtful. "I don't think that's the case. Serial killers are habitual. Very rarely do they change things up." He stared at the woman a moment longer. "He's playing a game with us. Trying to tell us that he's smarter than we are." Using his pen, he pushed back the hair from her face. She'd been pretty. He was about to stand when something caught his attention.

Frowning he looked closer. "Give me a light," he said without looking up. He held his hand up behind him. Behind him, there was a click as something was placed in his hand. Shining the light on the point he was staring at he brushed his finger over the small red dot.

"That. Right there. What do you see?"

Levi knelt down beside Lynn and leaned in. "Looks like a puncture wound. You think she was drugged?"

"I'd bet the farm on it. Look at her arm. More needle marks. We need to get her back to NOLA and have the ME look." Lynn removed his phone and snapped a picture of the wound and then a couple pictures of the woman's back.

"Do we know who she is yet?"

"Her name is Regina Kendrick."

Lynn turned to find a sturdy older woman standing beside the front door of the house.

"And you are?" Lynn asked, pushing himself to his feet.

"I'm Lizabeth Marceaux and dis my house," she said with a short nod.

"I'm detective Lynn Robichaud and this is my partner, Levi Moss."

"I know who ya are. You been all over the news."

"Did you know the victim?"

Lizabeth lifted her broad shoulders. "Somewhat. She used ta date my son, a few months back."

"And your son is?" Levi hedged, pen poised above his notepad.

"Jaxon Marceaux."

Levi jotted the name down and then excused himself. Lizabeth's sharp brown eyes followed him as Lynn stepped in her line of vision. "Were you close to the victim?"

"Not really. I knew'er well enough."

"Do you know of anyone who would want to harm her in any way?"

"Can't say I do."

Lynn nodded and looked around him. "Where were you and your husband this evening?"

"We went ta check our crawfish traps up da river a ways. When we came back we found dis girl layin' here like dis."

Lynn studied the woman. There was a keenness in her eyes that set him on edge. "Tell me, Mrs. Marceaux, what is it that you do for a living?"

"I'm retired," she said flatly.

"Retired from what?"

Lizabeth clenched her teeth together, her face tightening slightly. "I worked in child protective services."

This got Lynn's attention. "Did you know a Roux LaTour or a Travis Anderson?"

Lizabeth hesitated for a brief second before scratching her head and frowned slightly. "I can't say dat I can recall. I've worked with a lot of children in my day, detective. I don't r'member every case or child I worked with."

"I see." The tiny hairs on the back of Lynn's neck stood on end. There was something that this woman was not telling him.

"'Sides, even if I had known one of dem names, I couldn't tell ya anyhow. Dem files are protected."

"This is true, but both men are victims in a case we're working. A case that very well could be connected to this one here."

Lizabeth just shrugged her shoulders. "I don't know what ta tell ya. I barely knew Gina."

Lynn's brows shot up. "Forgive me, but Gina sounds like a name someone that was close to her would have used."

Unruffled Lizabeth didn't miss a beat. "As I said, *detective*, Gina dated my son for a minute. I knew'er as Gina, but that don't mean I knew'er well."

"Fair enough. Do you know where your son is? We'd like to have a word with him?"

"Not sure. Haven't talked to him t'day. If you have a card, I can tell'im ta call ya when I do."

He reached in his pocket and removed one of his cards. "Do you know why anyone would want to do this to you?"

She gave a bitter laugh. "Detective, I can tell you dis. Over my years I've pissed some people off mightly. Ta what extent, I honestly have no idea. Do I think one of the kids I took care of did this? Doubtful. One of their parents that I removed them from," she lifted a shoulder, "very possible. I've come across many a devilish people in my day, sir. At any rate, it's really too hard ta tell."

"Momma?! Momma?!" The sound of a frantic woman's voice caused them to spin around. A blond woman bounded up the steps and into the older woman's arms. Lizabeth hugged the girl and patted her head.

When the girl finally pulled away. "What's going on? Why—" Her eyes landed on the dead body and then flew back to her mother's face. "What the hell?"

"Ma'am, who might you be?" Lynn asked.

"Umm ... I-I'm Desire Marceaux. This is my mother."

"I see," Lynn said as he jotted something down. "And you sir?" He turned his attention to the man standing beside the young blond. His face had gone pale and his throat worked furiously, appearing as if he were about to be sick.

Finally, he tore his gaze away from the body. "I'm J-Jerry Alexander."

"Where you two this evening?"

"We were on our way back from dinner and saw the lights from the road. I was scared that something had happened to momma."

Lynn nodded. "What time did you go to dinner?"

"Ummm, around five or six and then we went to a movie," Jerry supplied.

Finally, Lynn closed his notepad. "If you can think of anything else." She took the card and nodded before ushering her family behind closed doors. As the body was being lifted onto the gurney, Levi made his way to Lynn's side.

"Looks like her boy Jaxon has done some time."

"What did he go up for?"

"Bootlegging."

Lynn frowned. "Is that all we have on him?"

"He has a handful of misdemeanor assault charges, unlawful conduct and aggravated assault, a couple drunk and disorderlies. I talked to the chief and it seems that Marceaux is a nice guy, for the most part."

Lynn snorted. "Can't be that nice with a record like that."

Levi lifted a big shoulder. "Seems like that's the case, though."

"Any of these charges been within the last little bit?"

He shook his head. "Nah. Most of them were before he went away. Looks like they happened mostly in his late teens and early twenties, but the last one was about six months ago. The charges were dropped and Marceaux walked away."

"Who filed the charges?"

Levi's mouth twisted into a wry grin. "Regina Kendrick."

Lynn's eyes widened and Levi nodded.

"Well, it looks like we need to be talking to this Jaxon."

"He owns a bar on the other side of town," Levi said.

"Well, I think I could use a cold drink, how about you?"

After making sure the rest of the crime scene was handled, Lynn and Levi climbed into the car and made their way down the long drive and headed toward Dead Water.

Inside the house, Cheri and Jax listened. Lizabeth stepped through the kitchen and into the living room. "Ya'll need to get outta here."

Jax nodded grimly. "It's only a matter of time before they put a name with my face. Once they do, they'll come looking for Cheri. They saw us today."

His mother frowned. "What do ya mean dey saw ya t'day?"

"Would someone please tell me what's going on?" Desire asked, frantically looking back and forth between everybody. "And why the hell is there a dead body on your front porch?"

"Desire, baby, not right now. Why don't you and Jerry go into the living room for a minute? Okay?"

"I'm not a child," she argued.

Jax stepped forward. "I promise we'll explain everything later, okay?"

Desire hesitated for a little bit longer before she grabbed Jerry by the hand and hauled him into the next room.

Jax stepped closer and lowered his voice. "We went up to N'Orleans to see Michael about the finger left in Cheri's freezer. They were leaving as we were going in."

She grunted. "They won't know bout Cheri," she said confidently.

Cheri felt sick. "They will."

All eyes turned to her. "What do you mean, they will?" Jax asked.

"I was Roux's emergency contact. It was listed under my married name, but they had my up to date address, and there were pictures of us together all over his place. If they've been to his house—especially those detectives," she said ticking her head toward the front porch, "they will figure out really quick. And if they draw the line between me and Travis. . . ." She trailed off, not able to even think about what would happen then.

"Dey only have speculation with Travis, *cher*. They can't prove you were da one dat he raped."

"They will see I was in the foster system and they will be able to draw the lines."

Lizabeth shook her head. "No dey won't."

Cheri looked at the older woman, confused. "But my files."

"Dey don't exist."

"What do you mean they don't exist?"

The older woman's eyes met hers. "I mean . . . dey don't exist. After you aged out of the system, I destroyed anything having to do with Cherilynn Deveau. As far as the government is concerned, you was never anything but the perfect citizen."

"Why? Why would you do that?" Cheri gasped, unable to believe that this woman in front of her would jeopardize so much.

"Because, child, the world done been unkind to ya. I figured I'd try to give ya a fresh start."

"You risked so much."

Lizabeth's eyes watered as she held her arms out and pulled her close to her chest. "I love ya, *bebe*. After everything dat man done gone and put you through and then Travis. It just wasn't fair," she said.

Cheri breathed in the scent of cinnamon and vanilla and smiled. When her own mother had hugged her, the only thing she'd been able to smell was stale cigarettes and whiskey. Finally, she pulled away and sniffled.

"Be that as it may, we still need to tell about the finger before this lands at our feet," Jax interrupted with a sigh. He raked his hands back through his hair, causing it to stand out in all different directions. If Cheri wasn't worried out of her mind, then she would have laughed.

"Jax, we can't. If we do that they will be able to tie me to everyone," Cheri said. "Why don't we just get rid of the damn thing? I mean seriously? It's too late to turn it in and if they happen to find it on us. . . . There's no way around it."

Jax nodded. "A valid point and we really don't need it anymore."

Cheri leaned back against the counter and crossed her arms. "We've got to do something to push their attention away from us."

"Why? We have airtight alibis. We were at the bar until late, a ton of people saw us there. Then today we were at the hospital."

"And if they ask about Roux?"

Cheri felt a pang of sorrow in her chest. "We will tell them that we went by there since we went into the city. Decided to drop by because he we hadn't heard from him."

"If you were as close as you say and you suspected something was wrong, why didn't you file a report?"

"We're both busy. Didn't think anything of it when he didn't answer or return my calls?" she offered, even though it was a balled faced lie.

He shook his head again. "Then why didn't you when you went to the house? There was broken glass in the back. You could have reported it then."

Cheri pushed her hands through her hair and let out a frustrated growl. "We didn't notice broken glass when we were there."

Jax shook his head. "They won't buy that. You just walked in, didn't notice anything out of the ordinary such as the fermented orange juice or the piles of mail or the fact that the cat bowl had been empty."

Thoroughly annoyed and frustrated she just closed her eyes. "Then what the hell are we supposed to do, Jax. Any explanation points right back to me. If not me, then you."

"This is what the sick bastard wants. He's playing a game with us. He's waiting for us to make a mistake and when we do, he will pounce." He leaned on the counter beside Cheri and draped an arm over her shoulder, pulling her into his side.

Jax stared at his mother, who just looked back at them with a calm, yet worried expression.

Cheri blew out an exaggerated sigh and scrubbed the heels of her hands over her eyes. "Jax, they will put this on you. You've done time, so they will look for a reason. It won't take much."

He shook his head. "They can't, not really."

She arched her brow and opened her mouth to say something, but Lizabeth made a sudden noise, causing them to turn their attention to her. "What is it?" Jax asked.

"Dis whole time, I've been trying ta wrack my brain. Somethin' just didn't set right. Dere was Travis and Roux and now Gina. Da first two made sense. Then I got ta thinking. There was another girl in dat house with ya, weren't there?"

Cheri nodded. "Yeah. G— Oh God." Cheri's eyes widened as things became clear.

"What is it?" he asked with a frown.

"*G* was what we called her—we didn't know her real name. I knew she looked familiar when I saw those pictures in your house, I just couldn't figure out why or how. It's been so long since I saw her. I mean we were just kids."

Lizabeth nodded, confirming Cheri's story. "I moved'er out shortly after I moved you and Roux."

"Did you know it was her?" Jax asked, swinging his gaze to his mom. "While we were dating?"

"No, I didn't cause if I did I shore would'a said somethin'. Dat girl was nothin' but problems fer me until she aged out. When she did, she up and vanished."

Jax removed a crumpled pack of smokes from his pocket and shook one out. Normally he wouldn't have smoke inside his mother's house, but things were dire. He rolled the flint and stuck the flame to the tip. It glowed to life as he took a deep soothing drag. Cheri watched as the muscles in his jaw ticked.

He exhaled and looked at his mom and then Cheri. "They're going to look into me and when they do, they aren't going to like what they see."

"Why?" Cheri asked.

"Well first thing they're going to see is my record." He pinned her with a gaze. "You know I have a record. It's not a secret, but they will look at it and see that a few months back, Gina filed assault charges on me."

Cheri frowned. "What? Why?"

"We'd gotten into a pretty nasty fight. It was the night we'd broken up. Things got a little heated. She punched me and when she went to swing again, I stopped her."

Her eyes widened. "You hit her?"

Jax looked momentarily hurt. "Of course not. She had a mean left hook—she broke my nose with the first swing. Anyhow, the second time she swung and I grabbed her wrist to stop her. When she jerked back, she lost her balance and fell. She ran to the cops and cried wolf. The next day, the cops showed up at my door with a warrant for my arrest. She'd told them I'd tried to rape her and when I didn't get what I wanted, I beat her."

"What happened?"

"She knew she wouldn't get anywhere, so she just dropped them."

"What? Just like that?"

Jax nodded. "It was obvious that she wasn't hurt. I had a broken nose to prove that I'd been the one on the short end of that stick. I'm not sure what changed her mind, but after I spent two nights in jail I was free to go. Hadn't seen or talked to her since."

Lizabeth's face turned red and she let out a string of Cajun curses that made Cheri's ears burn. "Dat cow is da one dat had you arrested? You didn't tell me."

He gave her a grim look. "Because there was no need in both of us being in jail," he said with a tired chuckle.

"And then she shows up dead on your mother's front porch."

Jax's face darkened. "They may have a motive for you with Travis, but they have a motive for me with Gina."

Cheri did not like where this was going. "And once they put all the pieces together, they are going to set us up as accomplices. I killed Gina for you because of the issues she caused and you killed Travis for me, or you killed Gina because she put you in jail and I killed Travis because he raped me." Her bottom lip trembled as she wrapped her arms around her waist. "But what about Roux. How does he play into this?" The thought of Roux being gone made her insides twist into knots.

Jax placed a comforting hand on her back. "First of all, we don't know he's dead."

She opened her mouth to argue, but he held up a hand. "We don't," he said firmly. "Which brings us to the scenario that they might think Roux was a lover caught in the line of fire?"

She snorted. "That's absurd."

"Is it?" he asked.

"What's that supposed to mean?"

"I mean, you two have this bond that goes back decades. He could have been in love with you and when he couldn't have you—"

Cheri held up her hand. "Just stop. I can't handle this. We've got to figure something out because if not, we're going to wind up in jail. That is if the sadistic bastard stalking us doesn't kill us first."

"Honey, she's right. Dey can't say anything about her wit Roux, but if dey figure out dat she's the one dat Travis . . . raped," she nearly choked on her words. "If dey figure dat out, dey 'ave a motive."

Cheri wanted to scream. She wanted to pull her hair out by the roots and scream until her throat bled. It was a game. Whoever was doing this to her was playing a game.

"They ain't got nutt'n on ya with dis girl. Ya'lls alibi is airtight."

"Until they get time of death."

She waved her hand. "Heard'em say it was between ten and one last night."

Cheri breathed out a sigh of relief. "We were both at the bar. There were at least three dozen people that saw us. Even Marvin was out there."

"Den ya ain't got nothing ta worry bout. Ya'll need ta get outta 'ere cause dey'll be out looking for ya. If dey done tink ya'll disappeared, it won't help none."

Jax pressed a kiss to his mother's forehead and grabbed Cheri's hand. Quietly, they snuck out the back door and kept to the shadows. Most of the commotion was around the front of the house. They waited until they saw the two detectives pull down the drive before getting in the truck and slowly following out. They drove with their lights of, completely hidden in the inky blackness of the forest. After the car pulled onto the highway they waited.

"I'd like to swing by my house to grab a few things," Cheri said as they watched the taillights of the cop car disappear over the hill.

"We need to get to the bar first. Then after we deal with the cops, we'll get your stuff."

"What if we didn't go to the bar? What if we went to my house?"

"Why?"

She lifted a shoulder. "Because they already know we were in N'Orleans. We just as easily be at my place or yours."

"That makes sense, I guess."

Silence weighed heavily between them as they drove down the dark highway.

"Roux' gone," she said softly.

"I keep telling you, we don't know that for sure."

She could see the slight flex of his jaw and she knew he was lying, but he was doing it to protect her. Jax remained silent, but she knew he was thinking the same thing.

Softly, blues music played in the background. It was a haunting song that drove chills the entire length of her body. It was an old song from the fifties and it was fitting.

"How's that for irony," she snorted.

Jax frowned and looked at her. "What?"

She ticked her jaw toward the radio. Reaching down, he turned the knob and the scratchy sound of blues grew louder. The haunting song of how a man came home to find sheets and pillows shredded all over the place and bloodstains on the wall reverberated through her head. *". . . better come clean, baby, cause soon find it out. Detectives gon be hanging round da door wanna know what it's all a'bout."*

"I don't know if this has anything to do with Carl now," she said as they turned down the road that lead to her house.

Jax shook his head. "I don't know how it could. You were already in the system when he was reported missing. You didn't know about his family so it's not likely they knew about you. What about your mother?"

Cheri flinched. "What about her?"

"Well, all you've said was that she never came home that night. Where was she? I mean did she not put up a fight when my mom took you in."

"I don't know," she said softly.

"What do you mean?"

She looked at him, the dash lights giving him an eerie glow. "I mean, I don't know. I haven't seen her since she left that day for work."

"She just vanished?"

She lifted her shoulder. She'd never really thought much about it. She assumed she'd just bailed, but now, she wasn't so sure. "I don't really give a shit what happened to her. As far as I'm concerned, she is the reason I am in this mess in the first place. If she would have kept her legs closed instead of worrying about her next fix, I wouldn't be here. We, wouldn't be in this situation." Venom dripped from her voice as a long-buried rage began to bubble up.

She'd spent days, weeks, months, and years cursing and hating her mother for what she'd done. At first, she'd tried to find her, but the café where she'd worked said that she'd never showed up to work. Later it was rumored that a female's body had been found in the dumpster. It was too badly beaten for an identity. Cheri had let it go.

When her own kids were born, Cheri had pushed that hate deep in the interior of her brain and refused to acknowledge it. Now, it seemed like all that hate was seeping out from the reaches of her mind. It was taking her to a very dark place, and she was getting extremely tired of it.

"If I find the person responsible for this, I will make sure their body is never found," she said vehemently.

Jax turned and gave her a look, and she cringed. He looked sinister. "Are you sure you want to go down that road?"

She hadn't been serious about killing somebody. Had she? She'd only been speaking out of frustration.

The more she thought about it, the more she realized that she was tired of being the victim. She'd been one since she was a child.

Cheri heaved a frustrated sigh. "I'm tired of being the victim, Jax. I'm tired of crying and I'm tired of being scared. I want this to end before more people I care about get hurt. That includes my kids."

He only nodded once. "Then that's what we will do."

She looked at him. "What? How?"

He blew out a long breath. "You're going to have to trust me, Cheri."

"But what are we going to do about the cops. They are entirely too close to this, Jax. One little slip-up and we'll both be screwed. Remember, Louisiana does carry the death penalty."

He pulled the truck to a stop in front of her house and let the engine idle for a moment. After putting it in park he turned and took her hand, holding it tightly between his. "It'll be okay. Let's just go in and get what you need. I'm sure when they don't find us at the bar they will come looking here first."

Either way, they needed to figure it out what their next step was, and they needed to do it quickly.

# 26

"Do you know when they will be back?" Lynn asked the little blonde behind the bar.

She shook her head as she continued to wipe the scarred surface with the wet rag. "Nah. Jax is off today. He usually doesn't come in on Monday's unless there's a delivery," she said with a shrug and looked up at them. Her steady blue gaze met his head on.

Lynn studied her, looking for tells for deceit and judging from her relaxed posture and the bored look on her face, she was being honest. It was either that or she deserved an Oscar. Finally, with a nod, he reached into his wallet and removed a card. "If you can think of anything, be sure to give us a call."

She took the card and without even looking at it stuffed it into the pocket of her denim shorts and continued about her duties.

Lynn and Levi stepped out of the bar. Lynn let go of a frustrated sigh and started down the steps. "What do you think?" Levi asked as they made their way down the pier, their footfalls echoing off the water below.

"I think that we need to find this Jaxon and Cherilynn," he grunted as they reached their car. They'd spent close to an hour at the bar trying to get answers, only to get absolutely nothing. Overhead the yellow light cast a muddy circle of light on the crushed shell parking lot.

Lynn settled behind the wheel and turned the engine over. A blast of cool air streamed out of the vents drying the sweat that had formed on his forehead.

"Do we have an address on her?" he asked as he put the car in gear and slowly pulled out of the lot. There had been a few patrons in the bar, mostly old weather-worn Cajuns enjoying a cold drink.

Levi flipped through a couple pages of notes and nodded. "Yeah, we pulled it from the information sheet on

LaTour's emergency contact list. It looks like it's 2736 Lumber Way."

Lynn programmed the address into the GPS and followed the direction.

"So what do you make out of this whole thing?" Levi asked as he flipped through the pages of Roux LaTour's file. Then he placed Regina's and Travis's beside it. What was the connection?

"It's hard to say. Something just isn't adding up. I don't know where the connection is between the three victims. Anderson was an ex-con with a love of amphetamines, while LaTour was quiet with no record and according to his file an upstanding citizen. Then—"

"We have Regina Kendrick. Not much on her either, aside from the charges she filed and then dropped on Marceaux," Levi supplied.

Lynn rubbed the back of his neck and focused on the road. Mentally he sifted through the clues they had with all three victims.

"What did the Marceaux woman say she did for a living?"

Levi thumbed through his notes. "She was a social worker." He looked at his partner and then frowned as he began to flip through the pages of Travis Anderson's file. "Foster care," he blurted out.

"Okay? Do you want to fill in those blanks?"

"It says in Anderson's file that he was in the system, bounced around from home to home until landing in juvie for raping a girl and then on to prison."

"And Marceaux was a social worker," Lynn supplied.

"Right. So what if Anderson was one of the kids that Marceaux handled."

"Okay, but her alibi is airtight and I don't see that woman murdering anyone."

"What if it's not about her? What if it's about his victim?"

"The rape vic?"

Levi nodded.

"I don't know. That seems like an awfully big leap. Besides, we have no way of knowing who his victim is. Docs are sealed."

Levi cursed and stared at the victims. "I don't know. I just have a feeling that this Cherilynn is the key to something."

"Why would she be? She's just the next of kin notification for LaTour?" Lynn couldn't really argue because he'd been thinking the same thing. What were the odds that they would run into them at the hospital and then see the same woman's picture all over a victim's home? If there was anything he'd learned during his years on the force, it was there were no such things as coincidences. There was something more there, he just couldn't figure out what it was.

"Do we have anything on this Cherilynn Bouvier?"

Levi frowned and chewed on his bottom lip. "I had them run a background check when we found out she was LaTour's emergency contact. Came back clean. Not so much as a speeding ticket."

"Nothing?"

"No, just that she's divorced with custody of two kids. Ex-husband is some sort of real estate broker or something up in Alexandria."

"Family history?"

"Nothing."

Lynn frowned. "Does it say where she was before she was married?"

"No man, I'm telling ya, there's nothing here. She is clean."

"Maybe a little too clean. Do we have birth records?"

"Not even that."

"Who doesn't have birth records?"

"Someone with something to hide?"

"Guess we're going to have to ask Ms. Bouvier to fill in some blanks."

"Looks like."

Hands flexed angrily. They never showed up. Why didn't they show up? They were *supposed* to show up. It's how it was supposed to go. Fury poured through veins as vengeful eyes watched the detectives walking down the pier. They were too far away to hear what they were saying. Overhead the muffled sounds of music drifted from the bar.

That bitch never showed up. An angry fist lashed out and slammed against one of the supporting stilts of the bar. Skin cracked and split open as blood dripped silently into the water.

It was almost over. They would all know the pain she caused everyone.

# 27

They sat in the truck a little bit longer, knowing they needed to get in and get gone. In the dim light, the house looked menacing, causing Cheri to question if she really needed clothes after all.

"What happened?" she asked quietly.

Jax turned and looked at her. "What do you mean?"

"I mean what happened? You told me you've killed before, but you've yet to tell me anything about it."

He shook his head. "We really don't have time for that right now. Let's just go in and get your things. Once we are back at my place, I'll tell you everything."

"Why back to your place?" she questioned.

"Because, whoever this is, has been in your house—on more than one occasion. He could be watching us right now."

She felt violated but taking a deep breath, she nodded. She was so sick and tired of feeling that way. She wanted to protest and stay at her own house but she knew that he was right. Staying with him until everything was figured out seemed to be the only thing that did make sense.

Finally, she gave a reluctant nod and as she did, he reached across the seat and took her hand once more. Lacing his fingers with hers, he gave her an assuring squeeze. "I'll go in with you," Jax said. For a moment she just stared at their linked hands. Her palm warmed from the touch as she moved her thumb against his. The strength he was lending her through his touch nearly choked her.

When she lifted her gaze, she found his eyes on hers, watching intently. She squirmed a little beneath their intensity. Her mouth felt coated with sand and her lips felt dry. Her tongue flicked out against her bottom lip and his eyes darted to her mouth, darkening hungrily. Butterflies took flight in the pit of her stomach.

*Not here. We can't do this here*, her mind screamed. He was leaning closer, or maybe she was. She really couldn't be sure which one of them was moving toward the other, but it had to stop.

Cheri dropped his hand and scooted back toward the door. "I can go in by myself. I'm not scared of the dark," she said teased lightly. Her attempt to ease the tension failed.

He didn't say a word as he studied her face for a few more moments. It couldn't have been more than a second, maybe two, but she was held captured by his eyes, making it impossible for her to look away. Finally, he put his hand on his door and shoved it open.

She didn't wait for him to reach her side of the truck before she leaned her shoulder against the door and gave it a hard shove. It came open on the first try, but she nearly fell to the ground. If the situation they were currently in hadn't been so serious, then perhaps she would have laughed. There would be no laughing until this nightmare was over.

The mugginess of the night clung to her skin. It was close to eleven and it was still miserably hot. She struggled to breathe as they began walking to the house. The air was so saturated with moisture, it felt like she was drowning. The smell of trash lingered on the still air.

The night around them was eerily quiet. The moon overhead was shrouded by thick clouds as rain once again threatened to fall. The only sound that could be heard was the crunching of dry grass beneath their feet. Not so much as a cricket or frog stirred.

"It's so quiet," Cheri whispered. The sound of her own voice startled her a little.

"N'other storm is rollin' in," he said by way of explanation.

By the time they reached the house, sweat was rolling between her breasts and down the center of her back. It was almost as if they'd hiked for miles instead of walking a couple hundred feet.

The house looked like a monster, lying asleep or in wait for its next victim. Their footfalls echoed on the steps and she winced, expecting them to creak, but when they didn't, she remembered that Jax had fixed that for her. She produced a key and slid it into the new lock. She'd told him that the lock was kind of a moot point considering the windows could be easily opened by peeling the cardboard box off of them. He hadn't been in the least bit amused.

After the tumbler in the lock gave with a soft *snick* Jax stepped forward, blocking her from the house. Before fully entering, his hand flattened against the wall in search of the light switch. There was an easy *click,* and muddy yellow light filled the living room.

He crossed over the threshold first and then she followed. Her nerves were pulled tight and the slow pace they were going was about to drive her insane. If anyone was in the house they were just going to have to get it over with, because she was sick and tired of waiting.

Annoyed, she elbowed by him and walked fully into the room. The cloying smell of mildew and mold greeted her. Without waiting for Jax, she walked down the hall in wide strides. She barged into her bedroom and flipped the switch. If there was someone hiding in there then they could just bring it on. Behind her, she heard Jax mutter something and quickly follow her.

"What the hell are you doing?" Jax asked as he grabbed her by the elbow and spun her around.

"What are you talking about? I'm getting my stuff."

"You know damn good and well what I'm talking about," he said gruffly.

She leveled her gaze on him. "I'm tired of it Jax. I'm tired of being scared. I'm tired of waiting for something to happen. I'm just tired of it. The bastard isn't going to be here waiting for me."

His eyes darkened. "You're so sure?"

"Yes!" she practically screamed.

"Why?" He crossed his arms tightly over his chest and pressed his lips into a thin line.

"Because. He's a sick, sadistic prick that is playing games. He's playing them with all of us. It would be too easy for him to be here waiting on me. He's getting off on making me scared and right now, it's pissing me off more than anything. I've been the victim my entire life. I'm so damn sick and tired of it, Jax. It's been one thing after another, after another, after another." She didn't give him a chance to respond as she went to the closet and jerked her old duffle from the top shelf.

She walked to the bed and turned it upside down, dumping the contents onto her bed. Some long-forgotten clothes fell out onto the mattress. Something else fell out and bounced to the floor. Kneeling beside the bed, she picked it up.

"What is it?" Jax asked as he took a step closer.

"It's a gift box like you'd use for a necklace or something."

"Have you ever seen it before?"

"No, I haven't," she muttered. Something on the inside rattled.

"Do you want me to open it?"

The only thing she could do was shake her head. Heart hammering against her ribs and fingers trembling, she gently eased back the lid. The hinges gave with a soft *pop*. The noise was enough to make her jump. A pair of thin, wire-framed glasses rested on a bed of white velvet. However, it wasn't just the glasses in the box. Her heart slammed against her ribs with such force, she was sure her they would break. For a moment her mind couldn't comprehend what she was looking at. Then everything clicked and she dropped the box. The glasses skid under the bed but the other item did not. It was in that moment she regretted wearing flip-flops.

The first thing she felt was the cold wetness of it as it landed. Her stomach rolled as she quickly shook her foot. It then fell to the floor with a sickening *splat* that caused bile to rise to the back of her throat.

She sucked in a sharp breath and just stared down at the offending object. Beside her, Jax knelt and retrieved the glasses and pushed himself back to his feet.

"Do you know where these belong?"

Cheri nodded as a lump formed in the back of her throat and tears burned her eyes. "They're Roux's," she said quietly. Then she looked down at her feet. "And that's *his* eye."

"Are you sure?" he asked as he knelt back down to get a closer look.

She felt herself nod. "Those are his glasses and I'm certain that is his . . . eye."

The floor seemed to tilt beneath her as she stared down at Roux's eye. It had once been the most beautiful shade of blue she'd ever seen. Always so kind and bright. Someone had stolen that light from him. The light was no longer there. Nothing was there. The blue eye was filmy as it stared up at her accusingly. The muscles and tendons trailed behind it like bloody worms. Her breathe died in her chest and her lungs felt like they were going to explode.

Jax retrieved the box and opened the lid once more. There was a bloody stain on the lining where they eye had been resting but something else caught his eye.

"See you soon," he read.

Too focused on keeping the floor from completely falling out from under her, she hadn't heard him.

"He wrote on the lid, 'see you soon.'"

The walls felt like they were closing in on her. Turning on her heels she raced from the house. The putrid scent of the dump attacked her senses as she collapsed to her knees. Her eyes watered as she angrily dug her fingers dug into the dry grass. She could feel her fingernails cracking and chipping under the pressure but she didn't care. Jax knelt beside her, his hand resting on her back.

Tears streaming down her cheeks climbed to her feet and angrily dashed them away. She was done. She'd had enough.

"Where are you?!" she screamed. Her throat burned fiercely but she ignored it.

"Cheri," Jax said in a warning tone.

She ignored him and spun around, looking back at her house and the shadows out beside it. She spread her arms out wide at her sides. "What are you waiting for?

Come get me you sick sonofabitch. COME ON!!!!" she screamed hysterically. "What are you waiting for?!"

"Cheri!" Jax said as he pulled her against his chest and tightly wrapped his arms around her. Her arms fell to her sides as she rested her cheek against the solid wall of his chest. She could feel the rapid *thump, thump, thu-thump*, of his heart. She didn't move as he rested his chin on the top of her head and stroked her hair—gently rocking them side to side.

"It's going to be okay," he said softly.

"No. No, it's not," she whispered. Any sliver of hope she'd been clinging to that Roux was still alive was just severed completely.

"He's gone," she whispered. She wanted to cry, but couldn't. She felt broken. Then a thought struck her, forcing her to move out of his arms. Her eyes grew wide.

"He knew."

Jax looked at her with confusion. "He who? Who knew what?"

"Whoever's doing this. They knew I'd be leaving. That's why he put it in my bag."

It made sense. Lightning flashed in the distance and was soon followed by the low rumble of thunder.

Anxiously, Jax looked around. His eyes scanning the shadows. A feeling of unease settled in his bones. He draped his arm over her shoulder and pulled her into his side as he guided her back to the house. "Come on. We need to get outta here."

It was as if she'd been put on autopilot as he led the way. Anger burned in the pit of his stomach and demons from his past began to creep up and clutch at him. His hands shook as he thought about those demons. No, now was not the time to think about them. Things were getting worse, and if he didn't watch their step, they very well could end up playing exactly into the killer's hands.

He guided them into her room, and she just sat on the bed. She watched as he moved around the room, throwing contents of the drawers into the bag. She knew she should be the one packing, but her brain was shutting down, and exhaustion was beginning to take over. She heard her name being called, but it felt like it was distant. Her eyes blinked rapidly as she tried to focus.

"Cheri!" This time she felt hands clasping her shoulder and giving them a jerk. The haze seemed to lift, and she saw Jax staring down at her. His face pinched with concern. Dark circles rested beneath his eyes, and she found herself wondering if she was the reason for them.

"Yeah?"

"We need to get going. I don't wanna be here no longer than we have too," he said as he slung the bag over his shoulder.

"Can you walk?"

The haze had cleared from her head, and everything around her was clearing up. She could still feel the pain in her chest, but she knew—deep down—that she needed to push through it. If she didn't, she was standing there dead already.

They were closing the door behind them when twin headlights washed over them before disappearing behind the truck. The car sat idling for a few minutes before the engine died, leaving the lights on.

"Shit," Jax muttered.

"Who do you think. . .?" The words expired on her lips. The two detectives slowly made their way to the house.

"What did you do with—" she said slowly from the corner of her mouth.

"In the bottom of the bag."

"Guess we're about to do this?!"

"Just follow my lead. Don't say anything about the finger or the eye."

"Pretty sure that's not exactly the kind of information I need to volunteer," she said sardonically. What are we going to do?"

"We're going to tell them the truth."

The four of them made eye contact, and the detectives stopped abruptly. It was hard to see the looks on their faces with the light at their backs, but if she had to guess, they were shocked. The tall one turned his head to the side and said something to his partner. The older one just nodded and turned back to face them. Cheri realized grimly that they'd just connected the dots. The detectives resumed walking as if nothing were wrong.

The kindness was gone from their faces as they watched them with accusing glares and guarded looks.

"I think it's about time we talked," Detective Robichaud said resting his hands on his hips.

She nodded. "I guess so."

Levi and Lynn pulled up behind a dark colored truck.

"Dark truck," Lynn said.

"Do you think it's the same that was seen at LaTour's earlier?"

"Don't know, but we'll run the plates later."

Both men climbed from the car and made their way around the truck. However, as they approached the house, they saw two people standing on the porch. Both men stopped.

"You've got to be shitting me," Levi said turning his head. "It's the same people from the hospital."

Lynn grunted. "This should be good."

# 28

Cheri unlocked the door and after reaching in turned on the porch light. She gave them the most genuine smile she could. "I would invite you in, but the air is broke, and last week, there was a water main break. Now, there's a black mold issue." She surprised herself by how easily the lie slipped from her tongue.

"Please, have a seat," she said, pointing to the chairs.

"It's okay. We'll stand," Detective Moss said as he eyed the chairs skeptically.

Cheri shrugged. "Suit yourself," she said as she took a seat.

"I'm detective Lynn Robichaud and this is my partner Levi Moss. We just need to ask you some questions."

Cheri nodded. "I remember seeing you guys earlier today."

"Can you tell me what the two of you were doing in N'awlins today?" Detective Robichaud asked.

"We were there seeing friend of mine," Jax said as he sat on the rickety table beside Cheri. His side brushed against her shoulder. She found comfort in the contact.

"Did this friend happen to be Dr. Michael Ross?"

"Yes, but you know that already," Jax said smoothly.

"What business did you have with the doctor?"

She watched as the hard look from Levi's face softened a touch when he looked at her. "Forgive me, but you don't seem the type of woman that needs implants."

She lifted a shoulder. "Maybe I want bigger tits," she said deadpan.

This caused the younger detective to cough and clear his throat, a light pink tint coloring his cheeks. If the situation hadn't been so tense, she would have found it funny.

"Can you tell us where you went after we saw you at the hospital?" Robichaud asked, resting his hands on his hips. The question was directed toward Cheri.

"After we talked to the doctor, we went to see a friend of mine."

"What's the name of your friend?"

Cheri felt a lump in her throat, but she swallowed it. "Roux LaTour."

Levi removed an 8x10 glossy photo from his folder. Bright blue eyes smiled back at her from behind wire-framed glasses. Her stomach rolled as she took the photo, careful not to reveal any emotions. It was the Roux she remembered—smiling, funny and kind.

"Is this Roux LaTour?"

"Yeah, that's him."

Their faces grew solemn. "I'm sorry to have to tell you this, but Mr. LaTour's body was found in the swamp early this morning."

Cheri gaped. "No!" Tears welled in her eyes and spilled down her cheeks. This was the one thing she didn't have to fake because the sorrow and grief were real. She felt Jax's arm circle her shoulders as he pulled her to his side. For a few moments she cried—genuinely cried. It was real, and she'd just heard out loud what she'd known in her heart all along. Roux was gone.

She could feel them watching her closely, gauging her response. After a few more moments, she composed herself. Lynn reached into his pocket and removed a neatly pressed square of cloth. He passed it to her and she wiped her eyes.

"Witnesses say that they saw a man and woman leaving his house this afternoon and getting into a dark, late model pick-up truck. Was that the two of you?"

Cheri nodded.

"What were you doing there?"

"I tried to call him on Sunday, like I did on most weeks, but he didn't answer. I didn't really think anything of it."

"Did he disappear often?"

"Sometimes he'd take off for a weekend and go to the casino or camping somewhere to clear his mind." *A lie.*

"How did you get into his house?"

"I have a spare key myself and I know where he keeps a spare outside. I went in and he wasn't home. Didn't look like he had been for a couple days. I fed the cat and then we left."

"If you were worried, why didn't you report it to the cops?"

Cheri tensed. "I wasn't really all that worried and I didn't want to cause a big freak out, especially if he was just gone somewhere and wasn't answering my calls."

"He ignored your calls frequently?"

"Sometimes. When he wanted to be left alone."
*Another lie.*

"Ms. Bouvier—"

"Cheri," she corrected.

Lynn nodded and started again. "Cheri, how often did you talk to Mr. LaTour."

"Once or twice a week. Sometimes not at all. Life happens, detectives, sometimes we forget to call the ones we care about."

Lynn removed his phone from his pocket and punched in a few buttons. "Were you aware that the back door glass was shattered?"

Her eyes grew wide. "No. We went into the kitchen and I fed the cat. That's all."

"You didn't go looking for him?"

"Why would I? It's obvious he wasn't home."

"Even after not hearing from him for a couple of days, you didn't search his home."

Cheri frowned, her anger was rapidly beginning to outweigh her grief. Jax pulled her hand into his and gave it a firm squeeze.

"Listen, detective. I didn't go rooting through Roux's place because I didn't feel like I needed too. I had no reason to believe anything was wrong. As I said sometimes he left for a couple of days. He was my best friend and like my brother—but we didn't share everything. If he needed space he took it, but he always came home. I was never worried."

Lynn removed his phone and pushed a couple of buttons. "If you weren't concerned then why does

LaTour's phone records indicate you tried calling a total of thirty-seven on Sunday?"

Cheri's heart slammed against her ribs because she knew what was coming next. Lynn pressed the speaker button and she listened as her scared voice played through the phone.

"*Roux, I don't know where you are, but something is going on here. I think someone—*" There was a brief pause. "*Roux, someone knows. I don't think I was imagining the other night. I think someone was really in here. I'm being watched. There's some weird shit going on. Just call me. Please.*" The line went dead and the four of them were silent.

"Care to explain what that was about?"

"I came home after work one night and someone had been in my house," she said as nonchalantly as possible.

"Did you report it?"

"No."

"Why not?"

"Because no offense, detectives, I don't particularly need unwanted attention from the cops."

"And whys that?" Levi asked.

"Because of my children. I'm trying to stay as low key as possible."

"And why's that?"

"My ex-husband is an asshole and he'd pounce on a chance to take the kids and keep me from seeing them."

"So you just shrugged off a possible home invasion?" Lynn asked. His dark brows furrowed. There was a tone of skepticism in his voice.

"Honestly, Detective, I wasn't that concerned. My son is a teenager. I've always kept my door unlocked because sometimes his friends like to crash here. Sometimes they may have had too much to drink. As long as they are respectful, I have an open door policy. Always have. I wasn't worried." She held her gaze steadily with his, silently willing him to believe her. Trying to calm her shaking hands, she placed them under her thighs and leaned forward, making her posture seem as casual as possible.

"It didn't sound like you weren't worried. In fact, it sounded quite the opposite." He played the recording again.

She shrugged. "I overreacted. We'd had a couple of drinks after work. I was a little tipsy. It was more than likely just one of my son's friends."

"You said *someone knows*. What did you mean?"

Her heart hammered against her ribs. This made her falter a little. What was she going to say? "There are a few things I'm not proud of in my past. I don't want my kids to think poorly of me because of some shitty mistakes from my past."

Lynn held her gaze for a few moments. It was a flimsy excuse and she knew it, but they hadn't asked about foster care yet and she most certainly wasn't going to offer up the information. Lynn jotted something down and then looked back up. His face was carefully blank, but she could see the wheels and thoughts chugging along in his brain.

"Did your ex-husband know Mr. LaTour?"

Cheri shook her head. "They met once when we were younger. Alex didn't like Roux and Roux despised Alex. I kept them from crossing paths as much as possible."

Levi made a note.

"How long did you and Mr. LaTour know each other?"

Here it was. This was what would connect everything together. Hopefully, the cards would fall in their favor.

"We grew up together."

"Where at?"

She hesitated for a moment. If she lied, it could throw them off, but for how long. They probably already knew Roux was from a home. "We were in a foster home," she said, knowing what was about to happen.

That got their attention. "You and LaTour were in the foster care together?" Lynn asked.

"We were. He aged out. He tried to hang around until I aged out, but I got bounced to another house."

"Why were you placed into foster care?"

She took a deep shuddering breath. "My father was some one night stand for my mother. She married a man when I was ten and we moved in with him. One night my mother never came home from work. When I woke up the next morning I was all alone. I haven't seen or heard from that man since and my mother's body was found in the dumpster behind the diner where she worked." It was the same story she'd told for years if anyone asked her. She'd been abandoned by two drunks, found by Lizabeth Marceaux several days later when she didn't show up for school.

"You never saw your stepfather again?"

"No."

"What was his name?"

She shivered. The power that that her stepfather had over her was maddening. Slowly, she pushed out the breath. "Carl Briggs."

"Did you know this man?"

Levi presented her with a photo of Travis Anderson. Her skin began to crawl. Though his hair was longer and greasier, he still had the empty, dangerous look in his eyes. There was no way to hide the repulsion that swam over her.

Carefully, she kept her face blank. "I did. It's Travis Anderson."

"What does he have to do with anything?" Jax asked, finally speaking up.

"Well, his body was found a couple days ago in the swamp. How did you know him?"

She took a deep breath. Here went nothing. "He was in the same house Roux and I were in for a while. He got removed."

"Why?"

She lifted her gaze, slowly meeting their gazes. "He was removed and taken to juvie because he'd been raping me."

Lynn frowned. "*You're* the girl Anderson was assaulting?"

"No, detective," she hissed vehemently. "I'm the girl he was *raping*."

"When was the last time you saw Anderson?" he continued.

"In court. I've not seen nor talked to him since. I didn't even know he was out of prison."

Both men nodded. "While you were in foster care, did you know Lizabeth Marceaux?"

She looked up at Jaxson. "I did. She was my caseworker."

"She was your caseworker and as it happens the mother of your boyfriend?" There was no denying the skepticism in his voice.

"It's true, but I didn't find out about it until Saturday night at his family reunion. We only started dating a short time ago. He asked me to work the reunion and I did."

"You work for him?"

"Yes, I work at the bar with him. Have for almost a week now?!" she said looking up to him for confirmation.

"Yeah, you started about a week and a half ago, closer to two weeks and you were quite the pain in the ass," he said. Cheri was impressed by the lovingness in his voice.

"Was Mrs. Marceaux also Mr. LaTour's case worker?"

"I think so, but I can't be for certain."

"What about Anderson's?"

She shook her head and lifted her eyebrows. "Again, I don't know. I wasn't really concerned with others at that point in my life. She helped me out of a shitty situation and helped me find a home that cared for me. I met my ex-husband just a little before I aged out and we were married.

"After that, I left and didn't look back. Saturday night was the first night I'd seen Liz in over two decades."

Robichaud jotted something else down and turned his attention to Jax.

"And how do you know Regina Kendrick, Mr. Marceaux?"

"We used to date."

"Are you aware that her body was found on your mother's front porch tonight?"

"My mother called and told me that she was."

"And you're telling us that it's a coincidence that the woman you, Mr. Marceaux, used to date was dead on your mother's front porch." Cheri looked up at Jax from the corner of her eye. If he was affected by the questioning, he didn't show it. She hoped and prayed that she was doing as well.

"I haven't seen Gina since we split some six or seven months ago."

"Not since she filed charges against you for assault," Levi added.

"And then dropped them," Jax said smoothly.

"Tell us, Mr. Marceaux, have you always had a hot temper on you?"

This time Cheri looked up at him, waiting for his answer just like the detectives were. Still, cool and collected, he lifted a shoulder.

"I'm a hot-blooded Cajun, detectives. Of course, I've got a temper, but I've never once hit a woman."

"But according to the report, Ms. Kendrick had claimed that you shoved her and bruised her wrists."

"I did shove her. Make no mistake about it, sirs, I will never hit a woman, however, I don't believe that should give a woman free reign to hit a man whenever she wants. After the third time she slapped me I did shove her. How she got the bruise on her wrists is beyond me."

Cheri flushed a little, remembering how she'd slapped Jax early on. Now she felt a touch of guilt.

"Did you know Ms. Kendrick?" Levi asked, bringing the conversation back around to Cheri.

"I did, but I haven't seen her in over twenty years, give or take."

"How did you know her?"

"We crossed paths in one of the foster homes we were in."

Both detective's eyes grew wide. "Was she in the same house as you, Mr. LaTour and Mr. Anderson?"

"For a time."

"Was she there during Anderson's attack?"

Cheri shook her head. "She left beforehand."

Levi was jotting notes furiously in his notepad. His bushy brows were drawn together in frown of concentration. Cheri's insides rolled and spun out of control. The entire time she wanted to look at the duffle bag. She kept having images of blood running from the seams and onto the worn porch boards by their feet. She knew it wasn't logical but how in the hell would she explain the eye?

"Can you both account for your whereabouts Friday night?" Lynn asked.

"We were at the bar until after closing time," Jax supplied.

"Which is?"

"Last call is at one. We close up around two. Sometimes a little later."

"Can anyone corroborate that?"

A smug smile tilted Jax's lips. "Yes, about two hundred or more people, my employees, the live band I had and if that don't work, the surveillance footage. Which also has dates and time stamps on it." This made Lynn frown and Cheri knew that they'd just been stumped. Their alibi was airtight.

Cheri looked up at him, shocked about hearing there was surveillance in the bar. He just smiled.

"What about Saturday night?"

"We were at my family reunion. We got there about three in the afternoon because we were catering. We set up and didn't leave until close to two o'clock. All my family was there, and let me just help you out with Sunday too. I brought Cheri home because after we were finished catering, we drank. She had a little too much. I crashed here and then got up the next morning to make some repairs around here. I know the lumber store owner so he opened the store up for me to purchase supplies. I have the receipts from all my purchases and you can see the repairs here. Cheri was here with me the whole time, and then, we went to work that evening. Again, we were there until closed."

"Did you then bring Ms. Bouvier home?"

Jax shook his head. "Her air was still on the fritz so I let her crash at my place."

"What time was that?"

"Left the bar somewhere around three-three thirty."

"And you just went back to your place?"

Jax nodded. "We did. She slept in my room and I slept on the couch. We got up the next morning and went to N'awlins, and here we are."

Levi was scribbling furiously. "Let me get this straight," he said, looking at Cheri. "The four of you, Ms. Kendrick, Mr. LaTour and Mr. Anderson were all living in the same foster home at one point."

Cheri slowly nodded. "For a brief moment."

"Was there anyone else, any other kids there while you were there?"

Cheri frowned as she searched through her brain. "There weren't any new kids that were brought in while I was there, but I think there was one more boy there. He was older because he aged out, or maybe he got moved, I don't really remember him. I didn't see him around much, only a couple of times and then when everything started happening--," she shrugged.

Lynn nodded his understanding. "That tends to happen. A victim of sexual abuse will block everything and everyone out. Do you happen remember his name?"

Cheri struggled to remember. "No. I'm sorry but I can't."

"Any little detail, no matter how small."

She shook her head again. "I'm sorry, but I don't remember much of anything from that house and forgive me for saying, I don't really want to."

"That's understandable. If you can remember it would be helpful." Lynn removed a card from his wallet and handed it to her.

She nodded and accepted it. There was nothing special about the paper rectangle and yet, it felt as if it weighed a thousand pounds. "If I can remember who he is, I'll call."

Levi looked at Lynn who was staring at Cheri. Cheri was holding his gaze steadily. She knew that if she so much as batted an eyelash, she'd look as guilty as she felt. When he finally looked at his partner, she let out a slow sigh of relief.

Both men nodded and walked away. It was only after their headlights were backing down her drive and then disappearing down the road that she was able to breathe. Cheri sagged against Jax's leg.

"You did great," he said looking down at her and stroking her head.

She looked up at him with a playful little frown. "I didn't know the Queen had surveillance."

"We had a break-in a couple years back. Stole a bunch of booze and emptied my safe. I put the cameras in shortly after. I don't typically tell people about it. Trixie, Cookie, and Marvin knows but that's about it."

"Do you think they bought all that?"

He lifted his shoulder and pushed to his feet. "We didn't lie about much."

"We didn't tell them the stuff we needed too either."

Jax stooped down and gathered the bag. After slinging it over his shoulder, he offered her a hand. Taking it, she allowed him to pull her to her feet.

"I'm following the don't ask, don't tell method. They didn't ask and I sure as hell ain't telling," he said as they walked down the front steps.

"What are we going to do ... with the eye and finger?"

"We're going to make sure they disappear."

Cheri flinched as he slammed the door and walked around the front of the truck. He jumped behind the wheel and turned the engine over. As he backed away from the house, she stared at the shadows beyond it. She had a distinct feeling that this was all going to be over soon. She just prayed that they were the ones who came out on the winning side.

As they made their way to Jax's house, she was quiet, lost in thought.

"Are you okay?"

Cheri jumped, a little startled by Jax's sudden intrusion into her thoughts. She frowned when she realized they were already at his place. Jax frowned. "Cheri? What's going on in that head of yours?"

She let out a frustrated sigh as she climbed out of the truck. Lightning fragmented the sky overhead and thunder rumbled as fat drops of rain began to fall. He followed and they walked up to his front porch. She stopped at the base of the steps and turned, looking up at him. "You know how there is something you know you need to remember but you can't?"

"I'm not sure I follow."

"Well, it was after that detective asked if there was another kid that had lived in the house with us. Until he'd brought it up, I never thought about it. In fact, I'd forgot about him."

"Do you remember who he was?"

She shook her head and frowned. "Not much more than I told them. He studied a lot and worked at the library. He seemed harmless enough, but. . . ."

"But what?"

"Jax, I don't know. It seems like there is something there I should know. Like it's right there in my face and I can't see it." Her brows furrowed as she concentrated on the string that was just outside of her reach.

"Hey," Jax said softly as he stepped closer to her. Reaching forward, he cupped her cheek. It wasn't an overly romantic gesture so much as it was one to give her comfort. He'd been doing that a lot lately. She closed her eyes and leaned into his touch, covering the back of his hand with her palm.

"You've got this. You're safe here with me," he assured her.

For a short moment, she left her eyes closed. She didn't want to open them because if she did, she was afraid that the moment they were sharing would vanish. Somewhere along the way, after the heated arguments, the snarky comments, and all the bullshit she'd been through, something was stirred to life, and she was certain that Jax was responsible for that little spark. It was that spark that scared her almost as badly as the killer.

Finally, she opened her eyes she gasped. His face was inches from hers. Her throat went dry as he moved closer. She kept her eyes glued to his and she could feel herself being pulled into their depths. Lightning flashed and thunder rumbled once more. In the bright burst of light, she could see the small flecks of gold in his irises. Funny how she had never noticed that before when he'd kissed her.

The rain was falling steadily now. However, just like the thunder, she didn't notice. She was rooted to the ground and lost in Jax. There was an intensity that had been building since the day they first met. It was had only been getting stronger and growing faster with each night they worked together and each second they spent together after that. The energy was kinetic, picking up steam and power until it threatened to destroy the both of them.

Her heart stammered around in her chest as he placed a hand lightly on her hip. She could feel the heat of his palm through the denim of her shorts. His other hand fell from her face. Rain was soaking them, dripping off the end of his nose, matting his hair to his head. Her hair fell in drenched strands around shoulders, sticking to her face.

Using the backs of his knuckles, he drew them down her bare arm. The slight touch caused goosebumps to rise.

Lips parted, breaths coming out in short bursts, she licked her bottom lip. When had she eaten sand? Better yet, when in the hell had she swallowed cotton? His eyes darted to her lips and a low groan came from the back of his throat. It was a sound that reverberated throughout her body and all the way to her toes. It was the last sound she heard as his mouth swept down and captured hers.

This time, she didn't fight it—didn't push him away. This time she allowed him to press her roughly against the support beam of the porch, pinning her there with the solid wall of his body. His hand reached beneath her hair and cupped the back of her neck. It was a firm and possessive hold and she found herself melting further into him. Thunder clapped loudly around them and the rain fell harder.

His tongue dipped and swirled against hers, teasing and tasting but always giving and never taking. She clung to his arms, afraid that if she let go, he would stop. It was in that second she realized that she didn't *want* him to stop. She needed this and she needed him. The thought of needing a man in her life should scare her, but for some reason, with this man, it didn't. Not even a little bit.

Jax's mouth moved from her lips, kissing along her jawline. When they reached to column of her neck she gasped and pushed her body into his. His hands skimmed the skin just beneath the hem of her shirt as he wrapped her in his arms and pulled her close. She stiffened when his fingers brushed against her scars. His lips stilled and he moved away.

His eyes, cloudy with lust, met hers. "Come on," he said, taking her by the hand and pulling her after him.

She frowned, confused. "Okay."

"I'm not going to do this out here," he said, tugging on her hand.

She didn't say a word as they walked up the steps and through the front door. As they did, he slammed it and spun around. Using his body, he forced her back against the wall. His fingers laced with hers as he lifted them high above her head.

Outside, their kisses had been one of longing and desire. Inside, their passion raged more furious than the storm outside. She gasped as he bit her bottom lip before attacking her neck once more. There was no going back. She was all in and in that moment she made the decision to just let the cards fall how fate intended for them too. If there was a chance she was going to die tomorrow, then she was going to live one hell of a night.

# 29

"What do you think?" Levi asked as he pulled the car out onto the highway that would lead them back to New Orleans.

Lynn reached inside his pocket and pulled out the package of antacids. He popped two of the chalky tabs into his mouth. "I think we have a connection now."

"All of them were in foster care. Do you think she's in trouble?"

"I think she is scared. She could be in trouble but with that big Cajun at her side, I don't see anyone getting too close to her."

"Do you think she's scared of him?"

Lynn frowned and thought about it for a second. "No. I don't think so. I mean I'm sure he has a temper, but I didn't get that vibe."

"And since that girl was deposited on the front porch of his mother's place, I'm more inclined to think it's about his mom than it is him."

"She was Cheri's caseworker."

"You do realize, that because it's the foster system, it's going to make everything that much harder. I don't think these people are involved, but you never know. We need to do some more digging, see if we can place them anywhere near the crime scenes.

Lynn shook his head. "Their alibis are going to check out."

"How do you know?"

"Because after doing this job for so long, you learn to read people. They weren't shifty or nervous. Cheri was shaken because of Roux and you can't fake that kind of emotion. They're not who we're looking for."

Levi grunted. "They may not be who we're look'n for but I'd bet the farm that they know more than they was sayin'."

"Maybe," Lynn said simply.

"Who we looking for then? Someone that knows about medicine and the foster system?"

"Lizabeth Marceaux fits one of those profiles but not the other. Dr. Ross fits the medical side but not the other."

"That we know of. The doctor is well-liked," came his grunted response.

"Sometimes those are the ones that make the best killers."

"I don't see the Marceaux woman dumping vic on her own front porch. Maybe it's someone that was in the foster system but also knows about the medical scene."

Lynn chewed on the chalky tablet before looking over at his partner. "Sometimes serial killers will inject themselves into the investigation. It makes them feel the power. They can manipulate the investigation any way they want. It would be easier for someone to get knowledge bout the foster system than it would be for them to on medical stuff, but then again, anything's possible with the internet."

"You're a profiler now?"

Lynn chuckled. It was a dry sound. "No, but I've worked with a few in my day."

"Mrs. Marceaux doesn't fit the profile of our killer."

"That's true, but it's not unheard of."

"I don't like her for this either."

"Me neither. These people are being targeted for a reason, and I have a feeling it has to do with their childhood. I want everything we can find on Cheri Bouvier and the others, births, birth parents. We're missing something."

"But you just said you didn't think she was responsible." Levi frowned, his bushy eyebrows drawing down over his face.

"I don't think she's responsible but if she was from the same house as the others—"

"She could be next," Levi finished.

Lynn nodded. He had a sinking feeling in his gut. Something very bad was about to happen. "We're looking for someone that has intimate knowledge of the foster system as well as a medical background. If the criteria fits, then he's somewhere between the ages of thirty-five and forty. He's going to blend into society and look completely normal. This killer is smooth and he knows it. I also want to look into that other kid she mentioned," Lynn said grimly.

"Where do we stand with Dr. Ross? I mean he did tell us about Anderson."

"I don't know." Lynn frowned. Until now he really hadn't thought about the doctor as a suspect, but now it felt like there might be a few missing pieces clicking into place.

"He's got a connection with Bouvier and Marceaux, he's smooth and well spoken."

"It wouldn't hurt to dig a little deeper. *Something* about him is off. No one can be that squeaky clean." Then Levi looked at him, with a cautious expression.

"What are you thinking?" Lynn pressed.

"What if the three of them are working together?"

"Go on."

"Well, Marceaux and Bouvier's alibis may be airtight, but if the doctor's isn't."

Lynn nodded and then added. "He could be taking them, like Anderson at the emergency room. He follows Anderson home, blitz attacks, and then kidnaps him. Then Marceaux does the deed and dumps him in the swamp. They do this to avenge the girl's rape."

"But then they decide they might like it a little bit more than they thought so they decide to go after LaTour."

Lynn shook his head. "No. The girl didn't have anything to do with LaTour. She was genuinely shocked about it."

"So when she finds out, maybe she takes it out on the ex-girlfriend?"

"I don't know, Levi. This seems all to cut and dry. Why would they kill people they have connections too in one way or the other? They can be all tied back to them.."

"One thing's for sure. We need to take a deeper look at that doctor." Levi grunted as he scratched at a spot on his cheek.

Lynn had to agree. It would make sense as to how the victims were injected with the paralyzing neuroblocker. The doctor had access to it. Maybe it did warrant another look. He wanted to kick himself for not seeing it earlier. Of course, the doctor would point them in a different direction. It would be simple for him to claim ignorance and only feed them the information they needed to know—just enough to keep them going.

"He seems like such a great guy, though."

Lynn snorted derisively. "Philip Markoff was in the national honor society and a member of the youth court."

"Philip Markoff? That was the Craigslist killer caught in 2010, right?"

"Yeah. The kid was a med student with a bright and promising future. Then there was Ted Bundy. That man worked a suicide hotline. The point is, some serial killers blend into society. They don't always, but can be upstanding citizens that are active in the community. Very seldom are actual serial killers the dregs of society."

"I guess," Levi muttered.

He cursed under his breath as he picked up his phone and tapped the screen. He dialed a number waited impatiently for the line to connect. "I need you to get everything you can on a Doctor Michael Ross. He is a plastic surgeon over at University." There was a pause in the line as the man on the other side took notes. "I want everything going all the way back to his childhood. Family history, the whole thing, and put a rush on it. We're running out of time."

He didn't wait for a response as he disconnected the phone and looked at the file on his lap. Levi pressed the gas, shooting them through the darkness and down the two-lane highway. Swamps surrounded them on both sides of the road. They were literally about as far south as one could get. Lynn watched the swamps as they were shrouded in heavy shadows and darkness. Rain began to pelt the windshield as lightning fractured the sky. It would be so easy for someone to completely disappear.

# 30

Cheri snaked her arms around his neck and deepened the kiss as he held her prisoner in his arms. His arms tightened around her as he walked through the living room and into the dark bedroom. Outside the storm raged on, but inside a different kind of storm was brewing.

After he placed her on her feet he took a step back and reached over and turned on the lamp beside the bed. There was a soft *click* and the room was bathed in warm, dim light. He moved to stand in front of her once more. She lifted her gaze to meet his and gasped. The intensity that she saw there stole her breath. Never in her life had she seen such an intense look.

He lowered his mouth to hers, but this time it was different. While the urgency was still there, it was a soft, lingering kiss. Her eyes drifted closed as she stepped closer to him. Other senses began to take over. She could smell the faint scent of his cologne mixed with the light scent of tobacco. It wasn't overpowering on him like it was on some.

Her hands rested on his hips, thumbs just beneath the hem of his wet shirt. Heat from his body radiated out and onto her hands. Slowly, she inched them up until her hands were completely on bare skin. He shuttered under her touch.

The stubble covering his chin scraped against her face. The sensual feel of it only teased her senses further. She closed the last little bit of distance there was between them and draped her arms over his shoulders. One hand sifted through the silky strands of black hair at the back of his neck while the other reveled in the feeling of tight muscles dancing beneath her palms.

Finally, he broke away, pressing his forehead against hers. Their breaths mingled, but their eyes remained closed.

"Do you want me to stop?" he asked in a ragged voice.

"What?"

He took a deep shaky breath and pulled away from her, but just a bit. "If you want me to stop, then you're going to have to tell me now." His voice was trembling as the hold on his control was slipping.

For a second she hesitated and then in that moment, she realized that she didn't want to hesitate anymore. There had been too much bad in her life. Jax was the first man ever that had come into her life expecting nothing. There were no ulterior motives, there was no force used, no mind games . . . nothing.

She had no idea what tomorrow or the next day was going to bring, but she would at least cling to the night. Somehow over the course of the last two weeks, Jax had become her safe place. She wasn't sure how or when it had happened, but it had. Somewhere amongst the bickering, fighting, and name-calling, she'd found herself falling in love for this man. It was a startling revelation and at the same time, it felt right. Everything had always felt forced with Alex and any other man, but not Jax. It was all natural.

She felt his finger under her chin, lifting her face to his. "*Mon Cher?*" he inquired softly.

Cheri's heart fluttered. The sound of French on his lips made her stomach tighten into dancing little knots.

Reaching up she cupped his face, whiskers scratching the palm of her hand. "I'm not sure of anything these days, but this," she took his hand and brought it to her lips, "I'm certain of."

A wide smile spread across his face and as the fire and hunger returned in his eyes, his lips captured hers once more. Hand skimmed her waist as he lifted her shirt up and over her head. His mouth returned to hers in a searing kiss that left her weak in the knees. Reaching behind his head, he pulled his shirt off. His beautifully tanned chest rippled in front of her. She licked her dry lips as she brought her hands up and gently flattened them over the muscles. His eyes drifted closed.

"Your hands feel so good," he said softly. When his eyes opened, they were cloudy with lust. Reaching for her, he wrapped his arms around her and pulled her into his chest. Flesh against flesh, the contact was something she had no idea she'd been missing until that moment.

As his hands roamed over her back, Cheri stiffened. Long calloused fingers brushed against the jagged scars marring her flesh. He pulled away and looked down at her. In that moment she felt completely vulnerable. Gently he turned her around and worked the clasps on her bra. As he slipped the straps over her shoulders he kissed the bare skin. She crossed her arms over her chest as he removed her bra and tossed it to the side.

Squeezing her eyes tightly closed, she pressed back the urge to cover her extra curves. She'd only been with one guy her entire life and he'd only shown disgust at her marks and size. This was a huge step for her and more than the murderer stalking her, it scared her.

Taking his time, Jax removed the elastic from her hair and allowed the waves to tumble down over her shoulders and to her back in wet strands.

"Beautiful," he murmured as he pressed his lips to her shoulders. The contact felt good but she was still struggling to let it go. "Turn around," he whispered.

Taking a deep breath, she slowly turned, keeping her arms crossed tightly over her chest. When she lifted her watery gaze to meet his, her heart tightened in her chest. She didn't see disgust or contempt. There was no look of repulsion in his brown eyes. There was only ... *want*. Pure and unadulterated want.

Reaching up, he brushed a strand of hair away from her face. The backs of her knuckles grazed against her cheek. She leaned into his touch as a single tear fell from her lashes. He caught the tear with his thumb and rubbed his fingers together. "Don't ever hide yourself from me," he whispered.

She had no words. The only thing she could do was stand there and stare at him. His hands grazed her sides, over her tattoo and rested on her full hips. "You're the most beautiful creature I've ever seen," he rasped. "You *never* have to hide from me."

It was the sincerity in his eyes that finally caused her to release the final barrier protecting her heart. There was nothing left. He now knew everything there was. Taking a deep breath and lifting her chin, she lowered her arms to her sides. For the first time in her entire life, she was allowing herself to be vulnerable to another human being. It was freeing and terrifying at the same time.

His eyes hungrily traveled down over her full form. Suddenly the stretch marks on her belly from carrying two babies were no longer visible. The extra padding at her sides no longer mattered. No one else mattered. It was just the two of them.

Jax scooped her up into his arms and then lowered her onto the mattress, kneeling beside her. "You're so beautiful," he said, voice gravely with desire. He lowered his mouth to the hollow of her neck and gently kissed, raking across the sensitive flesh with his lips. Cheri gasped and turned her head, allowing him more access.

From her neck he moved further down, lavishing her body with attention and driving her senses completely wild. Her eyes closed as his mouth found the tight buds of her breasts. Pleasure burst through her like tiny currents of electricity, causing her to gasp and arch away from the bed.

Jax watched as Cheri's eyes drifted closed. Her swollen lips parted as small sighs of desire slipped through them. She arched her back, granting him more access to her. His body hummed with excitement, urging him to take her fast, but the rational side of his mind reminded him that it's not what she needed. She'd been through too much in her life to be taken in such a manner. He needed to show her exactly what it was like to be treated like the beautiful creature she was.

Reining in his self-control, he plucked another nipple between his lips and tugged. The sound of her cries of pleasure only adding fuel to his own growing inferno. His body ached for release, his jeans having become miserably uncomfortable. It was a small price to pay to see and hear her pleasure. He would wait forever if that was what it took.

It was in that moment that he knew he would move heaven and hell for this woman. This little force of nature that had blown into his life like a hurricane, completely disrupting everything in his life and turning his world upside down. Since she'd literally run into him that day outside of his bar, he'd thought of no one else. As far as he was concerned, there was no one else.

He'd realized while watching her sleep in his bed last night, that somewhere along the way he'd developed feelings for her. Now, watching her writhe beneath him he knew, without a doubt, that what he had for her was more than feelings. His heart seized in his chest and his stomach tightened. He was in love.

It was only after the pressure of his mouth was gone and she was panting from pleasure that she opened her eyes and found him staring down at her.

"What?" she whispered.

He just shook his head, shaggy hair falling into his eyes. He moved from the bed, standing beside her. She watched nervously as he toed off his boots and worked the buttons on his jeans. Her mouth went dry and she licked her lips. This pulled a low grown from him.

"Do you know how tempting you are when you do that, *Cher*?" he said hoarsely, his hands stopping on his zipper.

She shook her head. "*'Bo bouch yo nan yon zanj, ta vire yon pechè nan yon saint*," he said, his voice thick with the Creole dialect.

Cheri flushed. "To kiss the lips of an angel, would turn a sinner to a saint," she translated softly.

"And every word of it is true." That was all he said as he pushed his jeans down over his hips and stepped out of them. For a moment, he stood in front of her, and she drank him in with greedy eyes. He was beautiful.

His narrow waist gave in to lean hips and an impressive endowment. Dark hair dusted his thighs and then she saw it. A long jagged scar running from the inside of his thigh all the way down his leg.

"It happened when I was in prison. We all have scars, *mon cher*," he said as he climbed in bed beside her. His lips gently found hers as his hands worked the buttons on her shorts. "It's how you let them heal that makes the difference," he continued.

The button gave with a soft *pop* and the rasp of the zipper followed. His fingers skimmed the lace of her panties before dipping just below the band. Inch by inch he moved lower until the calloused pads of his fingers found what they were searching for.

Jax leaned down and pressed his lips close to her ear as his fingers moved against her. A gasp tore from her lips as she arched against his hand. "It's time for us to both start heal'n."

The concept of time seemed to vanish as Jax moved to kneel between her thighs. Reaching up, he liberated her of the final barrier between them. He tossed her shorts to the side and leaned over her, stealing one more kiss. She eagerly accepted him as he positioned himself at her entrance.

"*Ouvri je'w*," he commanded softly.

It took all the energy she could muster but she opened her eyes, just as he'd asked her too. As she did, their gazes locked and with one swift flex of his hips, they were connected—not just physically but mentally and emotionally.

Cheri cried out as he hooked her leg over his hip pulling him tighter against her body. With one hand grasping the back of her thigh, he used the other to clutch the headboard above them. Her hands glided over the taut muscles of his back as they danced beneath her fingertips with each thrust.

Her breathing became labored as her body began to spin out of control. Pleasure threatened to consume her completely, and she welcomed the heat from the fire he was creating within her. Higher and higher it burned until she was crying out his name and her body was shaking uncontrollably.

Skin gliding against skin, hands teasing and touching, lips tasting and caressing, nothing else mattered.

# 31

There were no words. There was nothing that could be said that would explain exactly what Cheri was feeling. Together they lay beneath the sheets. Outside the storm raged on. Jax lay on his back, one hand resting behind his head while the other held Cheri tightly to his side. Her arm was draped over him, cheek resting on his chest as she listened to the steady rhythm of his heart as it slowed back to a normal pace. Her leg was lazily draped over his.

Idly, Jax's hand moved in small circles around her shoulder. Neither wanted to speak because neither had a clue what to say. They were content to lay there in the silence, and that's how they stayed for a long time. It was only after she'd finally began to slip into slumber that Jax's voice startled her awake.

"I'm sorry," he chuckled, kissing the top of her head. "I didn't mean to startle ya."

She giggled and snuggled tighter into his side. "What did you say?"

"His name was Ellison Cormier."

She frowned and looked up at him, resting her chin on the back of her hand. "What are you talking about?"

"The man I killed. His name was Ellison Cormier."

She nodded her understanding, knowing that he was opening up about something he'd never talked about. She just waited, letting him tell her on his own terms.

"Desire had just gotten back into town after one of her many journeys abroad. She'd run into this pole cat from N'awlins. Somethin' bout him just really set my skin on edge, but Desire said she was in love. She was rather insistent on it. So much so, that it caused us to have one of our biggest fights ever. She told me that I needed to mind my own damn business and stay out of hers.

"I did and more than anything I wished I would have followed my gut about that."

"What happened?" she asked softly. She searched his face but he stared at the ceiling, lost to the memory that was taking hold and pulling him under.

"I was tired of her ignoring me so I went out to Ellison's house. He lived way the hell out of town and since being back, Desire had taken to staying out there, knowing it made momma crazy. Anyhow, I went out there cause I hadn't heard from her in a while.

"At first nothing seemed wrong, but the second I stepped in the house I knew better. I heard something breaking from the bedroom and then my sister scream. I didn't ask questions. What I saw when I walked in that room was enough to give me nightmares for years."

Cheri's heart constricted as she listened to him relive the story as if it had happened yesterday.

"Desire was tied to the bed, naked. Her entire body was covered in bruises and cuts. The sick bastard had burned her with a cigarette. I don't know how long she'd been there but from the looks of it, it could have been days. I don't know where Ellison was and I didn't care. All I was worried about was getting my baby sister untied.

"He must have come out of the bathroom because I didn't hear him until it was too late. He'd hit me over the head with something. Hurt like hell but didn't knock me out. I don't really remember much else for a while. I remember seeing him and then flying into a blackout rage. The next thing I know, Desire is pulling me off of Ellison's body.

"I'd found a hammer and smashed his face in until there was nothing left. The bad thing about it . . . I felt nothing. I had no remorse for what I did."

"You were protecting your sister."

"And I would do it again," he said finally looking at her. He didn't have to say what he was meaning. She knew very well what he was meaning.

"What happened?"

"After I got Desire cleaned up, we bagged the body and cleaned the bedroom with peroxide. Then we burned the house. As it happened, it had been abandoned and Ellison had claimed to be fixing it up. We waited until nightfall and hauled his body a couple towns over to a massive pig farm."

"But do they eat a whole body?"

He only shook his head. She didn't have to press further to know that Ellison hadn't been entirely whole when his body was disposed of.

"We dumped his body and within two hours, there was nothing left. After that night, nothing was ever said about Ellison again. The story was that he'd left town. Desire supposedly had a car wreck but didn't want to go to the hospital. She lived with me for a long time, not wanting to be on her own and not wanting to live with our parents."

"Does anyone else know about it?"

He shook his head. "To this day, Desire and I are the only ones that know what happened. Until you."

"My lips are sealed."

"Speaking of my sister," he groaned.

She chuckled. "What?"

"She wants me to have lunch with them at the *Queen* tomorrow ya know, meet the new boyfriend," he said begrudgingly.

"He's not that bad," she said, batting his shoulder.

He frowned. "How would you know?"

"Met him Saturday night at the reunion."

"Oh yeah, that's right. Damn, that night feels like it was forever ago."

"Mmhmm."

"Anyhow, why don't you come with me?"

She lifted her head and looked at him. "Like a date?"

Jax chuckled and looked down at her. "I suppose you could call it a double date."

She scrunched up her nose. "Double dates are more fun in theory than actuality."

"This is true, but you wouldn't make me go alone with you?"

This time she laughed. "Is the big bad Jaxon afraid to go to dinner with his sister and her boyfriend?" she asked in a child-like voice.

"Yes, yes he is," he joked back.

She rolled her eyes and leaned up, placing a soft kiss against his lips. The contact sent small chills of excitement through her. When she pulled away, her lips buzzed with an electrical current. "Then yes, I'll go and protect you."

The pair laughed and settled into a comfortable silence—each lost in thought.

While she'd been working for Jax for a couple of weeks, the events of the last couple of days felt as if they had happened weeks—instead of days—ago. She listened to the steady fall of the rain as it slapped against the tin roof.

"There's nothing I won't do to protect ya. Ya do realize that, right?"

"I know," she whispered. She'd almost forgot that there was a raving lunatic out there killing people she knew. For a split second, everything in her life was completely normal.

His arm tightened around her as he pulled her closer. "I don't condone taking a human life, but if it comes to choosing the life of the ones I love when it affects the people I love? There are no limits."

Cheri's eyes widened. *He loves me?*

He must have sensed what she was thinking because he smiled and brushed the hair away from her forehead. His lips pressed against her and in one quick move, he pulled her on top of him. She sat up, knees resting on either side of his hips. The evidence of his arousal pressed firmly against her backside.

Their eyes met as she slid down the length of him, locking their bodies together once more. She braced her palms flat on his chest as a slow and steady rhythm was set. Pleasure was coiling in the pit of her stomach and still, their eyes remained on each other.

There was no longer anything between them. No secrets, no walls, no barriers. They were finally free to just be.

From the shadows he watched. He watched as the whore straddled him and threw her head back in pleasure. The soft pants and moans of pleasure mixed with the sounds of the swamp just beyond the shadows of the yard. It sickened him how he could hear them over the rain. His cock tightened as he watched her ride that bastard's dick—imagining that it was his him beneath her.

He imagined sliding his knife into the soft flesh of her belly. He imagined the look on her face as blood gushed from the cut causing him to get off as hot blood coated his naked skin. His nostrils flared as his jeans grew tighter.

A cry of completion pulled his attention back from the fantasy, and rage surged through him with a ferocity that would no longer be contained. He watched through the window as she was rolled onto the bed and the guy mounted her from behind. He pictured himself taking his place and as he did he would slice up the bitches back, opening each and every one of those scars with his blade. With each thrust into her, he would slice his knife deeper.

He could almost smell the blood—her blood. He'd been waiting long enough. It. Was. Time.

# 32

Cheri awoke with a start, body drenched in sweat. She scrubbed at her eyes and slowly sat up. Beside her, Jax snored softly. Desperately needing a glass of water, she slipped from the bed and grabbed his Jax's shirt from the floor. After pulling it on, she quietly stepped through the bedroom door, closing it softly behind her.

Outside twilight was giving away to morning as the horizon was slowly beginning to lighten. After grabbing a glass of water she stood by the window and looked out over the swamp. A layer of fog rolled over the water, concealing the cypress knees that lurked just against the water's surface. Spanish moss dripped from the limbs of the trees like tears. The whole scene was altogether frightening as well as beautiful.

She looked over her shoulder and into Jax's bedroom. He lay on his stomach, arms plowed under the pillows as he slept. The light blue sheet was draped over his backside but barely. His beautifully tattooed back was relaxed as he slept peacefully.

Her heart pinched in her chest as she thought about everything that had happened between them. They had been on a collision course for each other since the day they met. She'd tried to fight her feelings for him, even when she couldn't stand him. They were two broken people and it was only when they were together that she felt complete.

She smiled and for a brief moment—for just a split second—she imagined that she was happy. For the first time since she was sixteen years old, she imagined herself being happy—being happy with Jax. A coil of anxiety tightened in the pit of her stomach as reality came crashing down on her once more.

Trying to stop the panic attack before it come to full force, she stepped out on the porch. The morning air was already sweltering, thick with humidity thanks to the storm. She sat in one of the old Adirondack chairs and pulled her legs up to her chest. So much had happened over the last couple of days. She was having a hard time processing it.

She'd lost her best friend and gained a lover. While the gain didn't outweigh her loss, it made it a touch more bearable. Tears filled her eyes as she listened to the early morning frogs. She would never again see Roux's smiling face. Her stepfather was back but how on earth could he still be alive?

Cheri stared at her hands. It was almost as if she could see all the blood from all those years ago. If he'd died, there would have been a record of his death. However, there wasn't. Maybe he really was dead and it was someone else. But who? Who could hate her so much that they would kill Roux? Travis's death didn't affect her—with good reason—and as sad as it was, Gina's didn't hold that big of an effect on her. Even though it seemed to have affected Jax.

Nothing made sense, and no matter how hard she tried, she simply could not make sense of it. She pressed her fingers to her temples and attempted to ease the ache in her head but it didn't work.

The sky was shifting from cobalt to light gray, and Cheri decided that she couldn't stay still any longer. She needed to clear her mind. If anything, she needed to process everything that had transpired with Jax. He'd gone from being her boss to her friend to her lover in a matter of a few short days. Was what was happening between them just because he was there when she was vulnerable or was it real? Was it a case of white knight syndrome? She'd professed her love for him as they made love and he'd returned it. Was it just the heat of the moment?

With a sigh, she stretched her limbs and walked back into the house. As quietly as possible she retrieved her clothes from the bedroom and carried them back out into the living room. Quickly, she got dressed.

There was a notepad and pen on Jax's desk. She scribbled a quick note and walked back into the bedroom and placed it on the pillow beside him. He wouldn't be happy about her leaving, but it was almost completely daylight. They'd made it through the night without incident.

Silently she left the house. It was too far to walk back into town, and she didn't want to take his truck and leave him without a mode of transportation. Her eyes scanned the water, and she spotted the flat bottom boat. It was just a short ride to town by boat.

Her feet were soundless as she made her way over the decaying leaves and down to the water's edge. As she was climbing into the boat, the tiny hairs on the back of her neck stood on end. Her breathing hitched in her throat as she scanned the shadows of the trees.

She felt a sudden sharp pinch in her leg, and before she could register what was happening, the bottom of the boat was rushing up to meet her. Her head struck the aluminum siding of the boat and stars exploded around her eyes. Everything around her warped and distorted as she felt the boat shift. There was a loud roaring in her ears as she tried to focus. The water lapped at the sides as it tipped and moved around. Heavy black boots came into her line of sight.

Panic gripped her as she tried to push herself upright. Her limbs refused to work, feeling like they were weighted by cement. She tried to open her mouth to call out, but nothing happened. Her tongue was thick— refusing to work. She realized in that horrifying moment that she'd somehow been drugged. Suddenly her hands were roughly jerked together and bound with zip-ties. The hard plastic bit painfully into her wrists. Everything was bizarrely silent. The birds had ceased their chirping, and even the crickets and frogs seemed to have stopped their music. There was only the sound of water and breathing. Heavy breathing. Then the sound weeds and debris scraping the bottom of the boat. They were moving.

*Jax. Please wake up.* She pleaded. Then she realized with horror what she'd done. Hopelessness washed over her as she turned her head and looked up. Her vision was cloudy as she stared at the shape above her. The sky overhead was growing lighter and lighter, and yet the features of her captor remained shadowed.

Soon the whine of the engine filled the dense silence around them. It sounded like a shotgun blast beside her ear. It only meant one thing. They were far enough away from Jax's house now.

Her captor turned and sat back down, rocking the boat precariously. Then the face of her tormenter blurred and then came into view. Her stomach twisted, and nausea pushed bile to the back of her throat.

No! It couldn't be. Panic and terror surged through her veins as she stared at the malicious grin. How could it be possible?

"Why?" she croaked.

The only response she got was a maniacal chuckle.

Tears leaked from Cheri's eyes and dropped onto the floor of the boat. The last thing she saw before the blackness pulled her under was the smile of pure evil.

Jax awoke with a start, unsure of what it had been that pulled him out of his deep slumber. He couldn't remember the last time he'd slept so soundly. With a yawn he rolled over, expecting to see Cheri. When he saw she wasn't there, he quickly sat up. A piece of folded paper with his name scrawled on the front caught his attention.

Reaching over he grabbed the note and read:

*Jax,*

*I needed to get out and clear my head for a while. Don't worry, I'll be fine. So much has happened and I just need a minute to process. I will meet you at the Queen for lunch. Please don't worry.*

*Always,*
*Cheri*

Jax frowned and re-read the note. Looking over at the bedside table the alarm glared back at him. 9:43. How long had she been gone? He stood from the bed and pulled on a pair of boxers. From there he went out to the front porch. His truck was still where he'd parked it. Had she walked? No, she wouldn't have walked that far.

His gaze swung down to where he'd tied his boat. It was gone. He walked back into the house, unable to get rid of the gnawing feeling in the pit of his stomach. Unease urged him to quickly get dressed. If Cheri needed time to process everything that happened between them that was fine, but there was a killer on the loose, and she was his primary target. How could she have been so careless?

Once he was dressed, he stormed from the house hell bent on bending that woman over his knee. He jumped in his truck and turned the engine over. However, nothing happened. With a frown, he twisted the key again. This time it sputtered to life only to die once more.

"What the hell?" he muttered as he pulled the lever that would disengage the hood. He jumped out and went to inspect the engine. It only took a moment before he realized what was wrong.

"What the hell?" he muttered, looking for the missing spark plug. Spark plugs didn't just disappear.

The sound of crunching gravel alerted him to the presence of another person. He spun around, but it was too late. He couldn't move, and he couldn't dodge as something landed with such a force against the side of his head his knees to buckle. His vision blurred as someone stepped into view. He felt himself being hoisted up by the collar of his shirt and slammed against the front of the truck. Pain surged through him.

"You!" he rasped, trying to push through the pain. He tried to shake his head clear, but his arms felt like lead. A heavy blow landed in his midsection, causing the air to leave his lungs in a *whoosh*, doubling him over.

"Where's she at?" Jax wheezed. He struggled to his feet and swung his fist with as much strength as he could muster. His assailant easily moved out of the way.

Another blow. This time to his ribs. He felt them buckle under the force. He felt the sting of a needle in the side of his neck. "You'll see her really soon," rasped the voice. It sounded distorted in Jax's ears as he tried to focus on what was happening.

He was let go, and he fell heavily to the ground. His vision swam as he felt his arms being lifted. "I'm going to kill you, ya sick sonofabitch," he gasped. The muscles and tendons popped in his shoulders as he was drug across the ground.

There was a low, ominous chuckle that sent ice racing through Jax's veins, but his captor said nothing. He could feel the rough shell ripping into his shirt and scouring his back. Something was secured around his waist. It felt like a wide belt, but he couldn't be sure.

The edges of his vision blurred and dimmed to black, but he shook it off. He had to stay awake. He was floating, drifting in and out of consciousness. Then he heard the whine of a small motor hum to life. He wasn't floating, but being hoisted into the air by a winch and pulley system. *His* wench and pulley system that he used to put gators and other wild game in the back of the truck. The sick bastard was hanging him up like a gator ready for slaughter. Suddenly he connected with the bed of his truck. Something dank and heavy was thrown over him— smelling like urine and mold. He wanted to gag, but everything felt numb.

Cheri was the only thing he cared about. Where was she? Was she already dead? Sorrow filled his chest. He failed her. He'd promised to keep her safe, and he'd failed. The engine of his truck roared to life, and then they were moving. Jax could hold out no longer. He prayed that Cheri was safe as the blackness sucked him under into its chilling hold.

# 33

The sound of dripping water raked against Cheri's raw nerves. As the clouds began to lift in her hazy mind, she tried to focus on her surroundings. Sweat trickled down her forehead and into her eyes as she strained to listen. She heard someone shuffling around followed by a low groan. Close to her ear, a mosquito whined incessantly. Then she felt the bite of the insect against her neck. Synapses triggered in her mind, and she suddenly felt little bites all over her body.

She took a slow deep breath through her nose. The air around her was dank and musty with the unmistakable scent of swamp water and decay. It made sense considering the near constant buzzing of mosquitos around her.

There was a heavy metallic taste in her mouth as she tried to unstick her tongue from the roof of her mouth. What in the hell was going on?

She struggled through her hazy mind, trying to recall what had happened. Fragments of her memory started to come through. She'd been at Jax's house. Then the boat and—

Cheri's eyes snapped open as she looked around and horror, unlike anything she'd ever felt in her life, washed over her. Terror shook her to the very foundation of her soul as her surroundings became familiar. The room was windowless, the panes having been shattered long ago. Just beyond, the sky was growing dimmer. Had she really been unconscious all day long? Outside, the first sounds of evening could be heard.

Boards were missing in the floor beside an ugly old orange couch. It had been old all those years ago, it didn't look any better. The fabric had faded and worn because of the elements and the damp air, but also because of insects and rodents making it their home. An ashtray rested on the table, overflowing with cigarette butts—most of which looked new. The lingering scent of old whiskey and stale cigarettes clung to everything around her, even the sweltering thick air. It made breathing exceedingly difficult.

She was back in Carl's cabin. Her stomach rolled as memories swelled in her mind and began to crest forward. She could almost see Carl sitting on the couch, head back and passed out from his latest cocaine and Jack binge. His protruding belly covered by a stained white tank-top. Cheri swallowed back the bile that climbed to the back of her throat as she remembered being forced to sit on the couch beside him.

This couldn't be happening. They'd been so careful. How had he found them? Wait *he*. Something in her mind clicked, but she couldn't bring the blurry memory into focus. It wasn't right.

The sound of a low moan pulled her attention swinging around. There was a sharp pain in her neck as she looked for the sound. Finally, it settled on a figure slumped over in an old wooden chair. She gasped in horror.

"Lizabeth?" she whispered frantically.

The old woman moaned but didn't lift her head. Cheri began to struggle, realizing for the first time that she was bound to a bed in nothing but her bra and panties. Why was there a bed in the middle of the living room? She struggled more, the feeling of scratchy wool scraping against her bare skin. Horror filled every fiber of her being as she struggled wildly. The couch was facing the bed like some weird front row seating. What the hell?

"Lizabeth! Wake up. Lizabeth, you've gotta wake the hell up," she whispered harshly. She wasn't sure if they were completely alone or not. However, one scan of the run down cabin said they were, but was there someone outside, waiting?

Finally, the old woman slowly lifted her head. Typically, her hair was bound in a braid kept pulled back, however, now, it hung in thick limp strands sticking to the dried blood on her forehead and cheeks. The pallor of her skin was ashen. Dark circles ringed her eyes.

"Lizabeth," Cheri whispered again.

Slowly, the older woman turned her head and settled her eyes on Cheri. Finally, it seemed that some of the haze cleared from her eyes. "Cheri? Lord, chile. What is goin' on?" She lifted her head and winced. "*Mon Dieu,* my head hurts somethin fierce." She struggled against her restraints.

"I don't know, but we need to get out of here," Cheri said as she frantically tugged at her bonds.

Lizabeth did the same thing but after a few minutes of effort, nothing happened. Both women sagged with loss of energy.

"What happened?" Cheri asked as she tried to focus on Lizabeth instead of the burning pain in her wrists that her struggling was producing. Her head felt as if it were two times its normal size. She squeezed her eyes together, trying to clear away some of the fog.

Lizabeth shook her head. "I don't r'member. I was out in the backyard and den. . . ." She trailed off for a moment.

"And then?" Cheri pressed.

"Then someone was b'hind me. I heard d'ere footsteps and den I turnt around and nothing. I didn't get a chance to go no farther because next ting I know is I got whacked in da head with a board or stick or somethin'. Lord, who is doin' this?"

"It's Carl," Cheri said weekly. A sliver of dread ran up her spine and down her arms. Terror clung to her like the sweat coating her skin. Carl had finally made his presence known.

Lizabeth's eyes grew wide. "How can dat be? You killed him."

Cheri fought against the zip ties holding her hands together. "I don't know. Maybe he survived? I don't know. I was only thirteen."

The sound of a vehicle coming down the drive caused both women to go silent. Cheri's heart slammed against her ribs with a violence so strong, she was certain they would break. "Someone's coming," she hissed.

Lizabeth nodded and allowed her head to sag against her chest. Taking a deep breath, Cheri forced her body to relax. She had to figure out how to get out and get Lizabeth out with her.

She closed her eyes and listened as the rumbling sound of a truck grew closer. It wouldn't be long until they came face to face with the killer. It was the same man from her past, coming back to haunt her.

Her heart stilled when she heard the engine cut off, followed by the sound of a door opening and closing. Cheri held her breath, slowly counting and paying attention to every little sound.

Shuffling of feet.

The groan of exertion.

Muttered curses.

Then voices. Voices? Two very distinctive voices. However, one of them wasn't one she recognized, but the other . . . the other voice sent bone-chilling terror through her body. Then everything from earlier came rushing forward.

She was going to take the boat into town and clear her head, but she'd heard someone coming up behind her. They'd shot her with some sort of tranquilizer. While she lay in the bottom of the boat, she'd seen her captor.

Cheri opened her eyes and listened as footsteps climbed up the rickety old steps to the house. She was done being scared and she was tired of hiding. No. It was time she sucked it up and faced her fears.

She lifted her chin defiantly and stared at the front door as it swung open. A man wearing hospital scrubs and a baseball cap pulled low over his eyes walked in. A figure was slung over his shoulder and a lantern in his free hand. The light danced and bobbed with each of his steps.

She bit down on the inside of her cheek until the metallic taste of blood filled her mouth. The man roughly deposited the body onto the couch. A new kind of horror filled her when she saw Jax's bruised, bloodied and mangled body. Dust plumed out in a burst of clouds. Jax didn't move and she couldn't even tell if he was breathing.

The man straightened and worked his hands in the small of his back.

"*Mon Dieu*, that bastard is heavy," he said.

Tiny alarm bells sounded in her head. She knew that voice. Her eyes widened as he turned and removed his baseball cap. Her blood turned cold.

"You!?"

A sinister smile curved on his handsome face as he tossed the old cap to the side and watched her with wild, hungry eyes. The look on his face made her stomach churn with disgust as his eyes slowly traveled down her body. He licked his lips hungrily.

"*Bon yo wè ou ankò*, Cheri," he said politely, though there was nothing in the hungry way he stared at her even close to being polite.

"Wish I could say it's good to see you, too. I can't."

She opened her mouth to say something else, but the words fell short when another person walked through the front door. This was a face she recognized. This was a face she'd tried to forget for years. It was much older than the last time she saw it, but it was the same, never the less.

Cheri struggled against her bonds again, only this time it wasn't to get free, it was to wrap her hands around the neck of the person glaring back at her. There was such malice and contempt in one look it made her skin crawl.

Refusing to let either of them see her scared, she narrowed her eyes and lifted her chin.

"Hello . . . *mother*."

# 34

"I don't believe this. We're chasing our damn asses out here," Levi said angrily as he slapped the hood of the car. The parking garage was partially deserted. Lights began to flicker on as dusk began to settle.

Lynn stared at his partner over the roof and slowly shook his head. "There's nothing we can do. He's not here so we can't talk to him. Try his cell again if it will make you feel better."

"Damn it, Lynn. We've called his cell, his office, hell we've even called his country club—he's not there."

"The other nurses said he often goes hiking or mountain climbing," Lynn said with a shrug as he climbed into his car.

"We're at the ass end of Louisiana. Where the hell are there mountains 'round here?" Levi climbed in after him and slammed the door. Lynn stared out the window for several minutes and then turned.

"I just don't think he's who we're looking for." There was something that didn't fit. They'd gone through Ross' records going all the way back to grade school. While they'd found out that he and Marceaux were connected, there was nothing that otherwise pointed to criminal mischief. In fact, Ross was the model citizen.

"We know he was working in the ER the night Anderson came in. He could have very easily vetted him then and using his records find his apartment. He has access to the toxins and neuro-blockers and would know how to administer them properly."

Lynn slowly bobbed his head and stared forward. "It would have been easy for him to get Anderson and LaTour. They live here in the city, but want about the girl? What ties did he have? He comes from an upstanding family, happy childhood with no signs of abuse. There is nothing that points to him being who we're after."

302

Levi was about to respond when a pick-up pulled into the parking garage. The driver's side door pushed open, and Dr. Ross climbed out. He took one look at the police officers and made his way across the lot to them.

Both men climbed from the car.

"Detectives, I'm sorry to have kept you waiting. I just received word that you were looking for me?"

"Can you tell me where you were Sunday evening?"

The doctor nodded. "Of course. I went to a charity ball with my wife."

"And what time did you return home?"

"I'd say close to around four Monday morning?"

"That's some ball. Was your wife with you the entire time?"

"Yes, sir. Please, can you tell me what this is about?"

"What is your relationship with Jaxon Marceaux?"

He lifted his shoulders. "We've been friends since we were kids. Grew up down the street before his parents moved outta town. We talk every once in a while. Yesterday was the first time I'd seen him in a couple months."

"Where were you today?" Levi asked. He wasn't pulling any punches. The tone in his voice carried a hard edge to it. It was apparent by the tautness in his shoulders and his tightly clenched jaw that he was more than a little annoyed.

"I was over in Larose doing some work at one of the clinics there. Some of the families can't afford medical, so I volunteer a couple times a month. I can give you the number if you'd like."

Lynn stared at Michael as he talked to Levi. He was calm and collected. There were no markers indicating he was nervous or even lying. He hadn't even bothered to ask why they were questioning him.

*He's not who you're looking for.*

As Levi continued to talk to Michael, Lynn's cell phone rang. "Robichaud." He listened and the disconnected the call.

"C'mon, Moss. We gotta go."

Levi shot him a sour look but turned back to Michael. "Stick close to the city if you wouldn't mind."

Michael nodded. "Absolutely."

The detectives climbed into the car. As Lynn turned the engine over Levi looked over his notes and shook his head. "He's not who we're looking for."

"No. He's. Not."

"I'm about sick of this, man. This asshole is out there killing people, and we've got dick all. What was the phone call?"

Lynn pulled onto the street from the parking garage. Overhead the yellow streetlights began to flicker on.

"It was the station. Apparently, some kids were mucking around Big Charity earlier and stumbled onto something."

"Jeez, Big Charity? That place has been abandoned since Katrina, right?"

Lynn nodded. "Yeah, the city put up a chain link to keep vandals out, but it doesn't do any good. Any chances of them opening their doors again went out the window when University Medical Center opened."

"I remember Charity. It was a cool place."

Lynn arched a brow at him skeptically. "How would you know? You were probably still in diapers."

Levi snorted. "I was a junior in high school, jackass, and my mother used to work there. She took another job in Baton Rouge a few months before Katrina hit. So someone has what—broken in?"

"Most likely. That place is so big, it would be the perfect place—if it wasn't infested with mold and other structural damage."

"Do we have any idea what we are even going over there for? I mean what does it have to do with us?"

"Not sure yet. Just said that the kids found a room in the basement."

Levi let out an audible groan, and Lynn looked at his partner.

"What?"

"I just hate basements."

He pulled the car to a stop and looked at his massive partner.

"What?" Levi asked innocently.

"You can take down serial killers, slosh around in muck and stare at bloated dead bodies all day long but the mention of you going into a basement makes you squeamish. What are you, afraid of mice?"

"Haha, jackass," Levi grunted as he pushed from the car.

"Just pull up your big girl panties and be a big boy!" he snickered.

Levi flipped him the bird as they walked to where everyone was gathered. Lynn chuckled to himself as they walked. He'd learned a long time ago, that if one didn't find something laugh at while they were working, they would often forget how. It wasn't uncommon. The job wore a person down, not just physically but mentally. It got into their souls and just made them tired.

There were several units already at the scene as well as the crime scene as both men made their way to where the unit chief was waiting for them.

"Chief Beauchamp," Lynn said with the nod of his head. "What's going on?"

The chief rested his hands on his duty belt and looked at the detectives. "Some kids decided it would be a great idea to explore. They started in the basements."

"Aren't they still flooded?" Levi asked.

The chief shook his head. "No, the majority of the water was pumped out. Whatever was left just dried up over time, I guess. Anyway, they went through this door here," he said as he pointed to a heavily rusted door that had been pried open.

"A delivery bay?"

"Best I can tell it runs into the kitchen." They walked through the kitchen and to one of the several basement entrances. "Now, this hospital is two hundred and eighty years old, and some of the basements have been closed off."

"Closed off? How?"

"Some of them were completely bricked up. Supposed to have saved on costs, some such. Anyone, there's legends about this place."

"Some say it's haunted and that there are tunnels that run all over the city from beneath," Levi supplied.

The chief shrugged. "There's nothing in the city plans about tunnels, but. . . ." He hesitated and looked at the door.

"But what?" Lynn hedged.

"Apparently we were wrong."

"How so?"

"Just follow me, and you'll see," he said as he walked up the ramp and through the double doors. Just inside, halogen lights had been erected on tripods, shining their harsh light all around. Debris littered the floors, and the walls were covered with black mold. Somehow, one of the walls had been overtaken by ivy. It looked like something straight out of a horror flick. It seemed that time had forgotten the old hospital as food trays, papers and dishes lay scattered around.

The air was oppressive and smoldering hot. Sweat beaded on his forehead and rolled down the sides of Lynn's face. The smell of mildew, rotted vegetation, and stagnant water burned his nose. It was much worse than a swamp because at least with a swamp, there was open air. That wasn't the case here.

The men removed flashlights from their pockets and clicked them on. "Watch your steps. It gets pretty steep."

They began their descent and soon they came to the bottom. A long brick and rock-lined corridor stretched out in front of them. Water dripped somewhere as they swept the beams of light over the slime and moss-covered walls.

"This isn't the basement," Levi grunted as they walked toward the end of the hall. They could see a door open at the end with light spilling out. "This is the basement's basement."

After walking what felt like miles, they came to the door. Inside were two lab technicians gathering DNA and other samples.

"What the hell is this place?" Levi asked as they stepped into a small room.

"Best we can tell it was here long before the hospital was even built, possibly some sort of holding cell during slavery. There are other areas along the hall that look like they could be doors, but they've been sealed."

Like the corridor, the room was built out of brick and rock, but the walls looked to be in better shape. He took a step closer and looked.

"The walls have been scrubbed clean."

Slowly, he turned and looked at the medical equipment. "A gurney, heart monitors, intubation equipment, i.v stands. Whoever came down here knew what he's doing."

"The perfect place to carry out a murder." Lynn slipped on a pair of blue gloves and walked over to a small rolling cabinet. He pulled open the drawer. "Look at this." He lifted a nearly empty vile of white liquid.

Levi stepped closer. "Succinylcholine."

"There's nothing else in the drawer but this." Lynn held up a piece of orange plastic.

"A syringe cap."

"Looks like this might be our guy's kill room."

"Why not, it's the perfect place. The back of the building is secluded. Someone could easily come and go without being seen. There's all the time people coming to this place. It could be easily shrugged off as curiosity."

"That's a long way to get a body down here without anyone seeing."

"He can back right up to the bay doors and unload easily enough. If it's night time, it would be virtually impossible for him to be seen."

"Guys you need to look at this," the chief said.

They walked around to where he stood staring at the heart monitor.

"Property of University Medical."

"We were right. He works at the hospital."

"I've got something here," one of the uniformed officers called from the corner. He crossed the room and in his hands, were two items.

"Wallets." Lynn flipped them open and his suspicions were confirmed. "They belong to Travis Anderson and Roux LaTour."

"So where's he at now?"

"Working maybe?"

Lynn looked around the room. Something felt off. Slowly he turned. "What is it?"

"He's not done."

"Why do you say that?"

"Look around. There's no tools—scalpels, scissors, clamps. Nothing. If someone were using this as a place to torture, there would be instruments to do so."

Levi frowned. "You think he's going to strike again?"

A heavy feeling settled in the pit of Lynn's stomach as he nodded. "If not, why clean this place out. He wasn't worried about being caught because he left the wallets here."

"He wasn't worried because he's not coming back!"

"Which means our window just got a lot smaller.

"We need to get back to the hospital. Maybe Dr. Ross can help us narrow the list down and we can catch a break. At the very least, help us find the next victim."

"We already know who the next victim more than likely is."

"If it's not her, then someone else is going to die because we're wrong."

Levi crossed his arms over his barrel-like chest. "And if it is her we might be too late."

"Then let's hope that big Cajun can keep her safe until we can get there."

# 35

Levi's phone rang as they climbed into the car. The call was short. "So, they had to do a little creative digging with Cheri Bouvier's file."

"How so?"

"It seems like all her files mysteriously vanished."

"Convenient."

"And had it not been for modern technology, it would have been impossible to recover. Anyhow, everything Cheri Bouvier told us works out. Cheri Bouvier used to be Cheri Deveau. She was removed from her mother and stepfather's care after being found alone in her stepfather's cabin."

"What happened to the parents?" Lynn asked.

"Both vanished. No one has seen them since."

"We're missing something or someone." Lynn didn't bother parking in the garage this time. Instead, he pulled into a vacant spot in front of the Emergency Room. He was tired of waiting. All his patience had evaporated and they were running out of time.

They walked in directly to the elevator. Thankfully they didn't have to wait. The doors dinged open and both men rushed inside. Lynn just hoped that doctor Ross was still there.

"I'm still not sure what the doc is going to be able to help us with," Levi said.

"Whoever it is we're looking for is in the operating room. There are only so many people that can use that kind of drug."

"Surgeons and nurses."

"Yes, but they aren't the ones that typically do. Anesthetists are the ones that do that."

"So we can narrow the search by checking the files of all the anesthetists. He would be able to tell us which ones are which without us having to hike through tons of personal files."

"That's what I'm hoping."

The elevators didn't seem to open quickly enough as they rushed out. They stopped in front of the doctor's door and knocked. Doctor Ross answered the door a slightly startled look on his face.

"Doctor, can we have a word with you? In private?" Lynn then added when he noticed several people were staring and some were even whispering.

"Of course. Please come in."

The three men stepped into his office and he closed the door behind them. "What can I do to help, gentlemen?"

"We've narrowed down the suspect list to someone that we have reason to believe that works here. We found a room full of equipment from this hospital in the basement of Charity."

"Okay? I'm still confused as to how I can help."

"We're asking for your help in narrowing down our suspect list to anesthesiologists or personnel that can administer succinylcholine."

Michael's brows drew together. "If that's what's being used, then it would have to be administered through an iv drip. Otherwise, the affects would last four minutes, six tops."

"There was a partially filled bottle of succinylcholine there, as well as an iv pole."

"Then he's keeping them steadily on it."

"Which is what we already assumed. We just have to figure out who. I'm afraid our time is running out."

"What do you need?"

"Do you have access to personnel files?"

"Their in-depth files, no. I do have a roster of staff."

"That will take time we don't have," Levi said shaking his head.

"Not if I help." Michael turned to his computer and with a few key punches a screen popped up with staff and administration.

"Okay, let's start with the ones that are newer."

"Why newer?"

"Because whoever is doing this has been planning for a long time. They needed to insert themselves into a normal life. I'd say they've been here for a couple months."

Michael nodded and began to scroll down through the screen he opened six different links. "These are the ones that have been here six months or less."

They began clicking through the files.

"What are we looking for?" Levi asked.

Lynn stared at the screen, shaking his head but scanning the screen. "I don't know, but I--," His eyes widened as he pointed to the screen. Levi looked at the monitor.

"Sonofabitch," he snapped already heading for the door.

"What? What is it?" Michael asked following them.

Lynn spun around. "We know him. He was at two of the crime scenes. Thanks for your help doctor."

It was the last thing he said as he and Levi rushed from the hospital. "I didn't see it before, but he was in one of the photos at the LaTour house and then again at Marceaux's house."

Levi pulled the file out and scanned the picture. "Shit. He was there the whole time and we didn't see it. The bastard stood not four feet away from us last night. We talked to him!" Fury and insult rolled off of him in violent waves.

"Because *he* didn't want us to see it."

"Get on the phone to Dead Water and call everyone you can. He's gone back to finish the job." Lynn slammed his fist against the steering wheel as they got stuck in traffic. Even with his lights flashing, there was no way around the snarl of traffic.

"Shit!" he roared. He was going to be too late and there wasn't a damn thing he could do about it.

"Where do you think he's going to take them?"

Lynn stared ahead grimly. "Back where it all began. He's going home."

# 36

For several long moments, Cheri stared at her mother—feeling as if she were staring at a ghost. Once upon a time, Janice Deveau was beautiful. Her chestnut colored hair had once fell in long, shimmering waves down her back. The few times that her mother had acted anywhere close to maternal was when she'd tucked Cheri into bed when she was younger. She could remember the smell of the coconut shampoo that she used. Which probably explained why the smell of coconuts turned her stomach. Now, her mother's hair was almost completely gray and fell in lank, greasy strands around her face—looking as if it hadn't been washed in days.

In her younger years, it had been easy to see why the men always loved her—ample breasts and an hourglass figure. The woman standing in front of her was much, much thinner. Her once beautiful face was sunken in and sallow. Dark black circles—part days old mascara, part sleeplessness—circled her eyes. Her face was acne scarred and her body was twitching anxiously. "Time's been good to ya, *bebe*." Her tone was cold and unfeeling. Hollow eyes, void of love, stared back at her—occasionally darting back and forth.

"Can't say the same for you," she snorted. "You two've been working together?"

Both of her captors nodded, but it was Janice that spoke. "He took care of things in N'awlins while I handled things here."

Behind her mother's back, she could see Jax stir slightly on the couch. *Keep them talking. Give Jax time.* Cheri's eyes swung back to the man.

"Where's Desire?"

He shrugged. "Dropped her off a little while ago."

Cheri felt the color drain from her face. Had she gotten Jax's sister killed?

He rolled his eyes. "She's fine. I don't have issues with her." He licked his lips and slowly drug his gaze lazily up her body.

"*Bon yo wè ou ankò*, Cheri," he said again.

"I see your creole's improved, Jerry," she said bitterly.

He lifted a shoulder. "Or perhaps it was perfect all along."

"What did you do with Desire?" she repeated.

"I just told you I didn't have an issue with the little bitch. Though one more minute of listening to that insipid little girl and I couldn't promise the same result. However, as it stands, I've no issue with her."

"You didn't have issue with Roux."

Jerry's eyes narrowed. "Didn't I?"

"What are you talking about? You didn't even know Roux."

"Tsk, tsk, tsk, Cheri. I'm disappointed in you." He feigned disappointment while he clicked his tongue. Then he abruptly stopped and pinned her with a cold glare. "Well, not really, considering you were always such a stuck up little whore."

*Always? What the hell was he talking about?*

"You don't remember me, do you?"

"Should I?" Her brain spun and whirled as she tried to think about where she'd met him before, but she was still coming up blank.

His teeth clenched tightly together for a few moments as he tried to keep his temper in check. "Don't even remember one of your brothers."

"Brothers? You're going to have to speak English. I'm not fluent is psychopath."

"Do you know how many nights I watched you let that piece of shit Travis rut between your thighs? Do you know how hard I got wishing it was me instead of him? So many nights I thought about killing him, right there while he was on top of you, but I didn't."

"*I didn't* let Travis do anything," she yelled.

Then, tiny pieces of the puzzle began to click into place—Gina, Travis, Roux. It was all making sense. "Your name was Jer— No, Jerome Davis, wasn't it? You lived in the house with the four of us. *You* were the other boy."

"Ding, ding, ding," he said sarcastically as he began to pace the room. The boards in the floor creaked and groaned. She had no idea what kind of condition they were in, but judging by the gaping holes in different parts of the cabin, it couldn't have been good. He was growing more and more agitated. "I've watched you for years. When you met that prick Alex. When you had your son at Mercy and then your daughter." He stopped his pacing and turned mad eyes to her. "I could have killed you those times too, you know."

She frowned. "What are you talking about?"

"You were in distress, and Jeremy's heartbeat was dropping. You had to be put under."

Her eyes widened with horror. He'd been a part of her life without even realizing it. Her gut twisted and then another thought struck. "You were at the grocery store the day I was fired?"

"And in your house, while you slept. Do you know you talk in your sleep?"

Her heart rate spiked. "And Roux's yesterday?"

"I knew you'd come check on him. It was only a matter of time."

Tears burned her eyes but she refused to allow them to fall. She would not give him the satisfaction.

"I killed your beloved Roux," he gloated. "He begged like the pussy he'd always been. He felt every cut I carved into him. He felt every stitch of pain as I dug his eye out."

The joy in his voice made her blood curdle.

"And Gina?"

"That was me too. Your mother didn't actually kill anyone. She did the following and the phone calls."

Cheri's gaze swung to her mother, who was beaming proudly.

"You were the one that took Roux."

"He couldn't do what needed to be done because he had to be at the party, keeping up pretenses and all. I went to Roux's and he took care of Gina here."

"You called Roux while you were at the party?"

He flashed her a manic grin.

"Why Gina? She had nothing to do with this."

Jerry lifted his shoulders and pursed his lips. "She did. She caught me watching you one night and threatened to tell. She was gone before I got to kill her and then I aged out. So I watched her and saw her bedding the Cajun and knew she was no less a whore than you were. I took what I wanted from her before I killed her." He lifted a shoulder in a shrug. "Well, I didn't take anything that she hadn't given to everyone else when we lived together, even your beloved Roux."

"No! Roux didn't go near her." She felt sick.

Jerry's lips pulled into a broad, knowing smile. "Oh, but he did. I watched. He bent her over the living room couch and gave it to her. They thought no one was home, but then again, everyone always forgot about me."

Tears rolled from her lashes. She didn't want to think of her best friend like that. She didn't want to remember him in that manner.

She sniffed and lifted her chin. "That was so long ago. Why, after all these years? How did *you two* meet?" she asked, ticking her head toward her mother.

The smug smile fell from his face and he began to pace all over again. "You see, after I aged out, I went home. I found your mother sitting in *my* living room."

Cold terror blanketed her as she looked around. "*This* was your home? Carl . . . was your father? I-I thought he just had a daughter?"

"My sister led quite the life. She got out before I got the chance, though. She had it all—a family that loved and cared for her. Well, she did until a few months ago."

His eyes narrowed and rage colored his cheeks as he continued his story. "I'd come home to take care of him once and for all, only to find out that he'd already been killed. You stole my chance at revenge. After all the years that sick bastard tormented me—coming into my room night after night—all those things he made me do and did to me. It was all I could think about. I spent years fantasizing killing him—how I was going to do it. When I was ten I'd planned on killing him, but that old bitch took me away," he said pointing to Lizabeth.

"She removed you."

"You're a smart one. Imagine my surprise when I discovered that you were his stepdaughter. I wanted to reach out to you, tell you how I felt and that the pain would eventually lessen, but you were so self-involved, you didn't even notice me. No one did.

"So after I aged out and found your mother here, we decided to watch and wait. I went to college and got a degree, learning the perfect way to take care of all my problems."

"And Jax? What does he have to do with anything?"

"You let him between your legs just like you did Travis and Alex. Do you not think I saw you last night? How you were grunting and panting like a bitch in heat?" He spat to the floor. "You were always such a whore." His entire body trembled with pure rage. Things were rapidly beginning to escalate. He was starting to lose control as he relived his story to her.

She ignored the rough bedding as it scratched against her skin, the smell of unwashed bodies on the blankets beneath her. Her nostrils flared as she moved herself into a sitting position on the bed—never taking her eyes off her mother.

"Guess I take after my mother," she hissed. The words dripped from Cheri's lips like venom, and she took immense pleasure in the look that crossed the woman's face.

She'd been expecting the backlash, so when she walked over to the side of the bed and landed a sharp blow to the side of her face, Cheri hadn't been surprised. Stars flashed briefly around her vision as she felt blood fill her mouth.

Leaning over the side of the bed she spat the blood on the floor, feeling it roll down her chin. She couldn't help but to feel a little bit maniacal in that moment. This time when she smiled, it was wide. "That the best ya got?" she goaded.

"I should have killed ya when I had da chance ya pathetic little bitch."

"Pathetic? Me? You're the pathetic one, humping anything with a dick. You been screwing your stepson all these years too?"

Another hook landed just below her eye. This time it came with more pain. Her head snapped around and hit the iron headboard, causing her vision to blur and then double. It took a minute to recover. As she did, she looked at her mother with a hate-filled glare—ignoring the throbbing just below her eye.

"Did you know Carl tried with me? Did you even care that he tried to rape me?" Her bottom lip trembled and she cursed the sudden swell of betrayal she felt. Mothers were supposed to love and protect their children.

It was her mother's time to sneer. She leaned close—close enough for Cheri to see her rotting teeth and smell her rancid, whiskey-soaked breath. "Why do I think I left you with him that last night, huh? He'd begged me to have you but I wouldn't let him—not until you turned thirteen. Then, when you did, I told him he could have you as many times as he wanted. He even paid me quite well for it too," she said smugly.

Bile pushed up Cheri's esophagus forcing her to lean to the edge of her bed and spill the contents of her stomach, again. Her mother had sold her. When she sat back up Janice looked down at her with disgust, but Cheri refused to allow her to have the upper hand.

"Didn't count on me gutting the fat bastard like a gator, did'ja?"

Her mother took a startled step back, already pale face growing paler. She saw her opportunity, so she continued. She nodded her head and sucked her teeth. "That's right. That knife slid into his gut like warm butter, over and over again. You want to know what I did next? Do you want to know how I killed him? Do ya, momma? Because it wasn't the knife that did it." she practically yelled. Her chest was rising and falling rapidly as she felt the surge of anger that had been long buried rush forward.

"I stabbed him over and over again. Then, I rolled him into the swamp. I watched him get pulled under by the gators. I watched as they tore him to little greasy ribbons."

The mention of Carl's name sent Janice into a blind rage. With a wild scream, the woman pounced on Cheri and wrapped her hands tightly around her throat. She could feel the blood slowing, but she refused to show panic. Instead, she bucked her hips wildly, catching her mother off guard and sending her flying to the edge of the bed. With as much force as she could muster, she lifted her foot and drove her heel down into the woman's spine. It wouldn't kill her, but it would hurt like hell.

"I found his body, you stupid bitch," Janice yelled as she once again climbed on top of her body. "He was on the shore, half eat'n and bloody. I loved'im," she screamed. She grabbed a fist full of Cheri's hair and slammed her head back against the headboard. Pain ricocheted through her skull. Hot, sticky blood ran down the back of her head as her vision once more blurred. She wasn't sure how much more she could handle. She had to keep talking.

Cheri spat more blood from her mouth and stared at the other captor. "Janice, take a walk," he barked.

"B-but. . . ." she protested feebly.

"NOW!"

Janice jumped and scuttled from the room. While his attention was turned away from her she quickly glanced in Lizabeth's direction. It seemed that both of their captors had completely forgotten about her. Lizabeth's hands were working the bonds behind her back slowly as to not draw too much attention to her.

Finally, his attention turned back to Cheri. "I wanted to gut lover boy while he slept on your couch Saturday night, but I didn't. I want you to watch as I do it."

He took a step forward, removing a scalpel from the pocket on his scrub. The silver knife glinted in the dim lighting of the room as he walked closer. He leaned down and smiled. "It's my turn now," he said as he slowly drew the blade over the flesh of her stomach. This time there was no holding back the scream.

The pain seared through her with each slice of her skin. Warm blood oozed down her sides, soaking the mattress. She grew lightheaded and the room began to swim. She could feel her hold on consciousness slipping through her fingers.

Finally, Jerry placed the scalpel on the bedside table and climbed to his feet. He drew his palm over the fresh cuts, smearing the blood on her stomach and onto his palms. She watched in horror as he lifted his hand to his lips and licked away the blood—pure pleasure evident in his glazed eyes.

The urge to vomit again was strong, but she knew she had to resist. She need to reserve her energy. Unfortunately, the torment was just beginning as Jerry pulled his scrub top over his head. "Now, it's time to get from you what you've been giving out so freely."

There was no mistaking Jerry's arousal as it protruded behind his cotton pants. This time the urge was too strong. She wretched, barely turning her head in time to keep it from getting all over her.

He said nothing as he gripped himself through the front of his pants and groaned. "I'm going to enjoy every minute of this."

# 37

"No! Get away from me! Get off me," she screamed.

Cheri's ear piercing shrieks slammed through his head like an ice pick, but he was careful to remain still. The room was still spinning and his body ached all over, but he'd heard it all—each sick and twisted detail.

*Hurry! She doesn't have much time*, his mind whispered.

Again Cheri's tormented scream filled the cabin. He could hear her thrashing around, the bedsprings groaning and squeaking in protest. Jax opened his eyes into small slits, assessing the room. Jerry was climbing onto the bed and he knew if he didn't act soon, it would be too late.

He had to somehow save his mother and Cheri but how. He had to do it while Jerry was distracted, and that meant he had to let him get just a little bit closer to Cheri. His stomach hated that idea but it was his only chance. If he caught him off guard, then he stood a chance.

Very slowly, he began to inch up from the couch, keeping as quite as possible. Every inch of his body ached. His ribs screamed at each little movement. If he wasn't careful, he'd make one wrong move and they would all be dead.

He placed his feet on the floor and looked around for a weapon. There was nothing but the old glass ashtray. It would have to work. Taking great care, he pushed himself to his feet. It was now or never. He looked at his mother, trying to make sure she was okay. So far she seemed to be unconscious. Good. As long as their focus remained on one person, it would be easier.

Gently, he began to ease forward just as Jerry was kneeling between Cheri's struggling legs. Jax knew that the outcome of this fight wasn't likely to end well for him, but he had to make sure that he took Jerry down with him.

Cheri felt a renewed surge of energy as she watched Jerry climb on the bed and roughly shove her legs apart. Reaching over to the table he picked up the scalpel and slowly drew lines with the tip across the tops of her thighs.

"Tiny cuts. Tiny cuts," he sang with each new line. "The trick is to not cut too deep. Just enough for the tissue to bleed but not so deep as to nick any veins or arteries. Do you have any idea how many times it took me to get that right?"

Cheri stilled, pushing through the pain, she looked up at him. "How many?"

He smirked. "I lost count somewhere around twelve, I think."

"Twelve?"

He beamed proudly. "I traveled around a lot. Made it easier for me to remain under the radar. Now, feel free to scream. Feels better when they do," he groaned as he reached down and roughly cupped her breast through her bra. Pain splintered her nerves as he closed his vice-like hands around her.

Terror spiked through her and adrenaline surged through her veins. If she didn't do something soon. . . . A shift of movement over Jerry's shoulders caught her attention. When she looked, she realized it was Jax. His eyes were locked on hers as he communicated with a single look.

Her struggling ceased causing Jerry to look down at her. "Why'd you stop struggling?" Seeing him up close she could see the lines and wrinkles that came with age. He'd looked younger when they'd first met at the party..

She sucked in a sharp breath and lifted her chin giving him a bloody smile. "Because I think you're a weak, pathetic excuse of a man who will never get a woman without force."

His eyes clouded with rage. "Shut up!" he screamed as he locked a hand around her throat and began to squeeze.

"Pathetic," she gasped as his hold tightened.

Her eyes darted over his shoulder as Jax closed the distance.

"JERRY!!!!" Janice screamed from the door, launching herself forward. However, she didn't get far before Lizabeth sprang from the chair and tackled her. Jax swung the heavy ashtray with as much force as he could muster—connecting with the side of Jerry's head as he turned around. A satisfying crunch filled the room as he tumbled from the bed and collapsed onto the floor. Jax knew that Jerry wouldn't remain out for long. His main concern was getting Cheri out of there.

Tears rolled down her cheeks as he cupped her face. "Are you okay? Do you think you can walk?" he asked as he quickly worked the restraints at her wrist.

"I think so," she said as her arms sagged to her sides. Pain burned through them as blood rushed back into her veins. Slowly, she eased her legs over the bed, ignoring the burning in her legs and stomach.

Jax grabbed her clothes and thrust them at her. "Take my mother and get out of here," he said.

Her eyes widened. "No. I'm not leaving you. You can barely stand up straight."

"Cheri, trust me. I'll be fine."

She hesitated for a moment before nodding and racing to Lizabeth's side. Somehow, the old woman had managed to knock Janice completely out. Later she would think about how spry the Lizabeth was, however, now was not that time.

Cheri grabbed her by the arm and tugged. "C'mon. We need to get out of here." Lizabeth lifted her gaze, her face and hands were speckled with blood. Cheri's eyes darted down to her mother's bloody and bashed in face. Lizabeth had beat her to death.

"C'mon, we gotta go get help."

Both women raced to the door. Cheri turned to look at Jax and her eyes grew wide. "Jax, watch out!" she screamed.

Jerry sliced into Jax's side with the scalpel, causing blood to gush forward. "NO!!!!!" she wailed as his hands clutched his side. He fell to his knees in front of Jerry.

"*Bebe*," Lizabeth screamed.

"Run!" Jaxon gasped.

Looking over his shoulder, Jerry smiled at the women. Blood coated his face and his eyes were wild. "Yes, do run. It makes things so much more fun. Go on. I'll be along shortly."

Cheri's eyes held Jax's and she could see him pleading with her. *I love you,* he mouthed as Jerry brought his hand swinging down in a wide arc.

She didn't want to see what happened so she darted down the stairs, Lizabeth close on her heels. They crossed the drive, shells, and bits of gravel digging into her feet. She climbed into Jax's truck and turned the key, but nothing happened.

"C'mon, c'mon, c'mon," she begged as she turned the key over and over again.

"We gotta get," Lizabeth said. "Dis way."

Both women took off running through the woods. Cheri didn't slow down to put on her clothes. In fact, she dropped them and kept running. After a good distance away from the cabin and deep in the swamp. Upturned roots and cypress knees caught her toes and ankles as she ran. She was looking over her shoulder when her ankle turned and she went stumbling forward in the thick muck. All the recent rains caused the mud to become thicker—closely resembling tar.

She struggled to her feet but her ankles were stuck in a root snare. She tugged as hard as she could. The snare gave way and when it did, she realized it wasn't a snare at all. Her eyes grew wide and a scream bubbled in her throat as she held up the remains of a human arm. She screamed and tossed it to the side, scrambling to her feet.

"We hafta stop," Lizabeth said as she gasped for air.

"I need to go back for Jax," Cheri said as she struggled to keep her thoughts straight. Her head was light and she knew she'd lost a dangerous amount of blood. She pushed the image of the skeleton deep down in her mind.

"We gotta get outta dis swamp, chile. It's nearly dark an we don't wanna be out here in da dark," Lizabeth said as she sat on an old log.

Cheri nodded but there was no way in hell she was going to leave Jax in there. "Go on, I'm not leaving him."

Lizabeth was about to protest but the sound of a breaking twig caused both women to spin around. As they did there was a loud explosion and a bright orange ball of fire lit the swamp up around them. In that light, they saw the silhouette of a man coming toward them.

She placed her fingers to her lips and pulled Lizabeth behind a tangled briar patch. No more running. She refused to run from this man and her past. She was going to fight and this time she would not be the victim. Reaching down, she felt along the ground for something to act as a weapon. Her fingers skimmed the human remains.

With a jerk, she broke a bone away from the body. The tip breaking way in a jagged point. She lifted it to her eyes to inspect. It would work just fine. She watched as the figure crept closer. Cabin burning brightly in the background. Closer and closer he came.

Two more steps and he would be within distance. It was going to be a blitz attack that would likely get her killed, but it was her last ditch effort. It wasn't safe for them to run through the swamp at night. There were too many other animals that could end their lives. This was their best chance. If they made it out alive, they could go back and take the driveway back to the main road.

Her heart shattered, knowing that Jaxon was in that house. His body burning away to ash. Finally, Jerry stopped right in front of their hiding place.

Taking a deep breath, she rushed from her hiding spot, her bone weapon poised high above her head and ready. She brought it down, sinking it into soft flesh.

"Rot. In. Hell," she wheezed.

# 38

By the time Lynn and Levi made it to the crime scene the area was already flooded with emergency responders. On the horizon, thunder rumbled. The only thing left of the structure was a smoldering pile of char.

"What do we have?" Lynn asked as the fire chief approached them.

"Two dead inside. One male and one female."

"Any ids?"

He shook his head.

"How did it start?" Levi asked.

"Looks like a lantern was knocked over. This cabin should'a been torn down years ago. It was nothing but a tinder box waiting to ignite."

"Chief we've got something," one of the men said as he emerged from the swamps.

"What are your men doing out there?"

"We thought that there might have been someone else. We found two sets of footprints leading into the swamp."

"Did you find anybody?"

"No. We've been searching. We were giving up until we found this."

The fireman lifted a human skull for them to see. Lynn pulled a pair of gloves from his pocket and took it. "There's blunt force trauma," he said pointing to the caved in side of the skull.

"I need all teams to spread out and canvas the area," Lynn said.

When he turned he met his partner's grim eyes. "Do you think those are our vics in there?"

"It's not looking good," he grumbled.

They were too late.

325

A heavy knock sounded on the front door. "I'll get it?" she called.

"Da hell ya will. Don't ya dare move from dat couch," Lizabeth scolded as she rounded the corner from the kitchen and marched to the front door.

From where she sat on the couch, Cheri couldn't see the door. However, as soon as she heard the familiar voice, she turned.

"Hello, detectives," she said, as she closed her book and placed it on the counter. "What can I do for you?"

"We heard that Cherilynn Bouvier is staying with you."

"She is."

"Can we speak to her? It will only be a moment."

Lizabeth hesitated for a minute. "It's fine, Lizabeth. I can talk," she called.

The detectives walked in and settled onto the couch in front of her. She stared at them carefully. She didn't miss the slight hint of relief she saw cross the older detective's face. Was he actually happy to see her?

He cleared his throat and ticked his head at her. "What happened to you?"

"Was in an accident Tuesday night," she said with a shrug.

"An accident?" he asked, arching a brow at her in disbelief.

"That must have been some accident," he said. She knew he was referring to the stitches above her eye and in the bottom of her lip. In the four days since the accident, the swelling had gone down but the coloring still remained the same.

"Where's Jaxon?"

Cheri felt a tug at her heart and opened her mouth to respond, but was stopped short by a deep voice.

"I'm right here, detectives," Jax said as he walked in carrying a sack full of crawfish.

"What happened in the accident?" he asked, eyeing Jax's injuries and arm that rested in a sling.

"Well, after we talked to you Monday night we went back to my house. The next morning, we got up and decided to head back to N'awlins."

"Why?"

It was Cheri that spoke this time. "I wanted to go to Roux's place and get some things. I needed to be there in order to process. I needed to find my closure. On the way, we got into a wreck. A gator had managed to get in the road and Jax swerved to miss it. When he did he overcorrected and we rolled the truck and ended up in the swamp."

"Did you call the cops?"

"Why would we?"

"Because you had an accident," Levi said, his voice heavy with sarcasm.

She narrowed her eyes on the younger detective, trying to keep her anger in check.

"My brother owns a towing company. They called him," Lizabeth said. "I came in my own car and den took'em on up to see Michael."

"Where's the truck at now?"

"Parked out back," Cheri said.

The men exchanged a look and Levi stood walking over to a window at the back of the room.

"It's out there," he said. "How you walked away alive is beyond me. That thing is destroyed."

"Da Lord works in many a mysterious ways," Lizabeth stated.

"Why did you go to Dr. Ross instead of the hospital?"

"Because I don't have insurance, detectives. I can barely make my bills as it is."

They stared at her and she could tell by the look in his eyes that they didn't believe her. She rolled her eyes and picked up her cell. "We stayed with him until yesterday morning, but if you don't believe us—" She dialed a number and pushed the speaker button.

"Doctor Ross," came the reply from the other end of the line.

"Hey, Mike. It's Cheri."

"Hey, you. How are you feeling?"

"Sore. Listen, Detectives Robichaud and Moss are here. Can you verify where we were?"

"Of course. Jax and Cheri had been in a car accident. Miss Liz brought them to my home approximately around noon. I treated Cheri for contusions and abrasions and Jax for a dislocated shoulder and a few minor breaks and bruises. I've got it all logged in my notes and you can see on my security cam recordings that they were here."

Lynn shook his head. "That won't be necessary," he said.

"Thank you for your help, doctor."

"Of course." Then he said to Cheri. "Get some rest and come in to see me in a couple weeks. I want to make sure those cuts are healing. If I need too I'll go in and fix them further."

"Thanks, Mike. I'll talk to you soon."

They disconnected the call and she adjusted the blanket that was tossed over her lap. "Are you happy now?"

"I am," she said, unable to tell if he bought the story or not. While she remained calm and collected on the outside, her insides were a jumbled knot of nerves. Her heart sped through her chest like a frightened rabbit. "Now, what can we do for you?"

"You've heard about the fire at your old home?"

She slowly nodded her head. "Read about it in the newspaper. Can't say that I'm sorry to see it go. *That* place was never my home."

"When was the last time you were out there?"

She shook her head. "I haven't been out there since Lizabeth removed me."

"Dat poor child was out dere for days by herself when her momma and dat man disappeared. Why in the hell would she wanna go back?"

"We were just checking. Because two bodies were discovered in the charred remains."

"Oh?"

Lynn nodded, watching their expressions carefully. "Jerome Davis—you might have known him as Jerry Davidson," he said.

Lizabeth's eyes grew wide. "Jerry? That was my baby girls' boyfriend. I thought he'd gone out of town on business."

*Way to go with the acting, Lizabeth*, Cheri thought smugly.

"Turns out that he'd been killing his victims at an abandoned hospital and then burying them around the old cabin."

"Really?"

"There were a total of seventeen bodies buried around the swamp. They go back at least ten years from all over the country. One of the bodies found was Carl Briggs."

"And who was the other body you found in the house with Jerry—Jerome?"

"Janice Deveau."

"My mother?"

Lynn nodded. Still, Cheri showed no emotion.

"You don't seem to broken up about her death," Levi said.

"Why would I be? She left me with Carl. I heard her tell Carl the night she left for work that he could do whatever he wanted to me. I didn't even know she was still alive."

"And did he?"

She shook her head. "He tried but I ran into the swamp. I was out there for the rest of the night and part of the next day. When he left I went back to the cabin. He never came back and neither did my mother. I just assumed that they ran off together."

"It appears that Jerome and your mother had been working together. We found DNA from both your mother and Jerome Davis in the kill room at the hospital.

"They were the ones that killed Roux?"

Lynn nodded grimly. "It would appear so."

"But why?"

"That's what we've been trying to figure out. According to their kill patterns, they were working their way up to a bigger target. A target we believed was you."

Cheri's eyes grew wide. "So they were after me."

"They must have gone to your house and then Jax's. When they didn't see you there, they went back to the cabin. A lantern must have been knocked over, sending the place up in a blaze."

"I see."

Silence landed heavily in the room as the five of them stared at one another. Finally, Lynn pushed to his feet. "It looks like we're done here." He extended his hand to Jax first and then to Cheri.

"You guys take care of yourselves."

She gave him a small smile. "Thank you for everything, detectives."

"It's our job," Lynn said as he walked to the door. However, before walking through he turned.

"You know what was interesting about the bodies?"

Cheri's heart sped through her chest. "What's that?" she asked calmly.

"Both bodies were dead before the fire. They both suffered from blunt force trauma to the head."

"Maybe the rafters fell on them?" Cheri offered.

"Yeah. Maybe," he said with a wink and a smile. "Ya'll have a good night." They walked out of the house closing the door behind them.

As Levi and Lynn walked back to their cruiser Levi looked at him. "Why didn't you bust them? We know they were out there. We found Cheri's clothes and Jax's blood in the swamp."

"Did you see the ligature marks on the women's wrists? They'd been held captive. I don't know what happened, but whatever it was the killers were taken care of."

Levi stared at his partner in disbelief. "That's not how cases are handled, Lynn. You know that. We don't let people take things into their own hands."

Lynn blew out a long, tired sigh. "I know and under different circumstances, I would have pushed harder, but for the first time in my career, I wanted to see victims get the revenge they wanted."

"They murdered two people."

"We don't know that for sure. For all we know, Jerome and Janice got into a domestic dispute and things got out of hand."

"And you're okay with all of this?"

"I am. Is it right?" He shrugged. "Probably not. We are part of a system that helps uphold the law, but where were we when Cheri was being raped by that boy in foster care."

"Anderson answered for that. He was convicted."

"But that never gave Cheri the peace she deserved. That didn't ease the pain of growing up knowing that she'd been violated in the most horrific of ways. She would have never been in that situation had the system not failed her."

"The system didn't fail her. It saved her from Briggs and her mother."

"It saved her from one tragedy and placed her directly into another. Where's the justice in that?" He turned the engine over and turned to look at his partner. "Listen, kid, you do what you need to do. If you want to push this case through and bring them in right now, you do it. As for me, I turned in my resignation day before yesterday. This was my last case."

Levi was silent for a long time. "Everything in my mind is telling me that this is wrong. We don't get to choose who to persecute and who to let go. It's just not right and it goes against the oath we swore, but, if that were my sister in there on that couch or my girlfriend, I can't say that I wouldn't do the exact same thing. In fact, I know I would have done the same thing. I agree. I think we let this one slide unnoticed. The evidence is all circumstantial anyway. Right?"

"Right."

"Then as far as I am concerned, case closed."

"That works for me."

Lynn put the car into gear and pulled away from Lizabeth Marceaux's house. He was more than happy to leave this case far, far behind him.

# 39

"What are they doing out there?" Cheri asked as she climbed to her feet and went to stand beside Jax at the window.

"They're just sitting there."

"Do you think they bought it?"

Jacks shook his head and looked at her gravely. "Honestly? No, I don't think they did. They are entirely too smart for that."

"So what are they doing?" Cheri chewed on her thumbnail and pulled a cigarette from the pack in Jax's shirt.

"I know you don't think you gonna smoke dat vile think in my house, young lady."

Cheri flushed. "No, ma'am," she said.

Lizabeth nodded and walked back into the kitchen. Cheri watched in relief as the detective's cruiser finally pulled away from the house. As they drove away, they took with them the rest of the case.

"Is it over?"

Jax folded her into his arms and kissed the top of her head. She pressed her cheek against his chest, breathing in deeply the smell of fabric softener. "I think it is," he said. "If they wanted too they could have taken us in. I could see it in the older one's eyes. He knew we were lying."

She chuckled and looked up at him. "We weren't lying, per say. We told them the truth about Michael and staying with him. We just left out the part where you caught Jerry off guard by ramming your shoulder into him."

"And the part where I bashed his head in with his father's ashtray.

"And that the lantern *accidentally* toppled over."

"And the part about me finding you and my mother in the middle of a woods wielding human remains as a weapon," he added.

"And the part where your cousins helped us roll the truck off the bluff and then tow it back to the house."

"Everything else was the truth. More or less."

She smiled thankful for the man that now held her in his arms. Jax had promised to take care of her and that was exactly what had happened.

Jax lowered his mouth and gently pressed his lips against hers. There was a slight tug on the stitches on her lip but she didn't notice and she wasn't about to stop him. Her body began to hum with pleasure and when he pulled away, she whimpered in protest.

"I wasn't done with you," she whispered.

He chuckled and lightly kissed her forehead. "You're such a pain in the ass."

She smirked. "Are you talking about my ass? You must really like it."

He winked at her and gave her backside a firm little squeeze. "I do very much at that." They stood, wrapped in each other's arms, for what felt like hours. For the first time in her entire life, Cheri felt peace. The nightmares were gone and the anxiousness she felt had vanished.

The vibrating in her back pocket caused her to pull away. "That Jeremy?" Jax asked.

"He called last night while you were at the bar and I told him about the accident. He's on his way home."

"I finally get to meet the other man in your life?"

"You do and let me just say, he's not happy that you got us into a car wreck."

Jax smirked but the smile fell. "Are you ever going to tell him the truth?"

"Maybe one day, but right now, I—we—need to get on with our lives. I want to put this whole thing behind us."

"I think we can do that," he said as he brushed another kiss against her mouth. "Now, you need to get your cute butt back on that couch."

"Only if you'll lay with me."

A sexy smirk tilted his lips and a hungry look swam in his dark brown eyes. "I'd much rather take you home."

Heat crept into her cheeks as she bobbed her head.

"Momma, we're heading back to my place. We'll be back later."

There was a muttered curse about being young and in love from the kitchen. They both laughed as they stepped out of the air conditioning and into the evening heat. The humidity was miserable, as the mosquitos buzzed, but the only sweltering heat she could feel was her body's reaction to Jax's.

Not everyone immediately gets their happily ever after. For some, it takes a while to get there. For others, like Cheri and Jax, they just had to take the long way around.

*Murder's out of tune,*

*And sweet revenge grows harsh.*

~~WILLIAM SHAKESPEARE, *Othello*

# The End.

The END

Special note to the reader.

Thank you for taking this journey with me. While everything in this book was made up and a pure work of fiction, beneath it all, lies a very serious issue. Sexual abuse is a very real and traumatizing problem in the world. While some cases are reported, many aren't. Victims are shamed and made to feel responsible for the crime. It is important to know that you are not alone.

If you or someone you love believe that you've been a victim of sexual assault or are currently a victim call:

National Sexual Assault Hotline at
800.656.HOPE (4673)

You are not alone!

Check out other books
from Christine James:


The Chosen Chronicles:

*Risen*

*Bloodlines*

*Final Redemption*


Abroad

(co-written with author Amelia Cole)


The Guardians: UnderCity

www.ingramcontent.com/pod-product-compliance
Lightning Source LLC
Chambersburg PA
CBHW060008180626
46817CB00015B/273